The Island Prince

Gregory James Clark

Clink
Street

London | New York

Published by Clink Street Publishing 2019

Copyright © 2019

First edition.

ISBN:
978-1-913136-00-0 paperback
978-1-913136-01-7 ebook

About the Author

Gregory James Clark was born in Lancashire, England, in 1962. Educated at the Reading Blue Coat School he gained a BSc Honours in Maritime Studies (International Transport) from the University of Wales (Cardiff) in 1988 and an MBA from Manchester Metropolitan University in 2008. He was Editor of the *Quality Matters Newsletter* from 1989 to 2000, which was later compiled into the book *'Quality Matters: The Decade of Quality 1989 - 2000'*. He has recently worked as a teacher/trainer in Quality Management for the Chartered Quality Institute Certificate and Diploma in Quality Management, and helped to design and present The Programme for Global Quality Promotion (PGQP) in Russia and the African nations from 2005 to 2010. He also assisted in the publication of *'Deming and Juran: Gift to the World'* at Bradford University in 2007. He is currently Editor of *The Electron* Newsletter for the Institution of Electronics. Recreations have included ice dancing, ballroom dancing, golf, chess and snooker. Languages spoken include Dutch, German, Portuguese and Swedish.

By the same author

The Island of Dreams

In 2107 twenty-four-year-old Gary Loman is disillusioned with life. There are scant opportunities in the capitalist world that surrounds him. When he receives a prestigious invitation Gary knows that the change he has been waiting for has finally arrived; it's a ticket to fame and glory as a skater.

Leaving the old world behind, Gary embarks on a new adventure on The Island of Dreams led by the world's newest monarchy, where he is introduced to the woman who will become his wife and a wildly different social order, one which has evolved over the previous seventy years by virtue of a slow, quiet and largely unnoticed revolution. By 2107, however, The Island is poised to become one of the most powerful states in the world, acquiring, most notably, the territory of Kamchatka.

The Island Queen, Queen Katie of Kamchatka, with the help of her devoted Prime Minister and her faithful staff, then attempt to educate and train the 240 receivers of the distinguished Queen's Ticket, both for their roles as skaters and within the Kamchatskiy organisation, for whom they will be working under a completely new concept in political economy, based on quality rather than profit motives, and which is replacing Marxism as the world's rival to capitalism.

As Gary progresses on The Island, and as its Queen seeks out her new King, the world is on the brink of a breathtaking transformation.

Chapter One
Resignation

It was the first Wednesday in March 2108, and the Australian National Defence Committee had just commenced its Annual Congress, this year in Perth, Western Australia.

The country's Defence Minister, Aub Ryman, 33, had just stunned the audience, half of whom supported him and half of whom didnt, by using his Keynote Speech to announce his resignation forthwith. Some of his supporters were now pursuing him as he left the conference and made his way to the hotel entrance.

"You can't walk out now, sir," one of them said to him.

"I just have," Aub replied.

"Some of us are loyal to you, you know that," said another.

"Yes, and I know who you are. You will be amply rewarded when the time comes," Aub answered.

He was in no doubt that the course of action that he was about to take was by far and away the best, both for himself and for others. It was to be a great step forward, for it was a fact that others around him possessed neither the knowledge nor the capability to do what was required. The others knew nothing of The New Game and what was about to unfold secretly and behind closed doors. That was why he was about to become The Prince Regent of what was fast becoming one of the world's most influential and powerful entities.

A Kamchatskiy Silver Shadow limousine conveyed him swiftly through Perth's northern suburbs to the airport.

"Good luck Prince Regent," said the chauffeur as he alighted at the terminal building, his suitcase now in his hand.

A pathway had been planned for him to by-pass airport security before boarding the supersonic plane otherwise known as the Hebden Three, that would convey him to his Atlantic destination. This, however, did not stop two less informed security officials from approaching him.

"Excuse me sir," one of them said to him, "You cannot go there. There are no flights from gate six today. I'm afraid you must return to airport security at once."

It was just as well, therefore, that he was able to remove from his jacket the small case that his bride-to-be had given to him a year before. He opened it and flashed the bright gold on blue hologram of Saturn at the guards. It was so bright that it almost dazzled them, but, more importantly even these two ill-informed guards, who had somehow managed to miss that this sole passenger was scheduled to proceed to gate six without hindrance, knew without hesitation that the authority of this badge was not in question. It could only belong to one person.

"I'm so sorry. This way Your Royal Highness," replied one of the guards, who then directed him along a short deserted passageway to the awaiting plane, which was parked discreetly by gate six.

The plane was one of a fleet of thirty, but this one was special as it was owned by the girl that he was soon to marry, twenty-three-year-old Queen Katie of Kamchatka. It was sky blue and its tail bore the same Saturnian logo as his hologram badge. Inside it was much the same as the other first-class only Hebden Threes, only with a few more luxuries, as one might expect of a royal jet.

As the aircraft took off it followed a north-westerly path before reaching supersonic speed some one hundred miles northwest of Perth. From there it followed a more westerly trajectory as it headed towards South Africa before following the west African coastline northwards towards its final destination, The Island of Dreams, a small eight-mile-long island to the north of the Azores, yet a place that had recently gained enormous worldwide significance.

On The Island, from her sanctuary of The Great Dome, the slim, dark haired forty-one-year old Prime Minister Joanie Carmichael prepared to inform The Queen that her Prince would be touching down on The Islands beach runway, two miles northwest of The Town, shortly after two o'clock local time. The royal train, hauled by the aptly named steam locomotive Prince, would then bring her from her Royal Palace to meet him.

On board the aircraft the petite Korean hostess Su Lin greeted him first with a commemorative bottle of Prince Regent lager, on the label of which was an imprint of his face, and then with a document, which he scrutinised carefully.

He noted that the form had the effect of transferring ownership of the aircraft from The Queen to himself.

"What if I don't want to own the plane?" he asked.

"Then too bad. Queen will transfer it to you anyway," replied Su Lin.

"So the form is meaningless?"

"No. Form very important. It show Queen that you respect her wishes."

"I see. Then I suppose I had better sign it."

She offered him the pen and bowed her head. He noted the gesture, aware that should he refuse to sign the hostess would see it, rightly or wrongly, as a reflection upon her. He knew that, unlike with the budgets that he had been asked to approve a couple of hours earlier, he had to sign.

Lunch followed with a good choice of options that reflected The Island's fish and vegetarian tradition. No meat was served, but just about everything else was possible. Naturally The Princes favourite vegetable soup and lobster crepes were prepared in anticipation.

"Prime Minister want that you have great flight to Island and will have everything ready for your arrival," Su Lin continued. "If you look at screen you see coachman preparing horses for royal coach."

The viewing screen was revealed allowing Aub to see for the first time The Coachman carefully grooming the two black stallions that would pull the meticulously polished golden royal coach, with its star-studded black letter K, hallmark of Kamchatskiy Auto, clearly visible on the doors, just as it had been on the bonnet of the Silver Shadow that had conveyed him from the convention centre to the airport back in Perth. Then, presently, Joanie appeared on the screen, sitting at her chair in the centre of The Great Dome.

"Greetings Prince Regent," she said in her mild Anglo-Russian accent, "Her Majesty and I are so pleased that you have decided on this day to accept the new and great future that she has offered to you. You will know from our history what awaits you in the weeks and months ahead. You know that a lot will be expected of you, but we have every confidence that you are the man who can steer us forward. It is a decision that we are sure you will not regret, and we are honoured to have you. You are now officially Prince Regent and the band may begin to play."

The brass band on The Colonnade duly began to play the classic Entry of the Gladiators as selected members of The Island's staff of 500 began to march around The Town military style, in their distinctive sky blue uniforms with tapered jackets that each bore The Island's Saturnian logo embossed in gold on the back. They performed their ceremonial two-step, then, after three sequences, they all halted and turned their heads towards The Great Dome, and saluted The Island Prince. This then provided the cue for the outgoing setmates to leave their cottages and make their way towards The Square ready to greet their new hero.

"Setmates have one more week," Su Lin told him, "Then they will be leaving."

"That's good. At least I'll have the pleasure of meeting them. It will also be good to see the ones I enabled to go there this year. It's a shame I'm just that bit too late for the Carnival on Ice. Then I could have met last years as well. It will be a refreshing change, though, after the loons I've been cooked up with for the last five years."

During the second half of the flight Aub was able to watch the recording of Carnival on Ice, with its intricate turns and lifts serving to demonstrate the creative talent that ice skating trainer Jobine had nurtured and harnessed from the setmates during their time on The Island. He noted particularly the progress made by a certain Aborigine, Yvonne, recalling, as he watched her perform Silver Shadow, that fateful day just under a year earlier when he had given her his last Queen's ticket to The Island of Dreams. The flight was too short to enable him to see the entire performance, but edited highlights were enough for him to see for himself the results that Jobine had achieved with the setmates. Suitably impressed, he looked forward to meeting them and congratulating them all on their achievements.

At approximately 2.15 p.m. the plane touched down on the firm sand of The Islands southwest shore. The Prince thanked the hostess, pilot and co-pilot as he stepped out to meet The Coachman with his fine royal coach and horses as they stood at the edge of the dunes that peppered this stretch of coast. The Coachman approached the plane, ready to transport him in style along the winding single-track road that meandered its way through fields and orchards towards The Town.

As the carriage passed through The Triumphal Arch that led from The Japanese Garden, he saw the crowd, by now the entire population of The Island, cheering and applauding enthusiastically on a scale that he had never before personally experienced. It took him somewhat by surprise, having been far more accustomed to jeers and heckles than a celebrity welcome.

11

He looked eagerly for The Queen, but she was nowhere to be seen. She could see him, but he could not see her, as she looked down from her tiny observatory high up in The Bell Tower.

The carriage came to rest at the foot of the steps of The Great Dome, down which the reigning King Neville slowly descended in his Island robes along with his principal Queen Mary, The Queen Mother.

"Stand well back," ordered The Chancellor, as the carriage slowly came to a halt outside The Great Dome.

Dressed in his statutory top hat and tails he cleared a path through the throng to the base of the steps. The cheering intensified and confetti rained down as he shook the hand of The King and The Queen Mother. Then they ascended the steps and entered The Great Dome where Prime Minister Joanie stood ready to receive him, clasping his hands excitedly.

"Prince Regent, so good to meet you," she said, "After all this time it is really you, here on The Island. All the months of uncertainty are at last over. There is much to be done and I wish I was going to be here to see your great adventure."

"You're not?" said Aub.

"No. I thought you would have known. Now that you are here I have to resign and hand over my authority to The Queen's Ministers in Kamchatka, who will, one by one, apply their tests to you prior to awarding their Royal Acclamation. When that has been done a new Prime Minister will be appointed from among their ranks, whom you and The Queen must then approve. This is what our constitution demands, but I have had a wonderful six years here as Prime Minister, and it is only right that at some reasonable time I should stand down and hand over to someone else. I have been very privileged to have served in what many would regard as the best job in the world.

"It's not quite over for me yet, though. I still have the pleasure of showing you around the magical world of The

Island over the next week and, of course, have the honour of presenting you to Her Majesty The Queen. All has been made ready for you and I can assure you that all of my staff will do their very best to see that you are made welcome here and they will always be on hand to assist you. You already have more friends than you will ever know, and I know that you definitely will not regret making the decision that you did this morning. Your adventures are just beginning, and there is no doubt that you will have a very powerful and influential role in the future development of the world.

"I listened to your brief speech in Perth this morning and was so proud you stood up at last and said no at last to those backward thinking individuals. You will be your peoples saviour in the end, mark my words. There's nothing more important that you could have done for Australia."

"Some will still see me as selling out to the Russians."

"There's no such thing as selling out, Prince. It is the others who will sell out when the bidding starts. You will be the man who will introduce Non-Capitalist Economics to the Australian people, and, when they see it working on Bathurst and Melville, more will want it, and those old fogeys in the Australian Defence Committee will be where they belong, as footnotes in Australia's beleaguered past. So, come on then, tell me how much you enjoyed this year's Carnival on Ice."

"I can't wait to get my skates on myself."

"Well, I can tell you that The Queen herself has ordered her own personal maid to place a brand new pair of skates, tailored to your exact measurements, on your bed in Samurai Cottage, and ice time has been set aside for you."

"With the setmates?"

"With or without. You choose. Jobine, our resident trainer is eager to meet you. Hopefully she will be able to help you and Katie to become the world's first true skating King and Queen. Now that Carnival is over and the setmates have only one more week left here I have asked that she allows them to relax a little now."

"Then they go to Kamchatskiy, right?"

"Right, but we still have social night at the end of the week."

"I'd better get some practice in then. I'm very rusty compared to what I saw on the plane. I am pleased for all of the setmates, but especially for all those from Australia to whom I have had the honour of handing over The Queen's precious tickets personally. Yvonne was fantastic compared to when I saw her skate in Darwin. I'm so glad that I found the perfect person to give that last ticket to. I was getting seriously worried about what I was going to do with it. By the way, where is The Queen?"

At that moment The Chancellor created a distraction by wheeling in his trolley complete with tea and petit fours. The King then winked at him, careful to conceal the gesture from The Prince, for outside The Queen had descended from The Bell Tower and was mingling with the setmates.

"Sssh," she whispered as she quietly crept towards the steps of The Great Dome, dressed in a Tudor-style dress that gave her all the appearance of a fairy-tale princess. She ascended the steps, whilst The King and The Queen Mother engaged in conversation with The Prince, until, abruptly, they stopped. This provided the cue for the door to open and for Queen Katie of Kamchatka to enter.

"Now. I've got something to show you," said The King, "The blindfold please."

The Chancellor duly placed the blindfold over the Princes eyes.

"Now turn round," said The Queen Mother, who then removed the blindfold.

"Oh my God," exclaimed The Prince, "You look absolutely amazing."

"I now formally present to you, Queen Katie of Kamchatka," said The King, "otherwise known as The Island Queen."

She embraced him fondly as The Chancellor opened a bottle of Two's Company Island vintage champagne and dispensed glasses.

"To our wonderful Island Queen and to our future Island King," said The King, raising his glass and prompting the others to do likewise.

Katie gazed into The Prince's eyes, which had a distinctive sparkle and a strange penetrating quality.

"Only The Good Lord Himself could have blessed you with such beautiful eyes," she remarked.

"Only the Good Lord Himself could have placed me in love with such a special person as you.

Outside the horses that had pulled the royal coach enjoyed a well-earned drink as The Coachman and the crowd prepared for the re-emergence of the four royals, who would then be conveyed the relatively short distance to the railway station, opposite The Island's ice stadium, where the royal train awaited to take them along the four-mile long stretch of track to The Royal Palace.

Joanie hugged both The Prince and The Queen before leading the way to the balcony of The Great Dome. There they waved to the cheering crowd before descending to enter the magnificent gold Kamchatskiy royal carriage.

Cheers were spontaneous as they emerged and kissed symbolically on the balcony. They might as well have been married already, such was the intimacy and the surety. After all, it was all but a foregone conclusion that they would be married in less than a year. The Queen's Ministers in the Kamchatka Parliament would never dream of standing in the way of such a talented candidate for the throne, nor all of the people of the world who truly wanted to be part of the transformation that the second stage of The Island's slow, but well-paced, revolution was destined to bring. This said, they did have a remit to educate and improve where possible The Prince's capabilities for the unique and important role that he would have.

Chapter Two
A Royal Journey

The train steamed at a leisurely pace along its four-mile long track from The Town to The Royal Palace, allowing the four royals to talk amongst themselves in the single royal carriage.

"I want this marriage to be something really special," said The King, "When Mary and I were married back in 2083 the event was hardly noticed. It took place in The Island Church, and all of The Island's population attended. There was great celebration here and everyone had a wonderful time, but it was really just a local event. It didn't have any real significance as far as world affairs were concerned. We had only just established the Kamchatka Parliament some six years before as part of Mary's father, Ken David's, early plans for our revolutionary transformation of the world. Kamchatka, of course, was targeted for its cheap land, and enormous economic potential, particularly with regard to its extensive geothermal energy reserves.

"Everyone who threw their fortunes into the project had been at least an acquaintance of one or other of our great Founders. By 2077 their following was large and influential enough for the theory of Non-Capitalist Economics to be rolled out beyond the confines of The Island. The then Island King, Ken David, with his trusted Chairman Leo Harvey, who had devised the theory, formed the first Island Council of Kamchatka, which later became the Kamchatka Parliament following their brilliantly crafted deal with President Kasparov in Moscow in 2072.

"The deal made Mary and myself constitutional monarchs of Kamchatka when we eventually married in 2083, but it was not really all that significant. We had no real involvement in politics, but in the 2090s things began to change. The Kamchatka Parliament had by then set up its now renowned Political Academy and the first Ministers had started to graduate. They then passed an Act that empowered them to set tasks for The King such that any future Island King would be assessed by them in certain key areas of competence so as to guarantee that such a King would be certain to be capable in playing a leading role in the transformation. This was also in accordance with the Founders' original long-term plan.

"This means that you, Aub, unlike me, will be subject to the provisions of the Act, known as the Royal Prerogative Act."

"You don't have to tell me," Aub replied, "That Parliament in Kamchatka has become a huge driver for change and the influence of The Island on the world stage is now very considerable. Someone like myself is bound to be under a lot of scrutiny. The thing that amazes me is how so many of the world's politicians are still apparently oblivious to it. It's as if none of them want to admit to themselves that it even exists. This morning when I left Perth the Australian Defence Committee was still demanding that I approved budgets for a form of defence that's totally unviable in the modern age."

"You will face problems in Australia, there's no doubt about that," said Mary.

"Oh most certainly," Aub continued. "The people on Bathurst and Melville where I come from love Jacob Spence, the local MP and want him to represent them in Kamchatka's world-beating parliament. But I know that there are many people in Australia who view that as anti-Australian, undermining Australian sovereignty, reducing the power of our backward-thinking government and instead giving Moscow a foothold in yet another nation. Kamchatka means Kremlin as far as they are concerned. The fact that the strategy will greatly help Australia in the long term hasn't even entered their heads. I will have to prepare for some pretty vicious criticism in the Australian media."

"I wouldn't worry too unduly," advised The King, "Progress will be made one funeral at a time."

"I never thought of it like that," said Queen Katie, "That's probably the best way to look at it. Our revolution is at least slow enough to allow that approach to succeed."

"Absolutely," said King Neville. "Once the Australians of today see life as just going on as normal, and their own jobs just staying the same, those politicians of today that you left behind will soon forget all about you and Jacob Spence. In the longer term Australia will share in Russia's prosperity, as well as contributing to it and all will be forgiven. So you could say that the problems that await you as of now in Australia are nothing more than a storm in a teacup."

"Strange, isn't it," Katie added, "Russia is now by far the world's richest nation, yet it has the least aggressive leader in its history."

"That's because we helped save President Ulanov at a time when the Russian economy was failing," explained The King, "He is indebted to us. That's why he's standing down as President next year."

"He's what?" remarked Aub, astounded.

"That's what Vice Chancellor Bogodan told me yesterday. He's going to step down and become just Prime Minister of Russia, excluding Kamchatka, of course. Joanie Carmichael is Prime Minister of Kamchatka if only in name. This means that you, Aub, will become King of all Russia when you are crowned, just as my beautiful daughter Katie will be Queen of Russia as well as The Island Queen and Queen Katie of Kamchatka. It's a smart move really. By all accounts the Russian people have asked for it, as part of handing more power back to the people. In practice he won't be giving up any power at all."

"He may not be the most aggressive of Russian leaders," said Aub, "But he certainly knows how to roll the dice."

"Which brings me back to what I said about the wedding," The King continued. "It's going to be the most spectacular royal wedding ever staged. You will be married in the ornate St. Basil's Cathedral at the southern end of Red Square. This will then be followed immediately with the coronation, something that the world has never seen before. Then, outside, after the service, a spectacular ice show is to be staged in which you and Katie will form the star attraction."

"Oh my God!" exclaimed Katie.

"It's fine. It will be fantastic," her father assured her, "Jobine is going to be your exclusive trainer, and you know how good she is."

"I know the results that she gets from the setmates are outstanding," Katie agreed, "It's just the thought of all those people, millions of them, all over the world, all staring at us, not to mention all the expectations that the world is going to have of us."

She was slightly perturbed at the thought, but deep down, she was bright and confident enough to be one of those people who could easily grow to relish such a challenge. After all, who else in history had ever had such a fantastic opportunity?

"There is nothing to be afraid of," The King reassured her, "We are behind you, and Aub will be beside you. You have the world at your feet, as I'm sure you are aware. Both you and Aub will have to learn to be bold. The second stage of the revolution is almost upon us."

"And, after the ice show, what happens then?" Katie asked.

"That's something else," said The King.

*

As the train gently chuffed through Sabfelt, the memories of his last visit to The Island in December 2106 came flooding back to Aub. In the distance he spotted the outline of The Gun Inn and recollected the memorable evening that he had spent there enjoying Christmas fayre with The Island's Concierge, Patrick O'Rourke, and his accomplice The Reverend Duncan McIntyre, learning about the vital role that the pair was playing in shaping the second stage of the revolution. Thanks to them terrorism had not been forgotten, but had instead been reduced to mere theatre that served to educate rather than destroy.

"Everybody has a flash point," Patrick had asserted, "but it can be controlled and rendered harmless."

Aub remembered how he and Katie had watched and marvelled at the achievements of the pair in Chechnya. When Ulanov had been elected he faced a huge problem in Chechnya. Now, he was the President who could do no wrong, because Patrick and Duncan had wanted it so. All it took was the world's first true implementation of a Quality Supersystem that made life better for all.

A few minutes later the train passed slowly through Aldebaran station, where the Opera House and Astronomical Observatory could clearly be seen, prominently set back from the hamlet's single street with the visitors accommodation blocks beyond.

"Hey, there's the lovely Opera House, a mini version of the one in Sydney," Aub remarked to Katie, "I remember all those children queuing up for our autographs at the end of 'The Nutcracker Suite'. They were from The Leonovo School if I remember rightly."

"Yes," said Katie, "This year it's the turn of The Karaginsky School. They're going to come and perform Swan Lake for us."

"They're off into space next week aren't they? I wonder what The Concierge has in store in his lecture this year. I would still like to hear his 2107 lecture to the Leonovo School on The Electron-beam Probe."

"That is worth listening to, I agree," said The King, "I'll arrange for you to have a recording."

Chapter Three
Romantic Encounters

"I wonder if she knows," Aub said to Katie as they sat alone together over a special candlelit dinner that Bob, the royal chef, had prepared to order.

"I don't think she knows, but I think she suspects," Katie replied, "Not that I think she is really that bothered. My parents know some of the details of our romance, but they're not the type to want to pry into everything, despite my mother's strong adherence to traditional values."

"They know about our time on Bathurst?"

"They know you took me twice to your villa to meet your parents, but no more than that."

"And about how we first met three years ago at the Macquarie Ice Rink when you came to Sydney and we dined with your friends at the Deming Society luncheon?"

"Oh they know all about that. It was extraordinary really. I remember it well. There we were, two total strangers on a quiet morning session at Sydney's most famous ice rink. I had no idea you were a government minister. You had no idea I was a Queen. Yet it was as if we had been touched by angels on that fateful day. It was funny when the handful of mostly retired individuals seemed to all stop skating when we did our combined upright camel spin, our side by side pivots and three jumps and that European Waltz that just somehow worked. From that moment on I knew we were two people who were destined for each other. I liked the way they all stood by the barrier and applauded us as if they had never seen anything like it."

"I wonder if any of those people will still remember us when they see us in Red Square, and say to themselves Oh yes, that's that couple we saw that day at Macquarie?"

"That would be interesting. Maybe we'll get a tweet."

"Why did you take so long, though, before revealing to me who you really were?" Aub asked.

"I had to be sure about you, given the potential importance of the relationship, and how far our joint responsibilities were going to extend. I think that is where my parents' real interest lies. What we did on Bathurst and what we might do unchecked in our master bedroom is rather trivial by comparison, you have to admit. And besides, this is The Island of Dreams, and we can afford to have a few secrets. We aren't setmates, even though my mother might like to think we are. "

"So, what made you decide to reveal all and make the proposition to me that I should resign and come to this remarkable place, knowing that it would be impossible for me to refuse?"

"Well, there's a small word called love that springs to mind," she said, stroking his cheek, "But there's more to it as I'm sure you know. I knew quite early on that you are someone whom my father would be pretty certain to approve, and that was never going to be a given. I was under some pressure to make a choice somewhere and nobody compared to you. You also told me when we met the second time that you knew of The Island and its legendary status. You obviously were fully aware of the twentieth century teaching of Deming and Juran, very important to my father, and how The Island's Founders shaped it. It took a few romantic encounters, but love for me grew alongside the rational side. You were the perfect Island Prince in every way. But what did you think about me during our romantic encounters?"

"I loved you for who you were, the anonymous student of business and politics that just happened to like ice skating, and just happened to be The Island Queen."

"Skating has always been central to our culture as you can see from the murals on the ceiling of all of the great Torvill and Dean's twentieth century classics, beautifully painted by the wives, or should I say principals, of the Founders, representing the pursuit of excellence that has subsequently been built into all our consciences. And that's another attribute that I loved about you. It's still all too rare to see that quality in people. Yet the more romantic encounters we had the more evident it became."

"What made you choose to do your studies at Macquarie University?"

"I don't know really," Katie explained, "The Island's strong British connection played its part, but I didn't think I would fit in too well in the UK. It wasn't relaxed enough and its government is far too right wing, although I think I can do something about that. I had automatically been educated from age seven at the prestigious Kamchatka Academy of Political Science, and could have stayed, but I wanted something different rather than more of the same. The Kamchatka Academy is for people who intend to serve as Ministers in what is effectively my Parliament. I was expected to do more, so I chose Macquarie, mainly because it had its followers of Deming and Juran."

"Yes, I studied there myself for more or less the same reasons some nine years earlier. Then my father persuaded me to enter Australian politics, having no idea what I was letting myself into. The defence industry is awful, although at least with you by my side there should be some chance of one day wiping it out. Those romantic encounters on Bathurst were enough to convince me that now was the right time to get out. Tell me, why do the setmates have to wait until they are off the planet before they are permitted any romantic encounters?"

"That's largely down to my mother and her traditional values. But it's also down to the fact they have all come from different backgrounds and we just want to be sure that the couples are appropriately matched before such things develop. I don't see any of them regretting it when they see how stable and harmonious marital relations are in Kamchatka compared to places like the UK and America, not to mention your own country. On the surface it looks like a strict convention, but it works out for the best given that they know little if anything about our culture when they arrive. The total trust and cooperation that we have all known and respected for years still comes as a shock to them, even though they are the best candidates. As royals people like my parents expect that we should already be adapted and not need to go through that learning curve."

"Before Bathurst I know neither of us had experienced any romantic encounters," Aub continued, "I know that because we were both following the Founders' doctrine of right first time. And even then it was only one time and by then we knew where we were heading anyway."

"And where's that?" Katie whispered suggestively.

*

After the meal Katie led Aub by the hand to the front entrance of The Royal Palace directly facing the mile-long lake that lay at the centre of The Island of Dreams. There they held hands as they gazed across the calm waters that rippled in the moonlight. Aub looked to his left and saw what looked like a mysterious shape with a serpent's head raised from the shoreline. They walked towards it, and as they came closer he could see that it was in fact a gondola, carefully moored on a jetty beside a wrought iron gate.

"This is the gate to The West Garden," Katie explained, as she pushed the gates open, "Commoners are not allowed in here. That rule dates back to the days of King Ken and

Queen Justine, when it was decreed that this special place should be reserved exclusively for The King and Queen's romantic encounters, but it also allowed for a few others. All of The Founders, for example, were granted limited access with permission from the King or Queen, and today a similar provision exists for my chosen monarchs and world leaders. My father made that declaration in 2100. Tonight, of course, it is here exclusively for us."

They walked together hand in hand along the winding wooded cobbled path into which butterflies, nymphs and cherubs had been embedded in a variety of colours, not that they could be viewed with clarity in all their splendour in the semi-darkness. It came to an abrupt end in the centre of the Garden, where there stood a life-sized marble statue of Hermes and Aphrodite, which was surrounded by still water. As the couple approached Aub was startled as, all of a sudden, the statue became illuminated in a dusky pink light and sprays of water shot into the air.

"It turns itself on when people approach," Katie explained, "It's called The Fountain of Dreams. The water's very clean and pure enough to drink, and a few sips of it are supposed to bring you good health according to our legend. The water's also warm enough to allow for bathing unclothed."

Tempting though it was they decided that they would save the latter luxury for some future occasion, but they did each take a couple of scoops of the fine water. Then they continued along the path on the other side of the Fountain. Unlike the first path, this path was steep and even more winding than the other as it led down to a green where it branched out into several smaller pathways, each of which led towards an erotically themed statue. These were mounted on plinths of varying sizes and glowed in various colours as The Queen and The Prince approached.

"These, like the statue in the Fountain, were carved by Queen Justine's stonemason originally as an expression of freedom and liberalism hidden from the world," Katie explained.

They walked around for a while, watching the colours change as they approached each statue in turn. Then they returned to the centre where again The Fountain lit up and sprang into life. This time they paused and embraced as the moon cast the statues shadow over them. As they did so the surrounding trees rustled and Aub thought he could hear what sounded like laughter that came not from The Palace but from the woods.

"Did you hear that?" asked The Prince.

"What did you hear?"

"I don't know. It sounded like a strange deep laugh."

"Perhaps its Leo Harvey's ghost," she said, smiling as they kissed.

Chapter Four
Affairs of State

The following morning The Prince took the service train to The Town alone to meet The Prime Minister as had been planned. With the euphoria of his arrival now over, a standard driverless Kammie conveyed him the last quarter mile from The Town station to The Great Dome. The door opened automatically and Joanie was sitting predictably in her chair facing him across a plain oak table, with the illuminated screen behind.

"Greetings and good morning," she said, rising and pointing to the single chair in front of her, "Please be seated. I trust you had an enjoyable evening last night?"

"The best in years," replied Aub. "But beautiful though this place is, nobody comes here for all play and no work."

"Well, I'll give you an update and I'll start with the worst bit. Here's a copy of this morning's Sydney Herald. I don't think there is anything in it that you didn't expect."

The Prince scrutinised the front page and was not surprised to see his face alongside that of his trusted friend Jacob Spence, with the caption beneath that read 'Behold the traitors'. He continued to read the supporting headline article, which spoke of him and Jacob betraying Australia and selling out to the Russians. The article launched a savage attack on both of them for failing to respect Australian sovereignty, but it could have been worse.

"I'll give the paper its due," said Aub. "At least the article isn't entirely one-sided. I notice that in its latter stages that it acknowledges the fact that every country that has supplied MPs to the Kamchatka Parliament has ended up better as a result, and cites Trindade and Rocas with Brazil and The Falkland Islands with the UK as examples. I also see that The Australian Defence Committee has appointed Bernie Hamilton to my old job. I expected them to appoint someone far worse. I might even be able to work with Bernie."

"In the end they were forced to appoint a compromise candidate. It shows the old guard is crumbling and that they can't just appoint whoever they like anymore. You obviously have enough of your own supporters to block hard-line traditionalists and yes men. "

"The article is bad, I can't deny that, but it's far from disastrous. True, Jacob and myself are being accused of acting illegally and against the Australian constitution, arguing that we have a duty to serve our people from Canberra, not Kamchatka. It's not that long ago that it would have been impossible to serve our people by sitting in what is effectively a foreign parliament, but times are changing as we know."

"The article also seems to overlook the fact that it really is a great honour for any MP to be invited to serve in the Kamchatka Parliament," Joanie added, "Only representatives that have our approval can enter it from outside, and Vice Chancellor Viktor Bogodan, who is the person with the real power rather than ourselves, will be sure to keep it that way, because, for all its prosperity, it only has limited resources to share with other lands."

"I definitely agree with that," Aub replied. "Allocation of resources is and will remain a key issue. That's one major reason why the revolution goes at the pace that it does. The more prosperous a place gets the more it can use to help others, but this can only be done at a steady and controlled pace. Go too fast and it all collapses. Total Quality Management programmes were well-known for failing in the past because of this."

"I'm glad you see it like that," replied Joanie, "because Vice Chancellor Bogodan was most keen that I ascertained your absolute assurance that that you would be at one with him on that issue. Another problem is that of growing civil unrest in Northern Kamchatka where our territory interfaces with capitalist Russia. A similar situation is feared in Alaska and Baja California where our supporters continue to band together to purchase land and fly The Island flag."

"I know there are problems, yes."

"There's pressure on both sides. On our side we can only absorb small numbers of suitable people at any one time. On the other, people are amassing on the border, trying to cross from poor capitalist regions to our starkly contrasting non-capitalist side. To accompany this there is also the matter of soaring property prices and land values in the areas that are in close proximity to the flexible border in anticipation that the border will shortly move and allow residents in these areas to become absorbed onto our side and enjoy huge benefits as a result. I'll show you some of Sylvia Smith's latest footage."

The ensuing scenes on the screen were not a pretty sight. The Greencoats, far from being the gentle force that Aub had hitherto perceived, used some considerable force to drive back several hundred individuals from the thirty-foot high fence that separated capitalist Russia from the non-capitalist Island-owned territory. Russian soldiers, who were supposed not to exist, then acted from behind to round up those who were attempting to cross the line and remove them for sentencing.

"Sentences are getting necessarily stiffer," Joanie explained, "And you are going to have to sign the document that will place these people in detention for up to eight years in place of the present eighteen months."

"I understand," said Aub, shaking his head and appearing slightly tearful.

"Policing the world is never easy," Joanie said, "And I know that will be one of the hardest things that you will have to do once the crown passes to you. The argument of both Bogodan and Ulanov is that unless these people can be suitably deterred, there is the risk of total anarchy in the area. We cannot afford to allow our precious system to become destabilised. You will have to sign it and it's going to hurt."

"It will hurt because I have always devoted my life to improving the quality of life for others, not making it worse."

"More people will suffer a loss of quality if you don't sign. So you will have to, but, like the article, it need not be as bad as it looks."

"What do you mean?"

"Well, I have had a talk with our noble Concierge, and he is certainly open to a discussion on how to tackle the need for a deterrent with a combined strategy for improving the quality of life on the Russian side that will reduce the incentive for civil unrest."

"But I'm still going to have to sign a document that could potentially make me responsible for getting a lot of people locked up for a very long time."

"Nobody said that being The Island King would be easy," Joanie continued, "but now that's out of the way I'll show you something a bit more cheerful. What you see now is the debating chamber of the Kamchatka Parliament. You will note that there is no left or right, just a semi-circular arrangement with a single despatch box where Vice Chancellor Bogodan stands to read out the daily agenda and the levels of approval reached on proposed Bills and Action Plans. There are currently 676 MPs, of whom twenty-one, if you include the Parliament's newest member, sit on the Foreign Bench, which is located on the right hand side of the front row.

"You will see that the Ministers are taking their positions, except for one on the Foreign Bench between the Right Honourable Member for the last acquired territory of

Tierra del Fuego, Emmanuel Ricardo, and Mike Harris, the Right Honourable Member for The Falklands and South Georgia."

When all of the Ministers were seated the slim, pale faced Vice Chancellor, his blond hair neatly swept back, entered and faced them at the despatch box. With one stroke of his mallet he summoned the House to order. With a mild, slightly effeminate voice, he spoke first in Russian, then in English.

"Please be upstanding and extend a warm welcome for our new Member. Number of votes cast 675. Number of votes of approval 675. Ladies and gentlemen your approval is unanimous and I have great pleasure in welcoming to our Foreign Bench the Right Honourable Member for Bathurst and Melville, Jacob Spence."

"That was fast work," Aub remarked, as, surprised, he observed his colleague take his seat.

"This is happening live," Joanie emphasised, "As soon as you gave me his name I ordered a Hebden Three to be despatched to Bathurst Island to bring him to Petropavlovsk Kamchatskiy. He's about to be sworn in."

The Parliament building echoed to the sound of Waltzing Matilda as the small haggardfigure of thirty-five-year-old Jacob Spence emerged to be escorted to his seat.

"It gives me great pleasure and it is a great honour," he said, "To be the first Australian to serve in this, the world's greatest parliament. I am looking forward to working with all of you and I thank you all for approving my invitation to represent Australia here with such dedicated efficiency. I know our future King, whom I also thank for nominating me, will be watching as I speak. Ladies and gentlemen, Vice Chancellor, this is a massive leap forward for Kamchatka and for Australia. Thank you so much."

"Well, there he is," said Joanie, as she turned off the screen, "Your man now installed. Now I can tell you that the House has now approved the final selection of Ministers that are going to apply their tests to you. I can say that gaining unanimous approval from the House to become King and marry the Queen is not going to be in doubt. It's more the results that they will be interested in, to demonstrate the level of capability to solve problems that are of concern. The Island King always has to be seen as a key problem solver, acting with both credibility and integrity.

"I will now tell you a little more about what is going to happen. As you know next week I will be leaving The Island with the setmates for a land far away. In the meantime the selected Ministers will each set you a task. These will not necessarily be easy, but it's how you complete them that counts. There is no such thing as failure, just by how much you succeed. Remember that we are driven forever by constancy of purpose and a desire for continual improvement, and that it will be down to yourself and The Queen to guide us into the second stage of our glorious revolution. I will now bid you farewell. Lunch awaits you later in Government House. Then Jobine will invite you to take to the ice and show her what you can do."

*

Before lunch Aub had a little time to reacquaint himself with The Town and take in some of the fresh sea air. Then he took a look inside Government House, noting some of the portraits of famous British Liberals, including David Lloyd George, Jo Grimond, Paddy Ashdown and Vince Cable. He followed the time trail to the last portrait, that of Leo Harvey in 2036 and concluded that something significant must have happened to the party at that time as the year was clearly highlighted and, next to this particular portrait, was a jacket in a case that corresponded exactly with that in the picture. He noted the Liberal Democrat emblem of 2036 that had been carefully woven into the outer jacket pocket. Then he read the inscription beneath as follows:

'This jacket is one of the few surviving special commemorative Liberal Democrat jackets from the famous Cardiff conference of 2036. It belonged to the late Leo Harvey, first Prime Minister of The Island and Founder of the modern-day British Whig Party in that year, which later played a major role in the establishment of the now world famous Parliament of Kamchatka in 2077.'

Well I never knew that, Aub whispered to himself, as he began to realise that The Island held far more secrets than he could ever imagine. He walked around and peered through a door that led into a somewhat smaller room which contained a large table and a number of chairs. He approached the window and looked across the bay towards the west coast of The Island. The layout of the room told him that this was the signing room where The Prime Minister would be seated with delegations from various countries to sign treaties and conduct international affairs of state. Her position may have become merely symbolic, but the formalities were real enough to show that The Island really had become a truly powerful political entity despite the prominence and authority of the Kamchatka Parliament. He was moved by the extent to which this tiny room could change the destiny of the world, quite apart from being somewhat intrigued by its unusual British connection. Yet it was in here, most certainly, that he was going to have to sign the new Civil Disorder Act which in his heart of hearts he did not want to sign. Unlike with the Australian defence budgets, this would be a signing that was going to be unavoidable.

From Government House he walked past the statue of Atlas and Angel Cottage and on to The Town Hall steps, where another open door caught his eye. It was the entrance to The Wax House, which he had seen before, but now had one or two subtle changes. Straight away he spotted the newly added portrait of Joanie Carmichael, which now stood with the other past Island Prime Ministers, and the plaque underneath which read 'Joanie Carmichael, Prime Minister of The Island Territories 2102 to 2108'.

He then stepped towards the waxworks of The Founders and gazed at them, contemplating their achievements. He never ceased to be amazed at how such a small group of eccentric individuals could have come together and succeeded in making such a profound change to the world. He observed particularly Patrick Carmichael, The Actor and his principal Georgina, grandparents of Joanie Carmichael. Then there was the great Clifford Hebden, grandfather of the present Managing Director of Kamchatskiy Aerospace, Charlie Hebden. Then he looked to the first King, Ken David and the accidental Queen Justine to whom he owed his present position as heir to the crown, and Leo Harvey, architect of the system of Non-Capitalist Economics.

"How lovely to see you again," remarked The Curator, slightly startling him from behind.

"Geniuses all of them," The Prince replied. "If someone had said a hundred years ago that these people were going to achieve all of this nobody would have believed it. It's an honour and a privilege to be a part of it."

"They would be proud of you. You have all the qualities that they would have hoped for, especially that true desire and determination to make the world a better place in line with the plans that they envisaged. Come, I'll show you something new," said The Curator, leading him into the second hall, where he saw to his surprise a waxwork of himself standing next to Queen Katie.

"Well, do you like it?" she asked.

"A perfect likeness," replied Aub, noting that although the waxwork was not a perfect resemblance it did look very lifelike. "Where did it come from, as I don't remember posing for it?"

"The Queen commissioned it from a photograph that she took of you apparently on Bathurst Island. Lots of our waxworks are sculpted from still pictures."

"I see Joanie Carmichael has gone, not to the melting pot I hope."

"Not at all. She's being moved to a special place, I'll show you if you like."

Presently he was led to the distinctive waxwork of Joanie Carmichael, which stood apart from the display of past Prime Ministers.

"What's with this space commanders uniform."

"Hasn't she told you about her promotion?"

"No. I know nothing of it. I only know she is leaving The Island with the setmates at the end of the week."

"She's going to be the new Moonbase Commander, but sssh, don't tell the setmates."

"Wow. That's some job. I'd quite like that one myself."

With lunchtime approaching The Prince had just a few more minutes to wander around The Town a little more, and it occurred to him to perhaps visit The Church of The Founder Mary, where he had attended the Christmas service in 2106, but other than that it was one place on The Island about which he knew relatively little. He suspected that just maybe The Verger might be in attendance at this time so he made his way back past Government House to the somewhat flatter terrain beyond The Bell Tower.

From the air The Church of The Founder Mary could be seen to have a tree-like construction, which was just about discernible as one approached it from the steep bank from which an old stone path led down. Internally the altar was at the base of the trunk, whilst branches led off from each side of the aisle leading to small spherical prayer rooms, which collectively accommodated all of the world's major religions. The altar was bare save for the two-foot high brass statuette of The Founder Mary, which was mounted upon a three-foot high marble plinth in the centre.

As The Prince meandered his way down the path, he spotted an elderly gent wearing a cloth cap tending to some graveyard flowers, who presently heard him, raised his head, and walked towards him.

"The Church is open, please enter," The Verger said, pointing to the open door, "Our Church is always open you know."

"Always, even in the dead of night?"

"Certainly. Anytime anyone has time to pray they are free to enter. There are no thieves here. If someone really has a desire for something an agreement is always struck."

"Interesting," replied Aub, "Like the setmates I'm learning new things about Non-Capitalist Economics all the time. No thieving, no vandalism, hardly any crime apart from the occasional mild drunkenness, and everyone more or less having a fair way to obtain virtually anything within reason that they might want. Nobody overworked, but everyone in work. Everyone taking pride in their work. What more could anyone ask for? I see this graveyard is immaculate. I must compliment you in your work. I don't think I have ever seen a tidier cemetery nor a more pleasing arrangement of flowers."

"Well thank you, Your Royal Highness. I always try to make it presentable to visitors, and, of course, to Her Majesty. I know I'm very privileged to live and work in a place where Deming's Twelfth Point is central to every aspect of government policy."

"Remove barriers that rob people of pride of workmanship," replied Aub. "I know, I studied it at length, and in Kamchatka there is a whole Government Ministry devoted to applying it. Another reason why our Parliament is renowned as the world's finest."

"Quite. I have met Viktor Bogodan a few times. I was especially struck by how humble he is, just as Joseph Juran was once reputed to be. Even he has a secret fear though."

"Oh, what on earth could that be?"

"Being perceived as a dictator when he is anything but. People who are not acquainted with him only look at the power he has and are therefore fearful when there is no need. Others don't like the thought of having their power undermined. You'll have to watch for that yourself I'm sure."

The Prince knew exactly what he meant as The Verger led the way into The Island Church, where he counted a total of fourteen branches leading off from the main aisle.

"The whole Church is rarely used as most of the services are Christian," The Verger explained, "but all mayor religions can be found represented somewhere. The Christian prayer room is the largest, being subdivided into Protestant, Catholic and Orthodox. There are separate chambers for Mormons, Quakers and Presbyterians. Towards the rear you will see chambers representing Islam, with its sub-chambers, Buddhism, Hinduism and, right at the back, even atheism. I'll show you that one as its quite interesting and we do have quite a few atheists in our population. Kamchatka has yet more."

Aub gazed up at the convex roof of this chamber, which was of navy blue and depicted planets and stars in their courses. The prayer mats faced a model of Stonehenge illuminated in yellow, and the walls were adorned with Gothic-themed paintings embraced in The Island flag.

"Not as bare as you might have expected, hey," remarked The Verger. "It acknowledges a collection of non-religious viewpoints and celebrates our place in the natural universe. You'll even notice a prayer book, the first ever written specifically for an atheist congregation. You'll note the picture of Charles Darwin on the far wall, and in the prayer book you'll also find a section that prays for a healthy and kind evolutionary path for all humans and earthly creatures."

The Verger presently pressed a button on a remote device that he was carrying and soft music began to play, reflecting the style of the Druids.

"Quite relaxing, don't you think?" The Verger asked.

"I never thought there could be so much in it," Aub replied, "I've never seen a church with such an unusual feature."

"Neither had I until I came here. It's strange, religion has been around for so long, but it is only since the inception of The Island that theologians have contemplated incorporating atheist beliefs into what is otherwise a House of God."

They returned to the altar where Aub looked more closely at the statuette of the woman who had largely been responsible for what had, in the late twenty-first century, become a new concept in religion, one of the world's most ancient fields of study.

"One religion for everyone that embraced all other religions, that was The Founder Marys' vision," explained The Verger, "Now most of Kamchatka has converted to it, and the modern churches there have been built largely as replicas of the building in which you are now standing. This was the very first one, built way back in 2067."

"If Jesus really has watched over this world since His passing, as many Christians would have us believe, He must have been horrified and dismayed at the appalling cost in human lives that has derived from religion over the centuries, and its use as a smokescreen for politics and power.

"And we look to you to help us change it. Do read our Founder's book *Keeping the Faith* if you can. Finest book on religion since The Bible. You will learn a lot about one woman's dream of ending war caused by religion by preaching tolerance over bigotry. Through her we all keep our own faith, yet we acknowledge all others so that our Church is truly one body. A body over which soon you will preside."

Chapter Five
Onto the Ice

Samurai Cottage was a small, quaint, self-contained one-roomed cottage right in the heart of The Town, conveniently situated between The Great Dome and Government House. It was unusually private given its location, with a door that would open only for The Prince, The Queen and The Queen's personal maid. It had a bed, a table and all modern amenities should it be easier for The Prince to stay in The Town rather than The Royal Palace.

After lunch The Prince entered it and looked around, noting the pair of gold-bladed ice skates that had been placed at the end of the bed as Joanie had told him. He checked the time, then went outside to flag down a Kammie. He noticed that some Kammies had drivers whilst others did not. The one that stopped for him did have a driver, to whom he was able to request his destination as the ice rink.

Upon his arrival he made his way through the ornate entrance porch to the rinkside. Katie was already warming up on the ice.

"Great to see you again," said Jobine, as he put on his skates along with the training suit that had been laid out for him, "You'll need to break those boots in, but it shouldn't take long because they have been expertly tailor-made using the finest Kamchatkan leather. As you already know, for your Coronation Wedding we want to create the greatest ice dancing spectacle that the world has ever seen. I have therefore planned that you and Katie will master six six-minute-long routines to perform in Red Square. These will be interspersed with five slightly longer routines performed by a selection of top Russian, including Kamchatkan skaters, as well as schoolchildren from invited schools. All of this will take place next year on the Ides of March."

"Just as well my name's not Julius Caesar," laughed Aub.

"As you know," Jobine continued, "I have taught Katie since she was eight whenever I have not been otherwise engaged with the setmates, so I know exactly where she stands in terms of her standard. She should be able to help raise your standard when it comes to skating as a couple. When did you learn to skate?"

"Some years ago when I was about eighteen. Once I learnt more about The Island and its skating heritage I started to get more into it. So I made a point of skating whenever and wherever I could both as a student at Macquarie and in other places as a break from politics."

"This year, as you know, there will be no intake of setmates. One reason for this is so that I can give and Katie personalised tuition throughout the whole year whilst you are not on assignment."

"Six routines?" said Aub.

"Six for Red Square. There will be a seventh, but I will tell you more about that later."

"Right," replied Aub ponderously.

As Aub took to the ice Jobine could quickly see the difference in standard between the two skaters. Aub was quite definitely of a lower standard and out of practice by comparison. After he had performed a few basic runs and chasses she called him over.

"Yes, I can see that you are a good bit stiff," Jobine remarked, "and there is a considerable difference in ability between you and Katie, but it's not a big problem. When you're skating together many of the differences can be easily masked over time. We will need to match your free legs in terms of extension, and improvements in posture will have to be worked on, but we shall overcome."

"If anyone can get results you can."

"You'll be great, I promise," said Jobine, "Now I'll show you something new."

Jobine pressed a button on her hand-held device, which released a harness from above.

"Catch," said Jobine as she pointed to the descending line.

Aub turned his head and grabbed the harness.

"Now strap yourself in," she ordered.

He did as she said, and she then performed a final inspection to ensure that everything was in order.

"Katie is used to the harness," said Jobine. "You will need to get used to it. Don't be too concerned if you feel a little disoriented at first. Normally with the setmates I leave it a month or two before introducing the harness, but because your tuition is more intensive and Katie is already used to it, it makes sense to get you going with it right away. To start with I am going to lift you just one metre above the ice. I want you to get used to using your toe picks to act as a signal for the harness to provide partial elevation. Katie, I'm going to lower a harness for you also and I want you to practice reaching out to him."

Katie was raised to a slightly greater height, as if to draw Aub upward. Aub meanwhile gradually became accustomed to using his toe picks to act as a signal to the harness to raise itself. Then Jobine experimented with higher elevations.

"At the commencement of your first routine you will need to be able to descend," Jobine explained. "And this is an art in itself. We are going to imagine that the world is watching with eager anticipation after the coronation, wondering what is going to happen next. Then, to the audience's great surprise, you are going to descend from two different points overlooking Red Square, and come together, and it's the coming together that I want to work on with you. Once that's mastered, the rest of your opening routine should not be too difficult. You will touch down on the ice and begin the first of your six routines that will display your inner feelings for one another using a variety of rhythms, some fast some slow, some traditional some modern, some comical others passionate. The people will be totally mesmerised. Your first routine will take the audience by complete surprise. Your descent onto the ice and subsequent performances are to be a closely guarded secret until the grand day itself. Only then will they see the world's first ever real life skating King and Queen."

So the harnesses were raised such that Aub and Katie faced each other from two opposing platforms high above the ice. Upon Jobine's whistle they each used their toe picks to launch themselves towards each other. As Jobine expected, however, it did not go to plan and both were hopelessly off target when it came to attempting to combine with each other in a turning motion ready to land on the ice. It was possibly going to take several weeks to ensure that even just this single opening movement took place without error, so, with The Prince and Katie having gained a feel for it, Jobine left it after twenty minutes and returned to ice dancing from first principles.

"Ice dancing is all about two people skating together as one," she explained. "That is what distinguishes it from the other skating disciplines. I therefore want to get you moving together more as a single unit. In this you can either dance apart with synchronised action, or you can dance together in hold so that you move entirely together. Thus, I can turn on a Latin rhythm and ask you to dance singly, but in unison, to the rhythm, or I can put on a waltz and you can dance together with matching steps. Both will feature in your final performance. Both are contrasting forms of what we describe technically as ice dance. Once this is mastered we can add things such as props, or we can bring in more people as in formation dancing and various historical forms such as quadrilles, cotillions and minuets. Ballet can be performed using ice dancing, and as such is an applied form. But in your case you will be a newly married and crowned King and Queen, so our main focus is that of making two people skate as one and able to dazzle.

"Now, as I said there will be one more routine to master, and for this I will need you to wear special suits that have been specially created for the purpose. They are in the changing area and I would like you to try them for size. They will feel a little odd to start with. You will note that they are helium-filled. I need you to try them on now just in case we have to make any adjustments. They will help you to become used to skating at one fifth of normal gravity."

They tried the suits on and took to the ice. Somehow in these outfits they could perform steps, leaps and somersaults such that they could never have done before.

"Wow," said Aub, as he leapt in the air, tucked himself into a ball and then performed a double somersault. Then he performed the triple axel with ease. In fact he could perform quads, quintruples and even a sextruple Salchow.

"That might be easy enough," said Jobine, observing his newly discovered skill, "But the routine will be far from easy. You will need to make adjustments for the fact that your skates will also weigh less when you perform routine number seven."

*

In the evening social skating had been arranged such that The Prince and The Queen could skate with the setmates. There were opportunities for photoshoots as well as opportunities for them to meet The Prince informally and share experiences of their year on The Island.

"This is a very special year," said Jobine as she introduced the session. "For we now have our future King and Queen with us. Next year they will be crowned and married both at the same time. I'm sure you will all enjoy skating with them over the coming nights. They have said that they will endeavour to have as many dances as possible with all of you, and with that I shall now ask our resident organist and Chancellor to get things underway with our first dance."

The Prince circulated, shaking the hands of the setmates one by one. With the setmates already familiar with the company of The Queen, it followed that The Prince had more introductions to make. Katie, for her part, was invariably asked about how she had come to know Prince Aub, and where they would be going from here.

"We are going to have a world famous Coronation Wedding in Red Square," she said to all who were curious. "Then we are going to perform some great routines for you. So the story is just beginning, as it is for you."

"I saw your Silver Shadow routine," Aub said to Yvonne. "It was brilliant and I'm so glad I was able to give you my very last ticket, and you and your set can be very proud of what you have achieved."

He danced the Kilian with Yvonne, fast and smooth. As with the others with whom he danced, when she skated it was as if she had been skating with him a lifetime, not just one dance. He was that easy to skate with, not to mention The Queen, who was even better. The progress of the setmates could not be underestimated, though, as, under Jobine, they themselves had all become experts in their own right. This combination meant that, of course, this was no ordinary social skating night. It was a night for the stars.

He kissed Yvonne on both cheeks and embraced her before moving on to Marie, the French girl, for a Tango Especiale.

"So, you are Marie?"

"Yes."

"From Paris. Yes, I remember now. And how do you feel about your time on The Island of Dreams?"

"It has been an unbelievable experience. Joanie has given us all personalised diskettes of our best bits. I never knew we were being secretly filmed. I will treasure it for the rest of my life."

The other setmates all gave similar responses, combined with a natural slight sadness that it was all coming to an end. After all, it was a unique experience that they all knew they had been extremely privileged and fortunate to have had, and that was down entirely to The Prince and how he had distributed The Queen's Tickets. All of the setmates with whom he danced made a point of thanking him profoundly for having received their precious Ticket.

"I wish I could have given out more than 240," Aub said to Anne Clancy, after she had thanked him for hers.

Katie and Aub were naturally popular and with 240 setmates each by now highly proficient, there was obviously a need to restrict the number of people on the ice at any one time and not all setmates were going to have a dance with either Katie or Aub on the first night. Indeed many hadn't by the time Jobine brought the session to a close at ten o'clock.

A bell sounded as Jobine introduced the last waltz.

"So we must close for tonight," Jobine declared. "I therefore ask the next twelve couples to take to the ice. Don't worry if you haven't danced yet with Aub or Katie, because at least for now there's always tomorrow."

Chapter Six
A Round of Golf

The next morning The Prince and The Queen had breakfast with The King and The Queen Mother at The Royal Palace.

"Your parents and your brother Charles have both sent their best wishes for your future together," The King told them. "And I see there is great celebration on Bathurst Island following the admission of Jacob Spence to the Kamchatka Parliament. If you switch on your mobile device you will be able to see the jubilation. Also I can tell you that The Concierge has arrived and has sent you a copy of his 2107 lecture as you requested. I understand that he wants to brief you on a few things, and for that he has invited you both to join him for a round of golf on the West Links. He'll meet you at the clubhouse at ten o'clock. The Chancellor is coming up from The Town on the morning train and will take you to the West Links on the gondola when he arrives."

"I wondered when I was going to get a ride on that," replied Aub.

*

"So where did this beaute come from?" Aub asked The Chancellor as they began the half-mile cruise along the west side of the lake to the towpath that led to the clubhouse of the West Links.

The Chancellor then recited the story of how Queen Justine had reputedly taken a holiday with Ken to England's

Lake District and travelled on a similar craft on Lake Coniston.

"Ken, as you know was a master at building unusual ships," The Chancellor explained. "And Justine had told him how much she loved the old steam yacht gondola that had been carefully preserved at Brantwood, home of nineteenth century artist and political philosopher John Ruskin, author of *Unto This Last*. On learning this Ken then set about building a replica, which he then gave to her on her fortieth birthday in 2049. It's surprisingly fast across the water."

Hardly had The Chancellor had time to explain the story behind what was now Queen Katie's gondola, as it drew in alongside the jetty at the end of the towpath.

"Ahoy there, this way," came the broad Irish voice of The Concierge, as he waved his arms, gesturing to the royal couple to follow him into the quaint sandstone clubhouse that was adorned with photographs of golf games gone by, where The Island had played host to a range of monarchs and world leaders over the decades.

"Oh I see there the pictures Sylvia took of us last time," Aub remarked.

"Yes, the ones next to it are of me and the King of Spain," replied Katie. "I think he was a bit peeved that I beat him."

"You'll find the course quite challenging today," advised Concierge Patrick O'Rourke. "We've got quite a strong westerly coming in off the Atlantic and its set to turn squally later in the day, so I've packed waterproofs in our bags in case we need them. What's your handicap by the way, Aub?"

"Six," he replied.

"Then you'll get a stroke allowance for The Prisoner, the par three sixth that causes so much trouble for the unwary."

"I know. I took six shots on it last time."

"It's all those awful tiny pit bunkers all round the green. They're so hard to avoid," Katie added.

Of course Aub knew that there was far more to this than a mere round of golf. He knew that Patrick O'Rourke and his partner The Reverend Duncan McIntyre, were very much the spearhead of The Island's quiet revolution in the twenty-second century, and as such he was going to have to work closely alongside them to keep the revolution on track. They would be his closest advisors in the years immediately ahead, although with both of them fast approaching fifty years of age he was aware that neither of them would be able to continue at their present pace forever. Who was going to replace them? Aub asked himself. He put this question to Katie.

"They have led many teams," Katie reassured him. "Both have team leadership skills that are second to none, and, yes, they will be hard to replace, but you shouldn't be too concerned. Carl Lvov, the Minister for Teamwork has it all worked out."

"Don't they ever go on holiday?"

"Well, yes," replied Katie. "Every year they come here, Patrick blows himself up in a box, and, with the help of specially invited sixth formers, they both play a game of human chess on ice. That's as far as competition ever gets between the two of them, but it's always a closely fought contest."

"I named this hole Number Two," said Patrick, as they putted out on the second green, "Because I couldn't think of a name for it. But now I think I might call it Katie's Best. You read the wind just right. I don't think anyone will get a birdie on the next hole, though, with just water between the tee and the green and that fierce westerly. You can understand why I named this hole The Mariners Curse."

When they had teed off and walked along the rugged pathway by the shore Aub and Patrick engaged in somewhat more serious conversation.

"You know, Patrick," said Aub. "Joanie has always advised me to seek a second opinion when I have doubts about something. So here's one. What do you think about me having to give Royal Assent to the setting up of detention camps and the handing down of eight-year sentences for even just demonstrating in the vicinity of that rotten border that separates the magnificent Island-owned Kamchatka from the impoverished capitalist side, never mind risking their lives in an attempt to cross for quite understandable reasons?"

"Oh you'll have to sign the Bill," Patrick answered, "but that does not mean anyone is going to get locked up. To be sure the detention camps will be built and everyone will know they're there, but that does not mean anyone is going to be put inside them."

"What does it mean then?" Aub asked, somewhat confused by the logic.

"Ulanov has been heavily criticised in Moscow for not getting a grip of the problem. Some people are therefore seeing him as weak, and in The Kremlin there are still some around who are power seekers. It's not like the Kamchatka Parliament, not yet anyway. So, Ulanov has to be seen to be taking a hard line. At the same time he wants to appease his supporters, and Bogodan, who, like ourselves, have a vested interest in keeping him in office.

"From our point of view, we cannot afford to allow streams of unvetted people just to walk into our territory. People have to be educated to live under Non-Capitalist Economics. It's something you need to be trained to do, as you can see from the training that we give to our setmates, and they are, as you know, vetted before they arrive.

"So the camps need to be built and the sentences real, but in practice the problem isn't so much the border as the stark contrast in the quality of life either side of it. On the capitalist side are some of the most deprived and poorest towns in the whole of Russia, the world's richest country. The people feel neglected and let down by the Ulanov regime, which just hasn't been able to, as yet, bring their prosperity up to the standard achieved elsewhere. Russia is a huge country and it takes a long time for prosperity sometimes to filter through to the furthest parts from the capital.

"The solution therefore is to reduce the quality differential by a sufficient amount to raise the flash point at which civil unrest begins. When my teams move in, prisons become a thing of the past, but we need time to plan the operation. The tough sentences and evidence of purpose-built jails will buy us the year, possibly two, that we need, and if the judicial process is made intentionally slow, we could have the whole issue resolved long before anyone is actually interned. I'm far more concerned about the Mexican wall that the Americans built, but the Mexicans paid for. Now, the Mexicans say they paid for the wall, so it's theirs and they should be able to decide who crosses. Every year we see young Americans daring to tunnel under it, climb over it and fly above it. A handful make it into Mexico, but many are killed by their own side, because the American authorities regard it as a betrayal of their country. We can cure Kamchatka. We can't cure Mexico as things stand."

"What about Alaska? There are problems there as well, aren't there?"

"Sure, but there it's very different. There wealthy Americans have paid huge sums and paid high taxes in order to buy land on the Alaskan peninsula fair and square. The anger there is more like you experienced, resentment against nominated individuals accepting invitations to serve in the Kamchatka Parliament. The White House can only watch as elected representatives ditch Washington and represent American territory in a parliament that many Americans see, rightly or wrongly, as a satellite of The Kremlin."

Presently they approached the sixth tee.

"Now The Prisoner stands before you," said Patrick, pointing to the small, sloping green encircled by a ring of extremely small, deep, round pit bunkers. "Now you must land your ball exactly in the centre of the green, which in this wind could be difficult."

It did prove difficult. At first Aub thought he had done well to hit the exact centre of the green until, at the very last moment, the wind carried his ball just off course enough for it to land in one of the eleven pit bunkers that were notoriously difficult to get out of. Katie, knowing the hole well, and being more cautious, pitched her ball just short of the green allowing her to chip over the dreaded bunkers and at least obtain a par. Bogeys awaited both of the other players, but Aub did at least have his handicap stroke. With a handicap of just one, Patrick had no such advantage, showing that even the great Patrick O'Rourke didn't win every time.

"Tell me, Patrick, how many top-level teams do you have working for you worldwide?" Aub asked as they made their way towards the seventh tee.

"About 9000, all at your disposal."

"Nine thousand ! Me and Katie have about 200 agents, don't we Katie?"

"Something like that," Katie replied. "But comparing agents with teams is a bit like comparing apples with pears."

They played on, with Patrick enlightening Aub as to the whereabouts of these teams and the role that they were currently playing in preparing for The New Game. Patrick presently explained to Aub what the current status was.

"Well, the final draft of ISO 9100 has now been released. The International Sovereignties Commission, the ISC, looks as if it has finally reached agreement with The International Standards Organisation, ISO, on the full range of quality of life indicators against which successful bidding nations will be assessed.

"The auditing process will be very strict with successful bidders required to demonstrate year-on-year improvement on all of them from the point at which they take over office in the country concerned. An elite squad of third party international auditors appointed by the ISC and ISO will provide a continuous auditing regime across all of the indicators in all geographical areas that are under the sovereignty of the nation involved. Noncompliance will result in stiff financial penalties. Of course the sovereignty owners, the government, will have fair time to correct all deficiencies that are found, and there are bound to be some, but correct them they must.

"On top of this, all bidders, which may be foreign governments or multinational corporations, will have to show that they have a viable business plan and resources to comply with the standard in order to enter the bidding process in the first place. ISO 9100, as you know, has its roots in the much older ISO 9001 standard for industry that dates back to 1987, and its specifications vary according to whether a country is in the small or large nation category."

"It's linked to Leo Harvey, though, isn't it?"

"Leo Harvey famously chaired the ISO Technical Committee 176, previously responsible for administering and maintaining the ageing ISO 9001 in 2043, when it was in need of a serious upgrade if it was to maintain its credibility. TC 176 didn't have anything like the power that it has today. It was he who devised the concept of a quality supersystem, which would form the basis for a much more advanced standard related to the sovereignty of nations, with potentially transformational properties.

"It was many years in the making, but gradually it took shape, and it should only be a year or so until it finally gets tested in practice. Of course no leader or government can be forced to give up the sovereignty of their country, but they may well receive the opportunity to sell out and then take the money and go, allowing a more competent regime to step in and deliver real continuous improvement for its citizens. In this way some of the world's poorest and worst governed countries can be enabled to experience a dramatic improvement in prosperity and quality of life for the vast majority of their populations."

"You must realise, though," Aub replied "That there are lots of people throughout the world who are employed in defence related industries who would wreck this scheme if they had half the chance."

"Of course, but these people are mainly high-ranking ageing officials, as you have seen in your native Australia. Lots of younger recruits would rather work with the new ideology than against it, being well-placed to develop lucrative careers as auditors. On top of that there is a huge amount of public opinion now that favours it because most people would like to see war a thing of the past. Wars will be fought on the stock exchange, not the battlefield."

"Politics is alright in small doses," Aub said to Katie. "Administering that scheme is going to be a nightmare."

"It won't be easy to introduce," she confessed. "But you'll have 9000 expertly trained teams to call on, and if anyone can plot a course to victory its Patrick and Duncan."

"I know Bogodan has gone for TC176 like a dog for a bone," Aub replied.

"He knows what he's doing that's for sure," continued Patrick. "He knows TC176 is a powerful way of asserting his authority from a relatively benign quarter. He pushed that standard through with the help of Ulanov. He's such a humble man when you get to know him, yet he can go and do something like that, which is truly amazing. A few years ago almost everyone had forgotten about TC176 and ISO 9100. Yet there he was, quietly working behind the scenes where hardly anyone was looking. I've got to hand it to him. Leo's vision of a world without war suddenly looks as if it really could happen."

So they came to the short fifteenth. Aub teed off following a rare birdie.

"We call this one The Cat's Cradle," explained Patrick, pointing over the grassy dunes over which they would drive. "If you look carefully you will be able to make out the outline of a tabby cat resting from the shape of the dunes.

Mind the wind, though, you don't want to end up lifting and dropping from the third green."

Katie played the hole perfectly, once Patrick had helped her address the ball for this most temperamental of holes.

"That's what it needs, the gentle touch," said Patrick as he observed her clean, but not too strong, strike of the ball.

As they played on Aub continued to contemplate the enormous complexity of the administration of The New Game. He asked Patrick for a little more clarity on this thorny issue.

"Tell me Patrick, how are we going to train all of these auditors and keep the system consistent and corruption free? And how exactly do we assess a quality supersystem, given that it has never been done before? Are we really as well prepared as we think we are?"

"It won't be perfect. There is bound to be a learning curve, but I think we have enough good, honest, well-trained auditors to be able to at least start the process. I have personally made sure that all of the teams contain a fair and representative cross-section of industries and nationalities. Viktor wouldn't want it any other way."

"But some of the countries are huge with lots of terrain that is harsh and inaccessible. How are the auditors going to assess all of the quality of life indicators in, say, remote backwaters of Somalia?"

"They won't," Patrick explained. "A representative sample will usually suffice and not all indicators will be assessed in all cases. It will just be the most relevant ones, and often the sovereignty holders will not even know that the assessments are taking place. They will simply be advised of any major or minor non-conformances. Also, it shouldn't take the teams long to ascertain where the deficiencies are. Frequently, drone footage is all that is required to show if a place is below standard."

"And where do we stand in all of this bidding?"

"We will be acting as an enabler for the bidding process, helping the potential bidders and generally ensuring that the scheme does what it has been designed for, which is to prevent war and improve the lives of many of the world's poorest people. Massive improvements should be visible in just a few years. It's a chess game of a sort, with potentially many sides pushing for power, but if you were a poor person in any of the affected countries, would you really care who was in government, just as long as your own life and community continued to improve? For example, if you were a poor person living in Syria, and Syria was bought out by Jordan, and the quality of your life improved enormously as a result, would you really care if you were being governed by Jordan?"

"Obviously not."

"Everyone will be better off in the end as the system improves and the world's resources cease to be sub-optimised."

"TC176 takes over the world?"

Patrick laughed as he putted out with Katie who, having had more time to concentrate on the golf, won the right to tee off first at the last hole.

"Now the wind should be behind us," said Patrick as Katie prepared to drive inland back towards the clubhouse on the par four eighteenth. "You might even get a birdie here."

She did, and so did Patrick. Aub missed out slightly due to a hooked second shot, so settled for par.

"Now there is someone I want you to meet," Patrick explained as they entered the clubhouse ready for some well-earned beer and sandwiches, courtesy of the Aldebaran bakery. "This is Sheelagh, my principal."

She was a dark-haired lady of forty-three who was quietly sipping on an Irish coffee. She rose to shake The Prince's hand.

"You may only just have met me, but I have been a fan of yours for years," she explained. "I was in London last night and I saw that wonderful film."

"Oh, *The Making of Kamchatka*," Katie replied.

"Brilliant historical drama," said Sheelagh. "The acting is excellent and the script is almost exactly as it was. Lauren Lofgren is great as Rachel Harvey, daughter of Leo and first Vice Chancellor. Then look out for Alexei Kalinin as the young Viktor Bogodan. I loved assisting the film crew along with Maria, The Curator, who supplied a lot of the early historical information about The Island and its Founders that led to the acquisition of Kamchatka. It's Russian made, but in English, so should do well in the US. Believe it or not lots of people there actually do like us and many are curious to know more about how the Kamchatka of today came into being. Look out for the costumes too. King Ken is aptly dressed as Admiral of the Fleet and Rachel, well, a bit like a Queen really. I'll leave you to work out which one. The opening of the Kamchatka Parliament had all the trimmings of a fancy dress ball. It was just amazing, so informal yet so profound."

Chapter Seven
The Electron-beam Probe

That afternoon followed the same schedule as the previous one, as did the evening. The following two days were again the same, with Jobine teaching Aub and Katie, notably, how to act on the ice. Slowly she revealed more about what their six routines were going to consist of, with their contrasting themes.

"You will be acting as well as skating," she explained. "Red Square will be transformed into one great ice theatre, where stories will be told and legends unfold. The audience will wait in wondrous anticipation for the unexpected, the mysterious, the exciting, the passionate and the skilful. Here, take these."

Jobine presently handed to them each a sword.

"These ones are plastic props," she continued. "But on the day you will be dancing with real ones, and you will be dancing together as one, not fighting each other, but a common enemy. I want you to practice backwards crossovers in unison holding the sword in matching positions so that you can come together to do battle with your foe."

They practised, but Jobine could see that the swords did not match and they certainly did not come together.

"You need to gain speed on the crossovers," explained Jobine. "And for that the crossovers need to be smooth. Aub, you need to straighten up more and keep your eyes focused on Katie so you can match her. At the moment you are losing speed because you are scratching the ice. Quiet skating is good skating as you already know, but we will perfect this second routine. I'll play you the music."

As they skated, in The Great Dome Joanie prepared for her departure. Her personal effects were slowly being packed away ready for the long voyage ahead. The next morning Aub and Katie dropped by.

"Everything is fine," Joanie said. "I have had a wonderful time here and I'm looking forward to going on the SGV. I'll be sad to leave The Island, of course, but the memories are there of all the wonderful setmates that I have had the pleasure of coaching through The Queen's Ticket. I know, Katie, that it was your idea and I am pleased to have played a part in helping to make at least some dreams come true, as well as signing a few treaties. I learnt this morning that I am to have a special seat in the Kamchatka Parliament, the first ever representing a constituency that is not on planet Earth."

"We will meet again I'm sure," said Katie.

"Well, The Moon won't go away," replied Joanie. "And you have your own spacecraft."

"I take it that's an open invitation," said Aub.

"A warm welcome will always await."

"And likewise at The Palace," Katie said.

Joanie then described to the royal couple what her first duty was going to be in her new job.

"In just over a month I will be pressing the button that will make history by beaming a powerful beam of impregnated electrons to Sirius, the Dog Star, eight light years away. Also, take a look at my new house."

Aub and Katie looked toward the screen where the image presently appeared.

"But it looks just like this place," Aub remarked.

"It's a replica of this, The Great Dome," Joanie explained. "A dome within a dome, looking over a complete self-contained town, a fully equipped, fully operational self-sustaining community. Outside, in the Sea of Tranquillity, you will see the hundred metre diameter dish that will despatch the electron-beam probe to Sirius. Not too far away from it you will see an American flag with a wrought iron fence around it. That's the Patch of Honour that the Americans placed there in July 1969. A few weeks ago I signed the international preservation order that makes it illegal to trespass on the site, not that anyone would."

"I am fascinated with that probe," said Aub. "King Neville gave me a copy of the recording Patrick's lecture to last year's setmates. I'm even more keen to view it after seeing that."

"We can watch it later today if you like," Katie suggested. "There should be time before the social to go and see it at The Opera House."

*

"You can almost hear a pin drop in here," Aub remarked as Katie inserted the diskette into the playback unit. "Just like Sydney in miniature."

As the recording began Aub instantly recognised the setmates of 2106-07 at their round tables looking towards the stage on the SGV Katie.

"Oh I recognise some of these, that's Tara Branston," he said, recognising at once the dark-haired girl from Orange.

"You met her in Sydney, didn't you?"

"Yeah, The Defence Industry Congress was in Sydney in 2106. I gave her the last of your Tickets that year. She was a lovely skater and a good scholar too. Failed by Australia's atrocious education system of course."

"I remember a lot of them as well," Katie replied. "Paolo, Rhianna, Donna, Gerry, Michelle, Juan, Francesca and loads more. And those schoolchildren from the Leonovo School. They were a real joy to have on The Island."

Presently Patrick O'Rourke took his place at the lectern and was greeted as ever with spontaneous applause before commencing his lecture.

"Ladies and gentlemen, boys and girls, have I got a treat for you this year. Please give a warm welcome to Katrina Latkin, Headmistress of this years invited school, the Leonovo School, which, as the name suggests, is named in part after our great Founder Leo Harvey, who helped to establish the school in 2075. At the time it pioneered a completely new approach to Russian education along Deming lines."

"I remember her as well," Katie commented, as she and Aub watched her rise briefly at her table.

"Katrina, you're a star," Patrick continued. "Which brings me to my subject for tonight. You will observe on the screen a star chart with a small arrow pointing to one star in particular. Can any of you tell me which one it is?"

Several hands were raised and Patrick pointed to one of the boys.

"Aldebaran," he answered.

"Good try, but no," replied Patrick. "Anyone else? Girl on the left."

"Well, it's quite bright, so I think it could possibly be Alpha Centauri because that's quite near," she replied, clearly with a bit of uncertainty.

"It's the closest star to us certainly," Patrick agreed. "But it's not that. Here's a clue. Think of Pavlov."

More hands were raised and Patrick pointed to another boy.

"Oh it's the Dog Star, Sirius."

"You've got it. Now can you tell me how far away it is from Earth?"

"I think it is, er, about eight light years."

"You don't seem totally confident on that, but you're near enough right. It's actually 8.611 light years. Now I'll show you something else."

The star chart vanished and was replaced by a shot of the lunar landscape, with its array of recently built interconnected domes, with a hundred-metre wide dish beyond, which had a very pronounced antenna that extended outwards for about the same distance.

"Now, can any of you tell me what that enormous dish is designed for? Girl on the right."

"Send signals to outer space."

"Yes, and what else?"

The girl was unsure so Patrick invited one of the boys to answer.

"Receive signals from outer space."

"Yes, but there's a lot more. How many of you have heard of electron-beam welding?"

Quite a lot of hands were raised now.

"Many of you. But can any of you tell me who invented the process?"

The hands fell.

"No. Well, it was a German physicist called Karl-Heinz Steigerwald way back in 1949, and it took nine years from concept to complete operation.

Our beamer on Moonbase Alpha took rather longer. Its thousands of times more powerful than an electron-beam welding machine and huge by comparison. I won't tell you, Ms. Latkin, how many schools could be built for the monetary cost of this grand device, because it's Sirius."

The audience chuckled for a moment, then he continued.

"Over 200 teams were involved in its creation, and many more robots. It was shipped to the Moon in a number of segments, using our two freighter craft, and then pieced together by robots working on the unprotected lunar surface. On the screen you can see a sped-up version of the assembly process.

"We have to use the Moon for this project because it can only work to and from a location that has no atmosphere. Any atmospheric conditions would immediately disable our electron beam.

"As you know free electrons can be accelerated to a speed approaching the speed of light. Their paths can be controlled by electric and magnetic fields, which is useful because any decently sized planet may be expected to possess a significant magnetic field and so potentially be able to bend or even break our beam into chunks that, with the application of modern scientific techniques, can be tuned to perform a function, then re-energised so that it returns along its original path ready for our beamer to perform its second function, that of receiving the returning beam in the form of pulses that contain embedded data. That is why our device contains both the satellite dish combined with the electron beam apparatus.

"Look at the screen now and you will see a diagram that you may recognise. Can any of you tell me what it is?"

A couple of the older students raised their hands and Patrick pointed to one of them.

"It's an electron gun," replied the boy.

"It is indeed. And how does it work?. Well, as you'll see on the drawing a bank of metal bars is used to produce electrons in vast numbers by thermo-emission. These are then accelerated to ever-increasing speeds in a series of stages before being magnetically focused so that they can travel through a vacuum to their target, in this case Sirius.

"When the beam reaches Sirius the high magnetic field of the star will cause the beam to be deflected away from it and towards smaller bodies with much smaller magnetic fields, which are the beam's real target. The simulation you are about to see will illustrate.

"You will observe that the beam is designed to be attracted to these smaller fields one by one as it passes through what should be the solar system of Sirius. It will then begin to fragment, with pieces collecting around any planetary bodies that happen to be present. Note this can happen only after the beam has been disseminated by the star.

"So, we've generated our beam, it goes to Sirius, it gets broken, and the resulting beam fragments are drawn to planets. Now we have to make our beam do something.

Fortunately there is a property associated with electron beams that helps us in this aim, and that is the phenomenon of backscatter. Have any of you heard of it?"

No hands were raised.

"Okay, so what happens is this. When our electrons enter the atmosphere of a planet the ones at the front end will impact with the planet's surface and lose their kinetic energy, and this will be converted partly into heat and partly into light. The heat will be used to re-energise the beam so that it becomes a pulse. The light will be used to reflect an image of the planet's surface onto the rear end of the beam, which will recede as the planet's magnetic field eventually repels it back towards the star where, upon reaching a critical value, it will regain a sufficient amount of energy to be forced back along its original path. This process, however, does not occur naturally. In order to make our beam behave this way we have to do something with it. Can any of you tell me what?"

A few hands shot up.

"Girl on the left."

"Impregnate it," replied the sixteen-year-old.

"Very good. We have to impregnate it. If you watch the screen now you will see what we do to our beam as it passes through the various acceleration modules of our giant electron gun."

Patrick took the audience through the theory. As the electrons passed through the first accelerator they were laced with slightly more massive sub-atomic particles that, in particular, could absorb light to create a pixel effect. The same process continued in the remaining stages of acceleration such that these particles would be carried along with the beam to the star. On the planets, however, these slightly larger particles would be dragged towards the rear parts of the beam fragments. Each beam fragment would lose only some of its electrons. Then, at some critical point, it would be repelled by the planet's magnetic field having lost a large part of its negativity. Smaller and lighter, the pulses could be accelerated back to the Moon far more easily, and with much less energy, than the original beam. The magnetic field of the star was more than capable of doing this once the beam remnant was correctly placed.

"So now we have a sequence of pulses returning ready to be picked up by Moonbase Alpha," Patrick continued. "And our beamer, now transformed into a receiver, is specifically designed to draw them in with its reverse charged head. As each pulse is received it will go into the device that you now see, an image processor, where the beam remnants will release the light that they have stored so as to reproduce exactly the images that the backscattered electrons have effectively sprayed onto each one.

"Whole maps of planet surfaces should be able to be reconstructed electronically and to a high degree of accuracy in a way that has never been achieved before.

"A couple of months ago our scientists at The Clifford Hebden Research Institute tested this system to see if it would work. They rigged up a small-scale version of the experiment and despatched a beam to Jupiter. The beam passed clean through the asteroid belt as, fortunately, there are no significant magnetic fields there. Jupiter, however, has a very large magnetic field, sufficient to mimic that of a star, and so repel our test beam. It fragmented and was subsequently drawn toward the much smaller magnetic fields of the four major moons, Io, Calisto, Europa and Ganymede.

"If you look at the screen now, you will see two sets of images of the surfaces of these moons. One set was produced using a conventional probe, the other using our new experimental method. Now, can any of you tell me which is which?"

There was some shaking of heads.

"No. Because both sets of images are identical, proving that there is no difference between the quality of the results obtained by either method. The only difference is the time taken to gather the data. The set on the left took just over twenty months to obtain. The set on the right took three hours and ten minutes.

"What this means is that with our new toy we should be able to undertake a mission to map the surfaces of the planets of Sirius, and we know that there are at least three of these. Using the methods pioneered by Her Majesty's scientists at The Clifford Hebden Research Institute we have therefore been able to reduce the time needed to gather such data from the thousands of years that would have been required using a conventional probe, to just eighteen. That, ladies and gentlemen, is now a feasible project.

"It is, without doubt, the most ambitious and challenging space project that we have ever undertaken. To be sure there are still some fine details and calculations to be worked out, but all being well we should be firing the beam continuously for four weeks once the button has been pressed, we hope, sometime in the Spring of 2108.

"Now, as always on these very special occasions, we like to add an extra surprise to our visiting school. So, Ms Latkin, Her Majesty and I have arranged a special invitation for you and your school to travel to Moonbase Alpha to watch the firing of the beam and to experience life for a week at the base."

There were spontaneous cheers from the schoolchildren, quite clearly overcome with excitement at the prospect.

"You will travel on our super new flagship, the SGV Aub, and stay, yes, at The Electron Gun Inn."

The recording terminated with The Prince left spellbound by what he had just seen.

"That is outstanding," he remarked to Katie. "How did they come up with that? A virtual probe. Fascinating."

"True love and dedication," she replied. "Coupled with lots of ingenious thought."

Chapter Eight
A Fond Farewell

The next morning the royal couple was back on the ice. Jobine had asked Aub and Katie to skate a classical Tango Romantica, having ascertained that Aub knew the steps as a result of her observation of his skating at the social, although confessed to being a little out of practice. Katie, on the other hand, was ready for it having been told by Jobine that this dance would constitute the third of the six routines that they were expected to master for Red Square. She knew the dance well, and, furthermore, had had the opportunity to practice with Jobine skating the men's steps.

"This dance has special significance to the Russian people," Jobine explained. "It was invented in the 1970s by Lyudmila Pakhamova, Aleksandr Gorshkov and E.A. Tschaikowskaya, Russia's first recognised international ice dancers and today practically all Russian schoolchildren learn it as a matter of national pride. It will be a great crowd pleaser, and besides, as King and Queen of Russia, which in a year's time you will be, it is the one classical dance that you really should know because many people in the audience will. It is sometimes referred to as the king of classical skating dances. So, this dance is special and I want you to give it your best."

Jobine pressed her magic button and the music commenced. She then watched the couple skate three sequences of the dance before summoning them to attention with her whistle.

"Okay, you skated it," Jobine admitted, "but that's it. In Red Square it needs to be performed. At the moment it's just about good enough for a dance interval with setmates. You will need to learn to characterise the dance and Aub, your edges need to be much cleaner. Katie, you must kelp to assist him whilst at the same time allowing him to lead you. You are the stronger skater, but we must work to ensure that the difference doesn't show. The Russians like people that they can see are strong. They admire strength of character and this needs to show through in your skating because it's the first and most obvious thing that the people will see. Also, Aub, your facial expression was rather stern throughout the whole of that, to the point of looking strained. We don't want you looking like a soldier going to war. You're out of the Australian Defence Ministry now. You need to look regal, at least looking as if you are leading your Queen. Try again."

The couple tried to take on board the advice that Jobine had given, but it was clearly going to take time. After two circuits of the rink she stopped the music and summoned the couple once more.

"I can see you're trying and your posture was better second time around. Also, Aub, your facial expression was better, but ice dancing is all about two people skating together as one. Some timing issues will have to be corrected. Now, as the routine is designed to be six minutes in duration, I had in mind that after three sequences of the Tango Romantica it would lead naturally into an erotic Argentine Tango choreographed to our own composition. Hopefully, when we have pieced that together you will be able to blend the character of the Tango Romantica with that of our own dance to give a seamless transition.

"I will now return to your first routine, Fire and Ice. This needs to be a spectacle, a crowd-rouser, in contrast to the Tango Romantica, which is a crowd-pleaser. Later, I will introduce your fourth routine, which is going to tell the story of your love. This will be full of passion and, yes,

I'm sorry, but it will contain some difficult lifts mixed in with some intricate footwork.

"That then leaves routine number four. You know that throughout Russia today, pretty much every town and village has its own rink and its own skating club. Many of these are small and outdoors, but they are all centres for social gatherings. In many of these part of the club is devoted to a specific kind of skating that is based entirely around school figures. These routines are intentionally slow and intricate, enabling older skaters to make compositions in pairs and groups. It is all synchronised and as we speak a selected team of skaters at a club somewhere in Groznyy is rehearsing the moves that I have sent them. Your moves will be integrated with them such that everything is connected. I have yet to choose the music. Patrick rather likes 'Danny Boy', the Irish classic, as it connects with the strong Irish culture that he imported into Chechnya and would provide a regional flavour. This routine is intended to have more of a calming effect on the audience.

"For the fifth routine you will be joined by some old friends, the last two years' setmates from Kamchatskiy Auto, Kamchatskiy Maritime, Kamchatskiy Aerospace and Kamchatskiy Logistics. It will celebrate the achievements of Russian industry as represented by these four companies. The setmates will do most of the skating, but you will be their centrepiece and will skate a small section of each routine, for a minute and a half. That's four mini routines. Don't tell the setmates, though. It's going to be a surprise for them

"Routine number six will be A Fond Farewell which will begin with a sensual rhumba, then open out into a section from Holst's 'Jupiter, The Bringer of Jollity', that will incorporate The Island anthem 'I vow to thee my Island', before finishing with 'Neptune, The Mystic', finally waving goodbye and heading heavenward.

We will perfect these in the months ahead, then introduce routine seven."

*

The last night for the setmates on The Island finally arrived, and Joanie, as her last act as Prime Minister, had arranged a fondue evening in The Training Centre to which all of the setmates and Island staff had been invited. This enabled The Prince and The Queen to say a fond farewell to all of the setmates, something that Aub was keen to do, having only met many of them briefly. It also allowed staff members whom Aub had not previously met to introduce themselves to him for the first time.

This included notably Dr Adrian Schultz of The Clifford Institute, The Night Watchman, and Chief Trainer Mitsumoto-san, who, in the absence of a new intake of setmates for the following year, was to take the opportunity of having a years' sabbatical.

As the stainless steel cauldrons of simmering cheese were wheeled in by royal chef Bob and The Usherette, The Chancellor played a lament gently upon the old organ which had been placed at the far end of the room. There was much chattering and speculation amongst the setmates about the surprise that Joanie had promised them the next day.

"As you know I will be attending the graduation as I always do," Katie explained to Aub. "I will return as soon as it is over. It doesn't usually take more than an hour."

The Chancellor played for about half an hour. After he had played 'My Bonny Lies Over the Ocean' he stopped, although the chattering continued for a while, until Joanie finally brought a formal end to the evening.

"Well. That's it, apart from my one last surprise. I would like to say a big thank you to you all for being such hard working and dedicated learners. Tonight I especially thank The Queen's chef, Bob, and his team for keeping us so finely fed and watered."

Bob and his team of eight assistants bowed their heads.

"You are all model citizens in every respect," Joanie

continued. "It's been a pleasure and a privilege to have been able to train and equip you for the tasks which lay ahead. I will be seeing you again very soon. Sleep well, and remember, don't be late for the train."

"I wonder if any of them will guess," Aub remarked to Joanie after she had made her announcement.

"Not unless anyone has told them, and I don't think they have," Joanie whispered. "I didn't overhear or detect any kind of ecstatic reaction to the prospect of going into space."

"Are you sad that you're leaving?" Aub asked, as one by one the setmates drifted back to their cottages.

"Everyone who has served here is always going to feel a sense of sadness, but I'm pleased with what I have been able to do and have thoroughly enjoyed every minute. I'll be interested to see who you and Viktor choose as my successor. As for me, not everyone gets promoted to the rank of Moonbase Commander and to be the world's first extra-terrestrial MP is very exciting and special. So I can't complain in the least. Previous Prime Ministers have merely retired into obscurity."

The staff filed past, each wishing Joanie a fond farewell, with many giving her cards and small gifts. As Aub and Katie left for the sanctuary of Samurai Cottage, Aub made eye contact with Dr Schultz, and made a mental note of his expression. Something, he knew not what, told him to be instinctively suspicious.

Chapter Nine
Monopoly

The next thing that Aub knew he was being pursued by an angry mob up a grassy hill. Before him the executioner stood, poised to perform his duty. The Prince continued to run, but there was no escape. The mob soon had him, forcing his head onto the block. With just one strike the head was severed from the body.

A few seconds passed. Then The Prince found himself staring upwards, gazing into none other than the gazing eyes of Dr Schultz.

"You've had a bad dream, Prince, that's all," said Dr Schultz. "Just a bad dream."

"You might have told me that I had had my drinks laced," Aub replied.

"I have followed the procedure that Parliament has ordered. We needed to get you into the deepest level of sleep possible for this exercise. Behold The Dream Machine."

Dr Schultz turned to his assistant Polly, and asked her if she had recorded the fix on the locus of the dominant electron stream at the moment of impact.

"A perfect path," she answered. "I haven't seen one so good in any of the test experiments."

"We have to do this test," explained Dr Schultz. "As part of our ongoing research."

"What are you looking for?" Aub asked.

"R, S and T," replied Dr Schultz. "A trio of single cells in the brain that we believe are interlinked and perform a vital mental function. Find them and we will potentially unlock a completely new realm of neuroscience. The R cell we already know exists, because we are able to supply a sensory input once the brain is in its most relaxed state. We just don't know where it is located. We also know that there is a T cell, a transmitter, that allows an output signal to be recorded. In between is the S, or suicide cell, also known as the Sawicki cell, after the professor who first postulated its existence. This, we believe, has the power, upon receipt of the appropriate signal from R, to shut down the entire brain system, and induce an output from T."

"And when you have found it, what will that tell you?"

"Oh many things. To start with there are, even today, many unexplained deaths, especially in infants, and we think that some of these could be caused by a premature activation of S accidentally as the brain is formed. If this is the case then these deaths are preventable. But that is not all. We also believe not that we could prove the existence of an afterlife, but simply that it is possible that it could exist."

"How do you work that out?"

"If the S cell is activated and T is the last remaining cell, and it can transmit a code that could be picked up by an early forming R, then in theory at least, the time signature as we call it will be reproducible in a new brain, either here or elsewhere. If this can be shown, then it will demonstrate that it is perfectly possible for the signature of a recently deceased brain to subsequently become the time signature of a newly forming brain, thus giving it the same basic identity. In this way, not all dead souls may perish. Nature, not God, may so provide the answer to one of man's oldest and controversial dilemmas.

"With a large enough sample the fixes on the loci in simulation programs such as the one you just experienced, should eventually guide us ever closer to proving this miraculous concept. And its powers do not stop there. The theory could also help us understand the mechanics of other phenomena, such as telepathy, extrasensory perception and poltergeist activity. Do not underestimate the power of the electron.

"Now, with the first stage of our experts' program complete, I am going to return you to it, but don't be alarmed. The rest of it is designed to educate rather than stimulate. Tell me, are you familiar with the traditional board game of Monopoly?"

"I remember it from years ago, yes."

"Good. Then you will soon see how it works. You started on Old Kent Road, the worst square on the board, which represents the Medieval Zone. It is one of two brown squares. After that we move on to the light blue squares of which there are three. The transition from brown to blue takes us into the Industrial Revolution and beyond. On Euston Road we see the first moonwalk, Apollo 11, 1969. You will be placed, appropriately, on Pentonville Road, where we stand today. It's better than Old Kent Road, but still not a good square. You need to take the world off it."

"And how do I do that?"

"Each change of colour on the board symbolises breakthrough improvement of some kind. Each pair or trio of squares of the same colour represents control at the new level. The principle is classic Juran as you know. Within each coloured block, incremental improvement takes place. Juran's Trilogy Model will be used to guide you around the board.

"I will now return you to the sixth level of sleep and allow the program to continue from Pentonville Road. By the end of your reign you will need to have taken the world two squares forward, to Whitehall, second of the pink squares. The higher squares will test your creativity and application of knowledge, helping us to understand more about your true capabilities. The Science Ministry will then be able to gauge what they can expect of you."

The program restarted, returning The Prince to the virtual reality simulation into which he had previously been immersed. The fog cleared and before him stood The Prison Governor of Pentonville Road.

"Welcome to present-day Earth," spoke the gloomy pale-faced officer, pointing to the first of several cell doors of the shadowy prison that characterised this square. "And what a fine mess it is. In the cells behind me you will see many people who, for no apparent reason, have ended up locked into a world of fear, crisis, injustice, unfairness and cruelty."

The Governor unlocked the first door, which revealed a scene of devastation following a terror attack.

"It doesn't really matter what kind of attack it is," explained The Governor, "nor even who is responsible. It's the fact that it has happened and goes on happening. It doesn't matter whether it's an aircraft being blown out of the sky, or a blast in the middle of a city. It is a symptom of a lack of quality assurance in a population. You need to find where the motive comes from and how to effect remedial action. I know you have the skills and the intellect to find a solution."

The Governor then locked this cell and unlocked the second one.

"Here you see the beggar man who, by virtue of being locked into a cycle of unemployment, finds himself unable to contribute anything to the world, no matter how much he may wish to. Everybody loses as capitalism fails miserably to provide the much needed answer. Beside him you see the children who have nothing but the clothes on their backs, forced to flee from a barren land. Wrong place, wrong time. These people would work as hard as any other if given the chance.

"Now, I'll show you cell number three, full of armies and soldiers, not to mention defence ministers. I know you are well on your way to solving that one, but as you can see, the missiles are still there, the men are still being trained to destroy life, and the resources that could be going towards constructive ends continue, instead, to be invested in destruction. Be proud that you rejected it."

Cell four showed scores of broken families where children were beaten and abused behind closed doors, and relationships had collapsed leaving the rejected individual to pick up the pieces of a shattered life. Opportunities for cooperation were gone and sub-optimisation resulted.

"These are the results of a world in chaos," The Governor explained. "And as long as capitalism remains the dominant system in the world's political economy things are unlikely to improve in the foreseeable future. That is assuming that there actually even is a future. Take a look at cell five."

The Governor unlocked the cell and pointed to the rising mushroom-like cloud that rose from the ground.

"Hiroshima 1945. It may have been a long time ago, but the danger has not passed. It only needs one despot, in fact not even that. An accident could trigger it, such as the day a test goes wrong. Who is going to stop it? The answer is you. Fortunately you are not locked in, because you have a pal, The Pal of Pall Mall, first of the pink squares, whom you will now meet. I will bid you farewell, and hope that I do not have to meet you again."

The images faded and a new scene appeared. A youth approached him.

"Got a light?" he asked.

"Feed in 'No'," Dr Schultz instructed Polly.

"No," said The Prince.

"Well I have," said the casually dressed young man, who presently opened up a box from which light emerged that slowly cleared to reveal pictures.

Doors of different shapes and sizes began to open. Behind them battered, bruised and disfigured bodies were transformed into healthy individuals with smiling faces. Behind one door the terror incident that The Governor had shown him was wound back. It was as if everyone had been given a second chance.

"I have set them free," said the youth. "Pall Mall is a breakthrough square. The tide has turned. Now, unlike on previous squares, Non-Capitalist Economics is the dominant system. Observe, cooperation is now there for the battered woman and the child of the broken home. Secondaries have saved the day. The incentives for ruin are diminishing. We now have a Whig prime minister, and that makes many things possible that once were not. He will hold our gains, for sure."

Behind another door the tanks, guns missiles and bombs arrived, at a giant scrapyard.

"It has started," The Pal explained, "and you have initiated it. As you can see, they're going. There are still a lot out there, but at least the process has started, and these squares focus on solutions rather than problems, freeing souls instead of constraining them. Now, much of the repression has gone, but how much more can you remove?"

"We can change things, can't we?" came the voice of a man who was addressing a group of people.

"Yes. Yes. Yes," they shouted, as they waved their placards of Aub Ryman.

On closer inspection Aub was able to recognise the man as the slim, sprightly retired Colonel Francis White, leader of Britain's Whig Party. He winked and walked proudly into Number 10 Downing Street. The program made it clear that ensuring that this man did indeed enter Number 10 was a definite short-term objective for The Prince, one which potentially had great implications for the world. In his final act to The Prince, The Pal opened one last door, which merely contained the message With a Whig Government, Whitehall awaits.

The Pal vanished in a puff of smoke and was immediately replaced by The Wizard. The Pal had, however, left his box behind, and it was now The Wizard of Whitehall, complete with conical hat and robe of sky blue, dotted with numerous gold stencils of Saturn who was in control. He was dressed in The Island's colours of course.

The Wizard raised his magic wand and the box opened again. The bombs, tanks, missiles and guns were still there, but this time it took just one wave of the wand to make them all disappear in their entirety.

"Now here's an exercise for you, Polly," Dr Schultz said to his assistant, "I want you to use the input panel to direct an impulse to the R region of the brain that will make the subject reach out for the wand and read the inscription printed upon it."

"I'll try," said the petite fair-haired Polly.

Slowly Aub felt his right arm move toward the wand. The Wizard handed it to him and he read the inscription ISO 9100 that was etched on it. The significance of this was obvious.

"Now make him hand it back to The Wizard," Dr Schultz instructed.

The Wizard waved the wand again and the box disappeared, followed by The Wizard, leaving The Prince now standing on a large outdoor ice rink where children skated round in circles as if in celebration. Music began to play accompanied with the words War is Over. Katie was there by his side and he lifted her. He lowered her and they kissed. As they did so a flying horse descended from above, upon which was mounted a knight. The Knight whisked him away on his horse and they flew to a far off place.

"I am The Knight of Northumberland Avenue," said The Knight. "Now I will show you the world which your reign should have helped to shape. Observe the governments of every land now working together, not competing, joined together with constancy of purpose. See yonder the Kamchatka Parliament, now Parliament of the World, coordinating all of the others. Watch everyone working together to achieve the transformation. See management by fear obliterated, and the dark shadows of racism wiped out with my sword."

Shadows lurked behind trees in The Forest of Doom, but The Knight could spot them and kill them before they could do any harm.

"Preventive action is what you need," explained The Knight. "And you can't get that with capitalism because there is too much temptation to cut corners. But with Non-Capitalist Economics and One Party Democracy now universal it's very different. Everyone thinks differently now.

"See the whole world managed as a system. It's stable, it's optimised and there are no losers. You most probably won't be alive by the time the world reaches this square, but everyone will remember you as the King that empowered the world, ended war, ended greed, ended prejudice, ended injustice, whilst adding value and happiness."

The Knight pointed to an apartment block.

"See that building over there. That would have been burnt down under the old system. Capitalism would have led to a poorly run council willing to risk the lives of its inhabitants for the sake of cutting costs. Instead, quality is built-in, in every country on every continent. Fear ye not, citizens of the world, for on this square nobody shall lack for anything. Now, all that is left is to prepare for breakthrough. I will now fly you to Bow Street, first of the orange squares, to meet The Baroness."

If everything was as The Knight had said, what more breakthroughs could there be? As Aub lay intrigued Dr Schultz again turned to his assistant.

"He is in contemplative mood," Dr Schultz said. "I want you to track the current path here, it will help with our profiling."

The Prince found himself floating in a small cylindrical capsule that floated along a channel.

"Hello my charming Prince," came the voice of a petite blonde woman from behind him. "Welcome to the orange zone. Hope you like the transport, lovely and clean, just like the air. Totally renewable energy. We still have cars, buses and trains, but not on every street. As you can see, people are not stressed any more. The orange squares are completely stress free, for most anyway. Now, tell me how old you are."

"Feed in 'Thirty-three'," Dr Schultz instructed Polly.

"Thirty-three," replied The Prince.

"How old do you think I am?"

"Feed in 'Thirty-three' again," ordered Dr Schultz.

"Thirty-three," answered The Prince.

"Nearly," replied The Baroness. "One hundred-and-thirty-one and rising. Without the shackles of capitalism all sorts of possibilities arise, like increasing good health and life expectancy for all. No cost constraints. Only quality improvement."

Bow Street was no doubt a good square, but Marlborough Street was surely one better? The capsule veered to the right and The Baroness leapt out. The capsule stopped and a somewhat more straight faced gentleman got in.

"Marquis of Marlborough Street, pleased to meet you. Now I know you are keen to learn, so I am going to teach you something. It's all very well The Baroness promoting fine living and longevity, and breakthrough squares are good, but as Juran's Trilogy teaches, it has to be followed by a period of control at the new level. If not, you can lose everything that you have gained, and the last thing I want is to think of you being sent back to Pentonville Road. It may have escaped your notice, but between Bow Street and Marlborough Street is a Community Chest square in which two cards are waiting for the unwary. One says 'Go to Jail' and the other says 'Go Back to Old Kent Road'. You don't want either of them. Here's how to avoid them.

"On Bow Street everyone has everything they want. Here we have to think about how to sustain it. Too much too soon can itself cause problems as people grow to expect more and more. So here we think far more about the long-term. Too many people on Bow Street are just living for now and, at the same time, expecting the quality of life to just go on rising forever.

"So this is a control square where people do not think solely in terms of great expectations. We place an emphasis on standardisation to achieve stability. So remember, Bow

Street is a nice square, but it has its downside. Don't fall for it. Now, if you'll follow me down the stairs I will lead you to a narrow passageway, which is your only route off this square.

"That's the top end of Vine Street, last of the orange squares where The Viscount awaits your presence."

The Viscount was as gloomy as The Marquis was stern. Indeed these squares were designed to teach The Prince as much about avoiding pitfalls as making improvements. Even advanced societies would still face problems that had to be prevented.

The Viscount grabbed The Prince's right arm and dragged him forcibly into the narrow winding alley that was barely the width of two people. It seemed endless as it twisted and turned and led seemingly nowhere. It became darker and was eventually lit by torches. The Viscount stopped at an old doorway and unlocked the door. Then he led him upstairs to a small room overlooking the river, and began to present his lesson to The Prince.

"Whenever you have control at the new level you must also have Kaizen, incremental improvement. If you look at the screen I will show you what I mean. You can see three graphs. The first shows average life expectancy on Bow Street, it's a normal distribution, mean of 180 years. Next you see Marlborough Street, which looks the same and, purely on the basis of statistics you would deduce that both were the same, but you know different. Even though the distributions are identical, you know that Marlborough Street is more advanced than Bow Street. That's because The Marquis has put in place control activities that make the system less prone to failure. This means that you have increased assurance and reliability on Marlborough Street. Therefore, should you encounter two apparently identical curves like these again, do not assume that they are genuinely identical.

"I will now ask you to look at the third graph, which represents Vine Street. Tell me what you see."

"Why, it's just a single vertical line," Aub replied.

"A single vertical line," repeated The Viscount. "And you know what that means. Zero variation. The mean life expectancy has doubled, but, more importantly, it is no longer a mean figure, but an exact one. It is no longer the case that one person may live longer than another. Everyone gets 360 years. Then they will be judged on their contribution to determine whether they should be recommended to The Squire. Some people will make a better contribution than others, but all contribution adds value. Everybody knows that here.

"Vine Street is all about adding value. Marlborough Street adds some value, because control and standardisation add value in themselves. Bow Street adds relatively little value. Of the three orange squares Vine Street is by far the greatest contributor, which is why the rewards are potentially so much greater. Only from this square is it possible to gain access to the higher squares that follow. We have worked hard for our extra 180 year lifespan. Don't ever fall into the trap of building in control measures without Kaizen. Now, if you'll follow me I'll show you something very interesting."

The Viscount led the way back out into the narrow, twisting street that if anything became even narrower, to the point where only one person could just squeeze through. Then, suddenly, it just ended, giving way to a mist-covered lake, into which thin, frail, naked, colourless and featureless beings filed in an orderly fashion.

"These are the people who have received the call. Here they must remain unless or until their spirits are awoken by the sound of The Squire's horn."

Aub did not have to wait. The horn sounded immediately and the program threw him head first into the lake, from which he rose to find himself in a moat that surrounded a huge glass dome. Beside him stood a man on horseback holding a horn.

"Welcome to The Strand, first of the red squares," said The Squire. "Beware of it, though, because many an unwary traveller has become, dare I say, stranded here. It's got a nasty Chance square next to it, which contains two cards, one that reads Go Back Three Spaces, which sends you back to Marlborough Street, and one that says Go to Jail, which sends you back to Pentonville Road and makes you start all over again. The red squares are hard to get through, and I make no apology.

"So, if you'll pull yourself free of those murky waters, I will tell you what you have to do."

The Squire explained how The Prince should enter the dome strap himself into the adjustable harness and, when he blew his horn, begin collecting red tokens, then, when he blew his horn a second time, he should stop collecting tokens.

"Any blue tokens that you inadvertently collect will be deducted from your total. These will be subtracted from your good output. You must collect at least sixty red tokens, allowing for deduction of blue. Oh, and by the way, if you fail after ten attempts you will automatically be directed onto the Chance square and its game over."

It did not take The Prince long to deduce that this set up was a variant on Deming's Red Beads experiment. The program recorded the time taken for him to make this deduction.

"Let the fans commence," shouted The Squire, as he gave a blast of his horn.

For twenty seconds The Prince did as instructed, before The Squire blew his horn again. The Prince was lowered and the tokens in his bag were verified.

"You have collected seventy-three tokens," said The Squire. "Twenty-eight red and forty-five blue. That's a fail, but it's not all over. You have nine more chances."

"Now we'll see how much help we have to give him," Dr Schultz said to Polly. "I know he has the answer inside his head. Let's see if we can jostle a few cells, and see how many we have to touch before he gets the gist."

"What's the point?" Aub said to The Squire. "Presumably I will be suspended from the same height, the same number of tokens will be released in the same proportions, the fan speed will stay constant and my time allowance will be the same?"

"I didn't say that," said The Squire. "You can change them, but you have to make trades."

"Good," Dr Schultz remarked. "He's identified the fact that there are four variables that potentially affect the result, with relatively little jostling. Now it's a question of how long it takes him to complete the task. The Science Ministry will be interested in that. Feed in 'Optimise the parameters'."

"Optimise the parameters," Polly said, speaking into the machines audio input.

"There are four variables each with three settings," explained The Squire. "You might get lucky, but there are eighty-one possible combinations. You are only allowed nine more attempts to escape the automatic lock in and end your game on this square."

"So you have to cut down the number of combinations to reduce the amount of unnecessary experimentation," Aub replied, now sensing where the solution lay by recalling knowledge that he had gained somewhere in his past.

"He can do it," Dr Schultz said to Polly, "but my guess is he will need the prompt. Feed in 'L Nine Orthogonal Array'."

Polly did as instructed.

"L Nine Orthogonal Array," The Prince repeated to The Squire.

"Please explain," demanded The Squire.

"I want to test nine combinations of the four parameters."

"Very well. You have nine more attempts and I will accept your best result."

Genichi Taguchi's twentieth-century L Nine Orthogonal Array allowed for the optimum combination to be deduced in just nine attempts. The Prince therefore did nine trials. The contents of each bag were verified and when all nine bags had been counted The Squire announced the result.

"Congratulations Prince. In your top trial you managed to collect 108 red tokens and just thirty-seven blue, giving you a total of seventy-one red. Now, in return for your seventy-one red tokens I will give you one special token. This will admit you to the house of my and your Friend from Fleet Street."

"There are lots of reasons why The Science Ministry needs to know the extent of The Prince's mastery of Taguchi," Dr Schultz explained to Polly. "The next two squares are control squares, so they keep the same theme, but involve more complex tasks, as you can see. Fleet Street requires the subject to assess thirteen attributes on three levels, something which bidding governments are required to be able to do under ISO 9100, and for this he has to demonstrate proficiency with the L Twenty-seven Array. If you look at our output screen you will see he has a machine in front of him for which he has to optimise 1,000,594 trials. He is allowed twenty-seven attempts to find the one optimum combination that will make the machine work and print out a ticket to Trafalgar Square. I know he can do it, but how long will it take him and how much help does he require? That is what we need to find out. In real life he will be presented with many systems that he will need to optimise in this way, as well as guiding others to do so."

On Trafalgar Square, last of the red squares, The Prince was face to face with his Teacher, who looked rather familiarly like Joanie Carmichael, looking out to sea on a fine summer's day.

"Now we are at the summit," she said. "We can go no further. There is no finer world than this. Every system is optimised, and every being that has made it this far can be sure that he, she or it is faultless, just like the world in which they stand. Nature's cruelties have been tempered to the point of elimination. Every single test and challenge that nature has thrown at us has been addressed. Only space and time stand in our way. With lifelong learning, sustained over several lives, we have arrived at last at the point where world's divide.

"On the other side of this water is another dimension. Finally we have arrived at zero defects. Every brain is perfect, therefore it shall not perish, but shall enter transformation. Of course we never really get zero defects, so this square itself can be considered a myth, but we can take Taguchi's principles and take them as far as we can. On each of the plinths behind me stands a globe that represents a world in which everything is optimised, but in practice we all reach a point at which further efforts to improve the process and optimise our designs is itself suboptimal. At that point it becomes more worthwhile for the other side to accept those who have come thus far.

"Armed with this knowledge, and aware that you have applied the principles as far as they can reasonably be applied, you can progress to the yellow zone. But beware, you will be assessed at a much higher level, and you must avoid the Go to Jail square that lurks behind Piccadilly, and will send you back to Pentonville Road and end your game prematurely."

"Yes, The Science Ministry would like more," Dr Schultz remarked to Polly. "He should now know that he has to embed lifelong learning in everyone alongside Taguchi's methods. Let's see how he does on the yellow squares."

The Teacher raised her arms and the ocean parted to reveal a yellow brick road.

"Follow the yellow brick road. At the end The Lord, The Lord of Leicester Square, that is, will greet you."

The Prince followed the yellow brick road to the castle that stood at the end. Its portcullis lifted allowing The Prince to come face to face with the grey-haired Lord, dressed smartly in top hat and tails.

"You are going to be a great leader," he said, taking him by the hand. "Because you can work on the world rather than just in it. You are the trouble-shooter. Where great investments are faced with a perilous future, you can save them. You have the power of a saviour, wherever you wish to go. Usually the signs are there and as King you need to know how to recognise them. It's a fine art. Observe behind me the star that is about to implode in eight generations' time with a planet beside that contains brilliantly evolved beings. We have to flag that world, just as we have to flag those who are in danger of destroying themselves and place someone there who has the means to grow, learn and avert the impending catastrophe. Sometimes it may take more than one generation to do this.

"This is a breakthrough square because here your influence spans more than one generation. Everything may be optimised now, but that doesn't mean that it will stay that way. You have to be able to foresee and anticipate factors that can destabilise and affect even the most perfectly optimised system. At present these skills only just exist, but by the end of this zone they must do much more.

"Now, take my hand and I will take you to meet someone very special."

The Lord led The Prince to a brick wall, but when he shook his hand he was suddenly able to see through it and walk forward to the ancient stone staircase beyond. Candles lit the way upwards towards the little yellow door at the top, which was marked Coventry Street. The door opened and a small petite blonde lady greeted him. She was of similar appearance to The Baroness of Bow Street, only clearly older and somewhat wiser. She opened up a yellow umbrella and shook his hand.

"Welcome to Coventry Street," she said softly. "Come, take my hand. I am The Countess of Coventry Street. I appear as I do only so that you can recognise me. In practice I can take many forms, unlike The Lord of Leicester Square who only has one. One is enough for the basics, but not for everything. This is a control square, so nothing has changed, other than the fact that I can appear in the right form to the right beings, and deliver important messages to influential brains. I am what you would call a true spirit, acting often unseen, but bringing control to the forces offered by The Lord. He can identify, but not prevent. I am the missing link. I use my discretion, prioritise and then act, ideally without anyone knowing that I have acted. Under my umbrella you will always be safe, but once it has gone you are not. You face arrest on the next square if you cannot make the correct deduction. To help you I will give you a test. Here is a bottle of magic dust. You can use it, but it must be applied with care. Below you will see a child who is about to die, and the world will suffer enormously if I don't save him. So, scatter a small speck of dust on him, so you can prevent his great contribution of years to come from being lost. In your life you will be able to recognise your own magic dust.

"Even us spirits are not always right first time or even just in time. We don't expect that, but you should now have all that you need to go one step further."

The roof opened and The Countess held The Prince's hand. Above were only stars. Silently they left the turret and they flew ever higher, past planets and galaxies until a familiar image appeared in front of them. It was planet Earth, and as The Countess faded, The Prince saw his own face implanted into a bright embryo into which he merged. The Prince was now The Star Child, placed strategically above Earth so as to guide and protect it.

"Now," said Dr Schultz to Polly, "this is the moment of truth. This is a very hard square to pass. He has to identify and correct an unknown problem that could potentially destroy the Earth long after his lifetime before he can qualify to move into the green zone. I will use the audio to let him know what his job is, and we will see how long it takes him to work out the answer. Had we been using this program to train a student of the Political Academy we would simply terminate the program and deduct marks accordingly, but, as we are dealing with The Prince Regent, we cannot do this. He must pass the Go to Jail square."

Dr Schultz fed the instruction into the machine and The Prince picked it up. He soon realised that The Countess had gone and that he now had a task to perform. He was the Earth's great protector, and his role was to save it from impending catastrophe in a future generation. The nature of the catastrophe was not specified.

"The children who will need to enact your solution are not yet born. The disaster could occur in one, two or three generations time. You must solve it."

The Prince's first challenge was to identify that there actually was a problem. Of course a problem that was not going to reveal itself for many years or even centuries could not possibly be predicted, but it could be anticipated. Thus, a world that had become too reliant on any one thing could always be vulnerable to a widespread deficiency, especially if it could spread uncontrollably at some time, any time. This square was therefore all about dealing with the unexpected. The task assumed that the world was currently fully optimised, so sub-optimisation could not be assumed to be a cause, but a generation losing its focus could.

The Prince's mind was guided by the program toward the use of fully optimised electronic solutions upon which everyone had come to rely. Then, there was the potential for a rogue gang to emerge, with power seeking urges that defied the logic of optimisation. Was cybercrime dead in this supposedly perfect world? Possibly not, for even if it was currently nonexistent, the potential for recurrence could never be dismissed. Herein lay a possible answer to the problem. Fortunately he still had his magic dust to implant in a few critical brains that would give them the ability to, one by one, produce a piece of work that they would have the foresight to not only write, but store in a way that could bypass the electronic systems affected by a worldwide virus, that is to say ransomware that goes out of control such that even its creators could not control it. If it caught hold, it would render the entire world unstable, so destroying all of the optimisation of the past. Herein lay the power of The Star Child, to scatter the dust and form from it a book that offered the solution to a future problem that did not, as yet, exist, but one day could.

As soon as the book was released and hurled towards the Earth, the risk of arrest was gone. Instead a flashing light came toward him. It came ever closer until finally it revealed itself as a fellow Star Child, this time a girl with a gold halo shining brightly above her head. She pointed the way from Earth, then disappeared only to be replaced by another and another. It took five of them to bring The Prince to his new destination, The Archangel's Chamber.

It looked remarkably like the Kamchatka Parliament, except for those who were seated. The Supreme Archangel sat where Bogodan would normally have addressed the House, and Angels and Archangels occupied the benches. As The Prince walked in he was met by a man in green.

"I am The Regent of Regent Street, and you are hereby admitted to this House at servant level. This is a breakthrough square. If a world fails now, it is not your responsibility alone. The responsibility is now shared. At the moment The Archangels are debating the fate of a civilisation that has hit hard times as its world was struck by a meteor. Should they intervene to save it or not? We are one body and therefore one system, with far greater powers than a mere Star Child. As a servant you have no decision-making powers. You can only watch and listen."

"You have heard the evidence," said The Supreme Archangel. "You know it is but one world, but a heavy loss nonetheless. It's not a question of whether we intervene, but to what extent, to save something given that the catastrophe was not prevented. How valuable is this civilisation? It is time to vote. Your options range from one hundred per cent intervention to zero."

Their minds coalesced, then slowly the golden globe at the far end of the Chamber started to fade.

"The final colour will show the final level of intervention agreed," explained The Regent. "And also its distribution. It can never be one hundred per cent because there could always be another calamity. The universe is a big place. At the same time it can never be zero because the investment has been too great to allow it to fail completely. So, the colour stops halfway, but that's not all. The intervention will always include prevention costs for the future, and this also has to be voted on, knowing that similar risks exist on other worlds. Investing in the brains of the future will form part of that as you saw in the yellow zone."

The Prince observed.

"Now it's your turn," said one of The Archangels, pulling him towards the benches. "Sit here."

The bench was marked Oxford Street, showing The Prince that he was now on a control square.

"Use the sliding scale to show how much prevention cost to allocate," she instructed. "Get it right and you will be promoted to Bond Street."

The Prince surveyed the extent of the devastation, then adjusted his slider accordingly, taking into account what had happened, the optimal remedial action required and the risk of a similar occurrence happening again. Some of it was pure guesswork, but it did involve universal risk assessment capability. All possibilities had to be considered. The program followed his logic as he worked through the various failure modes that a world could encounter, combined with the proportion of prevention costs that usually accompanied any investment in quality.

When The Dream Machine was satisfied with its his evaluation it changed the name of the sign on The Prince's seat to Bond Street. At first he did not even notice the change, but soon it was clear. He noticed his hands change colour and a gold halo appear above him.

Bond Street was another control square, but it was a top level square. Now The Prince had to influence the decisions of the other Archangels. It was not enough for him merely to vote with the others. He now had much more control, and, with more knowledge, could see the need to exercise it. There was no substitute for knowledge, and the program at this point purposefully placed him in a position to spot knowledge gaps in the others for which he had to compensate. Thus, on this last green square, he influenced the vote as opposed to merely entering his own figure.

With The Dream Machine satisfied The Supreme Archangel showed him the way out along a secret passageway, at the end of which was a purple glow. The passageway bore the unmistakeable street sign Park Lane.

"Let's see what he makes of this," Dr Schultz remarked to Polly. "He's going to have to be a real visionary to make it to the last square. The Archangels can only maintain, they cannot create."

The Prince entered the purple room where The Principal sat. He was an ordinary looking stout man dressed in a purple suit, and the room was nothing special, just a quaint old drawing room. The man was not jovial, but instead was silent and melancholy, pouring over a drawing board upon which were drawn the plans of many worlds.

"Welcome to Park Lane," said the man, grimly.

"It looks like you have a problem," replied The Prince.

"I have. I have," replied The Principal. "A very big problem. Endlessly we can only watch from here and witness worlds fail, and huge amounts of work go to waste. We design them, we guard them, we do everything we can to save them, then we lose them, and why? Because we didn't get our designs right. It is said that God created man in His own Image. Yet God needs man as much as man needs God.

"You are here because your designs are good. I need you to design for me a world that will endure, a perfect world, a perfect design. Only that will satisfy The Master. Quality begins at the design stage. It's no good saying that it is someone else's fault when failure strikes. I want you to look at the design in front of you and try to identify as many failure modes as you can and their associated effects. Then I want you to prepare the prototype for The Master."

The Prince scrutinised the plan and considered anything that could go wrong, such as insufficient atmosphere, star too young or too old or too strong or too weak, poor atmospheric composition, not enough air or water, or the wrong combination of initial ingredients, or an evolutionary path with too many fault trees. It did not take long to see that the list was endless, and the number of orthogonal arrays required to optimise the design was far too great for Taguchi's theory to be viable.

"Do you see what I mean," said The Principal. "I must produce a design, but I have to live in hope, I can't be certain that the world that I create will ever be perfect."

The Prince did his best with the Taguchi L Fifty-four orthogonal array. This would give fifty-four prototype combinations in place of 1.7 million squared, and was the highest such array of which The Prince had knowledge. The Principal accepted the submission and led The Prince to the door at the back of the room, marked Master of Mayfair. As the door opened The Principal saluted then left. In front of The Prince was the old white-haired Master with a long silvery beard, who was dressed in a purple robe.

"Here you are at last, hey," spoke The Master. "I have before me ten designs for life-creating worlds. The Principal has approved all of them, but I need to be sure that at least one of them will make it through to becoming a spiritual world before it somehow fails. I'm still trying. How do I choose? You can take the bag of life-generating seed and distribute it in any combination. You can place it all on one world, or some on each world in varying amounts. It doesn't matter as long as we get one successful world."

"Now you see this one, Polly?" Dr Schultz remarked.

"Yes," Polly replied.

"As with the Park Lane challenge there is no correct answer. It isn't the answer that The Science Ministry is interested in, but the reasoning that the subject gives to his solution that is important."

The Prince scrutinised the designs and picked up the bag of seed. All of the planets had different characteristics and he checked the Failure Mode and Effect templates and the Fault Trees that The Principal had approved. The problem was every one had a high level of uncertainty built-in. It made more sense to place more seed onto the worlds that would appear to give it the best chance of survival, but also the best chance of evolving into something good.

One way of evaluating the suitability of each planet was to observe how the original designs had been conceived. Where mere guesswork had been used it made sense to leave that world, as a factual basis for decision making was absent. As for the failure modes, it wasn't just whether a failure mode existed, but what the potential effects would be. Then there was the question of by how much each failure was likely to fail. Taguchi's classical loss function could provide a clue here.

In addition The Prince looked at another of Taguchi's concepts, that of distinguishing between design parameters and noise factors. Design parameters were those nominal settings that could be chosen by a responsible engineer. Noise factors were factors that cause performance characteristics to deviate from their target values. Some planets were inherently less stable than others, whilst others were more prone to solar effects such as solar flares and meteors.

Tolerance levels on each planet were another question. In the end the final seed distribution would be a balance between classical Taguchi and risk management. Working on this basis led The Prince to an uneven distribution of seed amongst nine of the ten worlds.

This last act ended the program.

"Prepare for waking mode," ordered Dr Schultz.

The Prince awoke as Dr Schultz retrieved the analysis sheet from the machine.

"Excellent job, excellent job," Dr Schultz said to The Prince. "This machine is my pride and joy. Apologies for the uncomfortable beginning, but I'm pleased to say that was a really good performance. There is nothing in these results that should cause The Science Ministry any concern with regard to your competence. Understanding of concepts is good, recognition of applications is good, foresight and vision is good. I don't think I could have used an L Fifty-four orthogonal array on that Park Lane design challenge, no student has ever got that far. Most of them fail either on The Strand or Piccadilly.

"It goes without saying that kids love this machine when they visit The Island and I give them each a go on it. It has a huge potential for speeding up learning as you can imagine. Lots of basic knowledge will simply be able to be placed in a child's head, replacing years of schooling so that they can get to the complicated stuff much sooner. The kid goes in, the knowledge goes in, the kid comes out. The very latest in automated education.

"The Science Ministry will no doubt at some stage ask for your recommendation with regard to the commercialisation and exportation of these machines, for good purposes only, of course. You may well be called upon to assure that only good purposes can form part of the embedded system."

Chapter Ten
Breaking the Mould

Over the next two weeks The Prince and The Queen trained hard at the rink with particular emphasis on school figures and lifts. None of the moves were especially difficult, but they did require precision and control.

The school figures consisted largely of forward and backward figure-eights, with three turns, counters, brackets and changes of edge added later. Loops, which were confined to a small area of ice were added after that.

"We are going to combine all of these school figures together to form a routine that consists solely of school figures," Jobine explained. "This is rarely done at ice shows, but if performed well it can be a joy to watch. When you can do these simple figures well solo I will get you to synchronise them and we will add some gentle music."

The lifts were likewise confined largely to small shoulder height ones, with the exception of the sit lift which required Katie to spring off both toe picks into Aubs outstretched arms.

"It's actually not too difficult once you get the hang of it," said Jobine. "It's eye-catching and elegant as well. Strictly speaking it's a catch rather than a lift, but it makes sense to teach it with the lifts."

Jobine instructed Aub to stand with his arms outstretched, and before he knew it she was in a seated position across them. She then moved on to the side-by-side pivot in which both man and lady skated a pivot on a right back outside edge.

"If you get the timing right you should both be able to go into the pivot together and come out together," explained Jobine. "You can then either resume a dance hold or go into an embrace of some kind."

The couple practised for six hours a day for six days, with a rest day on the Sunday. Then Aub received the news that he had been half expecting. The Deputy PM summoned him to The Great Dome where he received his first royal assignment.

Inside, on the screen, Foreign Minister Oleg Rachkov, spoke to him via a video link.

"Greetings to you Your Royal Highness," said the fair-haired gent. "I am speaking to you because as you are no doubt aware the United Kingdom is to hold a General Election in just over a month's time.

"This is very important to us because the right result will greatly assist us in the commencement of the second stage of our great and glorious revolution. Our Founders were, as you know, originally from the UK and it was always their intention that when the time was right we should seek to influence political developments there so as to bring about much needed stability and constancy of purpose.

"Most of the world is still capitalist, but, during your reign, which covers the second stage of our revolution, the balance should slowly change. We want the UK to facilitate, not resist, that change. Tell me, do you recognise this man?"

A photograph then appeared on the screen of the man he had seen in The Dream Machine walking into Number 10.

"I believe it is retired Colonel Francis White," replied Aub. "Leader of the Whig party."

"It is the very same," continued Oleg, "and he needs to become Britain's next prime minister. As you are probably aware he has no chance without our assistance, so we need you and Katie working together to make it happen."

"How many seats did his party win at the last election?" Aub asked.

"Thirty-six," replied Oleg.

"And how many does he need to secure a majority?"

"Three-hundred-and-twenty-six."

"Don't you think it's a bit of a tall order?"

"Not at all. I think he could win at least 500 seats, and with that he would have a mandate for virtually anything we ask. So I want you to fly to London to meet him and explain to him our plan. To begin with you should not expect too many changes in the opinion poll ratings that currently predict him to have around forty to forty-five seats in the new parliament. Things will start to change when Katie becomes involved. She is going to visit the UK shortly before the election. Her good friends in the British royal family have given her a very warm invitation now that she has declared her intentions. It is you, however, who will hold the magic button."

That afternoon a Kammie collected The Prince from The Cat and Fiddle where he and The Queen had enjoyed a light bar lunch.

"Don't forget the parchment," she told him, handing it to him as he left.

Korean air hostess Su Lin welcomed him aboard the Hebden Three.

"Subsonic flight time to London Heathrow will be approximately one hour and fifty minutes," the pilot announced as he prepared for take-off from The Island's small, but adequate beach runway.

On the way The Prince was able to study in more detail the plans that Rachkov and Bogodan had hatched in order to ensure a Whig victory and it all made sense. The Prince's first task, however, was to convince The Colonel (retired) of the plan's viability, not that this should be too difficult, once he knew just exactly how much of the plan had already been implemented.

On arrival at Heathrow he was quickly escorted through airport security to the awaiting Kamchatskiy limousine that would covey him forthwith to the Whig party headquarters in London's Cowley Street. The Colonel was eagerly expecting him.

"Come in, come in, Your Royal Highness. What can I do for you?"

"I think it's more a case of what I can do for you," replied Aub.

"Yes, I understand you have come to help our election campaign and for that I am most grateful. What exactly do you propose to do?"

They sat down and a waiter brought over two glasses of brandy.

"How do you fancy being Britain's greatest prime minister since Churchill?"

The Colonel laughed.

"You must be joking. We had thirty-six seats at the dissolution of parliament. The opinion polls suggest this time we could make one or two net gains as a result of Anthony Brier's decline in popularity of late, but his vote is rock solid. Nothing is going to change that."

"Don't you believe it," said Aub. "You are making two seriously flawed assumptions, first that the opinion polls are accurate, and second that people, including you, actually believe them."

"I suppose they have been wrong before," The Colonel confessed. "But never so wrong as to distort the result to the extent that you're saying. Even if they were wildly out and we got, say, a hundred seats, there's no way I would be installed in Number 10."

"I beg to disagree," answered Aub.

"Well I'd love you to tell me how."

"In less than a year's time I am going to marry Queen Katie of Kamchatka."

"So? I fail to see how that is going to influence the result of our election in just a few weeks."

"Do you have any idea of the kind of following that my Queen has in this country?"

"She's very well liked, I know, but, well, she's hardly going to affect the election result."

"That's what you think. Let me turn now to the small matter of Orkney and Shetland, and its MP Oscar Munro."

"Yes. That was interesting," agreed The Colonel. "I think it was a fluke result personally."

"What, a sixty per cent swing in favour of your candidate with all of the other candidates losing their deposits? You think that was a fluke?"

"Oscar Munro is a very able Member of Parliament. He is extremely popular, but as you know, Orkney and Shetland is not representative of the country as a whole."

"No, of course not. Neither are the house prices."

"I know, they're the highest in the UK now. Nobody seems to know exactly why."

"I do, and so does my Queen."

"I've offered Oscar Munro the party leadership on several occasions and he has refused to accept it. Doubtless he would deliver a better election performance than I can, but he has publicly declared that he is not going to lead the Whig party. He doesn't want the job."

"You're right there. Perhaps that's because what he really wants is this."

Aub carefully removed the scroll that he had almost forgotten when he left The Island, and handed it to The Colonel, who examined it closely. He then coughed, almost mis-swallowing a mouthful of brandy. Then he stared, bemused, at The Prince.

"Why, this is an invitation to serve in the Kamchatka Parliament. This is a highly prized document. You cannot be serious?"

"I am being perfectly serious. You will observe that it bears my Queen's seal, my signature as Regent of Russia, and the signature of Viktor Bogodan, Vice Chancellor of the Kamchatka Parliament. His seat is already waiting for him. It's marked Orkney and Shetland and its placed on the

Foreign Bench between Mike West, MP for The Falklands and South Georgia, and my very own Jacob Spence, who represents my constituency of Bathurst and Melville.

"I take it you will agree to give this document to Oscar at the earliest opportunity?"

"Of course, how could I not agree to? But I still cannot see how you can possibly pull off a Whig victory at the election. It just isn't realistic. Also, why is it so important to you?"

"Well," explained Aub. "You may or may not be aware that some seventy-two years ago a small number of select individuals who, incidentally, were members of your party, founded a community on a small island in the middle of the Atlantic, with a plan to transform the world using a completely new system, through a steady-pace revolution that was programmed to take place over approximately three centuries."

"I know about my party's history, but I don't see how it links with this election. As you said, that was seventy-two years ago, and hardly anyone has ever heard of the place since. I know Kamchatka has links to my party, but as far as I can see it is only a distant link."

"That's because we are approaching the end of the first stage of the revolution and about to enter the second, where we need to start to get capitalist governments on our side. The Founders of the Kamchatka Parliament were all British, placing the UK in a unique position for us historically. We believe the UK is now ready to play a major role in the second stage of the revolution, and your party is the only one of the three main ones that has both the capability and the desire to do it."

"I don't quite follow."

"First of all, the UK has been woefully hampered in its economic development as a result of its corrupt and outdated first-past-the-post electoral system. Your party is the only one that is pledged to change it. You can. The others can't, or should I say, won't. We need OPD – One Party Democracy – rather than proportional representation, but if you are willing to accept that, which is virtually what happened in Orkney and Shetland, then I believe it could be perfectly workable in the UK after five years. Once the size of your election victory becomes clear on election night, hardly anyone will oppose it. Of course, the handful of opponents that you will have left in the House of Commons will still need to be kept under OPD, but I'm sure they will be happy to agree. After all, why should they not agree to keeping their seats permanently?"

"What kind of result do you foresee?"

"My opinion poll predicts that on election night you will have a minimum of 535 seats out of a possible 650."

"Oh come on, that's The Island of Dreams, not the British Isles."

"It's The Island King, The Island Queen, The Regent of Russia and the Vice Chancellor of the Kamchatka Parliament making you an offer.

"I have an elite squad of teams who will train every MP on managing the economy using Deming and Juran's theory within the capitalist framework. Everyone will see their quality of life improve. There will be no such thing as losers in the UK any more. That message you can take to the hustings.

"Stability of a system and constancy of purpose are what drives us forward, not lurching back and forth with individuals rewarded for winning elections and competing for power. England swings like a pendulum do, but not for much longer. Your party sits in the centre and can provide that vital combination of breakthrough, control and Kaizen.

"Another thing that my teams will help you to do is get the UK Government certificated to ISO 9100. At the moment the UK has made no provision for this. I know this because we have seen no interest from the UK in TC 176, which was once British led. There's interest in ISO 9001, but not ISO 9100. That has got to change. Britain needs to be in the first tier of bidders in The New Game. The UK could get certificated within five years with a little help. A little bird has also told me that by then Zimbabwe may well be ready to sell out to Westminster. Lots of people in Zimbabwe want to go back to Rhodesia, but without the racism. Millions of people will benefit."

"I'm sure I could agree to that, but please, do tell me Your Royal Highness, how this fairy tale is going to materialise?"

"Queen Katie of Kamchatka has more fans in the UK than you will ever know, and many of them are in strategic locations, marginal seats that can be easily swung. These people have made it their business to participate in media-driven opinion polling and, under my Queen's direction, have purposefully declared voting intentions that are deliberately bogus.

"I have, on my person, a small device, no bigger than a bar of chocolate, upon which is a little red button, which, when pressed, will deliver an activating text that will prompt all receivers to revert to their true intentions. They will then see that a vote for your party is, in effect, a vote for her. Who do you think these people love the most, Queen Katie of Kamchatka or Anthony Briers?"

The Colonel again stared deeply into the eyes of The Prince, knowing that armed with this kind of power anything was possible. Everything was slowly clicking into place. The only thing that he had overlooked was the possibility that Queen Katie of Kamchatka had a pre-stored message stating that a Whig vote was not so much a Whig vote as a vote for her personally that would allow her to help everyone.

"The reality is," continued Aub, "That people don't really care that much about who they vote for, but they do care about pleasing Queen Katie of Kamchatka, and if she sends a message asking for something as simple and cheap as a

Whig vote, I don't think any of her millions of fans will want to let her down. Some will know, of course, that for such a tiny action, the implications for Britain, as well as ourselves, will be immense.

"From the moment you become PM this country will never look back and future British history will record the fact that you, Francis, were the one who brought Britain back from the brink to become a leading rather than a falling nation. You will be the one responsible for breaking the mould of British politics."

*

In the debates that followed The Colonel had to make some subtle changes to his manifesto, but once he had briefed his party's members on the logic of campaigning on the basis of restoring stability of a system to achieve transformation, coupled with a commitment to creating a quality supersystem in line with ISO 9100, he had no trouble getting all of The Prince's strategy accepted. He did as The Prince asked, however, in mentioning not a word about the trump card of the magic button that was going to flip the election result and defy the opinion polls that were being secretly manipulated.

The Prince meanwhile returned to The Island to re-join his Queen to both continue with their skating and to follow the British election campaign in advance of both of them travelling to London to congratulate The Colonel on what was certainly going to be a night to remember.

The Opera House was filled to capacity in the evenings leading up to the General Election, as The Island's population joined to watch the televised debates. In accordance with tradition the leaders of Britain's main parties were invited to answer questions posed by a live audience. Some of these were of direct interest to The Island, and one of these was the stance that was being taken towards Oscar Munro. The compere of the show invited this question from a man in the audience:

"Oscar Munro, Whig MP for Orkney and Shetland, has recently announced that if he is re-elected he will take up his seat in the Kamchatka Parliament rather than Westminster. Does the panel believe that he should have the right to do this?"

"Anthony Briers," said the compere.

"No, I don't believe he should be permitted to represent his constituency in such a place, and when I am re-elected as prime minister I will ensure that a bill is passed prohibiting him from doing so. I think it is an absolute disgrace and it borders on treason. Kamchatka is a dangerous foreign power and no British MP that puts Britain first should ever even think of it. It is totally anti-constitutional."

He gained lots of applause, but was it genuine? He was booed rigorously in The Island"s Opera House, but with a bit of laughter thrown in. Tim Cosgrove, leader of the socialists, was invited to reply next.

"I don't agree completely with Anthony, I wouldn't call it treason in this day and age, and we have to respect the fact that Oscar Munro at present has the biggest majority of any British MP. I do, however, feel that going to Kamchatka is a bridge too far and, Francis, you should be stopping it from within your own party. I don't feel that Oscar should simply be allowed to walk out of The House of Commons, nor the Scottish Parliament, just because he feels like it. We have no proper procedures for it here and unless or until there are he should stay in Edinburgh where he belongs."

"What do you say to that Francis White?" the compere asked.

"Well, first of all the only people I have met so far that are against it are the two gentlemen beside me. Others understand what a huge honour it is to be asked to serve in Kamchatka. Nobody ever turns it down. I remember when Mike West in The Falkland Islands received a similar invitation some years ago. You two were against that, yet now look at the prosperity of that area. Orkney and Shetland are closer to home but the principle is no different. What I do know is that the people of Orkney and Shetland would not forgive Oscar if he didn't take up his seat there."

The people in The Opera House cheered. From the studio audience there was muted applause.

"Francis, you have no respect for British sovereignty," Anthony Briers interrupted.

"What do you think man in the audience?" the compere asked.

"I think we must respect the wishes of the people of Orkney and Shetland. They have voted in very large numbers for Oscar Munro and we cannot ignore that. All those territories with Non-Capitalist Economics are doing enormously well and we shouldn't lose sight of that. If that is what Orkney and Shetland want then they should be allowed to have it. This is 2108."

As the questions continued the people in The Opera House listened to the nature of the responses from the leaders, observing that apart from Francis White, the others frequently attacked each other, each blaming the other wherever they could find an opportunity to do so. Anthony Briers especially would seek to talk over the others, particularly Francis, in order to try to dominate the discussion. He wanted power and he showed it. If he could attack on personality rather than policy then he would. Could it possibly be that quietly he was beginning to fear Francis White's party more than the established opposition? After all, he knew where he stood in a two-horse race. He had no idea where a Whig presence in Kamchatka would lead. Thoughts of the power of Viktor Bogodan and Queen Katie of Kamchatka inevitably ran through his mind. For once he was the one who should feel afraid of defeat under Britain's unfair first-past-the-post system.

Another question that interested the people of The Island, not to mention The Prince, was the following, posed by a female student from Bradford:

"Does the panel believe that Britain's defence budget is being squandered unnecessarily on maintaining a nuclear arsenal and building yet more missiles and aircraft carriers rather than focusing on The New Game and what it has to offer?"

"Tim Cosgrove."

"We need to make sure that we continue to invest sufficient funds in our defence force. I do believe that the present government has got its priorities wrong by cutting back in key areas of defence at the expense of others. Nuclear, in particular, consumes too much of the national budget, but equally I don't believe that we can afford to do as Francis would have us do and rely on a foreign inspired unproven international standard to protect our shores."

"Plenty of applause there," Katie said to Aub. "But let's hear what our guy says."

"Francis."

"Yes, I do believe it is being squandered. All over the world there is a movement that is devoted to ending war and the threat of war. That is why a new standard called ISO 9100 has been recently released. We will need certification so as to become a bidding nation and not get left behind. If we do not invest in a Quality supersystem as required by this standard we will lose out. My party, unlike the others, is committed to making this investment. We must pursue it so we can help to bring about world peace."

Again there was some applause, but there could have been more.

"Anthony Briers."

"Britain needs a strong nuclear deterrent and Francis is frankly being an objectionable squirt by suggesting otherwise. We can't defend ourselves with a standard that doesn't offer any protection to anyone. And as for Tim's bullshit, let me remind you that it was his party's government that overspent on defence to the extent that it needed us to reduce yet another massive debt incurred by his party's crass ineptitude. His party can't govern and he knows it, and the Whig challenge is simply a joke a bit like him."

The compere then allowed the lady in the audience to respond as the crowd in The Opera House jeered at the much loathed Anthony Briers.

"I would just like to see all of the world's nuclear weapons dismantled and no more built ever again," she replied. "If ISO 9100 can succeed in doing that then I think we should give it a try."

There was applause for this in both The Opera House and the studio.

*

With four days of campaigning left The Prince and Katie left together for London. The lightning visit made immediate headlines, and the sheer number of people who turned out to catch a glimpse of them was enough to turn a few heads. Buckingham Palace warmly welcomed them, and, at Aub and Katie's request, Francis White had also been invited to attend the discussions on what the future might hold for Britain at a time when, unlike politicians, the monarchy was at an all-time high in the popularity ratings across the country. People were now beginning to see that this really could be a turning point in British political history. It was the monarchy, not the election, that was appealing to the interests of the people.

Afterwards Aub and Katie retired to their bed in Kensington Palace, with people again lining the streets in unprecedented numbers, sensing that something sensational was about to transpire.

"Now might be a good time," Aub suggested to Katie, as they lay together sipping champagne.

"Yes," replied Katie. "I'm glad we talked it through with the British royals though. I could not possibly have accepted going through with this without their support and full approval. But now that they have all agreed to it I think we can go ahead and change this country forever."

It took less than a second for Aub to press the red button that would release his Queen's message to all of her fans. It read as follows:

'This is a personal message to you from Queen Katie of Kamchatka. I love you all and I want to thank each and every one of you for your loyalty and devotion. I am deeply touched by it. I know election day is almost upon us. I ask of you but one small favour and that is to vote for me by voting for your Whig candidate at the polls.'

The message had a profound impact on the UK electorate that even The Island Queen had not foreseen. Now, for both Anthony Briers and Tim Cosgrove the first-past-the-post system was going to work against them. The result was not going to reflect the true following that both of them still had. Then again, for so many decades things had been the other way around.

Briers remained defiant to the last, insisting that his party was the only one that was fit to govern, but as the polls closed even he could see that the writing was on the wall. Even in his previously safe Enfield constituency his voice was dwarfed by the rampant cheers of the supporters of The Island Queen. In Torbay, Francis White's constituency, dancing and singing had started along the English Riviera well before the polls closed.

Everyone had until ten o clock to vote using their electronic keypads. Then at half past ten the result was declared. It wasn't long after that Francis White was on his way to Number Ten, outside which Aub and Katie waited expectantly. Sylvia Smith, The Island correspondent, provided the live commentary for The Island's audience in The Opera House. There was an enormous cheer as the result was read out.

"It looks as if The Prince Regent's forecast of 535 Whig seats was wrong. It's 536. For the first time ever it looks as if a serving British prime minister has lost his seat. It's only by a few votes, but he's out folks. I am getting reports of some scuffles in Enfield between supporters of our Queen and some of Anthony Briers' supporters, who are clearly unhappy with the result, but there is no doubt that the result will stand. I understand also that in Liverpool Garston Tim Cosgrove has just held on to his seat, but only just. Now Francis White is making his way to Number 10 and is set to make a short speech. In Torbay by the way he has what looks to be a thumping majority of around 40,000, which is enormous. People are now singing 'I vow to thee my Island' and waving hundreds of small Island flags. It's as if everyone knows that it is Queen Katie of Kamchatka who is Britain's best friend."

"I never even knew there were 40,000 people in Torbay," Katie whispered to Aub as they prepared to listen to The Colonel.

"This is history in the making folks," The Colonel declared. "A result like never before. It's a new chapter for Britain and for the world. Never more shall those in the responsible position of government be forced to compete for power. Never more will British workers be robbed of their right to pride in their work. We will deliver full employment and a much needed Quality supersystem, not warships, missiles and people trained to kill. The MPs that we have, of whatever party, will be trained to manage and manage well. Stability of a system is what will drive us forward, so Britain can become once more a prosperous and proud country. I thank everyone who has supported me throughout this campaign, and especially Queen Katie of Kamchatka for this opportunity, because I know it is her, not me, that is the worthy victor of this election. I shall not disappoint her or you. I have my brief and my policies are clear. Long live the revolution and God save the Queen."

Francis White then prepared to enter Number 10, and winked at Aub, exactly as he had seen in The Dream Machine's program.

115

Chapter Eleven
The Liberal Future

With the election complete and mission accomplished Aub and Katie returned to The Island. Aboard the Hebden Three they watched as Francis White (The Colonel) made the obligatory journey to Buckingham Palace to form a government, the first leader of his party to do so since David Lloyd George. In the Commons his first task was going to be how to fit five hundred and thirty-six MPs on the government benches.

"Please," laughed Tim Cosgrove, gesturing to those Whigs who were struggling to find places to join him on the opposition benches.

This was another first, not that it presented any real difficulty. With everyone working together one could easily envisage the opposition benches being a mere extension of the government benches from now on.

"Order. Order," shouted the speaker over the din, as eventually the House was somehow seated.

Aboard the plane Aub received a text from The Colonel, which read Help – what do I do with a full House?." He was largely unprepared, having only a few weeks before never anticipated to be in the position that he was. Fortunately Aub already had a message ready to return, complete with opening speech.

"Once all of this euphoria has died down we will have to see about inviting Francis to The Island so he can get some clear plans in place," said Aub.

"Patrick and Duncan have asked if we would have working lunch with them tomorrow at The Gun Inn," replied Katie. "They have been planning for this for years. A lot of hard work has gone into preparing for The Liberal Future as they have named it."

"Also, I see from the news today that all of the non-Whig MPs that still have seats, still a significant number, have all agreed to switch to his party. That's what he means by a full House."

"My God, look at Torbay," Katie remarked as the news continued on the screen, showing the people stretching for miles waving small Island flags.

"Somehow I don't think The Colonel is going to have a problem selling OPD to the British people. It looks like it's already happened in some places," Aub continued as he scrolled down the list of election results. "Looks like Orkney and Shetland is much the same, but The Western Isles are interesting, looks like they've done what Orkney and Shetland did last time. There's a sixty-one per cent swing to the Whigs there. Anthony Briers may be out, but his party still has forty-one seats, then there's Cosgrove's sixty-three, still significant. But they've all said they will work with Francis and join his party. That pretty much paves the way for OPD, which will help Patrick and Duncan."

Aub scrutinised the Enfield result as he watched the unfolding angry scenes on the screen.

"There's the man who was all for first-past-the-post," Aub continued. "Now, all of a sudden he finds himself squeezed out by it. He only lost by a few votes. Had there been proportional representation he would still most certainly have kept his seat. But, hey, the bugger deserves it. Arrogant and intolerant to anyone who disagreed with him, and generally epitomising everything that was bad about his party. Fortunately the forty-one that are left are mainly moderates that have been prepared to switch sides, if only to protect their own interests. They all know that with OPD there's no such thing as losing one's seat. A good few public sector workers seem to have remained loyal to Cosgrove, which is understandable."

"I wonder what influence that film had," Katie remarked, recalling the premier of *The Making of Kamchatka*, "because I'm still quite stunned by the number of people overall who responded to my request."

"That's a good point. I think there probably were a significant number of people who were going to see that film and conclude that if they took action it was not too late for Britain. The opinion poll that Patrick and Duncan prepared for me took account of that."

"More will be known about what Francis White intends to do over the next few days," came the voice of the reporter on the news station. "What does seem to be clear is that the royal family will be given a lot more in the way of parliamentary privileges with the ability to make decisions on certain aspects of government policy. Apparently there is going to be a White Paper published in the next couple of weeks called The Liberal Future, which will no doubt explain more."

"That's good. He's obviously picked that up from my download."

Meanwhile, on The Island's news station Sylvia Smith could be viewed giving an interview with Oleg Rachkov, Queen Katie's Foreign Minister.

"Mr Rachkov, what is the significance of this election result as far as Kamchatka is concerned?" she asked him.

"It's very significant," he replied. "First of all the UK is very much part of our heritage, and second this move will give us an important foothold in the capitalist world. We will therefore be able to transpose our model of democracy into an important capitalist country. We need this in the second stage of our revolution, not to mention the dismantling of Britain's defence industry. We need to see an end to British armed forces personnel continually being returned home in coffins.

Instead the UK can be a spearhead, with Quality the driving force, and we will help the UK to do it. There will be no more adversarial politics under The Liberal Future, and ISO 9100 can start to be implemented. Britain can now start to play a leading role in world transformation, which was the dream of Leo Harvey and Ken David all those years ago. Until now the UK has been working to an inferior economic model that has dragged both Britain and us down. Fortunately now the British people have seen that enough is enough. Too much of a gap has emerged between our achievements and theirs. Through our Queen the electorate has spoken."

"Thank you for that," said Sylvia. "Can I now turn to the invitation handed to Oscar Munro to serve in the Kamchatka Parliament. How significant is that?"

"As far as The Liberal Future is concerned it is very important. Lots of people have invested a great deal to be able to live in that constituency so that they can have the chance to live under Non-Capitalist Economics, and through Oscar we will deliver it to them. For years Britain has witnessed a continuous rise in the quality of life there relative to the rest of the UK, and we have managed to achieve that through our relationship with Oscar. The people there have indicated clearly that they want Kamchatka's rules and systems. They have already seen what has happened in The Falklands, where people have also invested heavily in order to be part of a society where everybody wins and the quality of life naturally rises as a result."

"True, but don't you think there is also a downside? Today the British media has been broadcasting scenes of people in tears in places like Thurso, Wick and Dornoch, fearful that Orkney and Shetland, which they love, will suddenly be closed off to them unless they can pay enormous sums for a visa that Kamchatka will impose, or worse, Greencoats with batons and detention camps in the North of Scotland for those who dare to violate the new rules."

"There are issues," Mr Rachkov confessed, "but the good news is we have the means to solve it."

A few heads shook in The Opera House as they were shown footage of several elderly ladies in Thurso who were clearly distraught.

"I am a Whig through and through and I love Queen Katie of Kamchatka like millions of others," she said. "But I can't live with the thought of not being able to visit my beloved Orkney. My sister lives in Kirkwall and I'm terrified I'm never going to be able to see her again if this new law comes into force. Please, please Mr Bogodan, don't take our islands from us."

"Oh we can't have this," Aub said to Katie. "I'm definitely not signing for any detention camps in the North of Scotland."

*

The next morning Aub and Katie took the train from the Palace Gates station to Sabfelt and made their way to The Gun Inn, where Patrick and Duncan were ready to greet them.

"I've ordered some whisky," said Patrick inviting them both to sit down. "I think it should be drinks all round for a job well done. We've prepared the plans, all that awaits is your approval. Francis may not be quite sure at the moment what he's doing, but it does'nt matter because one thing he does have in abundance is skill."

"What made you choose the title The Liberal Future? asked Aub.

"It was catchy," Patrick replied. "Also the title of one of Leo Harvey's most treasured books, written by the leader of the Liberal Party in the UK, Jo Grimond, in 1959. He speaks, for example of our failure to seize on the chance which science is offering us of getting away from the dreary caricature of a human race moved entirely by economic motives and the assumption that unemployment was unavoidable that proved so damaging. Man must act as though he could influence his own destiny was one of his sayings, as was a great deal can be done by mankind to avoid disasters. In *The Making of Kamchatka* you'll hear a few more quotes from this remarkable, but sadly long-forgotten book that Leo Harvey loved so much. In *Blueprint for the World* Leo Harvey carefully rewords Grimond's words on page twenty-six of *The Liberal Future* where he speaks of the crisis of the capitalist system having not arrived to read had not arrived.

"Grimond's argument that the failure of Marxism is a blow at the most luxuriant root of socialism coupled with the view that the most popular way out of the distressing success of the capitalist system is to call it democracy set Leo Harvey thinking when he was a member of the then Liberal Democrats in the early 2030s. Add to that the contributions of the Quality gurus, Deming, Juran and Taguchi, and you have a perfect recipe for the beginnings of what we see today.

"In *The Making of Kamchatka* the influence of Grimond on Leo Harvey's own philosophy becomes clear. When you see the film, take a look at the obscure photograph which Leo placed in the far corner of the Kamchatka Parliament. That's Jo Grimond, and that picture still hangs there today, in the parliament that has become the envy of the world, and where the offer of a seat is the greatest accolade that a politician can now receive.

"So, that's why Duncan and I decided on the title The Liberal Future for the White Paper that sets out our intended policies for the new Whig administration in Westminster. We mustn't let our man down by not giving him the right material to make the intended transformation. As you know, one thing The Island never does is fail. If we aren't sure that we can do something well then we will not pretend that we can. We amend or scrap the project well before there is any chance of failure. By the same token we accept that with any experiment, and The Liberal Future is an experiment, there will always be hazards and risks to overcome, but the good thing is we can overcome all reasonable obstacles."

"What are you going to do about Orkney and Shetland?" Aub asked Patrick. "People on the Scottish mainland are in tears because they fear that they will be prohibited from going there even to see friends and relatives."

"Media stunt," replied Patrick. "In our document we outline a simple procedure for going there, no expensive visas other than for those who want first class, as opposed to basic, products and services. It will be a very short-lived problem. It won't cost ordinary people any more than it does today. Only the rich will pay more."

"That's more or less the system Jacob Spence worked out for Bathurst and Melville," agreed Aub.

"Good. Then I think we're all agreed on a procedure for that," continued Patrick. "The next thing we need to consider is the training of the Westminster MPs for their new roles under OPD. For that I am proposing that they come here in five groups to be trained by some of my experts, on Quality concepts, including the provisions of ISO 9100, for which a special ministry will have to be established in London. In the absence of setmates it is perfectly possible for us to do this. Francis White is a former military man like yourself, and one thing he is good at is ensuring that people are properly trained for their tasks, so he will have no trouble being able to oversee this process.

"We will also need a Ministry for Benchmarking, as stipulated in ISO 9100, for all the professions and industry sectors, so Britain can implement best practice and, where possible, improve on it. Duncan, maybe you can say a little about the Ministry for Continuous Improvement?"

He showed Aub and Katie the plans he had created for a ministry that would be responsible for improving service delivery throughout the private and public sectors, pointing out that it would become an offence to award a contract on the basis of price without considering quality factors. Violation of Deming's Fourteen Points would also attract penalties. Proposals for a Continuous Improvement Act were laid out, placing a duty on all MPs to improve everything in their constituencies in line with the suggestions that people would submit under OPD. Patrick then took over on education.

"There won't be such a thing as a failing school," he asserted. "All children have talent. The examination system is a disgrace, delivering as it does unfair results and failing to reward true learning. Under our system children will complete log books of projects completed, and eventually exams will be scrapped. In Kamchatka they went out years ago, but it was a gradual process, so we won't be looking for that in the PM's first term of office. We will also make it a priority to discover underutilised talent, because that represents waste in the system."

On trade and industry Duncan added:

"Everybody who is able to work will work, just as in the Non-Capitalist model. The only difference is that workers will be paid. Unemployment is waste so it has to be eliminated as a top priority, albeit in stages. The transition from education to employment has to be smooth, and when there is a recession that is the time to get going with state-funded projects involving everybody who is not otherwise engaged. People will be able to work at a steady pace, no targets, just people able to show that they are working on projects. Any bonuses will be tied to quality indicators so that they are genuinely earned rather than being merely handed out. Profit without quality will be penalised and a new Non-Value Added tax will be introduced. To avoid the tax, those receiving bonuses will have to demonstrate value added. The proceeds of this will go directly into a fund for the improvement of quality in public services. Now, Patrick, I think you have some details about another proposed new ministry?"

"Yes, Dunc, it's going to be called the Ministry for National Cooperation and its aim is to ensure that, in the interest of adding value, people in organisations and elsewhere are enabled to cooperate with each other. In particular there will be new laws on the rights of workers to be transferred between companies, and to reduce the amount of competition that is allowed between organisations. This is aimed at reducing waste in the system that is caused through excessive and unnecessary competition. It will also, in the longer term, set out a framework for a national feedback and control system to balance supply and demand throughout society. Importantly, we will not seek to drive the process too quickly, because if we hit snags, and we inevitably will, then we must have the capability to slow the process down. Now, Duncan, what about policing?"

"That needs a radical overhaul in the UK. We have concluded that the legal system that we have in Kamchatka and teach our setmates is too advanced and complex to introduce to the UK at this time, but Deming's principle of ceasing to depend on mass inspection to achieve quality can be implemented and transcribed into the British policing system. Our plan, therefore is to integrate policing with health and safety, and for this we will form a new Auditing Ministry that will oversee the auditing of districts for potential deficiencies that could potentially act as root causes of crime. Where found they will become the subject of Improvement Orders, which will be highlighted to police and health and safety professionals. The Home Office will administer these Orders and be responsible for follow through. Less crime will require fewer police, a lower budget for policing and more satisfying work for police officers as they become problem solvers rather than firefighters. We have found the current levels of job satisfaction amongst British police officers to be absolutely appalling. Now, Patrick, transport."

"Thanks Dunc. In line with our overall policy of retaining private ownership of all property, goods, services and processes, we propose that the UK retains its privatised rail, road, sea and air network. Ever since the days of Leo Harvey and his interpretation of Grimond's *The Liberal Future* we have strongly opposed nationalisation. It is compatible neither with a well-managed capitalist system nor with Non-Capitalist Economics. Nationalisation is, by its very nature, waste creating.

"Transport provision, however, shall not be at the mercy of market forces. Where there is a lack of reliability in the system this shall be addressed through Non-Value Added Tax and the Continuous Improvement Act. Those who own transport resources must be responsible for their performance. Where there are bottlenecks or deficiencies in the standard of service provided, these will be subject to Improvement Orders under the Department for Transport. Failure to comply will result in tough penalties for those at the top. Private companies will, however, be enabled to improve their standards rather than being forced to cut back on services that clearly have demand. A fund will be set aside for this. Now, Duncan, health."

"Unfortunately our teams have had to conclude that Britain's health service is one of the worst that they have ever encountered. An obsession with speed and targets has led to a culture of arrogance and internal strife. There are botched operations and poor training everywhere and sweeping changes are needed. For this we are going to scrap all of the targets and start again with a privatised service. Again, as with transport, the Non-Value Added Tax and the Continuous Improvement Act will enforce improvement in service delivery. Those on low incomes will receive unlimited grants to cover any healthcare needs that they may have. For the rest a drastically reduced health budget should enable lower taxes to be collected by the Whig administration. Only the rich will have to pay more, and that money will be used to invest in the much improved training that is now imperative.

"Now, last but not least, your area Aub, defence. Patrick will sum up on that."

"As regards a policy for defence, our Liberal Future shall include a fully costed programme for the development, implementation and maintenance of ISO 9100. Provision shall be made immediately for planning of the new Quality supersystem, and the new Benchmarking Ministry will roll this out in a series of phases. Existing defence spending will be frozen and a programme for sustained disarmament established in accordance with the ISO 9100 Guidance Document ISO 9101. The Government shall then devise a programme of entry setting out its strategy for entry to The New Game and the sovereignty of nations. There should no longer be a requirement for foreign aid. Instead, everyone will share in the profits generated by the improved prosperity of the nations that are eventually bought out by the UK. This will stem from vastly improved management of all sectors, including governmental practices.

"The standard's requirements are very demanding, but with adequate funding and a high standard of training we are completely confident that the UK will be able to achieve certification within the lifetime of this parliament. We shall endure to provide any assistance that the UK Government shall require in order to ensure that timeframe is met and that ongoing certification is assured.

"So, Aub, that is The Liberal Future. All that is now required is for Your Majesty and Your Royal Highness to sign the document and approve it for submission to our friend, The Right Honourable Member for Torbay, so that he can commend it to the House."

Aub and Katie had every confidence in Patrick and Duncan, so a quick flip through the document was all that was needed for each of them to append their signature.

"Thanks for that," said Patrick. "And in return I will give you a gift."

Patrick then removed from his bag a book, the title of which was *The Liberal Future*.

"This was Leo Harvey's personal copy of Joseph Grimond's book that was said to have inspired him in his youth, and as such had a role in *The Making of Kamchatka*, which we shall be screening on The Island at a later date. Leo's daughter Rachel asked me to deliver this book to you and says that she very much looks forward to meeting you at the screening."

*

The first of June. Aub and Katie had just finished a morning of skating practice which had left The Prince now feeling far more confident in the harness. He had come to enjoy the sensation of flying with The Queen in his arms.

As they lunched together in the Training Centre they watched the parliamentary debate from Westminster, where prime minister's questions were surprisingly lively, given that everyone was now supposed to all be on the same side. In fact, in some ways, it was even more lively than in the past. The only difference was that the adversarial element had been removed. Instead, it was more a case of MPs seeking to extract from The Colonel the precise details as to how he was going to put into practice the revolutionary policies that he had set out in The Liberal Future. Fortunately, Duncan and Patrick had earlier supplied him with a list of as many conceivable questions and answers that they could reasonably foresee. All of the information was there at his fingertips. He did not realise it, but slowly and imperceptibly he was being trained to give answers in the style of Viktor Bogodan, greatly adding to his credibility. Far from being weak on policy, as many had predicted before the election, this government was anything but. With Patrick and Duncan's help, Francis White was able to communicate sound policies with unprecedented precision. Furthermore, he actually gave straight answers to every question. There were no politicians' answers or evasion of crucial issues, as had been the reputation of certain politicians hitherto. Indeed, politicians were being transformed into technicians, with the competence to actually make improvement a reality, as it would have to be if the UK was to achieve ISO 9100 certification.

One of the key areas of questioning concerned the implementation of OPD

"Will the prime minister please explain," said the Right Honourable Member for Barking. "What the role of MPs is going to be in this new electoral system, and how MPs are going to be equipped to put it into practice so that it does not smack of a totalitarian state?"

"Certainly," replied The Colonel. "MPs will be taken in groups to an undisclosed location where they will be trained in the methodology of OPD. Anyone who has observed it working in practice will know for certain that it definitely isn't totalitarianism, exactly the opposite. Any MP can be removed and replaced if the people in their constituency aren't completely satisfied in his or her leadership. It's only a job for life so long as continuous improvement continues to be delivered. Local councils that compromise on quality to cut costs will find themselves dismissed very quickly. You will have to work very hard to keep your seats under this new system, and it will be foolish to believe otherwise."

This led naturally to a question about the new political academy that will support it.

"This will be up and running within the lifetime of this parliament and will be open not only to graduates of politics and social sciences, but also to those in science and engineering. A rigorous period of training will then be required of up to six years, specialising in various governmental roles. It will be modelled on the Russian system and will provide a pool of expertly trained candidates who will serve initially in local government before becoming eligible to stand as sole candidates to be approved by this House as and when such vacancies shall appear. These candidates shall not be trained in adversarial politics, but in how actually to manage the country."

"Here, here," came the cheers from the Whigs, before the next question was taken, this time concerning the implementation of ISO 9100, which still remained controversial. The question was raised by one of The Colonel's close compatriots, the Right Honourable Member for North Somerset:

"Prime Minister," he said. "You have declared that the UK is going to be fully committed toward the achievement of ISO 9100 certification and the setting up of a Quality supersystem. Until recently hardly anyone had heard of this standard, yet you are prepared to allow it to dominate our defence policy to the exclusion of everything else. Can you please justify this and explain what you intend to do with all of our existing conventional and nuclear defence resources, not to mention those that are still in production for which a considerable amount of money has already been spent."

"Commitment to ISO 9100 will place our defence strategy in line with the most advanced and progressive in the world," the PM explained. "The Kremlin in particular has displayed great courage in dismantling all of its defence resources and declaring itself a non-nuclear state, even when the other major powers have not. Those that have not have subsequently found that they are wasting ever more resources with policies that are locked in to the last century. Millions of people are already gaining from ISO 9100 even though there have, as yet, been no certifications. It is my intention that the UK will be leading the way by being in the first wave of certifications. The cost of disarmament is actually a small price to pay. The Russians have already demonstrated that. My answer therefore is that if Russia can, so can we."

The debate finished with a somewhat more light-hearted question from one of the Members, although it had a serious side and prompted some jeering.

"Do you foresee a day when the UK will not need this House because everyone has gone to Kamchatka?"

"You refer obviously to the departure of my Right Honourable Friend the Member for Orkney and Shetland by Act of Parliamentary Transfer," the PM replied. "But the simple answer is no. The reason I say that is because I know that the Kamchatka Parliament would never allow that to happen. The Kamchatka Parliament is and will always be a very special parliament to which only politicians of the very finest calibre will ever be admitted."

"Well that looked like a credible performance to me," Aub said to Katie.

"Considering he's only just been elected I think he is doing brilliantly," Katie added.

Chapter Twelve
The Little Mermaids

One week later.

The Prince's next customer was a completely different kettle of fish. This time it was The Queen's Minister for Benchmarking, Mr Leonid Koshkin, a slightly balding fifty-one-year old, who summoned Aub to The Dome. He was seated in the chair and faced him.

"Be seated and observe," he said, pointing to the screen upon which was displayed a set of figures.

Aub scrutinised the figures and could see that the figures were in fact a set of quality indicators that compared the performance of two organisations, Kamchatskiy Maritime on the left and Frederiksen Shipping on the right.

"These figures," continued Mr Koshkin. "Show the performance of our organisation, Kamchatskiy Maritime, against the Danish conglomerate Frederiksen across a range of quality indicators. You will note that on every single indicator , from on-time delivery to operating efficiency to overall customer satisfaction, Frederiksen exceeds Kamchatskiy. Furthermore, these figures have been checked, verified and certificated as being correct and realistic by both our own benchmarking teams and by my own ministry. We have been benchmarking with Frederiksen for some years now, and all of the benchmarking protocols have been correctly followed. There is no question of these figures being fudged."

"What are you trying to say," asked Aub.

"Frederiksen's Managing Director, Olaf Frederiksen, has demanded that Kamchatskiy Maritime removes its motto 'never beaten on quality' from all of its advertising and correspondence on the grounds that it is false information and is misleading to customers and potential customers of both organisations' shipping services. He argues that either Kamchatskiy must improve and exceed Frederiksen's exceptionally high standards, or Kamchatskiy must come clean and accept that it is indeed second best. Naturally neither myself nor Viktor are happy with this situation.

"What the teams have established is that there are some very good reasons why Frederiksen is, shall we say, getting the better of Kamchatskiy. Much of it would appear to come down to leadership. The Danes think Frederiksen is probably the best leader in the world. We disagree, but there is a fundamental point to be made.

Frederiksen has cordially invited you to spend a few days with him in the Danish capital Copenhagen. You will find him a straight talking and amiable man, but don't be fooled. He will pretty certainly demand at some stage that you make a public admission to Denmark and to the world that when it comes to shipping Kamchatskiy Maritime is no longer top of the quality leader board. You must resist this pressure to make us lose face."

"So what do you want me to do?"

"I want you to take up his offer and see for yourself how that company is organised and how it works, and deduce in your own way why Frederiksen is scoring so much better than us on all of these indicators. I then want you to present your conclusions and recommendations so that I can outline a strategy for our own organisation to follow. Benchmarking is all about learning and we must learn from them. It is also about improving on best practice and not merely copying. Not that I believe you will want to copy Frederiksen once you have seen Olaf's model for leadership. Having said that, you will understand that losing face is not an option either. I will naturally accept whatever you recommend to us, so long as it avoids what I have just said."

*

A cool, foggy night in Copenhagen contrasted markedly with The Island's ambient Spring sunshine. Top class service and top class cuisine greeted The Prince at Frederiksen's very own Hans Christian Hotel, where Frederiksen's logo of two mermaids holding an anchor could not be mistaken on virtually everything from beer glasses to serviettes.

It was a hotel that was accustomed to catering for royalty, but the minute Aub arrived something troubled him. Perhaps it was in the behaviour of the staff. He couldn't place it, nor define it, but somehow there was something strangely artificial about this overt commitment to excellence. It was certainly not natural, as would have been the case in The Island's territories. His senses had been instantly alerted to the difference in perception that can arise when considering the notion of quality. The fact that customers could expect the highest standards of service in the world could not be denied, and there was no sign outwardly that employee satisfaction had been compromised. Indeed, all of Koshkin's indicators suggested the opposite, that if anything employee satisfaction here was even higher than at Kamchatskiy.

At first he wondered if some of the people may have been put up to providing inputs to the scoring system that would purposefully ensure that Frederiksen's scores came out on top. Could there be some kind of pressure being exerted perhaps? He thought about this possibility, but it was not long before this suspicion was confounded.

"My dear chap, how wonderful to see you," came a voice, just as he was about to start jotting down some initial thoughts.

A tall fair-haired man of about forty came towards him and quickly shook his hand.

"Olaf Frederiksen at your service," he said. "I trust everything is to your liking."

"Couldn't be better," replied Aub.

"That's great. I knew it would be. So glad you could come over. I've been longing to show you round. Copenhagen is a lovely city. It may be cool, but it is brimming with warm hospitality. You won't find anyone here desperate to change their way of life. I can assure you capitalism really can work, and better than you think. We have learnt an awful lot from you though. Benchmarking with Kamchatskiy has been the best thing we ever did. Without Kamchatskiy we would never have achieved what we have."

"How's that?"

"Well, you taught us to be systematic for a start, and showed us that there were better ways forward than mere adaptation. Your skaters, for example, are fantastic. Prior to benchmarking we didn't have anything like that to link to our brand. Now, as you know, our Little Mermaids are also world famous, just like the little one we have on our waterfront. Tomorrow night I have arranged a treat for you, in the royal box at the Olympic pool. Remember the Copenhagen Olympics eight years ago?"

"Yes, come to think of it I do."

"Well, the girls are fully grown now, and there are more. Just like the Kamchatskiy skaters. But we've also learnt other things, like building a social system in which the effects of marital breakdown no longer affect business performance. You'll see when I show you around tomorrow. I'll also show you our operations so you can see yourself how we achieve our world-beating, and indeed Kamchatskiy-beating turnaround times, forever improving on our previous best, and ensuring we are number one when it comes to reliability. You know full well that I am asking nothing more of you than to tell the truth as you see it, namely that Kamchatskiy Maritime has been beaten on quality and that you and everyone else now accept what has become an established fact. I shan't hide anything from you. Your own minister should have convinced you of that. If there is anything you wish to see, you shall. All you need do is ask."

*

The next morning the task fell to Frederiksen's Personnel Director, Peter Nielsen, to explain to The Prince how the company's work ethic is maintained.

"You will observe that in our organisation, unlike with Kamchatskiy, there is no trade-off between family life and work life. We have a completely sustainable and regenerative work force. Men and women are paired, just like setmates in Kamchatskiy, but where in Kamchatskiy family life is shared with work life, under our system it is not. Once pregnancy is achieved the relationship ends. It is no more. Emotions, therefore do not distract from the objective of improving quality.

"Children are cared for and educated at The Frederiksen Academy, such that everything they learn is geared in some way toward the advancement of the company. From an early age it is instilled in their minds that nobody beats Frederiksen on quality, not even Kamchatskiy. Emotion and family life require commitment to the point that efficiency is compromised. With us, all of that is programmed out, and our experience has shown that it is something that is no longer missed amongst our workforce.

In return for their services women retire at fifty with a generous pension. Of course they still see their children, it's just that we do not waste time with family life or an excess of emotion that would otherwise jeopardise productivity, which it does in Kamchatskiy."

"Do they have a choice?"

"Everyone has a choice," replied Mr Nielsen.

"Would you mind if I asked them, so I can be satisfied that this way of working is indeed what they want?"

"Be my guest. We call it Romantic Working, which means that whilst two people are together all emotional attachments are integrated with job roles. Come on, admit it, deep down wouldn't you really like to have the kinds of profits that we have? Go on, talk to our workers. Let them tell you for themselves."

Aub visited several departments including operations, on-board ship and at the port, office staff of various ranks, engineering and maintenance. Mr Nielsen also showed him The Frederiksen Academy, so that he could learn all about The Frederiksen Way. In every case there was a negative reply when workers and officers at all levels, male and female, were confronted with the question of whether they would trade their job at Frederiksen for one with Kamchatskiy. One girl's response summed it up:

"I would hate to work for Kamchatskiy," she said. "You are deceiving yourself if you think that everyone wants an unpaid job with a soft-centred company."

Aub understood the viewpoint, and the fact that he didn't like it was immaterial. Yet he could clearly see that these people had been brainwashed to the point of becoming automatons just like the robots that loaded and unloaded the cargoes. He told this to Mr Nielsen.

"Come on now, no need for resentment," came Frederiksen's voice from behind him.

Aub turned.

"Why are you here?," he asked.

"Just checking to see that all is well on your tour."

"I don't like it," replied Aub.

"I don't expect you do. But it is the way it is. What you call brainwashing is what we call education."

"What about the children? Is work the only thing they are going to be conditioned to live for?"

"They live to win," insisted Olaf. "Oh and by the way, they all learn the classic methodology of Deming and Juran. Us Danes have always been there to help each other and that is what they do. Nothing wrong with that I'm sure you will agree."

"Perhaps not. But I still don't like it and we are definitely not going to follow it even if it does make us second best."

"Then in that case perhaps you would be willing to speak out publicly and admit that that is what Kamchatskiy Maritime is, and also publicly declare that Kamchatskiy will henceforth remove its motto 'never beaten on quality'."

Aub carefully reflected on what Mr Koshkin had told him, and resisted the temptation to be drawn into making an admission.

"There will be no public about it," Aub said sternly.

"Oh come on now, you know Kamchatskiy has been well and truly beaten."

"Beaten maybe, and perhaps there is a case for changing Kamchatskiy's motto as it implies that there is some kind of contest. There isn't, because we have different values."

"You may not be in a contest, but we are," Frederiksen asserted. "It is our competitive spirit as well as our desire to cooperate to win that drives us forward. We will continue to benchmark with Kamchatskiy, of course, because it will help us to stay ahead. You will continue to benchmark with us, won't you?"

"Naturally. With that we both improve."

"Then we have a deal then? You quietly change Kamchatskiy's logo so that it no longer makes a false statement and we continue to benchmark."

"I think we could have a deal," Aub answered, knowing that he was going to have to concede something.

The fact was Frederiksen was driven by a profit motive whereas Kamchatskiy was not. This naturally made a difference to the company's strategy such that it necessitated a harder approach when it came to business. The souls of the company's people therefore had to be expected to be harder. This could not be altered because it was in the nature of capitalism.

*

The Prince's next port of call was Frederiksen's now world-famous swimming complex.

"Tonight's show will take place in the grand show pool," Olaf explained. "You can see that no expense is being spared on our sets and props. Just as your Kamchatskiy skaters put on theatre on ice, our synchronised swimmers bring theatre to the pool. You can see a few of them practising in the training pool behind. But our star attraction, naturally, is our Little Mermaids. Come, I will show you."

Olaf led The Prince to a gondola at the far end of the main pool, from where a tunnel, decorated with aquatic-themed murals, led through to the practice pool. The artwork was a careful blend of ancient and modern featuring the ancient gods of Neptune and Poseidon, which contrasted with watercolour portraits of recent Danish swimming and diving champions that reflected Denmark's current dominance of these sports, brought about largely from heavy investment by Frederiksen in training facilities for the country's young swimmers. Finally, there were the murals of The Little Mermaids, for which Frederiksen had become latterly famous.

As they reached the practice pool Aub could hardly believe his eyes. In it were some sixty mermaids, divided into five sets of twelve, replicating the format of Kamchatskiy Maritime. Equally divided between men and women they danced around each other in the water, their movements synchronised so as to form recognisable figures and routines. They danced around each other in pairs and groups so as to create intricate shapes and patterns, linking their arms and tails.

"Behold the world of Frederiksen," Olaf shouted, flinging his arms open. "And there are more where these came from."

"In some kind of genetic engineering factory?"

"Not at all," replied Olaf. "In fact it was your very own Dr Adrian Schultz who pioneered the life-changing surgery together with a team of very specialist surgeons. Very impressive, don't you think?"

"Impressive, having fishtails instead of legs, confined forever to live in water and perform like seals in a circus?"

"I don't think they would see it like that. All of these people had disabilities of some kind before they came here. We offered them the chance to undergo the pioneering surgery that would turn them into real-life mermaids. They could never have walked, other than with artificial legs, but look what they can do in water. They're a massive hit already in Denmark. They are already celebrities and looking forward to competing in our new talent contest Dancing in Water, which will see one of them crowned as Denmark's Supreme Mermaid. Do tell me though, what happens in Kamchatka when someone, for some reason, loses the ability to walk? Surely it must happen occasionally, even there? Do they get offered the chance to become celebrities by developing a fine talent, or do they somehow just have to get by the old-fashioned way?"

"Were working on it," replied Aub, attempting to be diplomatic.

"The old-fashioned way," was Olaf's response, clearly seeing through the attempt.

Aub was definitely on the back foot here, and it made him consider his report for Mr Koshkin. There was definitely a case for raising the profile of disability within Kamchatka, as they were most definitely behind Denmark here. He knew that he was going to have to recommend that the Kamchatka Parliament doesn't fall into the trap of believing that it led the world in absolutely everything. The message of subconscious arrogance, which was taught to the setmates, may have to somehow become reinforced amongst some at the very highest level. Furthermore, if Dr Schultz could help to create mermaids in Denmark, surely he could speed up the process of enabling those without natural legs in Kamchatka to grow new ones? Perhaps Dr Schultz should reassess some of his priorities for experimentation?

As he watched the mermaids perform he observed a precision and a finesse that, in its own way, easily matched if not exceeded that of the Kamchatskiy skaters. Ice skating was obviously a different discipline to synchronised swimming, but there were enough similarities at least to allow for some benchmarking to take place. Olaf knew that, and had clearly put the concept into practice.

A few moments later, however, Aub received another surprise. All of the mermaids suddenly stopped practising. One of them had recognised The Island Prince and had quickly signalled to the others. Before he knew it they all flocked to the side of the pool where Aub and Frederiksen were standing, waving pens, photographs and programmes for the evening show.

"I think they like you," said Olaf. "You might represent our rival company, but they like you. We may strive to be the best, but it takes two to Tango. It's like football. Where would City be without United?"

On inspection Aub could see that the photographs were of him and his Queen, and they all wanted autographs. The Prince duly obliged, and even gave the odd kiss on the cheek to one or two of the girls, struck by the joy that that apparently gave them.

"I've got some more programmes for you to sign, if you would be so kind," Olaf requested.

"Where do these Little Mermaids live?" Aub asked.

"In my Water Palace," said Olaf. "I had it specially built a few years ago. A private waterway links it to here. They have their own special transport vehicles, too, and I have purpose-built aircraft ready to take them on tour. Who knows, you might even be seeing them in Moscow or Kamchatka. I had thought of doing an exchange visit."

"I take it they can't have families?"

"On the contrary. They can have perfectly normal families. Dr Schultz saw to that. They go to The Frederiksen Academy like the children of all our other employees to become part of our sustainable workforce."

This aspect of the Frederiksen organisation still troubled Aub, so much so that he was interested to know how other Danes, outside Frederiksen, perceived both it and its questionable work ethic.

"What do other people in Denmark think about this sustainable workforce?" Aub asked. "I don't know of any other organisation in the world that has it."

"That's true," Olaf agreed. "Your best bet would be for you to go out and ask them. There are plenty of bars and cafes in Copenhagen, and you'll meet a good cross-section of the population. Some of them may even come to you. You'll be surprised how popular you and your Queen are here."

*

Olaf was right. As The Prince strolled around the streets of the city it wasn't long before people began to gather around him.

"I've come for the show," one woman said to him , as she asked for an autograph.

"What do you think of Frederiksen?," Aub asked her, seizing on the opportunity to ascertain what popular opinion was about this two-sided organisation. "I presume you don't work for them?"

"That's true, I don't, but I know a lot of people who do. Here Frederiksen is very dominant. He's so dominant that he practically runs the country, but most people here tend to think he does a good job."

"What about his work ethic?"

"It suits a certain type of person," replied one man. "Whether it is good or bad is a matter of opinion."

These views were echoed by the majority of the people with whom The Prince came in contact. Nobody had a bad word to say about Frederiksen, and many admired his determination to be the best and make Danish business strong. Several applauded his sponsorship of sporting events, and everybody knew of The Little Mermaids. One man, who worked for the Danish Government, made what Aub considered to be a very important point, and one that made him begin to reconsider his overall impression of Olaf.

"Frederiksen has made this country great again," he said. "And were going to need that when ISO 9100 comes into play."

"You have heard of ISO 9100?"

"Of course. We're not all still in the dark ages. I work for the Government and we recognise the importance of having a strong economy and of getting this certification early on. Frederiksen is committed to that. He's invested millions of euros in it, and without him I don't think we could get it. Anyone who supports The New Game has to support Frederiksen. He will help us achieve certification in the first wave. Then we can join the elite club that will end warfare once and for all."

Aub thanked the man for his input, and made a mental note that this point should also be included in his report. He then passed a group of schoolchildren on a tour beside Copenhagen's iconic waterfront, and overheard the teacher asking them what they might like to be when they grew up.

"A mermaid," several of them said.

He then turned and looked toward Copenhagen's most famous landmark.

*

Olaf greeted Aub warmly as he arrived for the show. He was duly escorted to the royal box, where the King and Queen of Denmark were already seated.

"Thank you for inviting us to Moscow," said the Danish Queen. "I'm glad you've been able to come and watch our show."

Olaf presently seated himself beside Aub as he continued to talk with the Danish royals. It didn't take long for him to establish that they were close friends with both his own Queen and Frederiksen, and so providing a definite link between Denmark and Kamchatka, despite the rivalry.

Announcements were made in both Danish and English to the full house in what was the world's biggest swimming and diving arena.

"Tonight," came the lady's voice. "We make history in Denmark. Not only do we have the finest all-star cast of synchronised swimmers and divers, everyone an Olympic medal winner, but we also present the inaugural World Premier performance by the one and only Frederiksen Little Mermaids."

The crowd cheered and applauded as the announcer paused. Then she continued:

"Five years ago there were sixty Danish children who, for different reasons, could not walk and did not know if and when they would ever find employment. Then a miracle happened. Thanks to that most important of Quality concepts, benchmarking, with our shipping contemporary Kamchatskiy Maritime, combined with pioneering medical science developed jointly between ourselves and The Clifford Hebden Research institute, our Founder Olaf Frederiksen provided the means for a completely new human creation, real-life mermaids, to be conceived and created. Now, with hard work and a commitment to Total Quality, we have a team that can give a performance like no other. Later we will see them perform for television for the first time, before they take off to live their dream as celebrities, doing what they wanted so much to do, and living as they never thought they would. First, however, please give a warm welcome to our reigning Olympic medal-winning synchronised swimming teams, bronze, silver and gold. We will begin with the bronze medallists."

The first of the three formation teams swam in from the tunnel and presented their routine to music, naturally with great precision, although predictably less precise than the following two teams. Various compulsory elements were quite clearly incorporated into all of the routines, including turns, twists and whorls in perfect time to the music. There were no dance holds in these routines. They were just compulsory elements set to music, hence the broad similarity between the three routines. This accounted for forty per cent of the Olympic Formation Dance mark. The remaining sixty per cent was earned from the more creative free dance, which did incorporate dance holds, simultaneous leaps and other figures that the swimmers could invent for themselves. Changes of tempo and an assortment of dance rhythms were expected, plus a story line, which had been the norm in ice dancing for over a century.

Very little splashing was observed, just as Olympic skaters would be expected to skate silently and on clean edges. In many ways the sport had, therefore, shadowed ice dancing in terms of its development.

The formation teams gave way to the single couple duets, which again mirrored ice skating, followed by the individual performances that took their lead essentially from free skating. These were somewhat more athletic with leaps, turns and twists that corresponded to the skating equivalents of jumps, spins and twizzles.

The divers followed, impressing with their contribution of airborne acrobatics , first singly, then together in pairs. This old discipline reached new heights as dives became ever more innovative and complex.

The interval followed during which Olaf gave to Aub a framed photograph of all of The Little Mermaids as he had seen them earlier. It opened and inside were the signatures of each of them.

"One good turn deserves another," Olaf said to him. "There's also a special greeting from them to your Queen, and her parents. In the meantime we are going to try to make this medical advance more widely available and, hopefully, get mermaid events introduced into the Paralympics."

The audience quickly settled as the announcer prepared to commence the second half of the show.

"And now, Your Majesty, Your Royal Highnesses, ladies and gentlemen, Frederiksen Shipping now proudly presents for the first time a unique show consisting of unprecedented talent. Please welcome the one and only Frederiksen Little Mermaids."

One by one the Mermaids emerged and took their positions until all sixty were assembled.

"What you will see now will amaze you," Olaf said to Aub, as the announcer introduced the first number.

"The year is 1803. Copenhagen ballet master Pierre Jean Laurent had been asked to provide dances for the Crown Prince and his sister to perform as part of a royal masquerade. For the occasion he choreographed, most notably, a famous battle dance.

"In 1997 the distinguished Danish dancer and teacher Jorgen Schon-Pedersen, with the gracious permission of Her Majesty Queen Margrethe the Second, revived it, and now it has been revived again as The Frederiksen World Shipping Company Dance."

The dance had been given a heavy pulsating rhythm that was designed to portray an air of triumphalism, and invoked determination on the part of its performers. There was scope for some of the original figures to be varied, just as The Kamchatskiy Skaters were able to do with their company dance Viva Kamchatskiy.

This opening dance gave way to a selection of three out of seven quadrilles that had also been created by Laurent and revived by Schon-Pedersen. Each was performed to music by three square sets of eight mermaids.

These dances were followed by duets, couple dances and individual performances, just as for conventional synchronised swimming. Classical pieces were mixed with more modern styles with a varying tempo that afforded the mermaids the opportunity to coordinate their skills of diving, turning, skimming the water, leaping and interlocking tails so as to add character. All of this then led to one finale, which enacted a fitting and appropriate classic fairy tale.

"Now our show is almost over," came the announcement. "But we have one last delightful piece for you. In this, all of our Frederiksen Little Mermaids will combine together to present their very own adaptation of 'The Little Girl of the Sea' by Sofia de Mello Breyner, one of the best-known writers of classical Portuguese literature.

"To set the scene, The Little Girl of the Sea, who has no name, is brought by a seagull to a beach at low tide where she is placed on a rock. There she meets her friends – the octopus, the crab and the fish, with whom she then resides in a beautiful cave. When the tide is out they play on the rocks. When it is high, they go for strolls on the seabed where there are forests of seaweed, gardens of sea-anemones, fields of shells, seahorses and mysterious grottos that are full of surprises. But one day a boy picks her up in the palm of his hand and takes her away.

"The Little Girl of the Sea tells him her story, then pleads to him to return her to her world, where the octopus, the crab and the fish are crying in each other's arms, longing for her to return. At the end she shouts to them 'I am here' and the story starts again.

"It is all set to original music and I'm sure you will love it."

This was a fifteen-minute formation dance, augmented with three-dimensional graphics that provided animation to accompany the dancing that centred around the four main characters.

The octopus tidies the house, smooths the sand and fetches food. With his many arms, each portrayed by a mermaid, he works very hard. The crab is the cook, who, in this adaptation, has assistants in the form of mermaids, who make broth from seaweed, turtle soup, foam ice-cream, algae salad and other wondrous dishes. The crab also has the roles of dressmaker and jeweller, and again the story was adapted so that more mermaids could act as the crab's arms making necklaces from conch-shells, coral and pearls. Then there was the fish, the Girl's best friend, with whom she plays. Again, to involve the whole cast, the story is adapted so that other fish form part of a dancing team, utilising a variety of dance rhythms and blending with the seahorses.

"Beautifully produced and superbly choreographed," remarked the Danish Queen. "You have to say they were magnificent."

"I wonder who thought of the idea," Aub added, intrigued, as he applauded.

Olaf just smiled and continued to applaud.

*

On his return flight to The Island The Prince reflected on what he had learnt during the course of his visit and began to draft his report.

First of all he had to concede, albeit reluctantly, that Frederiksen was right that Kamchatskiy Maritime could not claim to be never beaten on quality when in fact his own benchmarking team had been made to see otherwise. Perhaps Quality First may be a more appropriate motto to adopt. It did not have to be done publicly, as Olaf had initially demanded, just a subtle change.

Secondly, he had to consider the fact that a committed capitalist could not be blamed for following the money. That was not to say, however, that Kamchatskiy had necessarily to follow Frederiksen when it came to ethical considerations.

149

In the past there had been entrepreneurs such as Henry Ford and Frederick Winslow Taylor, who had unquestionably achieved results, but at what social cost? Frederiksen was driven by an obsession for efficiency and gaining competitive advantage to the point that he would stop at nothing to achieve it. His so-called sustainable workforce came with a heavy price for all those who signed up to it or were born into it. Family life had been well and truly undermined. Having said that, to a certain type of person this appeared to be perfectly morally acceptable. To this type it was Kamchatskiy's softer and gentler approach that had to be rejected, leading as it did to second best.

This line of thought led Aub even more than before to the conclusion that Non-Capitalist Economics had to work in harmony with capitalism, and apply benchmarking so that both systems could improve, rather than seeking to have one system replacing another as Marx and Engels had sought through *The Communist Manifesto*.

Kamchatskiy, he stated, should not seek to emulate Frederiksen, but rather should be guided by its own destiny. Kamchatskiy Maritime may have slipped into second place, but this was not necessarily going to be to its detriment. The future, he thought, should be more focused on developing specialisms that would give Kamchatskiy a greater comparative advantage in some areas. This would potentially deter Frederiksen from seeking to compete in them. In order to reflect this a broader range of quality indicators was recommended.

His journey through Copenhagen had convinced him that Denmark was not a country that was likely to want to embrace Non-Capitalist Economics. It did, however, want to gain ISO 9100 certification so that it could play a role in helping to bring peace to the world. In this area Frederiksen had to be encouraged. After all, he was a man of principle who was thoroughly committed to quality improvement, and perhaps there was reason to be grateful for the fact that in a highly competitive world, someone who was actually one's largest competitor was, in reality, willing to offer the warm hand of cooperation.

Finally, The Little Mermaids had to be commended. The fact that they were set to rival the Kamchatskiy Skaters had to be accepted, and it was now down to his own side to enact improvements in Kamchatka's strategy for the welfare of those with disabilities, and do more to develop technologies and opportunities. The old-fashioned way as Olaf had called it did need to be addressed, especially given that the technology that had given rise to The Little Mermaids had actually been pioneered on The Island itself and that had The Clifford Hebden Research Institute not worked with Frederiksen there was every chance that the theory would have gone precisely nowhere. This was not to mention the considerable amount of money that Frederiksen must have paid The Clifford Hebden Research Institute for its contribution. Sometimes one may have to work with capitalists like Frederiksen in the interest of progress, he concluded. Sure, he's won, but that doesn't mean that we have lost. He wrote, 'I think if Kamchatskiy Maritime must have a competitor I would rather it was Frederiksen and his Little Mermaids than anyone else.'

Chapter Thirteen
On Air

On his return to The Island The Prince made a point of visiting Dr Schultz with the purpose of requesting a full report from him concerning the joint work that had been undertaken for Frederiksen to enable The Little Mermaids to come into being.

"We provided the theory, they put it into practice," Dr Schultz explained. "And Frederiksen did pay us handsomely, so it was a project well worth investing in."

"What about doing more for our own people?" Aub asked.

"Good point. Sometimes we have to consider our exports first, even under Non-Capitalist Economics. But with what Frederiksen has given us I'm sure we will be able to do a lot more than we could have otherwise. Hopefully you can understand that."

"Oh I do," replied Aub. "But we must be sure to use the extra resources wisely. I will study the background as part of my report to Mr Koshkin"

"You must be tired after what you have been through recently," said Dr Schultz. "I've got just the prescription for de-stressing."

The Island Prince, however, was an individual who never really stopped in the pursuit of his goals. He was like Frederiksen in that respect. Only his Queen could persuade him to follow Dr Schultz's advice. She led him first to the royal jacuzzi, then to the bed of stones.

A small Japanese man prepared the bed of heated small white stones upon which The Prince was to lay on his back for exactly one hour.

"Lay on stone bed. Then you never have back trouble," directed the man.

It wasn't long before Aub began to experience the relief afforded by the magic stones, which were of a secret mineral composition that permeated the skin and subsequently absorbed toxins, so preventing accumulation over time. Regular use had been proven to prevent the onset of many previously incurable back-related problems.

"We make these stones on The Island," the man continued. "They are exported all over the world, but only we can manufacture them since Dr Schultz has the patent. He had our long-lost Founders Endo and Kai to thank for that. They developed the formula, which Dr Schultz subsequently inherited."

At the end of the hour Aub rose and noticed the now yellow colouration of the stones, and how much more relieved he felt, although he would never have guessed that this would have been the case an hour earlier.

"Now time for sauna," the man ordered.

Queen Katie was waiting for him in the sauna, where she massaged and comforted him.

"My father trained me to be a geisha," she said. "I may be a monarch but I am also a woman at heart. At least we can get back to some serious skating tomorrow. When you're away I just long for you to be back. It can get so monotonous just going through endless fan mail. I'm thankful, but I don't know of any other royal in the world who has to do that on such a grand scale. Did I tell you that next week I have been asked to do a tour of France?"

"No. I didn't know about that."

"My Foreign Secretary Peter Kalkin also wants you to go to New York to represent us in a live debate. He says he wants to see how you perform in a live political debate before he grants you his Royal Assent. I wasn't going to mention it so soon after your return from Denmark, but I thought if I told you now it would give you time to prepare."

"I'm glad you did."

"He's coming here on Friday to brief you. The debate is on the Sunday night."

*

At nine o'clock prompt on Friday morning The Prince made his way to The Great Dome to meet the slender grey-haired Peter Kalkin.

"I gather you know already that I want you to go to New York to take part in a live political debate?"

Aub nodded.

"The title of the event is 'If Russia can, why can't we?' It's a good opportunity for us to put our stance across to the Americans, as well as hearing what they think about us. It will also be a platform upon which you will be able to demonstrate to the world that, unlike other monarchs, you do and will have a major political role as head of state.

"As you will appreciate, we have historically had a somewhat uneasy relationship with the United States, which derived largely from The Island's early alignment with Russia in the last century. In the last century the Americans coined the slogan America First. We believe it should have read America Only because that's what it really came to mean. To us it has become a nation that is only interested in itself, rather than going out of its way to cooperate with other lands to help them to become stronger. The right to bear arms and a worrying undercurrent of racism are both serious deficiencies that will be hard to eradicate.

So you will have to expect some hostility, particularly from the media. This is unavoidable given the nature of things. Extreme poverty still persists in many no-go areas of American cities, and the US Government would love to put some of the blame for that onto us. Many commentators in the US have openly accused us of trying to wreck their economy. There has been a backlash against Kamchatskiy, with renewed calls for people to boycott our cars, shipping, planes and logistical services and instead buy American. Increasing numbers are complying. Observe the screen and you will see footage of Kamchatskiy cars being vandalised, Kamchatskiy yachts being set alight, and of mobs burning The Island flag."

Aub watched the short scene that followed, showing the expressions of anger that had erupted around America.

"There is also concern about our role in the recent British General Election result," Mr Kalkin continued. "The White House is jittery, because Queen Katie has a very large following even in America. That subject is certain to be raised. Indeed the subject of the debate was chosen because America's economy has reached a state of crisis. Our pouring of funds into Brazil and Mexico is bitterly resented and our acquisitions in Baja California and Alaska are despised by many American hard-line capitalists. Whilst Russia now has the strongest economy by far, with China just about holding on to second from the rising Brazil, the United States has now slipped to fourteenth, behind India and South Africa. Unemployment is rife and crime rates frightening. Yet despite this, you may well find that there is some cause for optimism."

"How do you work that out after what you've told me?"

"Well, The New Game is coming, and, although America has a lukewarm stance towards ISO 9100, it doesn't want to be left behind, just as you know deep down Australia doesn't. America still has a massive defence industry and, therefore, many Americans are in favour of retaining strong defence capabilities. But, as in Australia, there are also those that want world peace and want America to be in the leading pack of nations that will help achieve it. Some of these people are at the very top. We do have friends there.

You should expect a rough ride, but it's not all bad news.
  "Good luck."

*

From what Mr Koshkin had told him, The Prince was drawn
that evening to watch the latest Kamchatskiy Auto tour of
America , which, like the tours of other countries, aimed to
incorporate aspects of culture associated with the country
in question. Thus, Hollywood movie greats blended with
routines based on traditional American themes ranging
from jazz to country and western to others featuring the
names of great American cities.

The intention was to appeal to the American audience,
and to be sure the Kamchatskiy Skaters had no shortage of
fans. What Mr Kalkin had shown, however, was that there
was also a lot of anti-Kamchatskiy sentiment, albeit from a
relatively small right-wing minority.

The Prince greatly enjoyed seeing how his setmates had
progressed over the last few months under the Kamchatskiy
trainers, learning to act and skate perfectly in time, using
props and building on Jobine's teaching to broaden the
scope of their routines. It was after he had seen the routines,
however, that his joy turned to anger.

Commander allowed Aub to gain access to the setmate's
feedback, which was mostly positive, except for a disturbing
few. Embedded within the plethora of good-will messages
were, in particular, two death threats aimed directly at the
Aborigine Yvonne, that were clearly racist in nature. How
he hated these people. To him these were the people who
were truly behind America's economic demise. Yet racism
in America was very deep rooted historically, making it
hard to break even in the twenty-second century.

Further footage showed the Kamchatskiy skaters being
showered with stones, rotten fruit and other objects at the
end of their otherwise well-received performance in New

Orleans, where anti-Russian demonstrators had begun to gather in force. Placards read 'Russians out' and 'Down with Russia', and the flags of both Russia and The Island were burned simultaneously. This made The Prince think much more about how he was going to present his position at the forthcoming debate.

As he sat ponderously at his desk Aub looked up at the portrait of Joseph Juran, who had been a naturalised American, and recalled Juran's well-documented seething hatred of the Nazis during his lifetime and contemplated how wonderful he would feel if he were able to look down upon the Earth and see his teaching being used to crush such systems forever.

*

The relatively short flight from The Island to New York allowed The Prince to think through his strategy. Naturally he wanted to do all he could to preserve and encourage the much needed and valued goodwill that existed in the United States, as well as forging and preserving any links that would assist in the pursuit of achieving world peace through Quality. At the same time, however, what he had seen had convinced him that maybe he was going to have to be somewhat firmer in some areas than he had originally intended.

One thing that he was certain that he would seek to do was to set in motion the procedures for a worldwide application of Juran's Universal Sequence for Breakthrough aimed at eradicating all Nazi-inspired organisations that, in his mind, served only to contaminate the world with poisonous thinking. These organisations had no place in the twenty-second century and, with over nine thousand teams at his disposal, he was sure that a few could be assembled to undertake this important task and bring it within the remit of ISO 9100.

The Hebden Three touched down at New York Newark airport at just after three in the afternoon local time on the

Sunday afternoon. It was a quick shower and a quick change before the Kamchatskiy duly arrived to take him from his hotel for the night to the American Television studios for the debate.

Moderator Delores Dimarco, of Italian descent, conducted proceedings in which the panel of five, which included two opposing senators, Head of the Deming and Juran Society in America, Dan Sherborne, and one further invited guest American economist Ms Jordan Sheringham, would face a pre-set batch of questions from an invited audience.

"So, if Russia can, why can't we?," said Delores, opening the debate. "We all know, we have all seen, what has happened on the world stage since the turn of the century. Apart from American politics, everything else has changed. We are now lying fourteenth in the league of nations where once we were first. Jordan, you think the American economy is now in free fall. Would you like to get things going by telling us why?"

"Sure, it's all down to the balance of trade. To begin with China has, over the last few years, started to require us to pay back some of what we owe them. We should never have let our debt to them get so great. Then there is the small matter of Russia and the system of Non-Capitalist Economics that gets them out of trouble whenever there is a global recession, and there have been several over the last few decades. Each time they turn the screws on America, making us drop further down. We can't go on like this. Way back in 1980 a debate similar to this was held by NBC asking the question 'if Japan can, why can't we?' The problem is we haven't learned. Other nations have, and that's why we're now where we are. There's still time. We can still bring ourselves back from the brink, but our entire political make up is going to have to be completely overhauled if we are going to manage it."

"What do you mean exactly?" the moderator asked.

"Well, to begin with our politicians need to be trained to manage. Whether its capitalist or non-capitalist isn't the real issue. Where other nations have moved on, most recently the UK, we have not. We still have a highly competitive system that is basically adversarial with contestants trained to win power first and foremost. It's not going to work. Furthermore, budgetary control still revolves around price, not quality. Short-term profiteering continues to win at the expense of long-term investment in areas like healthcare and infrastructure. You don't see that in today's Russia. There the standard of everything just goes on rising year on year, and until we start looking at that we are just going to lag further behind. It's not their fault, it's ours. Sorry folks."

"Okay, Jordan, thank you for that. I would now like to take a question from a Mr Lloyd."

"Yes," said the grey-haired gent. "I would like to ask why it is that Deming and Juran were both twentieth-century American philosophers, whose legendary teaching is now ancient, yet our great country still appears not to have learnt from it. Is it not time now to do what we should have done decades ago and start deploying this teaching throughout our industry instead of letting others, particularly the Russians, do that for us?"

"Jordan."

"You make a very valid point. Russia, Japan, Korea, Mexico, and especially Brazil, have all invested heavily in our country and where they have they have achieved results. It's not by accident, it's by careful planning. Planning for Quality is central to their policy every time. We need to do the same."

"Dan, you're the Head of the Deming and Juran Society. I know your position is distinctly different from that of Aub Ryman. What do you think?"

"We are different, yes," conceded the dark-skinned forty-three-year-old Texan. "Our aim is to promote and apply Deming and Juran's teaching as widely as possible the way it was intended to be applied, within the capitalist framework. Deming and Juran had nothing to do with

Non-Capitalist Economics. That came much later. We don't support it, although a large number of our members do in some shape or form, usually by being members of Queen Katie's fan club, which is now big business in the US.

In answer to your question, yes it is time. As Jordan said, we are perilously close to economic meltdown in this country. Our industry can't compete. We can have all of the finest technology in the world, but if our thinking is wrong, and it is, we're not going to win. Look at the cooperation that went into Moonbase Alpha. Yet we continue to throttle ourselves with excessive levels of competition. It might be the American way, but it's going to kill us in the end."

"Senator Chas Miles."

"It starts in the schools, I'm afraid. We should have taught Deming and Juran when they were first brought out, not still be wallowing in ignorance 150 years later. For far too long our education system has been neglected. You ask a person in the street in downtown Milwaukee who Deming and Juran were and nobody will be able to tell you. That's how bad it is. By contrast you can go anywhere in Russia and its a rarity that you'll find anyone who hasn't heard of them, and Brazil and Mexico are much the same."

"Senator Brian Powell, your view is presumably different?"

"My view is that if Russia can so can we, but in our own way. We will preserve American values and American traditions and we will kill the beast that lurks in our midst. The man sitting next to me has his tenstacles everywhere."

"Sorry, did you say tentacles."

"I think you heard me correctly," replied Senator Powell.

"Aub Ryman, you are The Prince Regent of Kamchatka. What's your response to the question?"

"Chas is right. It does start in the schools, and that needs to be addressed. But what I also need to make clear is that we are not out to impose Non-Capitalist Economics on America, nor are we out to engage in economic warfare as one American correspondent would have you believe. We want to improve the world generally in as many areas as possible. We want the American economy to be strong, not weak, but unless you are willing to take on board what the past masters Deming and Juran taught the world all those years ago you will not win and you will become a nation of losers. We can't work with those who are determined to lose, but we can work with those who are willing to learn and I just hope that this great nation of yours will stop seeing us as some kind of fearful adversary and start seeing us as a valuable partner."

"Mr Lloyd, what do you think on the basis of what you have heard?"

"I think Jordan is right in that our politicians need to be trained to manage. I agree with Senator Powell in that we need to do things in our own way, but I also think we need to have a political academy like that in Kamchatka where politicians are trained to manage rather than being made to fight each other. At least the British have finally recognised that the electoral system is at the root of a lot of problems. They're going to change theirs now, and I think we should look seriously at reforming ours."

"What do you have in mind?" asked the moderator.

"A government-sponsored organisation that will be set up specifically to teach the politicians of the future how to manage the country, because the present lot couldn't manage a piss up in a brewery."

"On that note I will move on to the next question from a Professor Sheila Thomas, Professor of Royal Studies at Harvard University. Ms Thomas."

"Does the panel agree that the recent British General Election was manipulated, and, if so, could a future American Presidential Election be manipulated in a similar way?"

"She speaks of course of the spectacular rise of the Whigs in the UK, which was triggered by an email from Queen Katie of Kamchatka to all her fans. Aub Ryman, did your bride-to-be manipulate the British General Election so that the British Government would be subservient to Moscow?"

"Yes we did manipulate the election," Aub admitted, without hesitation. "But no, it was not so that the British Government would be subservient to Moscow."

"Then why did you do it?" interrupted Senator Powell.

"For the good of the British people," explained Aub. "We believe we can rescue the British economy and turn it around. The people there have shown that they trust us more than their old failed first-past-the-post voting system. The UK will now do what the previous questioner said America should do. It's all about trust and the sooner America starts to trust us the better."

"How many fans does Queen Katie have in the United States?" asked Delores.

This was a fact that The Prince knew that he had to conceal, so he simply said "A lot."

"Senator Powell, I see that you are desperate to come in on this."

"If that isn't a declaration of intent to take over this country then I don't know what is. Westminster is now the puppet of Moscow. The Whigs will never be dispossessed of power and the future for America is ominous. It is vital that we stop the same thing from happening here. I don't believe that it has anything to do with the good of the British people. It's a blatant attempt by Russia to install a government that will give Moscow the ability to dictate all government policy in the United Kingdom to its own advantage. But we can and we will stop it from happening here."

Aub shook his head as he read the extent of the ensuing applause, which told him that the volume of support for Senator Powell was considerable and would certainly present an obstacle to any kind of reform. The remaining panellists had mixed views.

"Any action that can get Deming and Juran's teaching embedded at the heart of government has to be for the good of the British people," replied Dan Sherborne. "As is the stability and constancy of purpose that will underpin it."

Jordan Sheringham, explaining from the economic viewpoint commented that "Something had to change in the UK" because the British economy, like that of America "is also in free fall."

"The trouble is, people no longer trust politicians," added Senator Miles. "They would rather trust a figurehead, even a distant one, than politicians who have successively driven a country to ruin. Perhaps it's time we had our own figurehead?"

This suggestion immediately struck a chord with the audience, sufficient to generate the highest volume of applause of the night. It was also sustained and accompanied by substantial whistling and cheering. Its impact would be felt well beyond the confines of the studio.

"Professor Thomas, what do you think?" The Moderator asked.

"I agree with Senator Miles. I think that what it has shown is that for some time now people across the world have started to look more to monarchs for guidance than to politicians who, as you have said, have been trained in adversarial verbal combat at the expense of managerial competence. Queen Katie of Kamchatka has played an enormous role in this and that's why so many people respect her and trust her to the point of being willing to act immediately on her royal command. I also believe that the same could happen here quite easily, that is to say she will decide who our President will be, if we aren't careful. The rise of Kamchatka, the subject of a recent film that has broken all box-office records, demonstrates how strong this type of government has become, and I believe the British people have chosen it because they know it's a strong form of government that will get them out of trouble. They trust Queen Katie to get them out of trouble and I believe she will, but I don't think she should be the one that chooses our next President."

Again there was substantial applause, before the Moderator moved on to the next topic, inviting John Slater, Professor of International Politics at Yale University, to pose the question:

"Does the panel believe that ISO 9100 will achieve world peace?"

"Chas Miles."

"Well as I see it the standard has good intentions, but we still need to protect our shores. I think we should start working on it, and if we were in government we would be, because we are in grave danger of being left behind. We can't afford that. Having said that, I don't think we should put all our eggs in one basket like the Russians, the Mexicans, the Brazilians, the Japanese and one or two others. You don't see the Chinese scrapping their entire defence industry for the sake of it. There is a real danger with ISO 9100 in that it is unproven and risky, but we would have two different defence strategies, like Prince Aub's native Australia, not like Senator Powell's party."

"Dan."

"Well I have to say I'm a bit sceptical also, even though I'm behind anything that encourages and promotes Quality. I agree with Senator Miles that it is unproven, although that could change. My other concern is that in many ways it is just a glorified version of the old ISO 9001 standard that has been in and out of favour for over a century. It still relies on different auditor's interpretations of the requirements. It's going to have to be corruption-free to a very large extent and we need more evidence to ensure that it is before we would give it full support. We will be watching developments very closely and will finalise our policy towards it once we see it in action. The issue of command and control in administering the standard needs to be carefully monitored and so I'm keeping an open mind."

"Jordan."

"Economically it makes sense and I can understand why many people across the world want ISO 9100. America could also do quite well out of it provided we bid sensibly and seek out the right sovereignties. There's plenty to go at in Central and South America before Brazil and Mexico get everything. Technically and in terms of resources the USA has the capability to become a strong and highly respected player, but we've got to get our own house in order first. We can't stay fourteenth and falling in the league of nations and expect to be able to meet the strict certification requirements. I'm inclined to agree with Senator Miles, we would be better going in later and stronger rather than risking everything from our present position. We aren't rich enough, simple as that."

"Aub."

"I think you all know my position. ISO 9100 has been developed by some of the greatest thinkers in the world. It has been in the making for over two decades and has been tested in several areas. Some countries are now very close to certification and others are coming through. All of these nations want to play a leading role in achieving world peace, which I believe this standard will do in time. Many of you will know that I resigned my post as Australian Defence Minister over this very issue. That was because I could not accept committing enormous sums of taxpayers money to the production and importation of armaments and weapons of mass destruction, the sole purpose of which is to destroy life. ISO 9100 may be experimental, but its potential to save life is enormous. No more wars, no more killing, no more lives needlessly lost in conflict. I say, please America, take this opportunity now and scrap those wasteful and destructive defence budgets. Just do it."

"Brian Powell."

"You're bad," he said, pointing to Aub. "ISO 9100 is an invention by Leo Harvey, and put into practice by Viktor Bogodan and the Kamchatka Parliament, the most dangerous parliament in the world, that threatens the security of every nation on the planet. Certainly as long as we're in government here we will not be committing any resources to it. Instead we will invest fully in our defence industry, with the help and support of our own Quality Assurance Committees. Now, Mr Ryman, please tell this audience and the American public just exactly how Viktor Bogodan came to have his tight grip over TC 176, how the standard was drafted by his people to serve his ends, and how he intends to use it to control the world by robbing nations of their defensive capabilities. What they are planning is dictatorship by the back door and America must stand firm and fight it off."

"Aub, you are shaking your head again," said Delores.

"Yes, because it's all lies. Do you really think that someone who was intent on becoming a dictator would really choose TC 176, a fantastic committee that has brought Quality to the masses, as the means to achieve that end? Of course not. Only someone who genuinely wanted to achieve world peace would go down that route, and if you support ISO 9100 that is what you will get."

At this point the Moderator invited some more general comments from the audience, which by and large reflected the spectrum of opinion given by the panel. The audience was notably and predictably lukewarm towards ISO 9100, with most people concerned about its long and costly list of stringent requirements, combined with its unproven history. On Deming and Juran there was broad agreement that more teaching was needed, but little consensus on how it would be achieved. On the issue of the role of the monarchy in politics, the American audience was unanimous that America should adopt a figurehead of its own that would represent America before Russia's newly adopted Queen started to gain enough support from her American fan base to oust the President of the United States.

Chapter Fourteen
Quest for a Queen

The next day at The White House.

America's President, Robert Broome, called a meeting of all his senior advisors, including Senator Brian Powell, Vice President David Brewster, and two other close advisors, Alan Tate and Charlotte Kaye, in the light of what had transpired in the debate.

"Well, we've all heard the debate, and we all know what is happening," explained the President. "And we can't let it carry on. We are now fourteenth in the league of nations where we used to be first. But it's not too late. You only have to look at Brazil, which eight years ago was fortieth and everyone said had no hope. It was lawless, had hyperinflation and couldn't be governed. Now look. Brazil is third, and who's paying for it? We are. Look around you at all our staple industries. Where do the detergents come from, and the aspirins and the kitchen utensils? Look at any one of them and the chances are it will say made in Brazil. Ladies and gentlemen this did not happen by accident. It happened because a certain woman was elected, nay, placed, in a position of power. She turned her country around and more besides, and how? Because she went to Queen Katie's mother and pleaded for assistance. Mexico did much the same.

What did come from that debate was the firm message that we have got to adapt to the politics of our time before it is too late. Furthermore the overwhelming message from the people is that we need to come up with something that will allow us to get in on the act in our own way. Fortunately it's still a couple of years until our next Presidential election, so we have got time as long as we act now. I have in mind a strategy, but first I'm going to ask you, Mr Tate, how big do you estimate Queen Katie's following to be here in America?"

"Research suggests that it is unknown and large," he answered.

"Would you say that it is big enough to have the capability to manipulate the next Presidential election?"

"Most certainly," Mr Tate replied.

"How is the fan base distributed?"

"Well, most of black America seems to be behind her, and many others as well."

"Senator Powell, what did you make of the position of Dan Sherborne?"

"Too close to Ryman for comfort. The only good thing about him is that he will at least uphold American values as long as they accord with Deming and Juran's theories. He won't support us, though, that's for sure."

"It wouldn't surprise me if he decided to run for President," Charlotte added. "I know Queen Katie is reputedly quite fond of him. And if that happens, well, my guess is we could end up going like Britain."

"So what's your answer?"

"Well, I was studying the reaction of the audience, and my greatest observation was how fervently they responded as soon as the idea of an American figurehead was raised."

"Exactly my feeling," replied President Broome. "David, what's your reading of the situation?"

"I think the only way you're going to stay in office is to somehow split Queen Katie's fan base in America. If we don't I think Dan Sherborne is likely to be our next President, and if he is he will destroy our two-party system and us with it. There is a way out, though. Take a look at Ulanov. He's stepping down as President and apparently demoting himself to Prime Minister. The people think it's great, and very popular for Ulanov. But in reality it's just a facade. He isn't actually giving up any power at all. It's just an illusion, and he's great at doing illusions. That's why Russia can and we haven't."

"Go on," said the President.

"We could do the same if we put our minds to it."

"You mean me stand down and become Prime Minister?"

"Exactly. Then we must have a quest for a Queen."

"And how do you propose that?"

"The good old-fashioned American way, with a competition. I've worked it all out. We will have a competition open to all women between the age of eighteen and thirty. They will compete for public votes combined with judges scores in ice skating, possibly gymnastics, singing and other performing arts, plus a special royal theme, since we can hardly have ladettes posing as ladies. So, whilst Queen Katie of Kamchatka may have millions of fans all across America, each and every one of whom would currently follow her cue, it is my hunch that a considerable percentage, let us say most, would opt to take their cue from our own home-grown Queen as opposed to a foreign one. The fan base would be torn and you never know, Queen Katie might even work with our Queen. They could become kindred spirits working together to patch over our differences with the Kremlin. The difference is, our Queen would be on our side."

"I like it," said the President. "As I said I had a strategy in mind and that would fit. I want the United States represented at the Coronation Wedding in Red Square, and I want that representative to start getting the results that Manuela has achieved in Brazil. We are not going to disarm, but we can start to reverse our appalling recent decline and convince the American people that we are still a party worth voting for. We will achieve transformation our own way and keep Sherborne well clear of The White House. As one American President once famously said, there can be no whitewash in The White House."

*

On his return to The Island, The Prince began to draft his report for Mr Kalkin, in which he gave a top priority to establishing a set of high-level teams, led by Patrick O Rourke, that would have as their aim to apply Dr Joseph Juran's Universal Sequence for Breakthrough to the problem of racism and Neo-Nazi behaviour at every level, beginning with the United States and then working outward towards other nations. This was one of the requirements of ISO 9100, but irrespective of the United States' stance toward the standard, addressing this problem and bringing the otherwise trailing USA closer to certification had to be a priority, even if The White House was totally unaware of the progress being made. It would suddenly dawn on the next generation of Americans how the Kamchatkan-inspired pursuit of Quality had made America strong again, and this was needed because a strong America would help to develop a stronger world.

At the rink Aub and Katie practised hard attempting to perfect their eagle lift. Then, in the afternoon, they took a walk to The Great Dome. As always the door opened automatically for them even though there was nobody there. Aub strode casually toward what had been Joanie Carmichael's seat and sat in it, swivelling around as he thought how unnatural it was to have the place absolutely deserted. Then Katie led the way up the ancient wooden spiral staircase behind the screen that led to the loft. The stairs were rickety and antiquated and rarely used. When they reached the top they saw The Eagle delicately perched on its iron bar. The giant mechanical bird stood motionless. Then it slowly turned its partly rusted head to face them, creaking as it did so and imparting a sorrowful expression. A few seconds later it turned back again to face the single panel of The Dome that could open, allowing it to fly free over The Island and nearby waters.

"I can't let my father do it," Katie said, defiantly as she took Aub's hand and stared sadly at the doomed drone. "It might be old, and a mere machine, but it's a unique creature. Its artificial intelligence is second to none and I love it."

"What's the problem?" Aub asked her.

"My father wants to scrap it. He says it has had its time and is no longer fit for purpose. But I disagree and want it preserved. This is its home, and it knows it. He says it's an ageing drone that no longer meets modern standards for autonomous aerial vehicles, and its brain is no more than an out-of-date twenty-first century computer. He also expressed concern that it wasn't safe to ride on anymore. The head and the wings are actually just part of a cosmetic frame that he says has now become very badly corroded, but I told him I thought it could easily be overhauled and renovated."

Aub struck its underside firmly with his arm and the resulting sound echoed vibrantly.

"Seems alright to me," he said. "I've seen far worse in the Australian military."

"Then will you promise to talk to my father and ask that he spare it from the scrapyard."

"I promise," he replied, kissing her.

Then they leapt aboard the mighty contraption onto the seat that separated its two wings. It screeched and the panel in front of them opened immediately in front of them. The engines hummed loudly before it soared out.

The royal couple waved at The Curator and one or two other members of The Island's residents as they went about their business. They felt and heard the wind as it whistled around them and the rusting metal wings raised and lowered with a regular motion that was accompanied with a deafening grinding sound.

Over The Island they flew, passing The Royal Palace and its lake, then on over the mist-covered peaks beyond, past the hydroelectric plant on the rugged northeast side of The Island, and over The Non-Olympic Stadium, the outline of which could only just be discerned through the haze through which they flew. The Eagle then turned and coasted back to base, its wings stabilising and falling silent as it re-entered The Dome. Finally it retracted its wings and bowed its head.

"Now you have to admit that was exhilarating," said Katie.

"Of all the experiences I've had I can't say that I have ever had one like that. Fantastic to see the whole Island in front of us like that."

As they dismounted The Eagle lifted its head and looked at him, taking him somewhat aback.

"It knows what you're saying," explained Katie. "If it could talk it would say please don't let them take me to the scrapyard. You can see that in its expression."

As the couple started to descend the spiral staircase back to ground level, Aub took one last look at it, noting the old-style Kamchatskiy Aerospace logo on its underside and talons.

"It would have been a great piece of engineering in its day," Aub remarked. "And I agree with you, well worth preserving."

"There isn't another one like it in the world," Katie explained.

"It won't be easy, but I'm sure there must be some engineers somewhere that could repair it."

*

That evening, over dinner at The Royal Palace, Katie's parents The King and The Queen Mother, were not happy.

"Now I've told you before not to go anywhere near that damned bird," said The King. "Don't you understand that it's unsafe?"

"It's for your own good," The Queen Mother added.

"It's condemned stock," continued The King. "The technology and the components are over fifty years old and, more to the point, it failed its last safety inspection. You can touch the filigree feathers and the metal will just crumble in your hand. And you, Prince, should have known better than to let my daughter, the future Island Queen, go anywhere near it let alone ride on it. Surely with all of your military background you know when a machine is quite evidently dangerous?"

"We have a saying in Australia," Aub replied. "And that's she'll be right, mate. Yes, you can tell when something isn't safe, and to me The Eagle may be old, and arguably obsolete, but not necessarily dangerous. It needs renovating, I accept that, but it's far too valuable a piece to simply scrap."

"Oh please save it," Katie pleaded tearfully.

She remembered how as a child The Eagle had been like a best friend to her in days when it had been in better condition. On her loneliest days, and when she felt low, The Eagle would pick her up on the seashore and let her climb on its frame. She would stroke its beak and it would talk to her in its own language, which only she could speak. She would ride over the mountains and the sea, often without her parents' knowledge. Unfortunately, however, in recent years it had become increasingly difficult to maintain, with modern engineers no longer having either the incentive or the training to learn the intricate skills of their predecessors who had been trained by The Eagle's architects Endo and Kai. So, it drifted into obsolescence. All of this she told to Aub.

"I'm sorry, but I'm getting a team of engineers in to dismantle it," The King insisted, shaking his head.

"Hang on," said Aub. "Surely there's a solution to this. The Eagle represents the best of 2040s art and science combined. It's priceless. Its technology is unique and the electronics in its brain so advanced that only one prototype was ever built. Wouldn't it be better to train a team of Kamchatskiy craftsmen in the old skills? After all, that bird is a true masterpiece of engineering."

"Alright," replied The King. "I will explore that option and leave things for the time being, but only on condition that nobody rides on it until all of this has been achieved and The Eagle can be certified as being entirely safe for operation."

"Thank you father," Katie replied. "It may be a mere machine, but I love that mechanical bird. It has always been my best friend."

"Right. Now that's settled," continued The King. "So, how did France go?"

"Fine," Katie answered. "I think we should keep the present President because at least he represents the centre ground. I don't think there is anyone else in France who's suitable. He very politely asked me if he could rely on my fan base in France to help him stay in office, in the interests of France, and help his government gain ISO 9100 certification, and I said yes."

"I second that," Aub added. "Any leader that's prepared to commit to ISO 9100 deserves to stay."

After dinner Aub and Katie retired upstairs to the television room.

"I don't know," said Katie, activating the television. "It seems I have the unparalleled power to approve or remove governments throughout the world, yet I haven't the power to save my best friend from execution. My father's going to destroy it, I know he will. I can't see any of today's engineers being able to acquire the skills needed to save it in the time that my father will give them."

"He might not be able to, but I can," The Prince reassured her. "As long as we can get him to agree to at least leave it until after our Coronation Wedding The Eagle will be saved, because when I'm The Island King it shall be fully restored."

She kissed him as they sat together on the sofa ready to watch the American news station, and the trailer for Quest for a Queen.

"Today, Television America is pleased to announce the launch of a brand new competition for all single ladies aged eighteen to thirty. Can you skate? Can you dance? Can you sing? If so Quest for a Queen could be for you.

"Week by week you will build up a portfolio of skills that will equip you to become America's first monarch since George the Third, a true royal representing the world's greatest nation, The United States of America, as President Robert Broome steps down to the post of Prime Minister in this our new America. If Russia can, so can we.

"As Queen you'll travel throughout the world on tour, meet some of the world's greatest stars, and enjoy nothing but the best. But it's winner takes all folks, as each week the public vote will be combined with the marks from our specialist judging panels in the various categories. There'll be sing offs, dance offs and skate offs, then a rigorous assessment of your suitability before our selected Queen is eventually crowned. Our top forty selected candidates will, over twelve weeks, be reduced to just one.

"This contest will also contain a new twist known as negative marking, so, if you don't like a particular candidate you can vote against her to get her out of the contest.

"Have you got what it takes? If so, apply now on your app for Quest for a Queen. Get yourself crowned in New York. Ride in the brand new Chrysler Stage Coach built specially for you, and take your place at the head of the royal household in the Grand Palace of Connecticut. Apply now for Quest for a Queen, but hurry, you've got just twenty four hours to get your application in."

"What an awful, unfair contest," Katie remarked.

"I know," Aub agreed. "But that's what the Yanks have done, and somehow I think we're going to have to find a way of supporting rather than opposing it."

"I can't think of a worse way of choosing a head of state. Bent judges, a fickle audience and a devaluing commercialisation of royalty. And what kind of candidate will they end up choosing?"

"Pretty certainly not the best one. But is that really going to matter? The President will still be in charge, just as Ulanov will when we are crowned in Moscow. What the contest will do though is generate huge amounts of revenue for America's communication conglomerates. And negative voting, I've never heard of anything more unfair and ridiculous, just to get more people voting regardless as to whether it is fair to the candidates."

"I bet it won't be long before a few other countries start coming up with their own versions of Quest for a Queen and then supply their own puppet," Katie added. "All because my fan base has ended up being such a mighty force that some leaders are bound to feel it needs undermining if they are to survive. My fan base will be split in America, but I don't know by how much."

"I know President Broome thinks we want to propel Dan Sherborne into The White House."

"What?" laughed Katie.

"It is laughable I agree. I know Dan and I know he wouldn't want to run for President. He's a Deming and Juran man, not a power seeker. No, my reading is we will have to support the Broome regime in the interests of preserving stability and safeguarding all of our citizens of mainstream America that have invested everything in Alaska. The last thing we want is a drop in America's quality of life indicators relative to places like Egegik that are close to our border."

"And what does that mean?"

"It means that Broome, and that dreadful Senator Powell, are going to have to be taught that we are not the foes that they think we are. A little hard cash here and there, generated through your friendship with their new Queen should do the trick. She may well even help us to help America work towards ISO 9100 and convince others of the sheer futility of spending billions of dollars on maintaining and renewing a pointless arsenal of weapons. That's why we have to surprise Broome and support Quest for a Queen, loathsome contest though it is, and accept it as just being the American way."

*

Over the following months Aub and Katie watched the competition unfold, with the candidates naturally pretending to be on good terms with each other, even though in practice it was dog eat dog. It was ruthless, and common to see contestants reduced to tears as the judges, whilst often helpful in their criticism, sought to add spice to the show by taking on bad guy (and bad girl) roles, hurling insults and personal jibes.

Every candidate tried her best to impress in her own way, and to avoid the negative marking and negative voting that provided a cruel twist to an already heartless competition.

The early sing offs saw off the first quarter of the candidates before they had even had a chance to prove themselves in the other areas, in group and solo numbers. Then it was dancing with a professional for three weeks which saw off the next quarter. Ice skating in the form of pairs, dance and freestyle followed to remove a further quarter, leaving just ten left to be trained in the royal duties that were essential for the role.

It was a strange thing though, that whilst Aub and Katie despised the nature of the contest, they warmed to some of the personalities that emerged in the final. The American public, as well as the judges, realised the importance of having an American Queen who could demonstrate devotion to duty and a high level of competence, as well as at least giving the appearance of being sincere in nature. Theoretically Katie could have used some of her fan base to attempt to influence the televoting, but in the end was pleased that she had refrained.

"I'm glad I have had no input to this contest," Katie confessed as the final approached. "None of these last three girls look as if they would be difficult to work with. They are all smart and essentially ordinary, despite being naturally competitive. As for the negative voting, that could even have had a beneficial effect in removing one or two of the more adversarial characters."

Quest for a Queen was big hit in America, forever in the news, and, of course, generating more revenue than any previously staged talent contest. It was by far the most popular contest for years amongst the American public and was always generating comment on social media in all its forms.

So, it came to the final three, only one of which could be crowned Queen of America, ending Queen Katie of Kamchatka's position as the world's newest monarch. Presenter Alexis Silver announced the results in reverse order.

"And so," she said, hesitating intentionally. "The judges' scores have been combined with the public vote from across all America and I can now reveal that the Queen of America is [presenter hesitates] Clarissa Danskin."

The audience in the arena cheered ecstatically as the result was read out and the slightly shy looking twenty-one-year-old stepped out onto the red carpet, making out that she could hardly believe the result. Her tears, however, were genuine enough. Back on The Island at The Royal Palace Aub and Katie also had cause for mild celebration.

"I didn't mind her," Katie confessed. "She's won even with Judge Rialto's negative marking. I think everyone's glad he didn't have his way in the end."

"You know why Rialto took marks off her don't you?," Aub said.

"No, I don't actually," Katie replied. "I thought she was the best skater, and someone who had ideas. She's different and stands out positively. I thought Rialto was completely out of order comparing her to a gazelle on heat and taking five hard-earned marks away from her that she had been awarded by the other judges."

"He marked her down precisely because she was so good. It was to provoke the people into voting for her to boost her score. Nobody wanted to see Clarissa lose, including me. I'll give Rialto his due, he's a master provocateur. He knows how to use provocation to control the masses. He's the sort of person you just love to hate. Everybody wanted Clarissa to win, so he took marks off her on purpose to force the public to vote for her, otherwise there would have been a risk that she wouldn't get the crown. Amazing."

"Clarissa Danskin," said Katie. "I don't know what she's really like, but I'm looking forward to working with her, the United States' greatest overnight sensation."

"She's got no real power remember," Aub added. "But that doesn't mean that she is going to be without influence. President Broome may not realise fully what an important step he has really taken. Quest for a Queen could yet be America's salvation."

Chapter Fifteen
The Brazilian Job

Halloween.

Normally at this time The Island holds its annual election under the system known as One Party Democracy, and The Prime Minister is symbolically lowered into a makeshift cauldron in The Square amidst a celebration of feasting and dancing. The Queen's 240 chosen setmates then have the opportunity to cast their votes (or not) for the single candidate, so learning how the system works. This year, however, was different. There were no setmates, and The Prime Minister, Joanie Carmichael had resigned in accordance with The Island's custom in the year prior to a coronation, ready to take on a new role, that of Commander-in-Chief of Moonbase Alpha, one of the most ambitious projects humankind had ever undertaken.

In order to ensure that The Island was not devoid of its usual life at this time, Queen Katie had arranged for a specially selected party of schoolchildren from three separate schools to arrive from Petropavlovsk Kamchatsky to come to The Island and act out their own ceremony, so providing a chance for the children to learn about OPD in a setting other than their own school. Three classes would participate.

They learnt how to form into sets and elect a spokesperson to read out a question to their teacher, who would act the part of the sitting MP and teach the workings of OPD, just as Joanie had taught the setmates. Then, the three teachers would take turns to descend into the mist-filled cauldron, whilst the children considered the quality of the answer that the teacher had provided to their question. Each question had to address some aspect of continuous improvement, either breakthrough or incremental, that affected the community in which they lived. As with the setmates, there were barbecues, magic lanterns were lit and floated on the rectangular pool in the middle of The Square, and The Island's resident folk band, Ten A Penny, played a medley of traditional folk songs from their repertoire.

Aub and Katie circulated among the children and spoke with the teachers. The smiles on the children's faces cheered them, particularly Katie, who was especially pleased to have brought The Island back to life.

The following day the visitors were treated to a tour round The Island , including The Royal Palace and a journey on the vintage steam railway, taking in the hamlets of Sabfelt and Aldebaran, the latter providing their accommodation. At six-o clock a party was organised in the East Garden and Aub Ryman was given the honour of reading out the results.

"For The Molensky School, you gave your teacher ninety-four per cent. The Chita Municipal School scored its teacher slightly less, but still a very creditable ninety. The best result was for The Vladimir Putin Academy, an excellent ninety-six, so very well done to all of you. As you may know in Kamchatka a score of anything over eighty-five per cent is regarded as very good for a sitting MP as the people rightly expect a lot, and the MPs can never please everyone, as even in our great principality there are always inevitably some conflicting demands between stakeholders in a realistic environment. Now, teachers, it is your job to enact as many of the improvement measures as you can, just as the MPs in the Kamchatka Parliament are expected to do."

Later that evening the parties were invited to join The Island's staff, and the royals to observe the real televised Kamchatka Parliamentary election.

"Most of the MPs seem to be getting around ninety per cent," Aub remarked to Katie.

"Yes," replied Katie. "It usually is about that across the board now. It didn't used to be. A couple of decades ago many of the sitting MPs struggled to get over eighty. A lot of the improvement has come from improvements in conflict resolution, and greater public confidence in our technicians to deliver results."

"Good results on the Foreign Benches too. Looks like my mate Jacob Spence has come in with a superb ninety-seven point eight for Bathurst and Melville. A very good ninety-three point four as well in Orkney and Shetland. Francis should be proud of that, now that constituency has been exempted from future British general elections. I'm pleased with those results, considering this is the first time OPD has been tried either in Australia or the UK."

"Wow, ninety-nine point nine for Viktor," Katie remarked as the Vice Chancellor's result was read out. "If it goes on like this there shouldn't be any de-selections or re-runs, which is good. Nobody really wants that when stability of the system is at stake. It's good news for you as well, since you will be the one overseeing this process from now on. Not that I can fault my father for his management of it, and the people are so good. That's what makes our Parliament so fantastic. Even when an MP retires the replacement candidate never disappoints. It has taken over thirty years, but now we have a system that really does work like a dream. Our challenge now is to help others to do likewise, which reminds me, we must start planning for next week's state visit to Brazil."

"Yes, The Brazilian Job is probably our greatest success story to date. Eight years from rags to riches. Manuela Raimunda has been truly amazing. The world needs more leaders like her. I remember when I was serving in the Australian military some of my colleagues called Brazil the biggest shithole on the globe. Now the Australian press is describing it as the most transformed nation on Earth."

"All through one remarkable woman."

*

The day before departure The Prince was summoned to The Great Dome where Vice Chancellor Viktor Bogodan faced him on the screen.

"Greetings, Prince," he said.

"Congratulations on your ninety-nine point nine," Aub replied.

"You saw the results then?"

"Yes I did. Jolly good show."

"It was good, yes. Shows everything is going to plan. We are now comfortably into the second phase of the revolution, which brings me to my reason for wanting to speak to you directly about the matter of your first royal tour with your Queen. You'll receive a very warm welcome in Brazil, I can guarantee it, but there's more to it.

"You will have heard of The Brazilian Job, that is to say the ongoing project to help President Manuela Raimunda to turn her country around. Eight years ago there was no such thing as Queen Katie's fan club to secure support from the masses. We had to pour in enormous sums of money, gained from our exports. Manuela was just another Brazilian President. Most people didn't think she would last more than a year in office. Katie's mother, then Queen Mary, met her and said to me that she had every confidence in her and urged me to back her, so I did. Since then our return on investment has been legendary. Brazil is now a very different place, some would say a money-making machine, which has made the United States especially very jealous.

Brazil today could be described as something of a hybrid country economically, capitalist, except for our islands of Trindade and Rocas."

"I know, I saw your MP Jonas Roneiro get ninety-six per cent."

"Indeed. What I need to inform you of is that once you have been crowned you will inherit from King Neville the responsibility of being Brazil's custodian. This means that from now on Manuela will be looking to you to assist her with major economic and political decisions. You could therefore say that The Brazilian Job is now yours. She is charismatic and one of the world's most admired leaders, even if some are a little envious of her achievements. Unfortunately, though, she does not always get things right."

"I don't know, I have never known her to slip up."

"That's because King Neville hasn't let her. Whenever The King detected that she had made an error, he quietly and tactfully covered it over. That's what I need you to be able to do, and why I want you to study the country and its systems of government very carefully. It's extremely important to us that we keep Manuela in power. Even if she does slip up, nobody must see it. When she started she had no idea who to trust and who not. She has a better idea now, but she is still not certain. You will need to study the people in government very carefully so that you can distinguish between the prisoners and the warders. Fortunately you have our Founder Eric's manuals to help you refine the skill, and my amendments applied to the Brazilian context. At the moment she has the upper hand, but only just. If she loses it her country will again be plunged into chaos and that mustn't occur. I have had to put some key players in whom we knew she could trust and I can supply you with the names, which you can turn to if you need to help Manuela get out of a crisis. You will then need to contact the person whom you feel is most appropriate from the list to give her the advice that she needs to make the rescue decision.

"Now, apart from Russia, Brazil is by far the wealthiest of all the world's capitalist countries. We discount China because it is Marxist and does not therefore fall under our remit for assistance at all, and won't until it both abandons Marxism and fully disarms. That won't happen for a good while yet.

"As for your tour, you will need to remember that Brazil is still Brazil, and Manuela is Manuela. You know you will receive my casting vote when it comes to your investiture, but I will be watching how you approach The Brazilian Job for all our sakes. I will be looking forward to reading your recommendations as to how you think we should continue to advise Manuela's regime and if we need to make any changes.

"Good luck."

*

As the Hebden Three prepared to touch down at the all-new Rio Santos airport, the royal couple could see instantly that they were arriving in a very special place. Where once the favelas or shanty towns had stood, there were now numerous gothic-style mock palaces that encircled a city that now had no shortage of wealth. What was more, this wealth permeated every level of society. There was no longer the harsh division between the city's richest and poorest, but, as the royal couple would soon see, it still had deficiencies that would leave it short of the high standards demanded by ISO 9100.

As the couple was whisked through airport security cameras flashed and expectant crowds gathered eager to catch a glimpse of the Kamchatkan Queen and her Prince, whom the people identified closely with their nation's new-found prosperity. The men in green, modelled on Kamchatka's Greencoats, bundled them into an awaiting Kamchatskiy. These modern replacements for the police had become more than mere enforcement officers. They offered a complete service to the public in line with ISO 9100, which stated must extend into the entire fabric of the community with crime prevention at its heart. In this area at least Brazil was compliant, one of the few nations in the world that was.

They waved to the many people who lined the grand cobbled lane that led to President Raimunda's palace right in the centre of Rio. Then they entered the courtyard, out of public view, and ascended the stone steps of the palace's ornate entrance where a large wooden door presently flung open to reveal the slim, dark-skinned woman in a diamond-studded white dress.

"Hello my darlings," she shouted, flinging her arms apart and beckoning them to enter.

Once inside she embraced them, then led them into a large lounge and sat them down in two leather armchairs alongside two old friends.

"Patrick. Duncan. Well I never," Aub said, not at all expecting to see them there sipping on the finest tequila.

Manuela clapped her hands and the butler duly brought a glass each for Aub and Katie.

"So, you have your itinerary," Manuela said to Aub and Katie. "Rio, Sao Paulo, Brasilia, Manaus, Recife, then some time to relax with Jonas in your very own Trindade and Rocas, before returning here for my finale. Tonight I have arranged for you to meet some of our stars of film and screen. We have a very lucrative film industry now in Brazil, thanks to Patrick and Duncan's efforts, helping us to make something more than the run-of-the-mill American action movies. Then, we must go downtown so you can see the real Rio."

The real Rio as she called it, unlike the night with the stars, was not anything that a royal couple would ordinarily choose to see, but this royal couple had to see it. Slowly and quietly the five of them were slipped through the back door of one of Rio's top gentlemen's clubs.

"They're not gentlemen you know," Patrick whispered to Aub, as they gazed around at the seedy array of leading male politicians and business leaders, being served drinks in small groups by waitresses who had been selected for their roles according to their looks. The otherwise cheerful Manuela suddenly turned a little more melancholy.

"I work with some of these rats," she whispered to Aub, who could quickly see that these so-called waitresses were obviously doing something rather more than serving drinks.

"When the sun goes down they change," Patrick added. "Many of the girls are not Brazilian, but immigrants from the poorer nations of Columbia and Bolivia, or else hookers that have found their way here from the United States in search of rich pickings."

It was a den of vice and sin, and it was obvious that it made Manuela sad, knowing that this unhealthy remnant of old Brazil was as bad as ever and hopelessly out of control.

"As soon as they see me and know I'm here, they will change like chameleons," Manuela explained. "Then, when they see I'm gone they'll be back to their old tricks. They think I don't know what they do, but I know only too well."

"You can see why she's got a problem," said Duncan. "The country needs ISO 9100 to enter The New Game, but this problem is on such a scale as to render any kind of corrective action virtually impossible to implement. Violent crime in Rio is now very rare, but other kinds of illicit activity, that has to be eliminated under ISO 9100 is still very much in evidence. That leaves our auditors no choice but to raise a major non-conformity and ask the question 'is this country fit to rule over others?' The answer has to be no when people at the top level are able to behave in this appalling way. People who by day work alongside Manuela and her advisors."

"It has taken me a long time to learn who I can trust and who not," Manuela added. "But I can only recognise a handful, and I only know of a few of these clubs. There are many more. This is only the tip of the iceberg. I have brought you here not because I wanted to, but because Viktor told me that I should. I could raise taxes on the bigger clubs, but if I do the problem will just go further underground and be even harder to monitor. Alternatively I could start closing them down, but if I do that they will simply reappear elsewhere. At least at the moment I know where a lot of them are. I can't win. Now, look, the mood is changing. A woman has shaken her head. She's a madam and one of her lookouts must have spotted us."

"I think I've seen enough," said Queen Katie.

"I'm inclined to agree," Aub added, as he escorted her towards the door.

*

The next day at Manuela's palace the group of five sat together to discuss the situation as it stood.

"I have over a thousand high-level teams in Brazil," Patrick explained. "And they have done a wonderful job. They have succeeded in reducing unemployment to zero point two per cent, where ISO 9100 currently allows for up to two per cent. They have also got the country fully disarmed and got rid of the guns. The incentive for crime has been all but removed. The teams have also reformed the police along the same lines following the same model that we used in Chechnya, and Brazil's housing stock is almost as good as our own. Unfortunately, however, the old cultural problem that we witnessed last night has proved to be a bridge too far.

Brazil also has a very serious immigration problem. It has a huge and largely uncontrolled border with several poorer neighbours, such as Peru, Columbia, Bolivia, Paraguay and Venezuela. Fortunately the country is big enough to accommodate these immigrants, and as soon as they arrive we put them to work, and we have got a lot of work done through them, but we can't go on forever, which leads me to my next question.

Let's assume Brazil gets its ISO 9100 certification, and it is going to need a lot of help from us to do so, even with its enormous wealth, it won't be able to buy out more than one country, two at the most. Which one or two does

Manuela choose? All of the countries that I have mentioned are keen to sell their sovereignty, not to mention Angola and Mozambique, which are also Portuguese speaking like Brazil. These two may also offer a lower price and offer more resources."

"As always, it's going to be a trade-off between quality and price," replied Aub. "What is Brazil going to get for its money?"

There was enough knowledge here, in combination with what he had seen, to set The Prince already thinking about what Viktor had said to him. Brazil did indeed still have problems even though so many had already been overcome.

"How have you managed to get unemployment so low?" Aub asked. "I'm impressed with these figures given that the country is so large and has taken in so many people."

"It's called organisation," said Patrick. "As the words on the Brazilian flag state order is progress."

"You have got me thinking," Aub continued. "If your teams can get all these people working productively, in a system that is fully optimised, then surely there must be some way to make better use of the talent that at least some of the women, not to mention the men, at that club either do or could possess."

"I'm sure that could be explored," replied Duncan. "But what do Katie and Manuela think?"

"Unfortunately some of them will never change," Manuela stated, shaking her head.

"Some of them," added Katie. "But what if enough of them could be tempted away from the ancient profession to bring Brazil at least to within the quite wide margin of tolerance that the standard allows? I've seen that section of ISO 9100 and I know it provides a lot of leeway in the cultural areas because TC 176 knows they are more deep-rooted and therefore difficult to address than some of the other areas."

"That's what I think," said Aub. "Get just enough of them out of it to meet the requirements, and then worry about the rest. The standard simply states that certificated nations must set a high standard of morality, integrity and honesty at a cultural level. It doesn't mention statistics like it does for example for unemployment or housing. So we just need to create some tempting high-level jobs to appeal to some of the women, and get those rich boys deploying their thoughts on something a bit more useful to this country's future. I'm sure we could put a few stimuli into their environment other than the ones they are accustomed to."

"So are you saying I should leave the clubs open?" Manuela asked.

"Leave them open, but reform them from within so that they become focus points for improvement, proper high-level quality circles, not vice joints."

"The auditors would fail us, though, wouldn't they, if they saw what we saw last night?" Manuela asked.

"They would raise a non-conformance, certainly," conceded Patrick. "And it would be major. But it would only prevent certification if we did nothing, and as Aub has just said, we can do something, and given that , you shouldn't fail on that alone. Fortunately we are in compliance in all of the other areas. Begging and homelessness, for example, are approaching zero all over Brazil, and I think we're almost there when it comes to having a management system that is responsive and fit for the twenty-second century. Business results are good in both the financial and non-financial indicators for health, transport, education and police. Corruption is still present, but the levels have been reduced to a level that only makes the non-conformance minor, and that can be worked on post-certification."

"You can do it, Manuela, I know you can," Katie said, seeking to encourage her.

"I don't know," Manuela replied. "The requirements of the standard are very strict. It might not be quite as hard for some of the smaller countries, but Brazil is vast and, although we have acquired great wealth, not all of it is distributed as equitably as the standard demands."

"No. But nobody is poor here," explained Duncan. "No other country can claim that. We are even having to work hard in Russia to reduce the differential between rich and poor, not least on our own doorstep. And look at race relations. Your country has scored higher in that than any other."

"What about all of those refugees though?" Aub asked. "My guess is that Manuela is going to have to buy out at least one of her poor South American neighbours to ease the problem. Colombia would be my favourite since they are the most eager to sell, more migrants are coming from there than anywhere else, and that would give the greatest gains in the shortest time."

"The people would certainly rather be run from Brasilia than Bogota," Duncan said.

"The price could be right too," added Patrick. "If you went for Colombia, you could possibly even consider Angola or Mozambique as well without being overstretched."

Manuela was visibly hesitant.

"One false move could end my presidency," she said.

"Don't worry," said Patrick. "The Russians wouldn't let it happen. It would be too damaging for trade. Furthermore, everyone here accepts that you are the right person to lead Brazil. They all feel, as do I, that if you were to fall the whole country would fall with you. Protecting you is one of our prime concerns."

This led Aub to the conclusion that Brazil's newly established Political Academy had to be strengthened. He made a mental note to include this in his list of recommendations to Viktor. Greater provision had to be made for the future leadership of Brazil, and for securing a natural succession, since Manuela had stabilised the country.

"You'll have ISO 9100 in less than two months," Patrick reassured Manuela. "You're closer than you think. Then, you'll have to play like a queen. Occasionally to get change for the better you have to be a little bit ruthless, even though

I know it doesn't come to you any more naturally than it comes to Katie. Your people will respect you for it."

"How do you mean?" Manuela asked.

"On the first of January 2109 the market for world sovereignties will be officially open, with the support of ISO," Patrick continued. "From that day all governments that have a certificated Quality supersystem in place will be eligible to bid for the sovereignty of nations that are willing to sell. I believe your country has sufficient financial resources now to buy out two countries in a single transaction. Then, just think, no more drug smuggling, no more bandits, and no more incentives for Columbians to risk everything just to get on that road to Manaus. Under your leadership our teams could work to transform both Colombia and Angola, and, when so transformed, the revenue that they will generate will be mightier than the Amazon itself. They are two pieces waiting to be taken."

*

With the business side of the state visit now addressed, the next day attention shifted to the royal tour itself.

"Oh my God," said Katie, as the royal couple entered Rio's Grand Central railway station.

She could not believe what she saw in front of her.

"I remember that thing," she remarked, as she gazed at the world's largest locomotive.

It was a magnificent giant steam-powered locomotive with a shiny silver tank that dwarfed that of any conventional steam engine. It was designed to run on a special wide gauge line that stretched from Rio to Sao Paulo, in parallel with the standard gauge line that carried the normal services. The engine had been named the Manuela Raimunda.

"I would love to ride on the footplate of that," Aub said as he gazed up at it.

195

"Your wish is my command," said a small black gent, who presently stepped down from it. "I will stand beside you and you can experience the ride. There's nothing like it anywhere in the world."

"I know that," Katie replied. "I remember my father taking me to the Kamchatskiy Logistics workshop when I was a small girl, and the Managing Director telling me that it was being built for a very special lady, but I didn't know who. It runs on finely cut anthracite that powers four turbines, yet it uses hardly any water."

"That's right, it doesn't," explained the man. "The water system is self-contained. Steam is captured and cooled back into water. Come. Step aboard the footplate."

The press was in abundance, photographing the royal couple as the small man assisted them aboard. Sylvia Smith, The Island's royal correspondent, was there and Katie beckoned her forward.

"Meet Sylvia," Katie said to the man. "I'd like her to come aboard so she can take some pictures to include in my Christmas broadcast."

"Now, Katie," said the man. "Maybe you can have the honour of pulling the lever that will fire up the Manuela Raimunda and open the hopper that will let the finely ground anthracite feed the furnace. You will see that it produces very little smoke and is very quiet, at least to begin with."

Katie pulled the lever and, after a few seconds the mighty locomotive began to creep forward, pulling with it the six deluxe carriages that comprised Manuela's special train.

"My God, this is something else," she said as it rolled forward.

Once the engine was up and running and had left the station the small man, the engine's custodian, invited Aub to pull the second lever. When he did so the engine suddenly wasn't so quiet.

"It will get to 450 kilometres per hour and then run at constant speed" said the man.

"You can hear the roar now of these four almighty turbines. Its deafening," Aub said loudly to Sylvia as the train began to accelerate rapidly so that it thundered through the Brazilian countryside.

After half an hour the train ground to a halt and the royal couple, along with Sylvia, descended from the footplate ready to undertake the rest of their journey in the comfort of the President's coach, but not before they had greeted each of Manuela's specially invited disadvantaged children who had been given a rare chance to experience the ride. It pleased them that they could help to make the children's day extra special, putting smiles on the faces of those who were destined to live only short lives.

The train rolled into Sao Paulo station at half-past two, and here again something innovative had been laid on. It was an ice-covered pavement, about four metres wide, upon which skaters dressed for carnival, filed in a procession past the royals as they signed autographs for the many people who had waited for many hours to get a prime spot. The bateria beat out the classic samba rhythm to which the passistas, or samba dancers, danced on the ice using small compact figures to express the character of the dance.

After this a hospital was visited, which showed that rich or poor, Brazilians could receive treatment and aftercare that few other countries could match, and this was all over Brazil. Patrick and Duncan had seen to that. Consistency was the name of the game, with wards that bore a closer resemblance to a luxury hotel than a hospital. There were no targets or quotas, just excellence in service at every level, under a privatised framework in which responsibilities were unambiguously defined and responsibilities assigned clearly as the standard demanded.

From Sao Paulo the royal couple journeyed on to Brasilia in a conventional unmanned aerial vehicle, otherwise known as a drone. This landed specifically on the landing pad of the country's National Political Academy. Its principal, Dr Joao Peranho, was there to greet them.

"Welcome to the Academy," he said, as he prepared to show them around the newly constructed complex. "This is where we will be training the leaders of the future. Manuela has decreed that it is our duty to provide for and supply a training programme that will guarantee a stable government for our future, as well as assuring the quality of management of all our organisations and services. The establishment of this Academy is, as I'm sure you know, a key requirement of ISO 9100, and it has to be demonstrated to the auditors that it does not just exist in name. I'm pleased to say that three weeks ago we had our audit and there were no non-compliances. Come, I'll show you the debating chamber."

Dr Peranho led the couple into a large hall where the trainees were practising their debating skills, taking it in turn to deliver speeches that discussed real issues.

"As in Kamchatka," Dr Peranho explained. "These people are being trained to manage rather than fight elections. Eventually it is hoped that they will be able to be elected under OPD, which is optional but not mandatory for ISO 9100. As you will appreciate, Brazil is a huge country, so getting OPD in place is going to take, I would say, the better part of a couple of decades to get going on the mainland. At the moment only your islands of Trindade and Rocas have it here. But you will see that our trainees are being purposely trained in being able to provide on-the-spot answers to questions that our trainers have raised, taken from real issues facing real people all over Brazil. They have to come up with ideas that will then deliver improvement. We see no reason why this element of OPD cannot be taught right away."

"I notice there seems to be a large proportion of women here," Katie remarked.

"There are, just as in the main parliament," said Dr Peranho. "Slightly more women than men. There is a reason, and that's down largely to the appeal of Manuela Raimunda. Lots of young women here want to be the next Manuela, and the emphasis on the soft skills side of Quality appeals to them. We are veering very much away from the macho style of management that did us so much harm in the past. Manuela has done a lot of work to try to make politics, if you can still call it that, an attractive career option for women, as well as making it appeal to a different kind of man than previously. Women's issues are also very firmly on the agenda, but these women are not feminists. Men and women work very closely together here, because everyone is trained to care intensively about everything that they do. Brazilians in the past had a reputation for being slow and slipshod. Not anymore. Everyone now works at a steady pace, not too fast and not too slow. Where fast decision-making is required people are trained to think fast, but where more thought is required to deliver the optimum result the training reflects that also. That way we get the full optimisation of talent as required by ISO 9100. Another reason why you see an excess of women here today is because today's topic is the role of women in Brazilian society."

"I can see you've come a long way in a short space of time," Aub commented. "But there just a couple of things that bug me."

"Oh?"

"First of all there is the issue of feedback to the main parliament. As I see it this place and the main parliament are operating as virtually separate entities. Then there is the matter of succession. It appears to be absent. If this is correct, then the role of this Academy definitely has to be strengthened post certification."

"Well, on the first point all MPs in the main parliament are required to study the output and views of the trainees, as ISO 9100 directs. I agree though, more probably has to be done to ensure that they actually do. Some take it more seriously than others, and I still personally doubt the integrity of some of our MPs, especially those that came up through the pre-Manuela era. That's a cultural problem."

"I know that," said Aub, recalling the gentlemen's club that Manuela had shown them.

The debate was in Portuguese, but Dr Peranho translated the essential elements.

"What this woman is saying," he explained, "is that women have a very important role to play in managing Quality. In many cases it complements rather than replaces men's roles. There must be no return to the adversarial battle of the sexes that scuppered the cause of feminism in the past. Women must therefore nurture and encourage those men that are genuinely working to improve the common good, rather than seeking to undermine them. We don't want macho men replaced with macho women or we will be dragged back into the past.

Now her colleague is supporting her with reference to Deming's Eighth Point, to drive out fear, as required under ISO 9100, emphasising the need for greater application in human relationships. She is saying that we must continue to use psychology to end violence and intimidation towards and by women so that men are no longer armed with adverse incentives. She says that whilst Brazilian men have been tamed, the journey is not complete. The thinking patterns and motivation of men and women both must be subject to the same scrutiny and continuous improvement as we are embedding in other areas."

Aub took on board some of the messages in this, ready to include in his report to Viktor Bogodan. In particular, in order to improve the role of women in Brazil, some changes were going to have to be made at the top. Had the right men hitherto been nurtured as the speaker had advocated? The answer was probably no, and in this case perhaps some subtle pressure in the right places was needed by the Kamchatka Parliament. The debate convinced The Prince that Manuela had a legacy problem, and that she herself may even have a hidden fear when it came to taking control of some situations. Where this could be identified there was definitely a need to consider intervention to support her. Perhaps it could also be time to afford a few of the trainees the opportunity to enter the world of Brazilian politics proper, and cast out one or two bad eggs? The only problem was that Manuela had to be enabled to have the courage to do it.

*

So Aub and Katie left Brasilia behind aboard what was now Aub's trusted Hebden Three, the one that Katie had given to him when he had left Australia on the day that changed his life. They were bound for Manaus where they would meet up again with their two trusted advisors Patrick O Rourke and Duncan McIntyre.

Manaus was a sprawling makeshift city set amid the Amazon rainforest. As soon as they saw it, Aub and Katie could see that it could only just support the high volume of people that occupied the many small, but adequate self-constructed dwellings that were laid out in long avenues. On arrival it was obvious that the majority of the inhabitants of Manaus were not Brazilian, but had drifted across practically without restriction from neighbouring countries, particularly Colombia. Nevertheless, they turned out in force to greet The Island Queen and her Prince, waving the many Island flags that Patrick and Duncan had provided in advance of the royal visit. The royals shook hands and signed autographs along a prescribed section of the route that led from the airport to the hotel where they would rest and talk with Patrick and Duncan about what had been achieved in this enormous region, as well as what still remained to be done.

"What we have created here," explained Patrick. "And what you will see tomorrow, is a perfectly controlled ecosystem. Manaus may not be the most elegant of Brazilian cities, but at least it is fully safe for residents and visitors alike. The constant stream of immigrants remains a problem, but by providing them with materials with which to construct their own comfortable dwelling places on their own plot of land, and by providing every one with a job and a wage that is fair in the circumstances, we have managed to do an exchange that has all but ended the previously uncontrolled input of drugs to the country."

The next day thus began with a tour of a sample of the many factories where the migrants had been put to work producing large quantities of the basic household and industrial products that were now being economically exported to the United States and elsewhere. The royal couple was pleasantly surprised. Working conditions were as good as they had seen anywhere, leaving no doubt as to why so many people wanted to make the long journey on the road to Manaus.

The workhouses may have been hastily constructed, but they provided a relatively comfortable existence for the migrants. In addition to the factories there were also small holdings that blended in with the rainforest that stretched for several hundred miles, reminding Aub of parts of the Australian outback, only on a larger scale, boosting Brazil's agricultural and freshwater fishing industry on a level that was staggering. It was truly grand scale, and simply grew as more migrants entered.

"Everyone is put to work, not too fast, not too slow," Patrick explained as the four of them toured a cotton mill, one of over a thousand that made Brazil now the world's leading exporter of textiles of every kind. No other country could compete now with Brazil in this and many other areas thanks to The Island's influence.

Aub and Katie chatted to some of the workers, shadowed by Sylvia Smith, who continued to compile material for The Queen's Christmas speech.

"We risked our lives to come here," said one man. "In Colombia the drugs barons are everywhere, but once we are over the border they cannot pursue us. The drugs have no value because our homes and jobs have all the value. Working here is so much better than being forced to work for them. Now we are doing something constructive. Thank you so much President Raimunda for giving us this opportunity."

"We will work hard, we won't let you down," said another man.

Reassuring though these words were, Aub could see that there was still an underlying problem that required resolution. The present situation was well under control. Patrick and Duncan's teams had made sure of that, but even a country the size of Brazil could only continue this way for so long. Colombia had to be bought out and quickly.

Later that afternoon, as the party flew across northern Brazil on their way to the coastal city of Recife, the sheer scale of the problem was brought home. Road after road criss-crossed this vast land, with small towns and villages popping up just about everywhere. It was well organised, but far too extensive for Aub's liking. As far as he could see there was only just enough time to prevent a humanitarian crisis from developing, and as for Colombia, that too was a worry since it had by now lost almost all of its best people. Things there could only get worse, and its government knew it. All of this had to be brought to Viktor Bogodan's attention.

"We have gone through this entire region upgrading and improving every city, suburb, town, village and hamlet," explained Patrick. "In the area we are over now we have set up no end of vast plantations so as to revitalise Brazil's coffee industry, and introduced some of the finest food processing technology in the world, bringing the very highest level of cuisine to Brazil and to the world. All of the revenue is ploughed back to generate further improvement, passing straight through The Island's financial management system and back again. The revenue just keeps increasing. The whole area has been audited to ISO 9100 and every non-conformance, and there were many, addressed and rectified. Life here nowadays is far from primitive, and the migrants have a clear progression from the workhouses into business. Manuela, on King Neville's recommendation, taxes them quite heavily, and some would say unfairly, but not until they have reached a pretty high level of earnings. There are few objections, because most of them are very thankful for what they have received, and can see much of the money being ploughed back."

As they flew over the state of Bahia they noticed a difference in the landscape, especially in the nature of the buildings. The many small self-constructed dwelling places gave way to what were clearly higher class towns. There was still manufacturing on a grand scale that rivalled China, but there was a higher level of prosperity that was detectable.

"It's amazing what can be done when people put their minds to something," said Duncan. "When we started out here some ten years ago this area was absolutely shocking. But we overcame the difficulties and got the place going again. The migrants in this area are all enjoying the fruits of their success, having earned the right to move further east."

The coastal towns of the north east, and the city of Recife were charming and welcoming to the royal couple, as ever, as they rode past in an open-topped Kamchatskiy. Then, it was on to the city's pioneering transport system. Once inside the transparent capsule Aub knew where the programmers had obtained the ideas for the Baroness of Bow Street in Dr Schultz's Dream Machine. The system as yet did not cover a particularly wide area, but it was fast, safe and efficient, with almost zero pollution.

"Recife did have a serious pollution problem at one time," Patrick explained. "But this system largely addresses it. As you can see, beautiful clean sea water runs along the channels powered by electric pumps. Recife is also a major recycling centre, thanks to our teams. It has the best sewage recycling facility in the world , providing cheap, affordable gas to the city. Our engineers at The Clifford Hebden Institute designed it as the warm temperatures here are ideal for it."

From Recife the royals travelled by steamer to The Queen's own island of Trindade, where her MP Jonas Roneiro welcomed them into the somewhat more tranquil surroundings of the palace which stood proudly in the centre of this relatively small island paradise. It was the ideal quiet retreat, where the locals numbered only a few hundred, but they were all there to greet their visitors. Modelled on The Island itself, it served as a reminder of home, the only difference being the twenty or so hotels on the coast that catered for some of Brazil's wealthiest tourists, providing them with the chance to experience life under Non-Capitalist Economics.

Here, away from all of the crowds and the ever-present media attention, the couple could actually relax a little and focus a bit more on each other.

*

The couple spent three days on Trindade before returning to Rio for Manuela's finale.

"Hello my darlings," she shouted, flinging her arms apart just as on the first night, as Aub and Katie stepped from their Kamchatskiy into Manuela's palace. They did not remain there for long, however, only long enough to consume a drink and collect Manuela.

"I have some more old friends who are eager to meet you," she said, as they all re-entered the Kamchatskiy.

"Where are we going?" asked Aub.

"Oh I don't say," replied Manuela, smiling and shaking her head.

So the car sped through the streets of Rio until it arrived outside the Ice Drome, where they were ushered inside by the watchful Greencoats. Inside they were led backstage where they were greeted by the familiar faces of the Kamchatskiy Auto setmates and their trainers.

"Wonderful to see you all again," said Aub as he and Katie embraced each of the sixty setmates.

"What do you think of Brazil?" Katie asked Anne Clancy.

"Incredible to see how this once lawless and failing state has been so transformed. Manuela reminds me of the legendary Wonder Woman. We've incorporated it into one of our routines. Yvonne plays Wonder Woman but don't tell Aub."

Aub greeted Yvonne and expressed his sympathy for the way she and the others had been treated in America.

"Tell me what happened."

"It was only a small minority of Americans and it comes with the territory," she replied.

"I know, but something has to be done about it. I can't have anything like this happening to any of my subjects. Did you see Quest for a Queen?"

"Yes. Loved the skating but hated the show. I think the best girl won in the end. I don't know how she will shape up as America's Queen though. Hopefully she'll be more than just a trendy doll."

"Oh she will," said Katie. "I'll make sure of that."

On the ice the setmates performed a variety of routines that built upon the training that they had received from Jobine. The basics contained more embellishments, however, and they had clearly learnt to transpose them from one routine to another so that they could now adapt their programmes to reflect the culture of different lands and continents. The Kamchatskiy trainers had, however, retained Jobine's principle of allowing each set of twelve to excel in a different skating talent, so nobody could claim that any one set was necessarily any better than any other.

Some routines used the Kamchatskiy as prop. Others did not. Here the Latin rhythms predominated, in particular the samba, including, for the first time, the classic Silver Samba, invented by Courtenay Jones and Peri Horne in London in 1963, performed in unison and set to the jazzy sound of 'The Peanut Vendor'. This latter dance came intentionally before the interval during which the audience, including the royal couple, Manuela and guest, the Managing Director of Kamchatskiy Auto, were invited to sample some genuine Brazilian peanuts, which, like the Brazil nut itself, had become world famous.

The programme closed with the Wonder Woman routine as a tribute to Manuela Raimunda and her government. Some catchy graphics helped to create the illusion of Wonder Woman spinning wildly before disappearing in a puff of smoke.

Chapter Sixteen
The Making of Kamchatka

The last day in November.

A very special guest was about to arrive on The Island, and, as was customary all of The Island's staff gathered in The Square to await the arrival of the royal coach from the airport. Everyone wanted to see this person who had had so much influence over The Island's history. After all this eighty-three-year-old had seen it all.

She did not disappoint, arriving exactly on time at half-past two, keen to greet all of her long-lost friends, many of whom she recognised, having not returned to The Island in over a decade. At her request the people would greet her first, before boarding the royal train destined for The Royal Palace, where Aub and Katie were eagerly expecting her. There she would explain to Aub all that he did not already know about the Kamchatka Parliament and her role in it, as well as the film that she had helped to make.

The now somewhat frail lady was none other than Rachel Harvey, daughter of Island Founder Leo Harvey. Aub had never met her before, and he was therefore naturally keen to establish just exactly how much he could learn from her, given that she had been the first Vice Chancellor of the Kamchatka Parliament, from its inception in 2077.

In the evening all of The Island's residents and staff joined the royals at the Opera House for a special screening of the film. Aub sat next to her in the front row. At half-past eight Patrick O'Rourke took to the stage to introduce the film that had acquired worldwide acclaim, with even the United States grudgingly accepting that this film deserved more than just a few accolades.

The film dramatised the story of how a small band of wealthy individuals, led by leading banker Leo Harvey, and shipping tycoon Ken David, came together in the early 2030s and between them developed a plan for the greatest Quality Revolution of all time. It would be neither fast nor dramatic, but would, over a long span of time that would extend way beyond their lifetimes, gradually change the way people thought, behaved and managed the world and its resources. At its core a system, known as Non-Capitalist Economics, would provide a viable alternative to capitalism that would completely replace communism, consigning the latter to history.

During the first stage of the revolution the Founders would purchase an island that they would call their Island of Dreams, which would have a monarch, and be governed by a prime minister, with the assistance of a chancellor. Here, Non-Capitalist Economics would be introduced and tested with willing volunteers. Then, once it had been proven to be a viable system, it would be rolled out in other places, small at first, then larger.

During the second stage of the revolution, the successes of the system would become evident and be made known. A Quality supersystem would be devised, embodied within a standard that would be related to the already existing ISO 9001, that would serve as a specification for leading countries to follow. The teachings of the renowned twentieth century philosophers William Edwards Deming and Joseph Moses Juran would be incorporated, driving both incremental and breakthrough improvement throughout the world. The Sovereignty of Nations would be determined by new rules, a New Game, rather than by confrontation and conflict. Capitalism and Non-Capitalist Economics would then ultimately converge so that the two systems would co-exist, creating a better world in the process.

"I am now going to take you back in time," Patrick continued. "Over seventy years, to when it all began. The film you are about to see tells the story of the rise of Kamchatka, from when The Island was originally purchased, through the great land acquisitions of the 2050s and 60s, to the eventual opening of the Kamchatka Parliament in 2077 by the absolutely extraordinary and fabulous lady that we are so honoured to have with us tonight."

Rachel stood up and bowed her head as the audience burst into spontaneous applause and cheering that was sustained.

"Rachel grew up here and I know has very fond memories of The Island from her youth. Rachel, please join me on stage."

The frail but sturdy lady slowly rose and climbed the seven steps onto the stage, where a chair had been placed for her.

"Now, Rachel, you are the daughter of Leo Harvey. You were also the first Vice Chancellor of the Kamchatka Parliament from 2077 to 2098. You selected and groomed your successor Viktor Bogodan, working hard to bring him out of his shell, and you played a major role in guiding the screenplay writers and the director in producing this magnificent film that has collected awards everywhere since it was released back in March. We are eight months on from the premiere, but this is a special screening that we can all enjoy together in this unique place that was so very much at the forefront of developments at the time. You saw it all, we are just seeing it for the first time here tonight. So, before we begin, maybe you could say a little more about the making of *The Making of Kamchatka*? First, what made you choose Viktor Bogodan from amongst what must have been a whole host of candidates?"

"Viktor was always a bit of a retiring sort of chap," Rachel explained. "I learnt over time that he was someone who would have all of the right qualities to be Vice Chancellor. The young man who plays him, Alexei Kalinin does so perfectly, and he bears a very good resemblance to what Viktor really did look like in the early years. He still has that neat, delicately combed blonde hair and the handsome looks. The important thing about Viktor was that I knew that no matter how much power he had he would never abuse it. That was critical to me."

"Sure, and what do you think of your part? How did it feel addressing that now famous parliament for the first time?"

"As you'll see it was more of a theatre than a parliament at that time. Even today you can still see a little of that, although we have dispensed with the costumes other than for ceremonial occasions. It was actually never designed at the outset to have much power. The Kremlin was the main authority. We were there more for show and to help The Kremlin make the region more prosperous. It was poor and largely barren in the early years, but my father and his friends, especially Clifford Hebden, whom you will also see played by John Fairbanks, saw the potential of Kamchatka's huge geothermal energy reserves. Exploitation of this led to very considerable wealth generation. I supplied a lot of the original drawings and CAD files to the film producers so that they could understand and dramatise all the projects, including all the teams that were set up. I see that under yourself and Duncan these teams are still thriving, only you now have ten times the number, and they are working internationally."

"Indeed and they are doing a fine job."

"Now the Kamchatka Parliament and The Kremlin are very much complementary institutions. As Kamchatka became rich, largely through Non-Capitalist Economics, and both Russia and the world fell into recession in the 2080s, we found that we were able to insulate Russia from it. So, as many other countries fell, we enabled Russia to rise, and ever since The Kremlin has had enormous respect for us. We virtually saved Russia at one point, and Ulanov."

"And there's a story of how Jo Grimond's picture came to adorn the far wall of the Kamchatka Parliament, isn't there?"

"Oh yes, that was funny. None of The Island's Founders wanted their picture on the wall. My father had a copy of Jo Grimond's *The Liberal Future*, published in 1959 and suggested him in the absence of all others. All The Founders agreed and so up went his photo, and it has stayed there ever since. I expect one day it will be replaced by a modern Russian, but so far nobody has suggested that, so the ancient black and white blown up photo of Grimond continues to remind everyone of the link between the Kamchatka Parliament and Liberal Britain."

"And the theatre hasn't entirely gone either, has it?"

"Not entirely, but nowadays we are definitely far more a parliament than a theatre. When you hear my speech on the opening day, and it is an exact transcription, you will see how we have grown to be exactly what my father predicted. Yes, though, to preserve our tradition debates are still sometimes conducted in costume to preserve the fun aspect. It helps to make us special. Interestingly I believe Manuela is thinking of introducing something similar in Brasilia. That's the only other place where you might see it. But if ice rinks can be turned into theatres, then why not parliaments?"

"Why not indeed? Another question that has been asked is how many shots have been taken straight from the 2070s as opposed to being acted?"

"Not many, but you will see a few, most notably the building of the parliament itself. There are some early scenes of The Island also, and I would like to thank especially The Island's curator Maria for giving me access to some of The Island's precious historical footage."

"Thank you Rachel for providing us with that. You have been a true inspiration to us all. Your Majesty, Your Royal Highness, ladies and gentlemen, the one and only Rachel Harvey."

As she returned to her place, duly applauded, the lights dimmed and the film commenced, opening from the scene from 2036 where the young Leo Harvey, played by Mark Holmes, made his now famous speech to the British Liberal Democrats at the party's Cardiff conference shortly after the party's thumping at the previous general election. Aub was intrigued, keen to learn more about the way British political history was about to change without anyone hardly realising it.

"This party," Leo said. "Has been through some difficult times, not least over the past year. Some of you may be content to allow this, our great party, to remain out of government, let us say forever, without any hope at all of ever breaking the mould of British politics. I am not, and neither are my associates. As far as we are concerned the losses we suffered at the last general election are the last that we can take. Enough is enough. We have therefore decided that as of today we will be forming a new party, but do not be alarmed. We will not be competing with you, in fact exactly the opposite.

"We shall be known as The Whig Party of Great Britain and what will distinguish us from the rest of you is our resolution that if we cannot be the government of the United Kingdom, and demonstrate our capability to deliver sound, competent and balanced government with built-in constancy of purpose, and it would appear that we cannot, then we shall do it elsewhere. We will, ladies and gentlemen, show the world just what a great party we are and what we really are capable of."

Applause rippled all round the auditorium, although many delegates were clearly mystified and visibly lacked confidence by their expression.

"Have you a plan?" one man asked in the question and answer session.

"Where will you go?" asked another.

"A plan, of course," Leo replied. "Where we will go, I don't know. But what I can tell you is that we will certainly go somewhere and we shall form a government."

"And then?" asked the first questioner.

"Then, we shall show what is possible with a new style of Liberalism, unlike anything anyone has seen before."

"And then?" the man asked again.

"Then, we shall return, and when we do it will be with a force the likes of which this country has never seen."

At this point the film's narrative took over:

"Many in the party were sceptical about Leo's proposals and when, or indeed if, any of them would ever transpire. The speech itself was not really remembered until some years later, when the name of Leo Harvey started to become well-known in areas that extended well beyond the realm of British politics."

Archive film was then featured showing the early years of The Island and its careful reconstruction from its dilapidated remnants of a staging post for Portuguese sailing ships en route to Brazil. It told the story of how Ken and Kathleen had stumbled across The Island and later made it their home, before tragedy struck and his beloved Kathleen was killed in a motor accident in Colorado. Then, in accordance with Kathleen's wishes, her best friend took her place to become the first Island Queen. Then the narrative returned:

"The Founders populated The Island with their friends, and there was no shortage of volunteers keen to participate in the new social experiment that they had devised. It was to be the dawn of what we now understand as Non-Capitalist Economics. Once the people could see a system in which Quality took the place of profit as the driver for success, few of them doubted The Founders' plans. "Unlike communism, this alternative to capitalism worked like a dream. All of the unfairness, waste and sub-optimisation associated with capitalism had been stripped away to leave a society in which everyone's effort was directed to improving the system, just as William Edwards Deming had taught almost a hundred years before.

"The volunteers included notably two Japanese engineers, Endo and Kai, both loyal friends of Leo Harvey and Ken David, who liked what they saw and lent their hands towards the building of what is now known affectionately as The Island of Dreams. They made many valuable contributions, but perhaps the most enduring is the *Stone Boat*, which still stands today."

"Now, David-san," said Endo. "Tell me if you can put to sea in that?"

"By 2050 Leo had become head of one of the world's largest banking and financial institutions, and became more and more isolated. The more he saw of the workings of capitalism, the more he despised it. Yet there he was, in a position that could not be more capitalist. But in 2051 he was to have one of his greatest strokes of luck.

"This was to come in the form of a move by the Russian Government to encourage more foreign investment in order to help overcome what were fast becoming serious economic difficulties. He saw his chance and took it. With the help of the other Founders he swooped in on the open market for cheap land in the otherwise barren and impoverished territory of Kamchatka, one of the places that at that time had become a major drain on Russia's finances.

"It took a lot, but with some highly skilful negotiation with The Kremlin, a deal was struck with a viable business plan to harness the enormous hitherto untapped geothermal resources of Kamchatka and to subsequently supply all of the power that Russia needed at a fraction of its current cost. It had to be said that Kamchatka had, and still does have, the most valuable geology in the world. It just needed the technology to harness the resources that it had to offer, and, fortunately, there was one Founder whose knowledge and expertise had apparently been rejected by Britain's Ministry of Defence, who would be key to the development of this most ambitious of projects. That man was, of course, Clifford Hebden, whom the world now respects as being one of the greatest scientists of all time."

Archive film then transported the audience back to Kamchatka as it had looked in 2051. It was a poor place, with largely peasant communities making a living from the peninsula's caviar industry, which had become only just sustainable. Local communities everywhere were protesting, with even officials expressing their anger at having been let down by Moscow. The drama unfolded as the Mayor of Petropavlovsk Kamchatskiy spoke out:

"This part of Russia has been starved of investment for decades. Nothing works here."

Leo Harvey, now appearing somewhat older than he did at the start of the film set in 2036, approached the man.

"I have a proposal," said Leo. "It's called Non-Capitalist Economics. Let me show you."

The laptop came out and the Mayor saw for himself how the pilot, on The Island, had begun to introduce optimisation of a system, and the concept of credit had been withdrawn, being replaced with a much fairer requisition system.

"I like it. I like it very much," replied the Mayor.

"This is what this land could be like," Leo explained to him. "And, what's more, The Kremlin has given me a free hand to implement it."

"I don't think you will have much objection to Non-Capitalist Economics from our people," declared the Mayor. "Most of them have never seen real money anyway. They would be more than happy just to be able to have a little more of what they wanted. If you can guarantee them an improvement in their quality of life, you'll soon win them over."

The narrative returned:

"Juran's teaching, of which Leo and the others were keen advocates, emphasised holding the gains each time a breakthrough was achieved, and Leo and his teams were excellent at doing this. The people of Kamchatka were unsurprisingly highly receptive, and initial worries that The Founders had of resistance to change soon evaporated. Drab towns and suburbs suddenly became great places to work. Infrastructure that had previously been notoriously unreliable, was turned into some of the world's best. Within five years Kamchatka had become Russia's powerhouse.

"In 2056 the King and Queen of The Island visited and it was not long before the people of Kamchatka welcomed them as their own. Fears that Moscow would object proved to be unfounded. In fact the opposite happened, and they received a warm invitation to The Kremlin at the end of their tour."

The royal tour was then dramatised, including the banquet hosted by Russia's then President Yuri Lemenkov, to which all of The Founders, plus The Island King and Queen were invited.

The narrative resumed:

"It was quite clear that King Ken and Queen Justine posed no threat to The Kremlin's authority in Kamchatka, and actually helped to reinforce it by ending the earlier protests against Lemenkov and his regime."

"You have obviously proved to be quite a hit," Lemenkov said to Ken. "What do you say to being offered the throne of Kamchatka?"

The narrative told the rest:

"They knew the offer was nothing more than symbolic, but to Ken and Justine it was the gesture that counted. They could not possibly decline Lemenkov's offer as a token of The Kremlin's friendship. It turned out to be a milestone in Russia's history and a highly astute move on the part of the Russian President, helping to relieve Moscow from what had previously been a liability. Now, with the help of The Island, Kamchatka was set to become Russia's greatest asset. The complete absence of all forms of finance in this territory meant that Russia now had a unique tool at its disposal when it came to countering the effects of recession in the global economy. Thanks to this one move by Yuri Lemenkov, Russia alone had an in-built immunity to recession. Other countries, particularly America, did not.

By the time 2070 arrived the economic league of nations in terms of GDP had shifted substantially. Russia boldly and proudly overtook the United States and China in quick succession, and in the summer of that year Leo Harvey was summoned to The Kremlin.

"Oh I remember that day," Rachel said excitedly to Aub and Katie, as the scene appeared where her father had met with Yuri Lemenkov. "He told me all about that."

"Tell me," said Lemenkov to Leo. "How is your Island governed?"

"Well, we have a monarch, a Prime Minister and a Chancellor, who supports the PM and manages our balance of trade with the world's capitalist nations. It's quite simple really."

"And how are they elected?"

"The Prime Minister is elected under a system that we call One Party Democracy. He or she sets their own target as to how many votes they feel that they deserve or should have to continue in office."

Leo then explained the workings of OPD, and how it had dispensed with competition between candidates.

"He or she has to be trained, of course," Leo continued. "But once trained they can then focus on the job constantly and forever so as to improve the system rather than having to fight to stay in power."

"That's what I want," replied Lemenkov. "I have an idea."

"What do you suggest?" asked Leo.

"I think that, on a purely experimental basis, Kamchatka should have its own parliament, with representatives elected under OPD. You shall oversee proceedings from The Founders' Benches. I am determined that Kamchatka should not be held back or impeded from delivering its full potential, and I believe there is more potential."

"So do I," answered Leo.

"Then we will begin planning now. My guess is it will take about seven years to get all of the machinery in place, including the necessary border controls that will be needed to ensure that goods produced in Kamchatka are not taken and sold elsewhere by crooks. Yes, we will have a single border that will cross the peninsula at the shortest distance between the east and west coast. Everything to the south of it will be administered by the new parliament. You will be free to develop your own policies and procedures in line with our own national guidelines."

The narrative explained what followed:

"The following year construction began. The Mayor of Petropavlovsk Kamchatskiy was delighted that Moscow had decided to empower the people of Kamchatka, allowing them to work to what had been proven to be a superior system politically and economically to any other in existence anywhere in the world. It just had to be rolled out on a much larger scale than The Island. By 2077 the project was complete. A new parliament had been created, something unique and special."

"Oh my God," Rachel said to Aub. "This is it. This is where Lauren Lofgren appears playing me in 2077."

"On July 9th. the stage was set. The Island already had a Prime Minister and a Chancellor," the narrative continued. "Symbolically they were in charge, but as they were strictly in charge of The Island only, it was decided that a new post, that of Vice Chancellor, would be created to oversee the running of the new parliament and its mighty challenge to roll out all of The Island's systems of government across the new territory that was Island-owned Kamchatka. But who was going to fill this all-important vacancy? With all of The Founders committed to other objectives, the task would fall to Leo Harvey's daughter Rachel, who, fortunately, had been at her father's side throughout the project and knew all about Non-Capitalist Economics and the secrets of its success. She was also conversant with all of the proposed workings of the new parliament as well as being young enough to be able to continue the role for many more years, something that The Founders also regarded as being important.

"On July 9th. The Kamchatka Parliament opened its doors for the first time. The Founders sat at their Benches, whilst the remainder of the House was populated by all of the government representatives of the territory that had previously sat in Moscow. Needless to say they were all delighted to leave. Queen Justine and The Island King, Ken David, took their places in the monarch's seats, dressed bizarrely as Alice in Wonderland and Horatio Nelson. Leo was suitably attired as Peter the Great, whilst his daughter, who would deliver the inaugural address, was dressed in the Tudor outfit of Elizabeth the First. The world had never before seen anything quite like it."

Rachel smiled as she watched the actress she had picked take her place in The Vice Chancellor's Chair and prepare to recite the speech that she herself had given on that now famous day.

"Good people, nay dear friends, for that is what you are. It is an honour and a privilege to address you today as Vice Chancellor of this, our magnificent Parliament.

"We stand united and unique upon the stage. We are united through our belief that Quality, not profit, is what will lead to a better world. We are unique in that we have elected, and been granted permission to, work to an economic model that is like no other.

"Capitalism is not our enemy, as some may have perceived, but it is unfair, at times cruel, and notoriously inefficient in delivering on optimised results. When viewed as a system this is something that the world can no longer afford. There is no holy rule that says that as human beings we must accept this bad and outdated model that in essence is no different to that which the Romans used. The world has moved on, and economic and political systems must move on also. Communism has been tried. It has failed, and it must be rejected, but the world deserves a choice, as my father has repeatedly stated in his many papers, books and presentations. He is a scholar like no other, and we must honour him as the true architect of this great House, what it is, and what it will become."

The House applauded at this point, before the young Rachel continued.

In The Opera House the real Rachel followed the speech using her own original transcription from which she had read the speech in 2077.

"Money shall be replaced. It is obsolete. It serves no useful purpose. Nor for that matter does credit. It serves merely to motivate people to take advantage of others rather than to serve the whole. Everyone shall, within reason, be entitled to anything reasonable that they desire. There shall be no wages, nor any prices to pay, just a selection of entitlements for each profession and level of responsibility. We shall not be classless, for we know that we need division, but in every case we will benchmark the best lifestyles in the world and match or exceed it using a set of defined quality of life indicators. We shall not be beaten on Quality, and a Ministry for Benchmarking shall be at the heart of our strategy, working alongside our Ministry for Product and Service Reliability.

"We shall also introduce a Ministry for Supply and Demand, whose role it will be to ensure that both are balanced. A Task Force shall be formed to manage the variation, as part of a complementary Ministry for Rectification. Firms shall not compete, but shall have transferrable skills that may themselves be requisitioned by the said Ministry or Force.

"We shall oppose nationalisation, for we have learnt that it impedes, rather than augments, the pursuit of Quality. The private sector has consistently outperformed the public sector in this regard and, therefore, all products, services, property and enterprises shall be privately owned, with due regard to accountability and responsibility.

"We shall have a pace of life that is optimised, neither too fast nor too slow, and we shall be driven by constancy of purpose toward the common objective of improving the system constantly and forever. Everyone shall work, but nobody shall be overworked.

222

"There will be no more competitive elections. Instead a Political Academy shall be established, under the jurisdiction of this House, in which individuals shall be trained to the very highest standards of managerial competence. When they have demonstrated their skills to the satisfaction of our Governing Board, their names shall be put forward so that they may stand as sole candidates, approved by a majority of the people they are to represent. Candidates shall be free to set their own targets for the level of approval that they believe they should achieve. Everyone shall participate in the improvement process. Everyone shall be encouraged to cast a vote for the candidate, but only once the voter has submitted his or her suggestions for improvement. The candidate shall respond in order to earn the vote. The people shall have the power to remove and replace any candidate that falls short of the high standards that shall be expected by this House.

"On decision-making we shall all make our decisions collectively. Once everyone is in agreement a consensus shall be reached. We shall all vote together save for those who may wish to dissent. The act of dissent shall be considered a right, and shall not attract punitive measures, although a fair and just reason for the dissent must be supplied. All just and fair reasons shall be considered with a view to a potential re-taking of the vote. Tyranny of the majority shall not be a feature of our society. Minorities shall always be entitled to fair outcomes.

"We shall trade with the capitalist world, including the rest of Russia, through our one single bank account which shall be managed by our own Harvey Banking Corporation. This will provide us with a balance of trade. Other than that banking shall not be a feature of our society.

"We shall be guided in our work by the long-established theories of the great twentieth-century Quality philosophers William Edwards Deming and Joseph Moses Juran. Both used Quality in complementary ways to drive Japan's

223

Quality Revolution, steadily, and largely without notice in the west, until ultimately a poor country was made rich. If it can be done once, it can be done again."

Again the Members applauded.

"This is our Blueprint for the World. As we look to the future we have in our sights the phenomenon of global transformation. For this, our glorious revolution is, as yet, merely in its initial stage. Once we have demonstrated our capability to the world, others shall undoubtedly wish to join us, as they seek to transform their lands. In the second stage of our revolution a Top Team of world leaders shall emerge, and we shall assist them. Conflict shall be no more, and this great Parliament shall become the envy of the world."

On the screen the House applauded, as in The Opera House Rachel quietly read aloud the last line, moved to tears by her memories.

The years rolled by and the faces on the benches slowly changed. The Founders' Benches gradually became less and less occupied, but one face stood out, namely the young Russian Viktor Bogodan. Rachel watched the dramatisation of how she mentored this rising star of the Political Academy through his final year there, and into the Parliament itself in 2090. The film showed him being coached by Rachel, her father, and the other surviving Founders.

"Oh my God I remember this," Rachel said to Aub, as 2097 came and she announced that she was going to retire and hand over to the man whom she had groomed for the post. "My father's health was declining and I wanted to look after him. It was the right time to hand over. Viktor was like a best friend, a very great comfort at the time. I still have an input occasionally to the Parliament, but not very often. Most of the advisory work is done by The King, whom you soon will be."

Rachel watched intently as the scene appeared where she was presented with a specially made golden goblet to commemorate her twenty years as Vice Chancellor.

"I still have that," said Rachel.

Viktor had appeared regularly in the chair of The Heir Presumptive prior to 2097, with neatly groomed blond hair, and distinctive black velvet jacket paired with pristine white trousers. Then, on 1st. January 2098 he took over from where Rachel had left off.

"Oh she looks good," Rachel said, as Joanie Carmichael entered the scene. "She was one of Viktor's best friends at the Academy, daughter of Founder Patrick Carmichael. She was born on The Island though, and always wanted to return to it. It was rumoured that she and Viktor had had a love affair during their time at the Academy. Joanie declined The Heir Presumptive's chair when she was offered it in 2098, preferring instead to hold on for The Prime Minister's post on The Island."

Shortly after this point Rachel suddenly became tearful, as the scene appeared which dramatised the funeral of her father.

"The real scene has been edited in," Rachel continued. "I don't think I want to watch it. The actress turns into the real me at the end, watching the burial here on The Island. His coffin was returned here in accordance with his wishes, because this was the place he considered home. The film flashes back after this to my father's role in ISO Technical Committee 176, which he chaired for a time in the 2080s, and his successful extension of ISO 9001 for companies to ISO 9100 for countries, at least in principle."

The narrative continued:

"Leo Harvey laid the foundation stone for a completely new concept in world politics, that of using a Quality Management standard to achieve world peace. For many years ISO 9100 was merely on the drawing board. ISO 9001 was the standard that everyone in Quality worked to, and many thought that ISO 9100 would be much too difficult to write never mind implement. It was, however, the new Vice Chancellor, Viktor Bogodan, who was to eventually prove everyone wrong, and successfully resurrected ISO 9100 at the turn of the century, following through his predecessor's aim of one day turning it into reality."

"That was supposedly the thing that couldn't be done," Rachel whispered. "I remember helping Viktor through it. He worked extremely hard as the film shows, but he got what he wanted, the respect and support of TC 176."

"As Patrick O'Rourke said to me, he went for TC 176 like a dog for a bone," Aub replied, as they watched the story unfold that had led Aub to where he was now.

"We can and indeed will make warfare a thing of the past," Viktor declared to the committee. "And this standard holds the key to doing it. It is the how behind the what, and with your support I believe my Parliament and this committee can together achieve the dream."

"What makes a man in your position so keen to take on this role?" the Chairman of the committee asked. "After all it is hardly a position of power."

"I don't want power," said Viktor firmly. "I have enough of that already. What I want is to develop this ageing standard that you call ISO 9001 into something that goes well beyond the confines of industry. I see enormous potential for a standard that could completely transform life for millions of people that can rid the world of war, and introduce an entirely new way of determining the sovereignty of nations."

"But what makes you think that you can make this highly ambitious scheme work?" the Chairman asked.

"I have read Leo Harvey's papers, and his book *The Sovereignty of Nations*. The theory is sound. ISO 9001 has stood the test of time. It's over a century old. We have seen how it has been able to transform industry across the world. The same principle can be used to manage countries as to manage companies. ISO 9001 is a fine standard, but the world needs something more. It needs a Quality supersystem standard, certification to which can show that governments have the competence to manage countries, and hence other countries. Too many governments are failing their people and that has to change. Managing countries is about assuring Quality in every discipline, not becoming adept at defeating one's opponents. A country, like an organisation, needs to be viewed as a system and my desire is to see through first of all a draft standard, then a published final version, that will enable this to happen. Then, once certificated, it will afford good governments the opportunity to buy out incompetent ones, and subsequently roll out the already proven good management practice. Only a variant of ISO 9001 could do this. I want to start to draft the new standard that will herald the beginning of a New Game in world defence."

"So ISO 9100 was born," came the narrative. "But getting it accepted and implemented was quite another matter. It took Viktor Bogodan another six years to complete his draft, and even then many people believed that it was far too complicated and complex a document ever to be able to be implemented in practice. Fortunately in Kamchatka a different view prevailed. One man in particular began to implement its provisions, with the help of a few friends.

"Oh my God, it's Patrick," said Rachel.

The narrative continued:

"So began the friendship between Viktor Bogodan and the Irish duo Patrick O'Rourke and Duncan McIntyre. Together they were able to do what many said couldn't be done. Viktor gave them his draft and the others immediately began recruiting teams to implement the new standard's provisions. They started in Kamchatka, then worked outwards to Sakhalin, The Kuril Islands, and later into Chechnya, a place that had long been a problem for The Kremlin. Unlike the other projects Chechnya was in capitalist Russia. It provided the first real opportunity to demonstrate the potential of this wonderful standard in a capitalist environment. It was a patchy and at times difficult process, but piece by piece it was done. The people prospered enormously and with a critical mass of people now supporting the standard, it wasn't long before ISO 9100 gained international acclaim, and a methodology for compliance to its provisions soon followed.

"Now Brazil and Japan are seeing the benefits of adoption, and have been for some years. But it is Kamchatka, with its snow-covered tamed volcanoes, that now leads the world. Nothing can compare with the Kamchatka Parliament. It has indeed become the envy of the world, and there isn't a politician anywhere that wouldn't, if only secretly, wish to be invited to serve on the Foreign Benches and become a part of it. Non-Capitalist Economics continues to be supported by many different people in many different parts of the globe, from Alaska and the Aleutian Islands, to the Falklands and Tierra del Fuego and beyond. The word is spreading and so are the territories of this amazing country within a country that is Kamchatka.

"Today, everywhere people are signing up to become friends of Kamchatka through its Queen, Queen Katie, with a pledge not of money, but of votes for centre parties. In 2109 the New Game will begin. In fact it is already upon us. Far from fearing the Kamchatka Parliament, people are desiring to share in its power and be a part themselves of the revolution that started on one small North Atlantic island, almost seventy years ago, that has been largely unnoticed, until now."

Chapter Seventeen
Advent

Rachel remained on The Island throughout the season of Advent as a guest of The King and Queen, having many a story to tell, especially to Aub. The people of The Island naturally knew Rachel well, as did the other royals, as she was a longstanding regular visitor. It was not the first time that she confessed to having a secret desire to retire to The Island once all her behind-the-scenes work at the Kamchatka Parliament had come to an end. Not that anyone would believe it, because, like her father before her, and others such as Patrick and Duncan, in practice such a person would be highly unlikely to ever give up work completely. Spending more time on The Island, however, was something else, and there was every chance that she may well do that, possibly even working more remotely from Kamchatka than hitherto.

The Advent season also gave Aub and Katie an opportunity to put more hours into their skating practice, with the pressure of political life now briefly softened. Rachel, naturally, had her own skates that she had brought to The Island and, despite her age, there was no shortage of intricate moves and figures that she could demonstrate to the royal couple. On school figures particularly, there were attractive combinations of figures that she could compile, acting as a source of ideas most notably for Aub and Katie's figures only dance that they would perform with the Groznyy Figure Club.

At the rink Jobine had prepared a checklist of elements for the royal couple and she wanted at this point to be sure that neither of them lacked any consistency in their performance. She was keen to ensure that when the big day came any probability of error would be confined solely to fine detail. Rachel skated alongside them from time to time, and with the people of The Island, taking instruction from Jobine that made a refreshing change to her life, reminding her of her youth and of the ice rink where she had been trained so many years previously. She was slow, but extremely precise, in every step, move and figure that she attempted. It was a rarity for her to falter. If she could not perform a move perfectly, she would not attempt it. Anyone who danced with her could easily feel that they had been dancing with her for years.

She watched eagerly from the rink side as Jobine went through her checklist with Aub and Katie.

"Side by side synchronised toe loop," she requested.

Aub and Katie then performed the said element.

"Matching free legs almost there," Jobine commented. "Now try with the synchronised three jump. It's slightly easier."

Again they performed the element and it was almost there. They continued with the other classic jumps, the Salchow and Lutz.

"You just need a bit more consistency," she emphasised. "But as long as you put in the hours it should be good enough by March. Now let's see the spins, the side-by-side camel spin, the synchronised sit spin and the synchronised cross-toe spin, variant of the upright."

Again they performed the elements, and again the elements wore performed satisfactorily, but were inconsistent.

"We need to work on your centring, Aub," said Jobine, noting that he was slightly off-centre each time. "I'll leave it for now, as it is the dance elements that I really want to focus on. Its time now for you to be able to show a good sense of rhythm, so that you can truly characterise the dances. When you drop down onto that ice pad in Red Square you need to really surprise those Russians with your skating skills. So, side-by-side double choctaws, open and closed, side-by-side mohawks open and closed, and side by-side twizzles with contrary arm raises and synchronised arm raises."

Aub and Katie did as directed, and again it was the consistency of the execution that Jobine focused her attention on.

"You're still tending to lean forward on the mohawks and choctaws, Aub. That needs to be corrected."

She then moved on to the lifts.

"You need to be able to replicate each lift that you are going to use to a precise and consistent standard. We need to remove some of the unwanted variation that we still have."

Jobine recorded each lift and then, off the ice, she dissected them one by one, highlighting each potential error point.

"I think you can see where the vulnerabilities lie. It's these points we still need to work on. Get the weak points mastered and the rest will follow. You'll have no trouble with the lifts, but you do have to show some passion on the ice. Your love for each other needs to be conveyed through the routines, including the rotational components of the lifts."

*

The Christmas lights and the many parties that took place during Advent allowed Rachel to relive old times, and Aub and Katie were keen to share in them, now that the setmates were not there. The Prince and The Queen made a point of inviting each and every Island inhabitant to The Royal Palace at some stage on the run up to Christmas. The Opera House also reverted to its original purpose as a venue for opera and theatre, put on by and for visitors by special invite. The British royal family visited, as did the royals from other European states, notably Holland, Denmark, Sweden, Norway, Belgium and Spain. Leaders also came, sometimes with more than just entertainment in mind. This was especially the case with Francis White and Milton Mbele, President of Zimbabwe. They were treated to a display of skating from The Russian All Stars, before getting down to business in Government House. Sylvia Smith took the minutes of the meeting.

"The people of Zimbabwe have spoken," President Mbele declared. "Our latest referendum came out clearly in favour of a return to Rhodesia but without the racism, which I understand that you are pledged to defeating. That being the case I and my government are prepared to step down and accept any reasonable bid from Westminster once the UK has its certification to ISO 9100. There can then be a formal handover of power, but I will only do it if I can be certain that London can deliver on its responsibilities to the people of my country. How long do you think it will be before the UK has its certification?"

"A short answer is about four years," said Francis. "And, yes, we are pledged to defeating racism. We have to be to get ISO 9100. No country can receive it without. Excellent race relations is a specific requirement. Juran's Universal Sequence for Breakthrough will be used to ensure that we pass on this requirement, and, of course, it will be rolled out in Zimbabwe as soon as we have the mechanism in place. Nobody more than I would like to see racism ended in Zimbabwe, and I believe we can do it and set a fine example to the rest of Africa. Zimbabwe can once more become Africa's bread basket. Knowledge and expertise can be shared. In fact we do not have to wait for certification to begin doing this. We can start doing it now. We will show you how it will work, then you can be convinced well in advance of making your bid that your move is a wise one. The only real change, apart from the international transaction will be the name change, Zimbabwe to Rhodesia, and your capital Harare back to Salisbury. I want you to be sure though that you are totally assured that we won't let you down."

"If anyone can do it, you can," replied President Mbele. "I think we can strike a deal. With a certificated UK I believe that Zimbabwe's underclass, black and white, can be removed."

"All will prosper I can assure you of that. Zimbabwe, or should I say Rhodesia, will never be poor again. I am very grateful to all the people of Zimbabwe who voted for this, and thank you also for allowing it to happen."

"Don't thank me. Thank Queen Katie," said President Mbele. "She can be very influential. You should know!"

Others too were locked in negotiations, some with more pressing time frames than others. The UK clearly had some time to get Zimbabwe on its track out of poverty. This was not the case for Manuela, who really needed to reach a deal with Colombia as soon as possible.

"Patrick has told me the teams can go in with your approval," Manuela said to Colombia's President. "It only needs your consent, and we can at least slow down the river of immigrants leaving Colombia."

"Of course I consent," he said. "It is ruining my country, and if my resignation is what will stop the rot then that is what I shall do, but as you know nothing formal can be done unless or until Brazil gets ISO 9100. I can't sell until you have it. That is the rule. When that happens I will naturally accept any reasonable price. My only other choice is probably ending up dead. We are losing all our best people. Colombia needs the Quality supersystem probably more than anywhere else at the present time."

That statement was perhaps true, although when the leaders of Israel and Palestine arrived there was maybe some doubt. The leaders of neither state had ever come together this way before, yet somehow Queen Katie, with the help of Patrick and Duncan, had managed to pull it off and got them at the table in Government House. This was exactly the kind of thing that Government House was set up to do, to allow leaders to come together and negotiate in a private and pleasant setting that was distant from the world.

"As you know Israel wants peace in Palestine as much as Palestine wants peace with Israel," said Alesha Shandecai, the Israeli leader. "And we want ISO 9100 certification. ISO 9100 demands that we disarm totally. If we did, and we got ISO 9100, would you be prepared to do the same? Would you be willing to work towards it with us? If we do it together we can be united in peace, fairness and equality. The rules governing the sovereignty of nations are changing."

"Of course we would," replied Yassar Mafoud. "We don't have the means to obtain ISO 9100, we are too poor. We couldn't do it without help. Patrick has more or less said to us if we accept Israel's offer he will make sure that both you and ourselves can have ISO 9100 jointly, because it will bring much needed peace to the region. Our only option is to work with you, and, as he is rarely wrong, I am inclined to believe him. Nobody wants bombs, guns and missiles threatening our lives when we can have Quality instead."

"As you have rightly said, he is rarely wrong. The one thing that seems to be uniting us is Queen Katie. I know her fanbase is as strong in Palestine as it is in Israel. That itself should draw us closer together. She has pretty much demanded that we sit here and work something out. I don't want to leave this table without a deal that is fair and meaningful to both of us."

Mr Mafoud rose and shook his opposite's hand.

"ISO 9100 it is. So long as we both apply together. Israel cannot bid for Palestine because it hasn't recognised us," he said. "We are therefore an unusual case. We can't sell out and you can't buy, but we can achieve something far more valuable and that's lasting peace. If we both get ISO 9100 I can accept Palestine as a part of greater Israel, no questions asked."

"And we can make your country richer and pleasanter," responded Alesha. "It's not an impossible dream. We can do it. In fact it's the only thing Patrick will accept. We must help you if we are to be able to help ourselves."

Each day a different pair of leaders were engaged in discussion. After Israel and Palestine it was the turn of Japan and The Philippines, the latter well aware of the fact that Japan was the most advanced country of all when it came to achieving certification. The Philippines, by contrast, was one of the world's poorest countries, and its leaders knew that their people longed for the quality of life enjoyed by the Japanese. They too had had a referendum that showed a clear preference to be governed from Tokyo rather than Manila.

"With ISO 9100 certification Japan would be obliged to bring the quality of life of all of your citizens to the level currently enjoyed in Japan if you agreed to sell out under the New Game," Japanese Prime Minister Iwai Takamoto explained. "Under the standard we would be obliged to be your servant as well as your master."

"When do you think you will be able to bid?," asked Don Aquino, leader of The Philippines.

"As soon as you are ready," replied Mr Takamoto confidently.

"Then all that is left to decide is the price."

"Our offer will be fair and can be made in stages. The Philippines covers a wide area and for us the process of transformation would be best undertaken piecemeal. We could work west to east or east to west, you choose."

"You know Patrick is going to act as broker. He will help us settle on a price, but I know he wants us to start our talking now. I trust him only to allow a fair deal to stick. Japan wants sovereignty, we need a better standard of living for our people. It's just a question of matching the equation."

"And we both want to be in Red Square."

On this they shook.

*

The negotiations continued for the next four days. Then, when they were complete, it would be down to The Prince to examine the deals that had been struck, so that he could see exactly what had been agreed behind closed doors.

King Neville, with the help of Patrick and Duncan, would then discuss strategy and how best to implement the plans. They met together at The Royal Palace to scrutinise the documents.

"Overseeing The New Game is going to be one of your prime responsibilities," said The King. "This is the mechanism by which we will achieve world peace using ISO 9100. We need to get all of them and more working collectively to build a better world. The world has waited a long time for this."

"I think we need some more informal networking between the various parties," Aub suggested.

"That would seem like a logical next step, now that at least the framework of the programme has been worked out," agreed Patrick. "I'll try and get some facilitators together."

"Also I get the impression that there appears to be something of a race on now to become the first nation to gain certification," added The King.

"Indeed," replied Patrick. "I don't think there is any doubt about who will be first. That's why Japan will be your next tour in the new year. It will be your first official royal duty to present the certificates."

"We must take care though that this rush to achieve certification doesn't develop into a race," Aub said, flicking through some of the signed agreements.

"It won't. My teams will ensure that," Patrick assured him. "The standard is designed to assure Quality and that is what it will do. Each nation will advance at an orderly pace."

"Isn't there a danger though that some countries might

feel that they have to get in quick when it comes to the bidding?" asked Aub.

"Unlikely with the leaders that we have secured in office," explained Patrick. "I'm confident they will all work closely with us. As you have seen with this first endeavour, deals will tend to be worked out well in advance anyway. The only bid that I expect in the first half of next year is that by Japan for The Philippines, and as you can see from the deal sheet, it will only be a part bid. Japan wants to make sure everything works to plan in the first segment before taking on the second. Manila isn't going to hand everything over to Tokyo all at once, and that's by Japan's request. One thing you can be assured of with the Japanese is that they will do everything with honour. The one thing they won't do is risk losing face by taking on too much too soon. Everyone has to win out of this. There must be no losers. The standard makes that very clear, and no country wants to lose certification after having gained it. Remember no country has to sell, and if they aren't totally satisfied that they will get a good deal, we, or rather you, will advise them to defer acceptance of the bid. That won't happen in the first wave though, my teams have every faith in the leaders that are driving the process."

With the first important phase completed the leaders were invited to a special banquet by The King to celebrate their achievements.

"Hello my darlings," came the now familiar voice of Manuela Raimunda as she rushed to embrace the royal couple.

The others followed and The Prince and The Queen made a point of congratulating them all on having achieved a major step forward for their respective countries. As they dined the leaders were encouraged to network with each other, so that they could all work together collectively to make what really was a very ambitious scheme a global success. Nobody wanted to see countries decline and wars break out. Everybody wanted to make poverty history. For Aub, however, there was something else that he had been advised to consider.

The next day the leaders, who had arrived essentially as strangers, departed as friends. One by one the Hebden Threes landed and left. Katie and Sylvia worked together at the Palace on The Queen's Christmas speech, using all of the material that had been collected, including the momentous scenes of Britain's historic General Election, then later the royal tour of Brazil. Scenes from The Queen's visit to France were also included. Aub meanwhile was stationed in The Great Dome where he faced Viktor Bogodan via video link.

"Glad tidings," said Viktor. "I trust all went well with the leaders' week."

"Excellent progress," replied Aub.

"I am addressing you today, rather than The King, because at this time there is a very important matter that requires your attention. I speak no less of the appointment of The Island's next Prime Minister. Joanie Carmichael has handed me a folder in which she has written the names of two possible candidates from this House that she would like to put forward. Both have indicated that they would like to be considered, but you can only choose one. Both are suitable and both are of Island descent, which is one of the key criteria for the post. I will now use Commander to despatch the electronic folder to The Chancellor. He will enter in a moment with a printout of it."

The printout duly arrived and Aub read it.

"I couldn't pick out anything that made one candidate any more suitable than the other, and I agreed with Joanie that either would be right for the role. They both have excellent leadership skills and are probably more suited to teaching setmates than participating in the more demanding arena of the Kamchatka Parliament. Equally, they both could serve in the Kamchatka Parliament in the Education Ministry for which they have been trained."

The first candidate was Martha Hertzberg. The Hertzbergs had worked closely with Clifford Hebden in the establishment of Kamchatskiy Aerospace and in The Island's space programme that had led to the construction of Moonbase Alpha. The second candidate was Philip Grant, grandson of Island Founder Colin Grant. He was familiar with the setmate training programme, more so than Martha, but was younger and also had a stronger background when it came to training for the Education Ministry.

"I need you to decide soon, because whoever you choose will need to be shown the ropes before Christmas."

Aub noted that Philip had a closer link with The Island's Founders than Martha. Weighed against that was the fact that Philip was also better suited for a senior role in the Education Ministry than Martha. Philip undoubtedly knew how to train setmates, and his background in psychology lent itself well to this, but this would also be useful in the Education Ministry. Martha, on the other hand, was noted to have performed well in hostess roles, which could be useful when it came to entertaining world leaders in Government House. He did not feel that any of Philip's skills matched this requirement and he already knew that the job of signing and ratifying treaties was The Prime Minister's job, not The Vice Chancellor's.

As Aub retired to make his decision he leaned towards Martha, on the grounds that she would be a bit out of place in the Education Ministry, yet she would be a teacher that the setmates would most likely quickly relate to. Philip was clearly high-powered, and potentially could quite possibly regret having what was really just a symbolic post rather than being active in the Parliament. Martha, on the other hand, was potentially a better teacher than a decision-maker. That fact, coupled with her hostess skills, finally made the choice for Aub. Martha Hertzberg it would be. He Shared his views with Katie and the next day he returned the electronic file to Viktor.

"I see you have chosen Martha," Viktor responded, again via the video link. "Good. I shall inform both of the candidates of your choice and your reasoning. Tomorrow you and Katie can return to The Great Dome and watch the approval. In the meantime you can ask The Deputy Prime Minister and The Chancellor to convey the news to The Island staff via The Island Times."

The next day Aub and Katie watched as the Kamchatka Parliament came on the screen with Viktor ready to make the announcement.

"I hereby announce to this House, that on the advice of The Prince Regent I am proposing that Martha Hertzberg be duly nominated as our next Prime Minister, replacing Joanie Carmichael, who is now Commander of Moonbase Alpha. All those in favour."

Viktor struck his mallet and immediately all heads were bowed.

"Carried unanimously. The House shall now rise and salute our new leader."

One by one all of The Queen's Ministers congratulated Martha and wished her well, the joy on the thirty-six-year-old's face being clearly reflected in her tears. Viktor invited her to say a few words.

"I'm going to The Island, I can hardly believe it. I really did think it would be Philip that would get the greatest job in the world. I'm so pleased I'm going to get the job of training the Kamchatskiy setmates and of making the dreams of 240 people come true. Thank you so much Mr Ryman, Prince Regent."

The Ministers cheered her as she left immediately for the airport and the Hebden Three that would shortly bring her to The Island.

On The Island the single sheet newspaper that was *The Island Times* was rolled off, the headline reading 'Martha Hertzberg is new Prime Minister' with the photograph of this 'lady with the frizz' positioned neatly beside it.

Later that afternoon The Prince's Hebden Three touched down on The Island's remote beach runway where The Coachman was waiting with his immaculate State Coach. Nimbly she stepped in.

In The Square the entire population of The Island waited to greet her, but it was Aub who was to receive the first embrace. The crowd cheered and threw confetti as the new Prime Minister stepped joyfully towards the entrance of The Great Dome, ushered in by Aub and Katie. The Deputy Prime Minister then stepped aside and descended the steps, ready to return to his more usual residence at the foot of the hill. The Chancellor meanwhile was inside ready to show Martha to The Prime Minister's chair, where he explained the workings of all of the various controls that were now at her disposal.

"She won't need any showing around The Island," Katie said to Aub. "She knows it like the back of her hand. The people know her also."

Katie then turned and went to a special file where she removed an envelope and handed it to Martha.

"So, Martha, congratulations on your new appointment."

"Thank you Your Majesty," she said softly as she gradually familiarised herself with all of The Prime Minister's controls.

"So. Here is your first task. Inside that envelope are my 240 Queen's Tickets. Each bears a name. Make sure that they are all there. Then I would like you to see that they each get distributed through the appropriate contacts, which you will find on your database, the one that The Chancellor just pointed to."

Katie then turned to The Chancellor.

"Chancellor, thank you for showing her the controls. What I would like you to do next is to take Martha through the programme for next year, so she knows what is happening and when. She knows the job, but she doesn't know the timing."

Martha smiled and made herself ready to take instruction

"It will seem a bit strange at first," Katie said to Martha. "But all should soon become clear. The Chancellor will take good care of you. Joanie Carmichael will speak to you shortly from Moonbase Alpha. She also wants to congratulate you. I look forward to seeing you at the party."

Having seen Martha safely installed it was time for Aub to put on his skates for some one-to-one tuition of his own from Jobine, who was keen to give him a little extra now, so as to attempt to close some of the gaps in his skating that still clearly lagged behind that of Katie. Katie meanwhile returned to The Royal Palace where Sylvia Smith was now making the last minute preparations for The Queen's Christmas broadcast.

"We can use the recording unit in the drawing room," Katie suggested to Sylvia. "I want the broadcast to go out in the morning this year, in order to avoid a clash with the British sovereign's message."

In the drawing room The Queen prepared to read her script, or at least part of it.

"Now, from The Royal Palace on The Island of Dreams, here is Queen Katie of Kamchatka's Christmas message to the world," Sylvia said as she read out the introduction.

The Island flag, with its gold Saturnian livery superimposed on a sky-blue background was then shown as The Island's anthem, which was also Kamchatka's anthem, 'I Vow to Thee My Island', rang out to accompany it.

"I can edit the scenes in as appropriate," said Sylvia as Katie read her opening lines.

"Loyal subjects. Good citizens. It gives me great pleasure today to be able to address more people in more countries than ever before, and I thank you all wherever you are for all of the continuing support and devotion that you have given to me over the past year. I have been greatly moved by the outstanding level of trust that you have all shown to me.

"The year of 2108 has indeed been very special. With the help of my devoted and hard-working teams we are drawing ever closer to the first certifications to ISO 9100, the new Quality supersystem standard, and I have recently been delighted to host a ground-breaking series of meetings with leaders from all over the world that has paved the way for transformational world peace to become a reality. We are not there yet, but we have definitely taken the first step."

Katie then paused the broadcast so that Sylvia could edit in the scenes of the world leaders relaxing and talking informally on The Island and at the banquet.

"Earlier this year we also saw a breakthrough in British politics with the election for the first time of a Whig Prime Minister, and few in the United Kingdom will forget the scenes that night. It was a remarkable result that astonished both myself and my Prince. I therefore thank especially all of the people of the UK that responded to my request for a change of government. I am now optimistic that real lasting and beneficial change will be made there, in the country of our Founders."

There was another pause as Sylvia edited in the election scenes.

"Another special moment for me was when I had the honour of helping to restore the French Government, thanks to all of my supporters in France to whom I am also profoundly grateful. As part of that visit I also had the privilege of being invited to The International Standards Organisation in Geneva, and of meeting with the multinational Technical Committee 176 that oversees the administration of both ISO 9100 and its sister standard, the somewhat older ISO 9001."

The Island Queen was then shown shaking hands and enjoying wine with the various members of TC 176. Then there was a message from its current Chairman.

"We are in the business now not just of improving Quality in industry, but of transforming entire countries.

That will eventually extend to continents and beyond. Through this great standard many lives will be saved. Through its provisions many countries have already seen the futility of continuing to throw taxpayers' money at the building of weapons and the maintaining of forces whose only purpose is the destruction of human life. It is money that can now be invested much more wisely."

"What he said could not be more true," Katie continued. "And I know the reason why so many of you who have chosen to support me have done so because you share my conviction to ultimately secure world peace by this method. But it is not just military offensives that are being removed by this standard. The standard also makes for a vast improvement in the quality of life of ordinary people with its stringent requirements for benchmarking, continuous improvement, reliability and the equitable distribution of wealth.

"Last month Aub and I saw at first hand how this had been achieved on a massive scale in one of the world's largest countries. During our tour of Brazil we didn't just enjoy the carnival atmosphere, or a memorable ride on the world's fastest train, interestingly powered by steam, but we also saw how large numbers of teams, each dedicated to the pursuit of Quality, were using ISO 9100 to realise improvements that a few years ago nobody would have believed possible."

Scenes from the Brazilian tour were edited in at this point, first in Rio and Sao Paulo, then in Northern Brazil.

"Not so long ago this country had a terrible reputation for corruption and crime. Now, there is a climate of almost total trust among its people. Once people could see what was possible, it wasn't as difficult as some might have imagined to spread the culture quickly and effectively across all states. Nobody wanted a climate of fear. Nobody actually wanted others to be poor. Nobody wanted to see mass unemployment and uncontrollable corruption. Fortunately the country, unlike some others, had a relatively good track record for racial harmony and cooperation. It wasn't difficult either to persuade many at the top to part with some of their wealth, once they could see that this would generate more wealth. Today Brazil is the world's third richest country, and not far off being second. It is currently on the verge of gaining ISO 9100 certification, and next year it is expected to become the first country in the large nation category to do so. I therefore have to thank all of the many teams that have worked so tirelessly to secure this achievement. In Rio I asked one man what the path to ISO 9100 certification had meant to him."

"The violence has gone. The drugs have gone. The shanty towns are no more. Our lives have been totally transformed. Everybody works together now. We live well, we have beautiful homes, we do not fear poverty or robbery. Nobody would dream of stealing from others today."

"And all through ISO 9100?" Katie asked him.

"All through ISO 9100. My local priest calls it a gift from God, but I know it is really the result of a lot of hard work and commitment driven by our wonderful President. Manuela really has proved to be a fantastic president for us, and that is down to you, we all know that."

The broadcast continued.

"My trusted friend Manuela has indeed done a terrific job. In the future others are set to follow her example. ISO 9100 demands constancy of purpose from governments and for all people to focus on improvement. For that reason, although it is not explicitly stated, it is implied that centre parties are required to maintain momentum and ensure balance.

"So, looking to the future, many of you will be aware that in March Aub and I will be married, and I can promise you that it will be an occasion not to be missed. We will, at the request of The Kremlin, prepare to take on the new throne of Russia, and to use it to guide the world into a new era. Together we will ensure that prosperity for the world is collectively quality assured.

"God bless and I love you all."

*

On Christmas Eve The Queen hosted her party for The Island's staff and residents. Without the setmates The Island was much quieter than in a normal year. The party did, however, allow all of the staff to meet and get to know their new Prime Minister, and for her to get to know them, as well as Aub.

"Ladies and gentlemen," said The King. "You will be aware that early next year my daughter will marry The Prince Regent Aub Ryman. A date has been set for the middle of March upon which they shall be married and he will be crowned. It shall be different to the past in that once crowned, by consent of The Kremlin, they shall thenceforth be not just King and Queen of The Island, nor of Kamchatka, but King and Queen of all Russia. This is unprecedented and represents a great step forward for us all, and reflects the adoration that the Russian people have for our sovereigns. I therefore propose a toast to Aub and Katie."

"To Aub and Katie," the guests repeated.

"Let us not forget also that we also have our new Prime Minister, who succeeds Joanie Carmichael, who, I understand is now settling in very well as the Commander of that most fabulous of engineering feats, Moonbase Alpha.

"Martha shall govern this Island and advise our Ministers on matters of state. She will also have the role of training the 240 lucky recipients of The Queen's Tickets for one year on behalf of the Kamchatskiy companies commencing in March, one week after the Coronation Wedding. I therefore propose that we offer a toast to Martha and wish her the very best in her new role. To Martha.

"To Martha," replied the guests.

Chapter Eighteen
The New Game begins

Christmas and New Year passed, with Aub and Katie for once able to concentrate on each other without the pressure of political and royal duties. They toured The Island and relished the serenity. Midnight mass was held as ever at The Island church, and New Year's Eve ended with a grand fireworks display at The Palace's East Garden. In a normal year The Non-Olympic Stadium would have been the venue for the annual Games Without Frontiers final, but this year the event was not held.

On January second Aub and Katie resumed their skating practice under the watchful eye of Jobine, still keen to improve the consistency of the couple. On one occasion the couple stumbled, and it was not for the first time. What Jobine did notice, however, was how the couple recovered from the fall. They had now learnt to perfect the art of recovery with some degree of success. This was all part of the learning curve that Jobine had set.

They continued practising for another week before Aub received his next call to The Dome, for the first time from Martha Herzberg.

This time it was the stocky Boris Marechenko, Minister for Certification, who appeared on the screen. His job was to update The Prince on the latest developments in The New Game, which had officially begun on January first, but first he needed to ask Aub one important question.

"Why did you resign?" he asked.

"Many reasons," replied Aub.

"To marry The Queen?"

"I said many reasons."

"Come on now, you can confide in me. Why did you resign?"

This time Aub did not answer.

"I like that," said Boris. "You have the strength of character to resist answering a question if you are suspicious of its motive. I know the answer anyway. It was because of this."

Boris then held up a copy of 'ISO 9100: Quality Supersystem Requirements for Nations entering The New Game'.

"This is the final version of the new standard," he continued. "Yes, you resigned to marry The Queen, but equally you resigned in order to be the spearhead of the revolution that will ultimately transform the sovereignty of nations. You want to be the person who ultimately ensures that the lives of servicemen and women the world over are no longer sacrificed for the sake of a result that favours one side or another. You correctly identified that The New Game is without doubt a breakthrough in world history because through it physical defence forces will no longer determine the world's destiny, and you want to be the man who leads it, with the help of our Parliament, ISO and some key individuals such as Patrick O'Rourke and Duncan McIntyre."

"I won't deny that. What's the latest?"

"Well, two countries have been audited and are about to receive their certification, Japan and South Korea. Brazil will hopefully be ready in the Spring, although we may have to relax some of the requirements in the large nation category to allow that to happen. That said, we can't not let it happen for reasons that you already know.

"Japan passed the audit first, and so rightfully Japan should receive its certificate first. As this is a landmark achievement in our revolution Parliament has deemed it appropriate that you and Katie should present the certificates. Martha will explain to you the itinerary to you both later today.

"Japan will formally buy out approximately one third of The Philippines at the end of the month. South Korea is expected to buy out North Korea at the start of next, given that North Korea, half by chance, seems to have inherited a playboy leader who would appear to have no interest in politics at all. He couldn't care less about the arsenal of weapons that he has at his disposal, and neither could his people. The whole thing is perfectly understandable. Pyongyang is ready to sell out.

"As you know, under ISO 9100 the certificated nation must completely disarm. If it then bids successfully it must then disarm the purchased state. North Korea has been a menace in the past, so this is a golden opportunity to dismantle and remove the threat before it has a chance to re-emerge.

"You will visit Japan first, then South Korea. It will be good experience because you will be able to see for the first time how a nation meets the requirements of the standard in practice. On your return I would be grateful if you could suggest some next steps, as Viktor is most keen that it should be you rather than him that is steering this process."

*

On the flight to Tokyo Aub and Katie studied the requirements of the standard. Aub was aware of the major provisions, as he had been familiar with the various drafts of the standard that ISO had produced over the better part of a decade. Some of the detail, however, was new, particularly with regard to the variations in auditing techniques that had been introduced to reflect the size, nature, terrain, economy and political systems of the countries under audit.

"God, the document's enormous," Katie commented as she browsed through its contents. "No wonder it took

249

so long to write. I take my hat off to ISO for having the determination to see this project through to the end."

Aub scrutinised the two submission documents.

"Looks like Japan and South Korea benchmarked each other when it came to the supersystem itself," Aub remarked. "The submission documents certainly contain many similarities. I'm not surprised because benchmarking is a key requirement. They clearly learnt a lot from each other during the certification process as they both had to pioneer the greatest single Quality improvement project since *The Making of Kamchatka*."

Aub had been used to inspecting military personnel, and dealing with politicians, but nothing had prepared either him or Katie for what was to greet them on their first morning in Japan.

From their hotel they travelled in a driverless Kamchatskiy to the Japanese Parliament. There the Emperor greeted them, bowed his head, and symbolically laid down his sword in front of the royal couple. Prime Minister Iwai Takamoto then approached the slightly bewildered royals, shook their hands, and explained:

"He is laying down his sword to symbolise the end of an era. Thanks to you he no longer needs his weapon. Under ISO 9100 we must disarm completely, so that is what the Emperor has done. Our country has learnt only too well about the horrors of war and what they can do. Today the Emperor lays down his sword with pride, as a tribute to those, including yourselves, who have been willing to devote their lives towards the objective of creating a better way of determining the sovereignty of nations."

As the Emperor placed his precious sword at the feet of the royal couple there was spontaneous applause, followed immediately by the releasing of exactly 176 white doves.

"One-hundred-and-seventy-six," said Prime Minister Takamoto. "The number of the Technical Committee in ISO that has developed this wonderful standard. The

Philippines, Indonesia, Borneo, New Guinea, all will be much stronger in time. Quality management was born here, so it is right that Japan should lead it, with the help of our friends, of course."

Mr Takamoto then proceeded to lead the couple past the entire Japanese Government. The ministers each bowed their heads in turn as the couple passed by, standing proudly as they did so. At the end of the line Japan's Minister for ISO 9100 Certification stood with his team, the men and women who had been responsible for implementing the standard's many provisions. Mr Takamoto took his place next to them as they posed for the press. Sylvia Smith, as ever, was there, collecting pictures for The Island Times, and for The Queen's next Christmas speech.

The Chairman of ISO TC176 then emerged and walked toward Aub and Katie with the prized certificate, ready to hand it to them to present to Mr Takamoto. A microphone was then handed to Aub in accordance with the itinerary.

"Good people," he said. "It is an honour and a privilege for us both to now be able to present to you the world's first ever awarded prestigious ISO 9100 Quality Supersystem certificate. This truly marks a landmark day in the history of Japan and the world.."

More photography followed as the certificate was formally presented. A gong then sounded, providing the cue for the royal couple to begin their walkabout, shaking hands and signing autographs for the many people, many of whom had queued for days to gain a good vantage point for this world first event. The depth of feeling that this country had for this achievement, and its sense of pride gradually became more and more apparent to the visiting royals. They could tell that this was no ordinary royal visit.

The next stop was the concert hall where, still clutching his certificate and holding it aloft like a trophy, Prime Minister Takamoto again walked beside Aub and Katie, who sensed increasingly that the certificate represented not just achievement, but also power, the likes of which Japan had not known for a very long time.

The Minister for ISO 9100 Certification gave his televised address to the invited audience:

"Today is a very important day in Japanese history. It was here, over a century and a half ago, that two great philosophers, William Edwards Deming, and Joseph Moses Juran, whose teaching remains at the heart of this glorious standard, first proposed a new approach for the management of industry that has now been transposed into the management of society and eventually shall be the preferred method for managing the world and the sovereignty of nations.

"In 1945 we had nothing. The horrors of war had flattened our land. All we had was our people. Then, in the following decade Deming and Juran came, and, despite being American, were willing to devote their lives to helping us. With their guidance we became strong again, and fit to lead others. We have built on that. We have maintained the momentum, held the gains, and latterly moved up a gear such that we can now contemplate a Quality Management strategy that will not only give us more strength, but will also deliver strength and prosperity to other lands that are in desperate need of it.

"For the last eleven years, nay longer, we have dedicated ourselves to the task of building a supersystem that makes us fit for the challenge of becoming a bidding power in The New Game, the first such nation to do so. If the price is right we shall purchase sovereignty and, as Deming said, improve the system constantly and forever both in our country and others. Everyone shall be put to work to achieve the transformation, as the standard expressly demands.

"Poverty shall disappear. You will not see it anywhere in Japan, and soon you will not see it in The Philippines either. We benchmark the best in the world in every social aspect, and we have implemented the self-policing state to replace dependency on inspection to achieve law enforcement.

"Your Majesty, Your Royal Highness, over the next three days you will see how we have put ISO 9100 into practice. It has not been easy rolling out over 200 clauses, each one highly specific in its requirements, across every sector of society and covering every aspect of Quality. There are stringent criteria, for example, covering reliability and fitness for purpose, not just of products, but also services and systems, such as administration, from the largest town to the smallest hamlet. At zero point two per cent our unemployment matches the world's best for a capitalist state, and we meet all of the standard's requirements when it comes to providing value and opportunity.

"Self-discipline and continual improvement are built-in in every aspect of training and education. There is no such thing as a Japanese criminal.

"Your Majesty, all over the world your many supporters are either placing or maintaining centre parties in power. Here it is the latter, and we thank you for placing your trust in us to deliver what is required and to make your dream of achieving world peace and the end of warfare across the globe a reality. Only centre parties, elected by OPD, can secure for everyone the constancy of purpose that Deming told us that we needed all those decades ago. His Fourteen Points are now enshrined in our constitution. Nobody here wants to experience the shame of doing a bad job or no job, and we are pledged not to let it happen, just as ISO 9100 demands. We do not dispense welfare payments, but guarantee opportunity, just as the standard directs.

"We believe and desire that any country would welcome rather than fear, the prospect of a Japanese-led government. Thanks to ISO 9100 we now have a free rein to make poor countries rich and give some of the world's most deprived people the improved quality of life that they so richly deserve."

From the concert hall the royal couple was escorted round Tokyo's famous shopping complex, the Ginza, where they were exposed to a new way of doing business.

Elsewhere in the capitalist world traders would compete to maximise their own individual profits. Not here in 2109. Instead, all of the traders collaborated to maximise customer satisfaction. There was no competition, just a commitment to provide variety, reliability and functionality that would yield value to as many customers as possible, and with poverty eliminated, there was never going to be any shortage of customers. It was an eye-opener to Aub and Katie, showing what could still be achieved with capitalism. It showed that capitalism and Non-Capitalist Economics could quite easily coexist. Japan had proved it, and Aub noted this as something to enter in his report to Boris.

In Tokyo the royal couple continued to visit shrines, met autograph-hunting schoolchildren, and travelled on the famous Shinkansen Railway that showcased the cutting-edge technology of the frictionless linear air track that was the feature of Japan's latest Bullet Train. It did indeed fly like a bullet along its specially shaped graphene-covered channel. It could be argued that it was not really a train at all, but a self-propelled frictionless single carriage powered by air that rippled at high pressure from within the channel upon which it floated. In this respect it was definitely a very different train to the one that the pair had ridden on in Brazil.

All over Japan people flocked to get a glimpse of Aub and Katie. Nothing compared, however, with the reception that they received in Hiroshima. When they arrived they were greeted by what could only be described as a sea of people. It was perfectly understandable, for here were still the remains of the ancient relics from an age when war had completely devastated the entire landscape and cause the most horrific loss of life that the world had ever witnessed. As long as there was war on Earth, and the technology to produce the most destructive of weapons, everyone knew that there was always going to be the risk of a repeat somewhere. To the citizens of Hiroshima and Nagasaki Aub and Katie were not merely foreign monarchs. They were people of God-like stature.

This realisation came as a real shock to the system to Aub and Katie. Neither had experienced anything like it before.

Passing through the mass was not difficult. The cortege easily passed along the path that had been cleared for it.

"This can't be real," Katie remarked to Aub as the gold-plated Kamchatskiy slowly inched its way along at a snail's pace, so that as many people as possible could see them.

"I expected people," Aub replied. "But this is an entire population. Surely we can't be that important."

But they were. To these people they were saviours. Even to the Samurai class they were the sword that would kill the beast. Through them Japan would be set free again, but in a completely new kind of way. ISO 9100 was a constructive, rather than a destructive, weapon.

When the Kamchatskiy reached the rotunda it stopped and the royals were led out. Aub was given a microphone and Queen Katie a wreath. She laid it at the base of the monument to the fallen, that provided a permanent reminder of what had happened on that terrible day in 1945. The Prince was suddenly placed on the spot with all eyes upon him, and not all of them were Japanese. Viktor Bogodan and Boris Marechenko watched with interest from the state apartment above the Kamchatka Parliament. Words, however, just came naturally to The Prince as the whole city stood in silence before him:

"For centuries nation has fought against nation. For centuries sovereignty has been decided on the killing fields by force and coercion. The arrow, the gun, the poison gas, the bomb, and, ultimately the nuclear missile, have all played their part, manufactured to destroy life. Empires have risen and collapsed. Millions have lost their lives through time without reason. If I were God I would be weeping to see such waste, and the gross sub-optimisation that that the ultimate form of competition has inflicted upon the world.

"The pair of us are honoured and deeply moved that you have all turned out in such numbers on this cold January morning. You look to us, and we will help you in every way possible to make what you have achieved a success, but you should also look to yourselves for it is yourselves and your Government that have brought you to this point and placed your country on course for a glorious future. Those who perished in the dreadful events of 1945 did not do so in vain. From the ashes has eventually risen the phoenix. The New Game will be the spearhead that rids the world of war once and for all."

It had to be said that this was the biggest display of unity ever seen in Japan. Many of the people raised placards of Aub and Katie, along with the Japanese flag that represented a new-born sense of patriotism. After all, this was the first time that Japan had had an opportunity to extend its sovereignty since the end of the Second World War, but this time in a way that the whole world would be pleased to accept.

*

The Japanese part of the tour concluded with an ice show in Tokyo, which showcased the very best of Japanese skating talent. Seated next to Prime Minister Takamoto, Aub and Katie watched the national champions of Japan past and present perform their routines in ice dancing, pairs, duet and free skating. There was, however, one distinctive feature of this skating display, and that was the display from the National Figure School of Japan.

The National Figure School consisted of a team of fifteen specialist skaters whose work involved skating four routines that comprised solely of school figures. Each routine was skated on clean ice to the traditional Japanese Koto music. Counters, brackets, loops, three turns and changes of edge were all combined together in synchronised movements, with the skaters passing between each other and turning around each other, but perhaps the most striking aspect was the tracing that was left at the end of each of the routines. In each case, as the skaters departed, the lights were dimmed allowing the audience to take pictures of the resultant tracing, each one providing the outline of a familiar object, such as a fish, a flower, a rabbit or a bird. It was intricate and impressive, and definitely something for the connoisseur.

"I hope the Olympic Federation adopts this at the next Olympics," Katie said to Iwai. "It's really super stuff."

"Please, do recommend it to them," Iwai replied. "I'm sure they will listen to you. Everybody else does."

*

The next day the Emperor's drone conveyed the royal couple from Tokyo to Seoul, where the presentation ceremony was similar, but less elaborate. President Ki San Wang proudly received his certificate and held it aloft. Again the press was in abundance, Sylvia Smith, of course being granted the prime position as The Queen's royal correspondent.

As in Japan the people turned out in large numbers to welcome Aub and Katie, although not on anywhere near as grand a scale. That was, of course, until they reached the border with North Korea. Then, everything changed.

All along the border people gathered in what seemed like an ocean of faces. It was awesome, and at first Aub and Katie did not know what to make of it. As they crossed into North Korea waves of confetti rained down on their Kamchatskiy. It looked and felt very similar to what they had experienced in Hiroshima.

People lined the roads and threw flowers all along the route to Pyongyang as they passed through towns and villages that were quite obviously much poorer than those in the country's southern neighbour. The difference between the now ISO 9100 certificated South Korea and the impoverished North was stark. It wasn't so much that the people were restricted from crossing to the South, they weren't, it was simply that the quality of life and the much needed investment had not come to the North. This particular North Korean Government just hadn't cared. The South wanted to help, but, of course, the North's rulers were not going to do anything until a deal had been struck that permitted all of them simply to leave as very wealthy individuals. Under The New Game sovereignty came at a price and everybody knew it, but at least the price was not in the form of human life.

The smiling faces of the children and the expressions of joy on the faces of the adult population conveyed the message of liberation. They were in no doubt that Queen Katie of Kamchatka, and her Prince, would not let them down. ISO 9100 would compel South Korea to upgrade every aspect of Quality in North Korea to the same level as in the South so that the two countries would be as one. The people were cheering in vast numbers because they knew that within a few years their land would be transformed into one of riches. In the longer term, naturally, the whole nation of Korea would be larger and more powerful as a result of the unification.

When the royals arrived in Pyongyang their first stop was the parliament building. Aub and Katie were swiftly escorted inside, and were slightly nervous, unsure of what kind of reception they were going to get inside, knowing full well the reputation and character of North Korea's leaders of 2109. The feeling became even more intense as a single tank rolled past them. Neither Aub nor Katie knew just what to make of that. For a few moments it certainly did appear that there was something a little disconcerting about exactly what was going on.

Slowly and tentatively they entered the North Korean Parliament only to find a completely empty chamber that appeared to be entirely deserted, except for two familiar gentlemen who sat side by side next to the leader's seat. Aub and Katie stood motionless, hardly believing what they saw.

In front of them Patrick and Duncan sat.

"We've bought them out," said Patrick.

"They wanted to go so we bought them out," added Duncan.

"In the entire national interest the President dismissed his ministers," Patrick explained. "He saw no reason why our teams shouldn't get to work right away. He just wanted his money, so we brokered the deal with Ki San Wang, and the entire North Korean Government then vanished. We have been looking after things since January 2nd."

"What was that tank doing outside?" Aub asked, curious about its significance.

"North Korea's last tank," said Duncan. "It's being driven to the National War Museum. We have control of the country for the time being until Ki San Wang is ready to be installed later in the year. The sooner we can transform this country the sooner the profits will start rolling in. The Island will make on the deal in the end, as we have negotiated a share of Korea's profits in exchange for getting on with the job quickly. Ki San Wang wanted to minimise the delay before his country started to reap the benefits. Kim Lam Zam may have been a playboy with no interest in politics, but he has actually done the greatest favour ever for the North Korean people. This is going to be a rich country sooner than lots of people think."

"So how will the payment be managed?" asked Aub.

"The Island paid off Kim Lam Zam. Ki San Wang will pay us, with an additional amount that is linked to the profits of the joint Korean nation. You could say we have become a shareholder in Korea. We are going to put in the investment and bring about a swift transformation, with the help of a bit of recruiting. Compared to Brazil it will be a doddle. The Kremlin has also backed us, so some of the profits generated will go there. Since you are going to be the King and Queen of Russia anyway, that won't be an issue, and it will help Ulanov, who in turn helps us. A quick start will also give our teams a bit of much needed time to get used to the lie of the land. Many of them are already at work. Some outlying areas of Pyongyang are already seeing some quick gains from some inexpensive, but vital projects."

"Our Quality planning phase is well underway," Patrick continued. "The military has completely disbanded and all personnel have been signed up to work with our teams. It will be The Brazilian Job but on a smaller scale."

"So for the time being it's just you two running North Korea?" said Aub.

"Just us," Patrick confirmed. "You'll enjoy touring this place. It's full of fascinating history. Look out for the fireworks too, displays will be taking place all across the land on Friday to mark Unification Day and the establishment of the Republic of Korea. The people of course don't know that it's just us in charge here. Ki San Wang is nominally in charge. Our deal is largely a secret, but is in accordance with international protocol."

Chapter Nineteen
American Coronation

The first Saturday in February.

All eyes were on America, and in particular New York for it was here that the stage was set for one of the grandest events that the USA had ever staged.

All over the United States people of all ages and backgrounds proudly waved their nation's flag and held special parties to commemorate the great day that was the American Coronation.

The winner of Quest for a Queen, Clarissa Danskin, made the finishing touches to her dress, and to her skating outfit as she prepared to make the most important journey of her life from the Palace of Manhattan to Times Square, where in a few hours' time she would be crowned before revealing to the world for the first time the skating routines that she had choreographed specially for the occasion.

On The Island The Opera House was again full as everyone gathered to watch the crowning of the American Queen in the event that had been designed specifically to rival Aub and Katie's Coronation Wedding that had been scheduled for March 15th. Aub and Katie sat in the front row with her parents, and Patrick and Duncan. The Island Times bore the headline 'Broome steps down: new Queen to be crowned'.

In Times Square American TV presenter Alexis Silver stood in the place where it would all happen, meeting some of the many people who had camped out for the better part of a week in order to occupy the prime viewing spaces.

"The atmosphere here is like nothing anyone here has ever experienced," she said. "The American flag is everywhere, people are spontaneously singing the national anthem, and behind me you can see the giant ice pad where the skating will take place with a star-studded line up. I am now on the red carpet that stretches all the way to the centre of Times Square where you can see the golden throne of America and the golden crown next to it.

"The minute she is crowned President Broome will be Prime Minister Broome and, perhaps more importantly, his party will become the Royalist Party, which is a real landmark in American history."

There was no doubt that Robert Broome had trumped up his stepping down as President. Most people accepted that, knowing that what he was doing was little different to what Sergei Ulanov had already done in Russia to make way for Aub and Katie. Some had argued that it had trivialised monarchy, but was that what most people thought? Alexis posed this question to some of the onlookers.

"Do you think this trivialises monarchy?" she asked one gentleman.

"Not at all," he replied. "I think it's great for America. Everyone here knows we've gotta do something to get our country back on track. I think it's fantastic that were goin' to have our first monarch since King George the Third. We need it."

Alexis then asked the same question to a lady next to him.

"I don't think it trivialises it. It changes it certainly. We need more royals involved in managing the world. Clarissa's going to work with Katie and that has to be good."

"Are you a fan of Queen Katie?"

"Absolutely. And in the next American election I will be voting for Broome, although if he had not done what he has I certainly would not be."

"That seems to be a recurring message across the country. Let me ask this guy if he feels the same."

"Definitely," replied the man. "It's plain for everyone to see. Broome votes for Katie, the people vote for Broome. He can't lose. Katie's fans will now vote for him. Those who are not Katie's fans will probably still vote for him. And if he can pull off what Ulanov has in Russia, boy will he be on a roll, and so will his party."

"And do you agree?" Alexis asked another woman.

"I sure do," said the coloured woman. "This country has to play catch up and fast. All the countries in The New Game are tearing ahead of us and we have to keep up or go under. The sooner everyone sees that the better."

"And do you think Queen Clarissa is the answer?"

"Yes I do. She's got what it takes. Through her Broome's going to get Moscow on our side. The years of rivalry are over. With a bit of luck she'll change the way our Government governs. She'll get people cooperating at last. Ulanov's not our enemy, why should we still be pointing missiles at him? He's not doing it to us. But I agree with the others, I'm voting for Broome now, even though I never thought I ever would. This move will throw the whole of black America behind him."

"This is a once in a generation event," said another man. "It's fantastic to be a part of it. And the best bit is that she's American, not like Aub and Katie who have no connection with Russia at all."

"That raises an interesting point," said Alexis, turning to another man. "What do you think about that?"

"Quest for a Queen came as a response to the debate, 'If Russia can, why can't we?' Everyone knew President Broome had to listen to the people or face certain defeat. He did listen, and this is the result. We can and we will, and we will do it the American way, not the way other people do it or say we should. That's why it matters that our Queen is American born and bred."

"Absolutely right," Aub said to Katie. "It's essential America retains its identity. There could be nothing worse than them simply trying to copy us. We need to get accepted by the American people, and through her we have every chance. Without her we would be struggling forever to win over the Americans, and they would drag the world down something rotten."

"My view exactly," said Katie.

The audience then saw Clarissa dressed in all of her finery as she left the modern-day Palace of Manhattan and travel in a specially constructed gold coach. The scenes presently appeared on the great screen in Times Square.

"We can see now our girl, soon to be America's Queen, leaving the Palace of Manhattan," Alexis continued. "In a coach that is entirely American, and, as you can see, it is every bit as grand as anything that Kamchatskiy could have made. It is definitely not a Kamchatskiy. It has been produced by Chrysler by some of America's finest craftsmen.

"You can also probably make out behind the throne all of the finalists from Quest for a Queen, as well as some of America's finest singing talent, not to mention the skaters who will skate alongside our Queen."

All along the route from Manhattan to Times Square people turned out, just as they had done elsewhere for Aub and Katie, cheering and waving the American flag with an astonishing display of patriotism. Security, however, was intense. Unlike in Russia, America's right to bear arms was still embedded heavily in the national culture. Nobody could rule out the risk of assassination in such a place, and so, while the Chrysler carriage may look grand, it was also heavily protected and built to withstand attack, unlike its Kamchatskiy counterpart. It was therefore both bombproof and bulletproof, and there was no shortage of armed cops facing toward the crowd as the carriage passed by.

As the carriage approached Times Square the throne was prepared and a small dark man took his position beside it.

"This is Reverend Elijah Thomas," continued Alexis. "He's a familiar figure in the Evangelist movement, and has been chosen specifically for his pro-American stance and total conviction to the Church. He's expected to deliver a rousing speech later, but the American Coronation itself is, I'm told, going to be relatively short and simple. There will then be a flypast by the American Air Force that will serve as a reminder that they are very much alive and kicking, with no intention of abandoning their duty to defend America and its interests.

"Also taking their places are President Broome, soon to be Prime Minister Broome, a number of senior senators, and behind them the judges from Quest for a Queen. The jeering that you can hear is for judge Rialto, who notoriously deducted marks from Clarissa. During the contest everybody assumed that Rialto had deducted points to try to stop Clarissa from winning. Now it appears that a second theory has come to light, and that actually he really wanted her to win. By deducting marks lots of people were apparently inspired to vote who otherwise quite possibly wouldn't have bothered. He later admitted on my show that he was indeed a keen fan of Queen Katie of Kamchatka, a fact that he had previously kept secret, and later admitted that in his opinion Clarissa was indeed the girl whom he thought was best placed to work with Queen Katie to get America back on track. That, he said, was all down to personality and likely compatibility.

"Beside the throne you will see the beautiful amazingly hand-crafted golden Crown of America. Some people have called it the Mickey Mouse Crown, but many others have stated that it is far from that, highlighting the pivotal role that Clarissa will play in helping America to recover economically. Her first job will be to try to reduce America's shocking inflation rate of seventeen point six per cent. The point is, like it or not, Broome desperately needs Aub and Katie's help and Clarissa will provide the link."

"I told you Rialto was really doing us a favour," Aub said quietly to Katie.

"So it seems. I could never quite make him out, but now I understand perfectly. Looks like I had an unknown secret admirer with influence."

"He certainly spurred loads of your fans to vote for her because she really was the right girl. I'm looking forward to working with her."

They continued to watch the live event and cheered with the audience both in The Opera House and in Times Square as Clarissa stepped down from the Chrysler coach onto the red carpet, allowing people all over the world to glimpse the girl's stunning coronation dress for the first time.

"Now we finally get to see the dress," Alexis continued. "It's studded sequins set against a blue background with the red and white stripes of the American flag clearly represented in the trail, which is being held by two of America's top junior skaters, who also won a contest to have the right to undertake this prestigious task. I can hardly hear myself speak now, the roar of the crowd is just deafening as she mounts the three steps up to the throne beside which preacher Elijah is standing, with the crown on his right side. The crown, by the way, has been valued at some hundred million dollars, with diamonds set in gold on seven pointed heads. There's nothing like it anywhere in the world, it's entirely modern, yet it bears a resemblance in style to the crowns of ancient kings. It's a fascinating object."

The cheering intensified as the trail was released and Clarissa duly sat upon the throne. Then there was silence as Elijah began to give his address:

"Ladies and gentlemen, good people of America. Heaven has sent us an angel."

He paused and the crowd cheered.

"God has spoken to us. He has shown us the way, the truth and the life, and we have listened. This is a turning point in American history. This is our chance to change, and the opportunity to turn over a new leaf. I am proud of our armed forces and what they have done. They have served our country well and we will remember with dignity all those who have sacrificed their lives for this, the world's greatest country."

He paused again and there was further cheering, accompanied with intensive waving of the American flag.

"This is the world's greatest country and we must continue to believe in both that and our core values, just as others believe in theirs. If we don't believe in ourselves, how can we expect others to believe in us? We will not be a nation of losers. God is on our side, but we must accept that He is also on the side of others. God will not abandon those who are doing good work in other lands seeking to make His world better. We have therefore to work with these people not against them. Let us remember always that life is a two-way process. God needs us as much as we need Him.

"We have seen it all before. In the sixteenth century it was the Spanish Armada. In the twentieth century it was Nazism. God rejected them because they were evil. He did that by providing a means for them to be destroyed. In the Second World War millions of lives were lost, but in the end evil was defeated. That was, and still is, the will of God. He doesn't want us to fight and destroy each other. He wants us to work hard together so that one day we will be worthy of being reborn in His image.

"Ladies and gentlemen, if Russia can, so can we. But let us not make Russia our enemy, for if we do, mark my words, we will be defeated and with every good reason.

"In front of you sits our new Queen, a Queen who has been chosen to represent us, with a constitutional right to rule over us, to guide and protect us in the name of our Lord, our saviour Jesus Christ. Every God-fearing person in this country is behind her, and nobody, no matter where, can suppress that power because it is a power of Divine stature, and the will of God shall always prevail."

He turned to Clarissa and held his Bible aloft.

"Do you Clarissa Amelia Danskin, swear by Almighty God to serve and to protect the people of the United States of America, to be its lawful monarch and to uphold the doctrine of America First?"

"I do," Clarissa answered.

"And do you further swear by Almighty God, to act in the name of Quality so that all American citizens may thrive and prosper in the face of adversity?"

"I do."

"And finally, do you Clarissa Amelia Danskin, promise to use all of your bestowed powers to act in the name of justice and of peace, forsaking any and all temptation to place self-interest before the will of God, the interests of America and the interests of the world?"

"I do."

"Then it is my honour and duty herewith to place the Crown of America upon your head, such that you may go forth and serve the Lord in the interests of all of the people of America, so that good shall prevail over evil. The Lord bless you and God bless America."

"God bless America," the crowd chanted repeatedly as Reverend Elijah Thomas reached for the crown and slowly placed it upon Clarissa's head, at which moment the whole scene appeared to flash as photographs were taken by the thousand, both from media representatives from all over the world, and from the many onlookers, each eager to catch the defining moment.

Seven US fighter jets then flew overhead as a squadron, leaving in their wake trails of red, white and blue in the clear sky above.

Then, as it cleared, the choir began to sing on the makeshift pews to the right of the throne. They sang the very same hymn that had been sung at the conclusion of the Memorial Service held for Dr W. Edwards Deming on 29th. December 1993 at his beloved St. Pauls Parish Church in Washington:

Alleluia! Alleluia! Alleluia!
The strife is oer the battle done;
Now is the Victor's triumph won;
O let the song of praise be sung:
Alleluia!
Death's mightiest powers have done their worst,
And Jesus hath his foes dispersed;
Let shouts of praise and joy outburst:
Alleluia!
On the third morn he rose again,
Glorious in majesty to reign;
O let us swell the joyful strain:
Alleluia!
Lord, by the stripes that wounded thee,
From death's dread sting thy servants free,
That we may live and sing to thee,
Alleluia!

Confetti then rained down from on high, partially masking the new Queen so that the crowd could barely see the harness being placed around her waist, and the coronation dress being removed, nor the fastening of her skates around her feet.

As the last of the confetti fell to the ground Queen Clarissa was revealed not in her coronation dress, but in a catsuit, again coloured in the stars and stripes of America.

Suddenly the American Queen, her crown carefully removed, flew across Times Square from the throne at one end to the ice pad at the other. She landed in the centre of it. There was no time for a warm up, but she was used to that. She had rehearsed the coronation drill on several occasions in the grounds of what was now her Palace of Manhattan, a modern-day Regency-style palace that formed part of the prize for whoever won Quest for a Queen.

Alexis Silver resumed her commentary:

"There she goes, across Times Square ready to land on the ice as the world's first official skating Queen. Even

Queen Katie of Kamchatka has not yet been seen skating in public view. You can hear the crowds here, it is absolutely ecstatic. Prepare to be dazzled."

Throughout Quest for a Queen and afterwards Clarissa had mastered the combined skills of free skating and dance, but the style complemented that of Aub and Katie. Where Aub and Katie were in essence dancers, and therefore skated as one on the ice, Clarissa was far more of a solo artist. This did, however, include solo dancing, a new Olympic event, whereby skaters performed solo routines that were essentially dance routines, devoid of the obligatory jumps and spins that distinguished the two disciplines.

Clarissa had mastered all of the standard double jumps, and in that respect was a step ahead of Aub and Katie. She was also fully conversant with the use of props and the harness, both of which had been put to the test in Quest for a Queen.

Clarissa's first routine was packed with vitality, recreating the style of American street dancing that had a long association with New York. She was the centrepiece of what was essentially a group number.

"The young skaters that you see alongside Clarissa in this opening routine are all from the New York Street and Commercial Ice Dance Academy," Alexis explained. "This is fifteen minutes of sheer brilliance. She's mastered the style and, of course, it's a truly American style. You'll also see that Clarissa, with the help of the top trainers that were assigned to train the winner of Quest for a Queen, has blossomed into an amazing mime artist, and you can clearly see this in her American Street."

"I love that style," Katie whispered to Aub, as she removed her hand-held device from her bag.

"What are you doing?" asked Aub.

"I'm going to send a text to her congratulating her on her coronation and on her wonderful skating, and to say that I'm looking forward enormously to seeing her in Red Square."

"Don't forget to add my name," said Aub. "The more I see of her the more I like her. When I first saw Quest for a Queen I didn't think anything that came out of that show could possibly be good, but thankfully I've been proved wrong. Broome's just secured himself another term in the White House."

"Throughout the performance you'll   see Clarissa reaching out right across America, that's what she said she wanted to do when I interviewed her when she won Quest for a Queen," Alexis continued after the opening number had finished. "She'll be back soon, but first we are going to meet a few old friends that came from a time when America led the world. It's a tribute to the colourful world of American animation, which will be augmented with some virtual reality. Cartoon characters will be projected onto the ice and will interact with the skaters. You'll see Disney greats like Mickey Mouse, and others such as Officer Dibble turning over a new leaf to Top Cat, and Tom and Jerry playing cat and mouse, and making up at the end. It's all about happy endings, which is, of course, the underlying theme of the coronation. Look out for Queen Clarissa as Snow White and later as Batgirl. There's some clever trickery as the cartoon characters skilfully switch from projected images into real skaters."

There then followed a demonstration of America's equivalent of the Tango Romantica, the Yankee Polka. This dance was invented in the 1960s by James Sladky, Judy Schwomeyer and Ron Ludington and first skated at the Skating Club of Wilmington, Delaware in 1969. It later became a compulsory dance in international competition. Alexis Silver introduced it as follows:

"Now, every child learns it. It's danced at skating clubs all over America, and it has become our national skating dance. It is, of course, the dance you all remember from Quest for a Queen. Yes, it's the Yankee Polka and Queen Clarissa is going to skate it with one of Americas top ice dancing professionals,

Tommy De Lacy to the classical piece 'The Yellow Rose of Texas'. Watch for the rocket at the end that carries her to the Moon, symbolising the launch of the Apollo missions at the same time as the Yankee Polka was first being performed. There's a significance in that as she has she has pledged to give America a stake in Moonbase Alpha following a deal that she has struck with Queen Katie of Kamchatka in exchange for a promise to reform America's gun laws. If you go back a few years you will remember that the Russians initially excluded the US from the project, but things have changed and now there is a much more relaxed feeling in Moscow that could see America become much more involved."

So Clarissa skated her only couple dance of the show, proving that where Aub and Katie had mastered Russia's national dance, she had mastered the American equivalent from the historical section. Then, at the end, the rocket appeared as a prop onto which she was lifted.

"Lift off, we have lift off," came the commentary. "Off she goes. She'll be back later. Next though it's off to San Jose to meet some of her friends. Please welcome the San Jose Formation Dance Team for some California Dreamin'."

"You've completed the deal then?" Aub asked Katie.

"I've invited her to Moonbase Alpha in July for the 140th anniversary celebrations of the first Moon landing of Apollo 11. Joanie Carmichael has approved it and said she would stage a banquet for her and a number of guests. We will be there along with Patrick and Duncan to discuss the setting up of a new American quarter on Moonbase, along with a strategy for reducing the number of guns in circulation in the US. I take it you approve?"

"You know me, I want full disarmament," said Aub. "But it's one thing at a time I suppose. I'd like the Americans to have a presence on Moonbase anyway. They may not have invested in it because they were largely prevented from doing so, but if it helps us to achieve American disarmament eventually then it has to be worth doing."

The ice show continued with routines to Mississippi and the Streets of Philadelphia, as well as some tributes to the legendary jazz, blues and rock greats of the American music industry. Clarissa returned to present her self-choreographed Louisiana Blues, displaying in particular one of her original steps that had helped her to win the Quest for a Queen final.

This was a deep-edged choctaw that led straight in to an outside edge twizzle and a backwards closed chasse. The crowd recognised it and immediately applauded as she danced the move as part of the intricate solo dance routine that was characterised by its slow timing and long, deep flowing edges and subtle turns.

Clarissa's show then moved to Chicago and Tennessee before finishing where it had started in New York. Clarissa joined the New York Formation Ice Dancers for the classic New York, New York before finally the message That's all folks was revealed on the great screen.

"What a fine end to a magnificent show," Alexis said as she made her way along the red carpet to the rink side. "I am now going to approach Queen Clarissa because I think she has a few closing words. What I can say is that the party is only just beginning all over America. It's the biggest this country has ever seen. We like to do things big here, but this is really big.

Your Majesty, that was out of this world. I'm now going to hand over to you so you can give your first address as Queen of America."

"Good people, loyal subjects," said Clarissa. "I hope you enjoyed the show."

The crowd cheered.

"You voted me to be your first American Queen. When I received the crown I agreed that I would place America first, as has been enshrined in the American constitution, and I shall, but it means what it says. Remember America first does not mean America only.

"I love my country and I love all of you. I shall serve you and I will do my utmost to save this great country. Hopefully I will be able to demonstrate to you that it is not too late. If Russia can, so can we. As your Queen I shall not leave it to others to carve up the world between themselves as we continue to squander our precious reserves on weapons of mass destruction that serve no useful purpose. We can and we will be part of the revolution that is transforming the world, and, yes, I shall be representing America in Red Square on March 15th."

"I look forward to meeting you," said Aub.

Chapter Twenty
Coronation Wedding

The 15th of March in Red Square.

For the past week Aub, Katie and Jobine had been residing at an undisclosed location on the outskirts of Moscow. They had rehearsed the Coronation Wedding event and had travelled the route that their Kamchatskiy state carriage would follow from the Church of All Saints in Kuliski to St Basil's Cathedral via the Zaikonospassky Monastery Church, Alexandrovsky Gardens and the north bank of the Moscow River. Katie had chosen this route in order to allow as many people as possible to line the route and see the carriage.

An ice pad, similar to the one that had been placed in Times Square, had been laid in Red Square beside the so-called Place of Skulls, whilst in Alexandrovsky Gardens three large screens had been erected so that events inside St Basil's Cathedral could easily be seen by the people.

The event was as unusual as it was grand, the world having never previously witnessed a royal wedding and a coronation simultaneously. It had happened before in the private confines of The Island, but this was very different. Russia would soon have a royal couple of its own.

As in Times Square, many people had camped out for days, braving the remnants of the cold Russian winter in order to gain a vantage point for the spectacle. At two o'clock, one hour before Aub and Katie were due to arrive, Island correspondent Sylvia Smith spoke to some of the people on and off the main route.

"What do you think about Russia having a royal family?" she asked on gentleman.

"I think it's great," he replied. "Just what this country needs, and we couldn't have better people. Aub and Katie deserve to be King and Queen of Russia for everything that they have done for us. We still have problems, but without them we would surely have had far more."

"The good thing is they're ours," added a woman who was standing beside him, holding up her child. "They represent the people. We can form a bond with them. We can't do that with The Kremlin. It's too impersonal. You only have to look at the UK and how people there turn out to see a royal wedding or a coronation, and to be able to see both at the same time is unique and fabulous."

Not everyone, however, shared the same view. Some distance from The Kremlin Sylvia spotted a group of elderly gents who, apparently, were completely oblivious to the events around them.

"What do you think of the Coronation Wedding?" Sylvia asked them.

"Not a lot," one of them replied.

"Why's that?"

"Because I don't know these people. They are nothing to do with us. They aren't even Russian."

Such views, however, were largely confined to the older generation who had grown up during a very different kind of era.

"Does it matter to you that they are not Russian?" Sylvia asked a somewhat younger group of individuals that had taken up positions in Alexandrovsky Gardens.

"Not at all," replied one young man. "They have done far more for us than any Russians have. The fact that we are going to have an Australian King is neither here nor there, and, as for Katie, it was her ancestors that set up the Kamchatka Parliament, now the world's finest institution, which stops recession from hitting us. Moscow is by far the world's richest city, and it is through her, not Ulanov or anyone else in the building behind us."

Sylvia moved on, this time to a group of men and women who were waving a combination of two different flags.

"Now, I see you are waving two sets of flags, the Russian flag and the Queen's Island flag, why is that?"

"Because they are both important to us," answered one of the women. "We are from Kamchatka and The Island flag is everywhere there, but of course Kamchatka is also part of Russia, so we wave both with pride."

"How long are you here for? Sylvia asked.

"Well, we came here on a Basic Tourist Exit Visa, which is valid for ten days. It expires on the 20th, so we must be back by then, but it's great because it covers all basic costs such as hotel, meals and economy class travel."

"That's interesting, could you hold it up so the viewers can see what one looks like?"

"Sure."

"I see it has The Island logo top left, and the Queen's head below it. Then to the right are the words Basic Entitlement, and below the valid from and to dates, plus the scope of validation, which in this case is Greater Moscow, so this is the only place where it is valid. It also has your photograph and an ID number. So you don't need any money?"

"No, but we can use it to draw out small amounts. It has a small credit allowance and these days pretty much all places just scan it."

"So that's how it works coming from Non-Capitalist Economics into a capitalist state?"

"Yes."

"And you like it?"

"Definitely. I wouldn't be without my exit visa, most importantly because it lets me back into Kamchatka. People from outside in general can't afford to go there. The entry visas are much too expensive. It needs to change really. That's why there are still some problems at the frontier."

"I know all about that," replied Sylvia, as she recollected the unsavoury scenes that she had witnessed at the movable border between Non-Capitalist Kamchatka and the rest of Russia, which was still a matter of concern to both authorities.

"But the King and Queen will sort it, I know they will."

Sylvia moved on around the west side of The Kremlin to face the mighty Moscow River.

"The carriage will pass along this road behind me," she said, speaking into her selfie camera, which she now carried on a stick. "And then along this short stretch of riverbank. As you can see scores of small boats have taken up temporary moorings so that they can get a prime view of the carriage as it passes along the Kremlyovskaya and Naberezhnaya before turning left at the Bolshoy Moskvoretsky Bridge and finally coming to rest outside St Basil's Cathedral. There you will see assembled The Moscow Philharmonic Orchestra, as of today renamed The Royal Moscow Philharmonic Orchestra, which will play first the Russian national anthem and then the Queens own anthem 'I Vow to Thee My Island', set of course to the music of Gustav Holst's 'Jupiter' from *The Planets*."

Inside St Basil's Cathedral the guests of honour were already assembling as the golden state Kamchatskiy carriage, a replica of the royal state carriage in London, save for the Kamchatskiy logo embossed on its doors, was poised outside the Church of All Saints in Kulisky ready to receive Aub, Katie, Neville and Mary.

The cameras were ready and waiting as the world would see for the first time the Queen's bridal dress of sky blue, studded with sequins and decorated with a hundred gold imprints of Saturn that featured on The Island's flag. Alongside they would see also The Island Prince's robes, also on show for the first time.

Television coverage shifted to All Saints as the royal couple, along with Katie's parents transferred from their

Kamchatskiy limousine to the carriage, which was duly hauled by four white stallions.

Large crowds lined the route as the coach made its way north westwards along Prospekt Serova before turning left at what was once the KGB headquarters into the Teatralny Proezd, and continuing thereafter south west past the Alexandrovsky Gardens where the majority of the spectators were stationed. The final stretch took the royals east along the north bank of the Moscow River before coming to a halt outside St Basil's Cathedral. Here, of course, access was restricted to the invited guests of honour, although some members of the public had been able to purchase tickets in advance for seats in the temporary stand that had been erected at the opposite end of Red Square with a commanding view of both it and the ice pad.

As was the custom, the bride's father, in this case the retiring King Neville, led his daughter toward the uniquely presented altar where The Island King's crown was prominently on display beside the newly-created throne of Russia. According to the schedule the coronation would immediately follow the royal wedding. Sylvia Smith provided the English commentary:

"The wedding service will be a traditional Russian Orthodox wedding service, which of course is just one of the major religions of the world that is incorporated in The Church of The Founder Mary, the Island faith that embraces all recognised religions of the world, and which now exists in most countries.

"We see notably among the guests the proud parents and brother of the future King, Aub Ryman, who have been flown in specially from Bathurst Island in Australia on Aub's very own Hebden Three, which was gifted to him by his Queen. Beside them we can also see the secondaries of the royal couple. These are interesting because in Kamchatka there is something called the Set Formation Act, which provides legal powers for designated couples

279

with loose attachment to the principal couple to intervene should the marriage run into difficulties downstream. It has to be said that this Act does seem to have had a profound effect in reducing the instances of marital breakdown in Kamchatka, and whilst the Act does not apply in the rest of Russia many young Russians are increasingly voluntarily choosing to adopt its provisions in order to protect their marriages. The divorce rate in Russia has fallen markedly in recent years and many expert sociologists are attributing that as the reason.

"Next to them we see Aub and Katie's personal skating trainer Jobine van der Eigt, a very special woman, known for training the setmates, 240 a year, who, each year except for this, are invited by The Island Queen to her Island so that they can live their dream of becoming skating celebrities.

"Beside and behind them are various monarchs and world leaders, whom we will see in the procession later. Meanwhile we hear 'Here Comes the Bride', Neville walking Katie down the aisle, which, by Island tradition, will be his last act as King. Her younger brother and sister are holding the dress trail, whilst the trail of the Prince's robe is being carried by two of his young cousins. The Master of Ceremonies, who has the unique role of both marrying the couple and of crowning the new King, is the highly respected Archbishop Karelinski. He will join them in Holy matrimony after reciting a short reading in Russian. There will then be an aria from the St Basil's Cathedral choir. After that all eyes will be on the adjacent throne where Prince Aub will sit ready to receive The Island King's crown, a beautiful ornate object with an interesting, if relatively short history. It was made of course back in 2037 for Ken David, first King of The Island. It's a much more decorative crown than the one we all remember from Queen Clarissa's coronation last month, and also is much heavier. You can just about make out Queen Clarissa sitting behind Aub's parents in somewhat plainer dress. She is actually sitting between President

Manuela Raimunda of Brazil and President Alberto Pedro of Mexico. Even she admitted on Russian television a few days ago how astounded she was at the way in which all of the of the other leaders have rallied round her to help her to solve some of America's deep-rooted problems."

The exchange of rings was duly followed by the aria. Then, after another short reading Aub took his place on the throne of Russia and Archbishop Karelinski prepared to conduct his second duty, that of crowning the King. For this Queen Katie did not alter her position, but merely turned around to face the congregation. The throne, of course, faced the congregation rather than the altar. The Archbishop addressed the congregation in English as follows:

"Today two people have been joined together in holy matrimony to reign over us. We have now witnessed the first half of this world-first event. In a few moments I will ask Prince Aub Ryman to take the oath of Allegiance to the Russian People through which and by which all rights shall pass to him and his Queen to become joint heads of state of this, the world's greatest nation.

"With this power comes both an authority and a responsibility to manage and approve our governmental rulings by way of Royal Assent. For this power to be bestowed the Ministers of the Crown of the Parliament of Kamchatka have collectively, jointly and unanimously submitted their approval, having indicated their complete satisfaction that the said King is of both the calibre and stature, and has complete capability to undertake the tasks and duties that shall be his to initiate and complete.

"With the approval mentioned, The Kremlin has decreed that, notwithstanding any event, this entire country shall revert to a constitutional monarchy with all due processes and protocols that shall apply to such a state.

"It is therefore with great pride and honour that I shall shortly pronounce the said Prince Aub Ryman King of all Russia, and that his Queen, Her Majesty Queen Katie of Kamchatka, shall by default also assume the same said authority and responsibility, acting forever together with our King to continue to guide and direct this our glorious nation in the way of peace and prosperity. Although we are many, we are all gathered here today as one body to serve the Lord our saviour and to preserve and protect all that is good in the world wherever it is to be found.

"It now remains for me to recite the Oath of Allegiance to our new King, such that he may take his rightful place as our appointed monarch and custodian of the rights of the people."

The Archbishop then turned to Aub and read out the Oath:

"Do you Aub Frederick Ryman promise that from this day forth you will use the powers that are hereby bestowed upon you to act and take decisions to the best of your ability to safeguard and enhance the prosperity and security of this our motherland for the remainder of your life on Earth save for any unavoidable impediment?"

"I do."

"And do you further promise that from this day forth you will discharge any reasonable duty as may be deemed necessary by the parliaments of this land to ensure that the integrity of this our glorious nation is preserved and enhanced whilst discharging also your absolute duty to bring together the nations of the world and deliver them from conflict and internal strife?"

"I do."

"And do you also promise that from this day forth you shall undertake the management of the sovereignty of nations in the manner that has been agreed between this our glorious motherland and the other participating nations of the world, and to provide leadership and dedication to the principles and objectives that have been laid down to ensure the effectiveness of the said management both now and in the future?"

"I do."

"Then it is with the greatest honour and pleasure that I hereby place upon your head the Crown of The Island King, as of now the Crown of All Russia, so that you may use its powers wisely for the good of both the motherland and of the world."

"It's interesting to compare this Oath with the one that Queen Clarissa swore to in Times Square," Sylvia continued. "There are some subtle differences. The Russian Oath is very much more detailed and contains some very clear prescribed requirements relating especially to the duty to preside over The New Game. Lots of people are placing a huge amount of faith in this man to deliver, but the good news is he also has lots of people to help him. Russia first was not mentioned explicitly, but is clearly implied, alongside a more general duty to help all of the nations of the world. We can also note that the word integrity was used rather than quality , but quality improvement is definitely incorporated in this section of the Oath. The Oath itself of course was jointly drafted by The Kremlin and the Kamchatka Parliament and subsequently approved by both, as well as being agreed well in advance by Aub and Katie as being very much in accordance with their own wishes. We have heard it for the first time, but there is nothing in it that anyone really didn't expect.

There will now be an interval of around twenty minutes as the King and Queen leave St. Basils Cathedral to take their places on the balcony above Red Square. From there they will observe the procession as it files past, marking the dawn of a new era in world politics."

Aub and Katie took their respective positions on The Kremlin balcony alongside Sergei Ulanov and Viktor Bogodan and Katie's parents Mary and Neville. Dressed in their finery they saluted the dignitaries as they filed past from the very spot where once Joseph Stalin had stood to wave to the people, but what a different world it was.

As the procession passed through Red Square, Sylvia Smith again provided the English commentary:

"Now we can see the procession led first and foremost by the veterans of Russia's armed forces. Some have prosthetic limbs, a few of the older ones are in wheelchairs, others are marching slowly behind. They have all lost comrades whom they remember and they all march with pride, proud to have served their country. The armed forces no longer exist here, but they are remembered for the work that they did in their time defending the motherland. They command enormous respect here, even though these former servicemen and women are pleased themselves that they are now passing into an era where their roles have become effectively redundant.

"Behind them is a much larger contingent, the thousand-strong men and women in smart suits who lead the mighty auditing squad of The International Standards Organisation, who have effectively replaced them, ensuring that the exacting requirements of ISO 9100, the international Quality supersystem standard, are met. They are taking over where armies have left off. They are multinational and led by two highly respected men from Ireland, the Supreme Auditors Patrick O'Rourke and Duncan McIntyre. They will take a few minutes to pass.

"Next we see the leaders of the world who will each play their part in leading the transformation, each carrying their respective flags. Prime ministers, presidents and monarchs are walking shoulder to shoulder. All of Queen Katie's centre party allies are present, all part of what Archbishop Karelinski referred to as the one body that will lead the world in a new direction. It really is a historic moment.

"Leading the way we see the British royal family accompanied by Britain's Prime Minister Francis White, who is holding the Union Jack proudly aloft. We can all recall how he was swept into office in spectacular style last year and it has to be said that Britain is now just beginning to show signs of economic recovery.

"Behind them walks the newly-crowned Queen Clarissa of America, proudly holding her country's flag, demonstrating that the USA very much has a welcome presence here. Beside her is President Manuela Raimunda of Brazil, who has befriended her enormously here. One senses that Brazil really is going to help America in the next few years by helping the US to make more things under a new, much more favourable licensing agreement. Manuela empathises with Clarissa because, as some of you may remember, when Manuela first came to power in Brazil her country was in a far worse state than ever America is today.

"President Pedro of Mexico is behind them, and behind him we see the leaders of Japan and South Korea, the first nations to have achieved the much coveted ISO 9100 certification. Both have done an incredible job. Behind them we see the Danish royal family followed by the royal families of Spain, the Netherlands, Belgium, Sweden and Norway, along with the French President for whom Queen Katie recently secured re-election.

"Now the next pairing is really interesting, the leaders of Israel and Palestine walking side by side with their flags. Amazingly they are walking together with a display of solidarity that is unprecedented. It has taken a long time and a lot of negotiating to bring them to this point, but for both the potential rewards offered by The New Game have proved to be too great for either of them to maintain their old division of mistrust and fear.

"Some countries are noticeably absent, more are set to come on board in the next few years. China remains a problem, and will continue to be so until it shows at least some willingness to disarm. So far its leaders have shown no intention of abandoning their old Marxist philosophy, but that could change if more countries cease trading with them. India and Pakistan likewise have a disarmament issue into which they are both locked, but there is greater hope for Australia, New Zealand, Canada and Portugal. Watch also Finland and Iceland as they are not far off achieving ISO 9100. Aub and Katie may well be looking to secure some re-elections there, which, oddly, could also happen for President Broome in America, thanks to Queen Clarissa.

"Eastern Europe for its part is being drawn forever closer to Russia. Most of the leaders there are now seeking rather than resisting what is now being seen as the warm hand of friendship. There is already talk of Poland, Romania, Serbia and Ukraine wanting to adopt the rouble as a first step to a more lasting bond with Russia. Don't be surprised if all of Eastern Europe isn't trading with it in a few years' time. Collectively all of these countries are moving towards the centre with their leaders hoping to secure re-election from our new King and Queen. None of them are expected to sell out to Russia. Russia is not looking to buy, but closer attachment looks to be virtually certain.

For now, though, we can look forward to lights, camera and action as Aub and Katie prepare to take to the ice."

*

As dusk approached there was a deep rumbling sound in Red Square and the previously largely unnoticed set consisting of volcanic snow-covered peaks suddenly became illuminated. The stand shook as Katie, now dressed in a silvery grey catsuit, and made up as the ice queen, flew across from the balcony, as did the similarly dressed Aub, so that they met with an intended collision a few metres above the ice pad.

They intertwined as the harnesses were gently lowered, giving the impression of two people turning together as they descended. Sylvia Smith continued her commentary:

"Now we see from on high, as the distant volcanoes rumble, releasing their spirits, the mysterious Queen of the east, with her King, descending into the centre of Moscow. Beneath, on the ice, the spirits make their way for them as they present their contrasting world of fire and ice. Watch as

286

the colours change during this wild and intricate dance. The spirits are played by the junior division of the world-famous Russian All Stars. As the routine progresses the volcanoes quieten and the spirits are tamed. The rumbles stop and start throughout the dance, but grow forever fainter.

"The music has been specially composed for them by the master modern Russian composer Vladimir Vushenkin, who has composed a number of modern-day masterpieces, I think about eleven in all. It's all about contrast and the taming of nature, turning that which is wild and unstable into something that is manageable and stable. The concept is clear enough, but the way in which Jobine has trained them to express it is quite remarkable. It's a great contemporary opening routine. As the spirits rise they are immediately tamed again. Aub and Katie are very much the controllers of the piece, having complete control of the ice. It is as if they are conducting an orchestra, and I expect Vushenkin had this in mind when he wrote the piece. As we reach the end we can see fiery moves gradually change into frozen moves, with all of them skating in unison rather than independently. So Aub and Katie freeze with them at the end. Great stuff and highly original.

"Now, beneath where I am sitting is what was once Lenin's tomb. It's now serving as the changing room, and as one group of skaters leaves the ice another will enter. The skaters at this event come from all over Russia, including Kamchatka, which is where the next troop is from. These are the Petropavlovsk Kamchatsky Ice Dance Formation Team and they will be skating a variety of dances all of which are set to local folk music and designed to reflect a different aspect of local culture. These are traditional folk dances transposed onto the ice. They're colourful, and exciting to watch with lots of changes of hold and elegant on-the-spot turns. It's very traditional, but also very eye-catching."

Aub and Katie followed them, this time dressed as warriors:

"So Aub and Katie return," Sylvia continued. "This routine is set to Gustav Holst's 'Mars: The Bringer of War', but what exactly are they fighting? This routine is intentionally deceptive to the observer. First it looks as if they are locked in combat with each other, but then, suddenly, they find themselves no longer fighting each other, but a new enemy. The soldiers that you see emerging are again played by the junior Russian All Stars. It looks at first as if they are rising against our two warriors, who now have to focus on their challenge and fight together. But are they really fighting our two heroes? Slowly we see that they are starting to fight each other, but it soon becomes apparent that they are not actually fighting at all, but instead delivering a warning. As the routine progresses we see that there is, in fact, a much stronger enemy against which all must rise. Look closely and you will see the fire-breathing dragon slowly appear, and it's real fire that it breathes out. It's a wonderful model that brings everyone onto the same side in the end. The idea is that the dragon represents war itself personified. Finally it runs out of fire and stops functioning.

"Lots of applause for this routine like the others. I can hear the cheering from Alexandrovsky Gardens as well. There's a fantastic atmosphere there I can tell you. Also if we look over to the other side of the ice pad by the Place of Skulls, we can see the veteran ex-servicemen and women, clearly moved by the philosophy that has been woven into that routine, not to mention the skill. Aub, Katie and the other skaters all had to have perfect timing with their moves in order to avoid the jet of flame, which came at fixed time intervals. Not that Aub flinched in the slightest, after all he is an ex-serviceman himself, something else that has gained him a not inconsiderable amount of respect from the Russian veterans.

"Next onto the ice we welcome a slightly older group of skaters from the Groznyy Figure Skating Club. Aub and Katie will be skating with them to show their mastery of school figures, something that trainer Jobine is especially keen on. There are lots of matching and contrasting moves in this routine, which is to two pieces of music. The first is the classic Irish folk song 'Danny Boy', which has been chosen to reflect the city's now strong Irish heritage, which has been created almost entirely by the intervention of Queen Katie's supreme auditors Duncan McIntyre and Patrick O'Rourke. It's now the most prosperous Russian city outside Moscow. The routine consists solely of school figures and the skating is highly precise, with skaters coming together exactly in time on their figure eights. You'll see three-turns timed impeccably, whilst the eights themselves are totally in unison and contrasting.

"'Danny Boy' is followed by 'How Great Thou Art', which has rather more in the way of expression, with lots of synchronised arm movements used to express the character of the music, and you'll see quite a bit of rise and fall. Aspiring figure skaters note how the rise is used to gain speed, whilst the fall is used to bring about a very controlled slowing down of the skater's momentum. As the skaters meet at the centre of the eight they rise onto a straight leg, touch hands, and then start a new eight. Some of the eights start on backward edges, some on forward edges, some are carefully timed to achieve symmetry with other eights. There is no attempt, however, to create fancy shapes as some of you may have remembered from Aub and Katie's royal tour of Japan. Artform skating is a different and more difficult discipline of figure skating altogether, and the Japanese are currently the world's masters at that. This is more like a branch of ice dancing. Look out for the counters, brackets and loops all being combined together to make what is almost a formation dance."

The Russian Olympians followed them, showcasing the finest Russian talent and contenders for the top Olympic medals in free skating, pairs, and dance, including the newly introduced duet event. They were then followed by Aub and Katie. Sylvia continued:

"Aub and Katie now return to the ice to skate Russia's national ice dance, the Tango Romantica. They will skate three sequences of this one-time compulsory Olympic dance that was invented right here in the 1970s. It's from the same era as America's newly-adopted ice dance, the Yankee Polka. Both dances are now classified as historical. Watch though as Aub and Katie finish the third sequence because the dance doesn't end there. They have choreographed their own Argentine Tango, which we are told is very raunchy and full of passion and energy. It's a sensual and erotic dance with a strong steady beat upon which you will see some very clean turns and intricate footwork. Watch how they come together as well, and observe the lifts. Each is four beats long, and watch how they freeze at the end.

"They will be followed by four of the Kamchatskiy Company Skating sets, one from each of the four Kamchatskiy companies, Kamchatskiy Auto, Kamchatskiy Maritime, Kamchatskiy Logistics and Kamchatskiy Aerospace. These skaters are dome of the skaters that Aub and Katie chose last year to train under Jobine to live their dream as skating celebrities. They come from a variety of different countries and now train under the Kamchatskiy company trainers.

"The managing directors of each of the four companies, and the trainers are in the VIP enclosure in the stand to my left, and also there are the remaining Kamchatskiy sets. First to skate will be Kamchatskiy Auto, showcasing the company's new car, the Silver Shadow. Then you'll see a lovely old sea shanty from Kamchatskiy Maritime, and some excellent use of moving props from Kamchatskiy Logistics. The last routine, from Kamchatskiy Aerospace, celebrates the rise of Russia's space industry from Yuri Gagarin and the launch of the Sputnik programme, through to the building of Moonbase Alpha, a modern-day miracle of engineering. Here you'll see some spectacular lifts, and note how each set has mastered a different set of skills, so no one is any better or worse than any of the others. They all contrast with one another."

After this Aub and Katie returned to dance their sensual Rhumba, a slow-paced classic dance with plenty of turns, lifts and long flowing edges. They succeeded in focusing all eyes upon them. A perfectly timed death spiral led on to a winding sequence of cross rolls followed by a matching pair of spread-eagles.

Next, the Russian All Stars returned this time to celebrate the world of Russia's world-famous ballet heritage. Sylvia explained:

"Now Russia is of course world-famous for its ballet, the Bolshoi in particular, and one thing the Russian All Stars are famous for is their ability to transpose ballet onto ice. In leading this tribute, they will perform extracts from Swan Lake, Sleeping Beauty and the Nutcracker Suite, three all-time classics. For sheer professionalism this is a fantastic display. No other skating company can match the All Stars in this area, although many have tried, including several in Kamchatka. The fact is ballet on ice is the province of the Russian All Stars. The music for this is going to be played live by the Moscow Philharmonic Orchestra, which is stationed just to the right of my commentary box at ice level."

This brought the show almost to a close, save for one final routine that had originally not been planned:

"So they leave the ice to a standing ovation. The fabulous Russian All Stars. And that's about it, except for one last routine, which actually replaces the one that Aub and Katie had originally rehearsed. At their request, they have choreographed, with Jobine's help, a completely new routine over the past week. For it they have chosen another of Vushenkin's celebrated pieces, his version of 'Utopia', taking its name of course from Thomas More's famous book of 1516, and now the theme to the recently-released movie *Utopia*, which was filmed right here in Moscow. The filmmakers have assisted with the wonderful graphics, but there is one more thing that is special about this routine and that is the fact that for the first time, it is an ice dance skated by three people.

"Aub and Katie quite unexpectedly asked Queen Clarissa if she would like to skate with them a completely new kind of dance, set to the music from 'Utopia'. Clarissa said that she would be delighted and so, in the space of just one week, this amazing routine was pieced together. As you watch the dance you will see that there are very few breaks in hold. Clarissa is lifted three times by Aub and Katie, but the hold is retained throughout. What they said they wanted to do was to take ice dancing into another dimension by demonstrating that it is indeed possible to have three people, as opposed to just two, moving together as one. There are several shoulder holds in which the three of them turn together, and there are some very cleverly timed twizzles with only momentary breaks in hold. Aub turns them both at one point, then he is lifted to shoulder height by the two girls.

"Now they are taking their starting positions. He is supporting the two girls who are facing in opposite directions to start. Reading into the philosophy of the routine you may spot the deliberate parallels between 'Utopia' and Total Quality Management. Both are eternal goals that are never ending. The crystal ball that appears in the centre of the ice contains images that build up as the dance progresses. The music is now starting and the three of them are just beginning to move. The introduction is very quiet, but the pace gradually increases, building up to something special, towards which the skaters are forever reaching.

"It is quite an intense piece of music, as anyone who has seen the film will know, representing the shape of things to come through skill, hard work and cooperation. Everyone works together. There is no conflict in Utopia. Watch the skaters as they carefully intertwine. The changes of hold in this dance are absolutely magnificent. Jobine has just drawn out the skating talent of all three skaters to a new level. The dance holds are continually changing, but, with just the handful of exceptions mentioned, there are no breaks at all. The three of them are totally connected.

"In the last scene we see images of the real world that gradually become coincident with those of Utopia. The skaters want to join the two, but of course they can't because Utopia is imaginary whereas the real world is not. The result is perfection on the one hand and imperfection on the other, but through this wonderful dance they bring the two so close together that they do indeed merge, and the differences become harder and harder to spot. Watch for the entirely deliberate errors, intentional stumbles, followed by recovery, symbolising corrective action followed by improvement. The final message is that we can build Utopia, but as soon as we do it evolves into something even greater. The skaters in the end are absorbed by it and the illusion of their final disappearance from the ice has been very cleverly crafted by the filmmakers.

"If you get the chance to see the film, it's well worth it. It's based on Thomas More's classic, but has a modern slant, and these three incredible skaters have just added something extra. We have entered a very much more refined age in this century, one where people can do more than just dream about a better world.

"For now the show is over, and Aub and Katie are about to embark on their honeymoon. That too is something special and if you think the skating is over think again. I'm told Aub and Katie have one more skating routine to perform, but we will have to wait three days before we can see it. Once again it will be a skating first.

"From here they will travel to Samara, once home to Russia's great space programme. In the twentieth century it was off limits to tourists. Then it was opened up, but hardly anyone went there. Today it is a much revitalised part of

Russia's infrastructure that has been specially adapted to accommodate space going vessels, or SGVs, that can safely take off and land there.

"A Kamchatskiy limousine will take the new King and Queen to Sheremetyevo Airport where the King's own Hebden Three is waiting for them to take them on the short flight to Samara. You can still hear the cheering crowds here and as the three skaters bow we can see that everyone around us is standing to applaud that incredible routine. But the party is just beginning here."

Again the crowds lined the streets and many threw flowers as the Kamchatskiy made its way through the Moscow suburbs prominently displaying the message 'Just Married'.

Chapter Twenty-one
Moondance

At Sheremetyevo Airport the royal couple was escorted quickly to the awaiting Hebden Three, but not before Aub and Katie had paused to sign a few autographs to a handful of fans that had managed to assemble in the public gallery. Hostess Su Lin welcomed them aboard and, all of a sudden, the world appeared so much quieter. At last they were alone together watching the world pass by on the short flight to Samara. As they approached the spaceport they could see the mile-long ramp very clearly with its row upon row of giant LED lights that pierced through the freezing fog that was beginning to engulf the site.

A special bus took the couple from the aircraft to the top of the shaft where a brightly lit glass elevator awaited ready to descend some five thousand metres to the chamber where the newest and finest of Kamchatskiy Aerospace's three space going vessels, the SGV Aub, stood, fully primed, ready for its first non-test flight to the greatest achievement of human engineering to date, the incredible Moonbase Alpha.

Take-off was relatively silent for an SGV. Largely unseen, the SGV Aub accelerated to escape velocity, a little over 25,000 miles an hour, in just over forty-five minutes. Afterwards its trajectory stabilised and in another forty-eight hours it would be docking in its very own purpose-built landing bay on Moonbase.

For safety reasons the royals had to remain in the take-off and landing lounge for the duration of the acceleration, although they did not have to be strapped in as would have been the case with the older SGVs. This was due to the fact that in this vessel the gravity unit that compensated for the weightless conditions of space had now been configured to additionally provide compensation for the considerable G-forces that inevitably arose whenever a vessel such as an SGV accelerated at such a high rate. This could not be done throughout the vessel, but in a few areas such as the take-off and landing lounge, the bridge and the galley, it had been engineered.

With the Earth now behind them they had the restaurant, which could accommodate up to a hundred VIP guests, all to themselves. A candle flickered on the sole table that had been set aside for them, and for the first time in months they could actually relax. All that lay before them was the vastness of space, or so Aub thought.

Aub was just about to tuck in to the finest moonfish when he noticed an unusual flashing light some distance from the vessel on the port side, and seemingly heading toward them.

"What the hell's that?" Aub called out.

"What?"

"That light. It's not part of the vessel, and whatever it is, is pretty big."

Katie laughed.

"It's the freighter vessel Gagarin," she explained. "It's heading back to Earth. There's another freighter, the SFV Sputnik, running currently about one hour behind us. They operate a system a bit like the policemen in Victorian London. Every freighter is always within range of at least one other so that if there were to be an emergency on one of them, another could come to its aid within a maximum of two hours."

Aub watched ponderously as the eerie looking craft, which was entirely dark save for a few windows, passed silently by.

"Have there ever been any incidents on any of them?"

"Not major ones. There was a fire on board one a few months ago, but the vessel didn't require any assistance. That was traced to a fuel link arising from a fractured O-ring. The links have since been modified. Apart from the SGVs they are the safest craft ever built."

The royal couple naturally had the honeymoon suite in which to bathe and rest. Only the Earthlight shone in from above. For a moment it reminded Aub of the night he and Katie had kissed in the West Garden of The Royal Palace back on The Island, which itself was a world away from the frustrating life that he had previously endured as Australia's Defence Minister. The ornate four-poster was as much a relief as a luxury at the end of what had been a very demanding schedule. An eleven-hour sleep was only to be expected once the passion had subsided.

*

With the arrival of morning, or what passed for it, a champagne breakfast awaited followed by a full day in which to explore the many delights of this extraordinary vessel. Apart from the wide assortment of delicious food and beverages from around the world, plus a few lunar specialties, there were challenges such as walking upside down and learning to dance in a weightless environment. This was of course in addition to the cinema and what was soon to be a tourist information unit advertising the many attractions of Moonbase Alpha as well as displaying its many amazing construction phases. The whole project fascinated Aub, who had known of it for some years, but not otherwise appreciated just exactly what had been achieved. He now had to comprehend the fact that the whole of this place would now be part of his realm. He contemplated how far The Island, one tiny island, had come since the inception of its Non-Capitalist revolution that had started with just a handful of people meeting at a party conference in Cardiff in 2036.

Together they viewed some of the many facets of Moonbase Alpha, the centre of which had been partly modelled on The Town on The Island nestling within its transparent globe in the Sea of Tranquillity. Then there were the seven freighter craft, each named after a milestone in Russia's proud history of space exploration. Moonbase Alpha, of course, required a constant stream of supplies throughout its construction, from diggers and rovers, to building materials and light provisions for personnel. Now, however, it was almost complete, albeit ongoing, representing the pinnacle of The Island's silent revolution and a true masterpiece of civil engineering.

The extent of Moonbase Alpha was around fifty square miles, and the fact that most of its inhabitants had not yet arrived did not alter the fact that in reality its layout was comparable to that of a major city on Earth. It was equipped with every facility, yet was completely protected from harmful cosmic rays by virtue of its system of interconnected transparent domes that permitted the permeation only of the natural sunlight that the ozone layer allowed on Earth.

A key attraction of Moonbase Alpha was undoubtedly the now much talked about Electron-Beam Probe, the ultimate in space exploration. On board the SGV Aub, Aub and Katie were able to learn much more about its design and function than Patrick had explained in his somewhat simplified lecture to the setmates of 2107. It would not be long before the rich and famous would be flocking to see it as part of the lunar tour that would generate some much needed revenue from the capitalist world to help with its upkeep. Not everything could be taken care of by Non-Capitalist Economics, although it went a long way.

Aub and Katie pondered as they listened to scientists speculating about what Sirius' solar system might look like. It was anybody's guess, but the question that everybody wanted to know the answer to was could there be life?

"Life on other planets," Katie remarked. "It's amazing to think that this wonderful instrument of modern science inspired by our very own resident geniuses Patrick O'Rourke and Adrian Schultz could enable us to be the among the first generation of people to find out if there is something out there."

"The results will be astonishing whatever they show," Aub added. "I can't wait to actually get close to that thing."

As the second night approached the Earth appeared very much more distant than it had on the first, whilst at the same time The Moon grew ever larger. This was a new experience for Aub and Katie. Never before had either of them witnessed the panorama that was unfolding before their eyes. The mountain ranges and craters that characterised The Moon's surface now appeared so much clearer.

As they lay once more on the four-poster The Moon suddenly seemed enormous. Moonlight now illuminated their quarters, although it could be shaded out. It was, however, the perfect night for lovers, and who else had ever been in a position to experience love in such a setting? So, at least for the time being, The Moon was not obscured.

*

Some nine hours later, in what passed for morning, The Moon was no longer a bright object shining above them. The spacecraft was now cruising above it. By breakfast time the vessel was gliding just one hundred miles above the lunar surface. It reminded Aub and Katie of the ancient images that both of them recalled from their childhood, when, at different times, old film clips of the Apollo missions had been shown to them at school. Now they were experiencing the same reality.

At eleven o'clock Island Time, or Central Atlantic, the SGV Aub approached its landing site. Aub and Katie returned to the take-off and landing lounge from which they would disembark into the gravity-compensated tunnel of the space terminal. The thrusters were activated and the craft gently hovered above its landing circle before lowering itself precisely into position. Then the docking procedure commenced, whereby the tunnel that led to terminal reception was connected to the entry and exit door of the SGV, with the pressure equalised before release.

The dimly lit tunnel gradually broadened out to give way to the most peculiar terminal building that either of them had ever seen. It was permanently bathed in a strange shadowy sunlight with the sky otherwise totally dark. As they stepped out into it a familiar face greeted them.

"Joanie, oh my God!" Katie exclaimed as The Island's former prime minister Joanie Carmichael proudly advanced toward them in her prestigious Moonbase Commander's uniform of blue and gold that prominently displayed the red star, a feature that was unique to the jacket of the Commander.

"Hello," said Joanie as she embraced both of them.

"Great to see you again," replied Aub. "How are you liking your new job?"

"Proud to serve," she replied. "And pleased to know that I still actually have a seat reserved for me in the Kamchatka Parliament, the only one reserved for a constituency that's not on Earth. Come, I'll show you round your quarters. Then tomorrow we can take a trip around the base. You'll see lots of empty houses, but they'll soon be filled. You'll need magnetic shoes, though, as most areas have lunar gravity. We couldn't build massive gravity units everywhere in this massive complex."

As they left the terminal they stepped aboard a Kammie that was large and spacious. It was a VIP coach, made by Kamchatskiy Auto specifically to convey VIPs from the terminal to their Moonbase accommodation.

Over lunch Aub and Katie met some of the officers who served under Joanie Carmichael, each responsible for a different aspect of the base's operation. Most of these were middle-aged and notably had been among the last recruits of the now disbanded Russian armed forces. Aub quickly identified with the parallels that existed between running a military command unit and running a base such as Moonbase Alpha. Prior military service was clearly an advantage for such personnel who had to ensure that every action was timed with precision and perfectly executed. There was definitely no room for errors in what was, after all, still a potentially lethal environment compared with the Earth. Systems had to work exactly to specification, as the consequences of failure could be disastrous. Poor quality of all kinds was not an option here.

The officers, like Joanie, wore their uniforms with pride, honoured to have been given roles and responsibilities on Moonbase Alpha.

"We are proud to serve here, Your Majesty," one of them said to Aub. "Far better than wasting our lives in a pointless war. Now we can put our skills to good use rather than bad, even though we still have a largely military structure. Moonbase Alpha is a great place to live and work."

As the couple spoke to each of the thirty senior officers they received a broadly similar set of opinions from all of them. Despite having been trained initially for potential combat, all of them were glad that the armed forces had been disbanded, but pleased that their training had still been useful for the management of a constructive project. It was not that their skills were obsolete, more that they would be applied in a different way.

In the afternoon Joanie escorted the royal couple in a moon buggy that took them out into the suburbs where robots were busily at work performing the finishing touches to various outbuildings.

"Now you've got to be prepared for a shock," said Joanie as they prepared to leave the central area.

Up to this point the ride had been relatively smooth, but once they hit the outer roads the buggy jolted and the way ahead was somewhat more bumpy.

"We are now out of the gravity-controlled area," Joanie explained. "A few of the buildings have gravity units, but most don't and are work places staffed by robots working under lunar conditions. The pavements in these areas are magnetic and there is air so people can walk along them, but the roads are just dust tracks and the gravity is lunar."

As they approached the perimeter of the base they could see the vast fields of solar panels that permanently soaked up the sun's rays to provide electrical energy throughout the base. Robots could be seen charging themselves at various points, ready to take over in shifts in the fully automated factories that made products of all different kinds, some for use on the base, others ready to be shipped to Earth for onward use or sale.

"The good thing about robots is they don't need feeding, they don't consume oxygen, and they don't even need gravity," Joanie continued. "They just have to be programmed to work in the lunar environment. They don't need to sleep either. All they have to do is recharge and return to work. There's no such thing as day or night here, but all the houses and dwelling places for humans have gravity units and what we call simulated night. The further away from the centre we go the more robots and the fewer people you will see. They can look after each other though. If one of them develops a fault another can soon diagnose and fix without requiring human intervention. Even when the Moonbase is fully operational the robots will outnumber the people by over two hundred to one."

As they headed back towards the central zone the ride suddenly became smooth again and the people returned in ever increasing numbers. Houses replaced factories and the robots tended to be the smaller domestic types as opposed to their much larger industrial counterparts.

"We couldn't have built a place like this without Non-Capitalist Economics," Joanie explained. "No nation on Earth could have afforded it. Only by bypassing capitalism did it become realistic, but it does solve many of the Earth's problems and certainly contributes towards making the Earth's resources more sustainable. We can do lots of things here that simply aren't possible on Earth. With the help of robots and our exceptionally well-trained personnel we can either make what we need here or ship it in using the freighters. The freighters can also take things back to Earth. Strange though it may sound this place could even become profitable within a few years, with its relatively low running costs and a huge range of manufacturing and service industries that's largely operated without a human work force."

At the interface between the central zone and the outer zone large warehouses could be seen where long slow-moving trains docked to unload their wares. Warehouse robots then performed various unloading, sorting and storage functions such that human personnel were needed only to specify items to be retrieved.

"As you can see, we can mass produce with high reliability at a level that no country on Earth, even China, can match. Whole industries are brought together as one with round-the-clock operation," said Joanie. "And you'll note our waste disposal system. One thing that can be done much more easily here than on Earth is rocket launching. From beyond our perimeter rockets can be launched cheaply and effectively straight at the sun providing the ideal location for some of the world's most toxic substances. Through this base we intend to make pollution on Earth a thing of the past. Other things, such as sewage, can be perfectly recycled to produce renewable water and gas. Symbiosis in the plant houses also helps us to produce oxygen, so we only need top-ups from Earth rather than large quantities.

Now I'm going to take you to a special part of the base that I know you have been longing to see."

Joanie drove the buggy along what was at least recognisable as a street, complete with bungalows. At the end was a mighty dish.

"Oh my God that's it," said Katie.

"That's it," repeated Joanie. "The mighty Electron-Beam Probe. In a little over eighteen years it should be showing us what the solar system of Sirius looks like."

They paused for a moment to look at and walk around the cylindrical base of the massive construction. As they did so they observed two engineers screwing a plaque into the iron wall of the building where the beamer was housed. Joanie took a photograph of them as they stood beside the door of this wonderful triumph of engineering. Katie quickly read the words on the plaque before the pair of them stepped aboard the buggy for the short smooth ride to their final destination.

"Now the tour is almost over," explained Joanie. "I'm going to take you to something you will recognise, but with a difference. There you will also meet a couple of familiar friends."

It was only a matter of yards from the Electron-Beam Probe to the Moonbase Alpha Ice Emporium where the couple disembarked. Ready to meet Aub and Katie were none other than Jobine and Sylvia.

"How was the journey?" Aub asked as he and Katie embraced them.

"Absolutely fabulous," said Sylvia. "We've only just arrived."

"We came on the humble freighter," Jobine added. "But it was a fantastic experience. Those craft really are remarkably comfortable. We were given one of the senior officers' quarters and were truly pampered."

"We experienced weightlessness and were even washed by robots," Sylvia continued. "They might be functional, but those freighters are lovely to travel in."

"Let me show you the ice," said Jobine as she led Aub and Katie through the entrance porch to the rink. "On the surface it looks like any other and feels like it when it is in ordinary operation. It's when it isn't that the fun starts. I've only just got used to it myself, but if we stick to what we've practised there shouldn't be too much difference between skating on this rink and skating with the harness on back on The Island. I'll explain how it works. Basically beneath the ice surface is a variable gravity unit. Gravity can be varied under operator control, or per-programmed to vary at different points in a piece of music. Under normal operation it is set to Earth gravity. In the off mode it is set to lunar gravity, which is just twenty per cent of Earth gravity.

"Obviously that means that you can perform things on this ice rink that you couldn't perform on Earth. Tonight and tomorrow we are going to practise so that you can get used to the ice and its characteristics.

Then tomorrow evening at six o'clock Island Time, you will perform your special routine once through before the cameras. It will be beamed back to Earth. I will be in the commentary box, the first person ever to use it, so I'm really excited."

*

Practice began with two side-by-side toe loops, the first under normal operation, the second under lunar gravity. With their weight reduced to one fifth the triple toe loop suddenly became quite achievable. They could jump five times higher than on a conventional ice rink on Earth.

"The hardest thing is the timing," Jobine explained. "You have to be ready to take off at exactly the time the gravity changes and land exactly on cue for your next figure. This rink really comes into its own when it comes to the jumps, but the variable gravity is also useful for other things. Remember the sequence where you take off together on both feet using your toe picks, then meet and descend intertwining?"

"Yes," said Aub. "I remember we practised it using the harness back on The Island."

"Which helped you, because although you were not aware at the time, the settings on the harness were exactly set to reproduce the effect that you will experience here. It effectively simulated the lunar gravity for you in order to make this routine easier to perform."

So they sprang themselves skyward and Jobine adjusted the gravity controller immediately to its off mode. Aub and Katie rose above the ice to a height that exactly matched that which they had achieved using the harness. They met, then intertwined, turning all the time as they descended slowly back onto the ice.

"Know your sequences," Jobine urged. "During the performance the music will tell you when the gravity is about to change. Also remember that in some parts, such as when you do your airborne walks, an intermediate setting may be used. Where this is done the gravity will be set to one third of Earth, but again it follows exactly the setting that we used with the harness on The Island. Tonight we will just practise the elements under manual control. I will use my hand-held controller to adjust the gravity levels. Tomorrow we will rehearse the entire six-minute routine."

*

With the practice complete the couple returned to Moonbase Command in a moon buggy, this time driven by one of three of Queen Katie's personal chauffeurs. They passed through the iron gates that led to the royal couple's private Moonbase apartments. The courtyard resembled the Town Square on The Island in every detail. The rectangular pond was even stocked with well-fed goldfish and a replica of The Colonnade had been constructed to perfection. The same had been done with The Great Dome where Joanie lived and worked. Government House was also there ready for the day when world leaders would eventually assemble to attend major summits.

There, however, the similarity ended. There was no bell tower and certainly no beach, although there was a secret garden behind the royal apartment. Inside the apartment the

King and Queen's personal servants resided on a full-time basis, carefully recruited from the remnants of the Russian armed forces in much the same way as the Beefeaters were at the Tower of London.

Aub and Katie met them warmly as they lined up before them. The Queen's very own Moonchef then entered and revealed what had to be the finest set of meals ever prepared on The Moon to date. It was not large, but it did offer the widest possible choice, excluding meat of course, which was in accordance with The Island's convention. There were, however, a few items that were labelled as lunar specialties, prepared entirely from lunar ingredients. These were unique in character and taste. Moonfish, grown purely from cultivated fish flesh, was one such example.

As the couple sat down to dine by candlelight, the restaurant bathed in Earthlight, the head waiter opened the very first bottle of lunar wine that had been produced from the now extensive lunar vineyards using robot-harvested grapes and a completely automated wine-making plant.

"This may be the first bottle Your Majesty," said the Frenchman. "But there are plenty more where this came from. Tell me if you approve."

"I certainly do," replied Aub as he gently sipped the white Semillon.

"Then I am most pleased," said the waiter. "It won't be long now before we start exporting these to Earth."

"You know one thing I love about all of this," Katie said to Aub as the waiter quietly retired.

"What's that?"

"The fact that our love for each other doesn't die the moment we step off the ice. I'm so grateful for that, knowing that we can still have a good life and a family without skating or politics taking over our lives to the point of obsession. Yet I'm still glad we can express our love on the ice. Not everyone has the opportunity to do that and to experience the joy that that brings."

"It's made all the better by not having to be spurred on by competition. I feel some sympathy for those people back on Earth for whom competition robs them of that joy."

"Thankfully though expressing love on the ice is a growing trend at least in some places, Russia particularly, helping to extinguish the depressing reign of the seedy nightclub."

*

As the royal couple's first day on Moonbase Alpha drew to a close, Aub and Katie could not resist the opportunity to explore their secret garden, complete with magic mushrooms and Stone Boat. Their romantic encounters were revisited as they kissed, this time under the Earthlight. Nothing stirred and all was silent, for The Moon was without wind and the trees, although present, were but young saplings. There was, however, a stream with stepping stones that led to a miniature castle at the top of which The Island flag hung motionless.

"I must thank the engineers who designed this," said Katie as she and Aub stepped across the stream. "Very creative."

As they approached the castle the drawbridge lowered allowing the couple to cross the mini moat. They then ascended the forty-foot high mock Medieval stone staircase to the large round bedroom at the top. There they threw themselves onto the heart-shaped bed that was almost calling to them lie on me.

"This is absolutely amazing," said Aub. "We can even make our own tea and it looks as if there is a small kitchen here with some food and a minibar, all for us. It's as if our old Island engineers Endo and Kai had built it for us."

"They did," said Katie, smiling. "The two robots that constructed it are named after them. I've seen photos of them. They're only small, but they're very strong."

*

The next morning the royal couple strolled back to their quarters for breakfast with Joanie, Jobine and Sylvia, before the Kammie took Aub, Katie and Jobine to the rink for the rehearsal. This afforded them one last chance to familiarise themselves with the various gravity transitions that were incorporated into their routine. Two hours was sufficient for a routine that would only last for six minutes and would be the only routine to be performed.

At six o'clock Island Time the stage was set. It was a strange warm-up in a strange rink as they were the only skaters to perform. There was, however, a fair-sized audience consisting of some five hundred Moonbase personnel. Jobine and Joanie occupied the VIP box, the first people ever to do so. Sylvia Smith duly took her position in the commentary box, which had several unoccupied seats that one day would be filled with international commentators. She provided the commentary in English:

"Greetings mother Earth. This is Sylvia Smith beaming live from the Moonbase Alpha Ice Emporium where soon Queen Katie and King Aub will be performing live their specially choreographed Moondance, telling their story of love and passion, which extends beyond the ice into their real lives. Two extraordinary skaters are about to perform on one extraordinary ice rink.

The rink is due to open officially to Moonbase staff next week, and should be opening its doors to visitors from Earth in about six months. Now Aub and Katie have just completed their warm-up and are just coming over here I think to say a few words."

"Hello Earth," said Katie. "This routine is dedicated to all our fans around the world. It is called Moondance. We hope you like it. We love you all."

They then returned to the ice and assumed their starting positions, standing back to back. Sylvia then continued:

"This programme may not be long, but I can tell you that unofficially it has the highest worldwide television audience ever recorded, yet another measure of the enormous popularity of this amazing couple. No wonder they can influence elections. All over the world people have paused whatever they are doing, employers have allowed workers to stop their work, and even the traffic has stopped so that the world can watch the Moondance.

"The music starts fairly quietly, again it is a composition by Vladimir Vushenki n. To start with they are moving in different directions, Katie is following one path whilst Aub is following another. Both appear to have lost their way in a wooded forest. Everything is completely dark, except for the moonlight. The graphics are great here throughout, but right now we see a beautifully simulated full moon that casts its light down on them. This opening section is very contemporary and there is no connection between the skaters, until the sun rises and a dove of peace, wonderfully projected in three-dimensions, descends and draws them together. Now we will see for the first time the this rink's unique feature.

"How is it that a couple that can only perform single jumps now, all of a sudden, can rise to a great height and perform triples? The answer lies of course in the fact that The Moon's gravity is only one fifth of that on Earth and this rink is equipped with a variable gravity unit underneath the ice surface. With the gravity now set to lunar their weight has dropped by four fifths. Already the gravity unit has been described as the greatest twenty-second century scientific invention, although the Electron-Beam Probe that's just a stone's throw from this rink surely rivals it.

Now for a while The Queen runs from her Prince, and he can't catch her because on her side of the rink gravity is set to full lunar, whilst on his side it is set to just one third. She can therefore achieve a much greater height than he can as they both use their toe picks to achieve elevation.

Cleverly, she now disappears and he thinks she's gone, only to find that she re-emerges at the other end of the rink. This time they both rise high under full lunar gravity and meet exactly over the centre of the rink. He holds her and as the words say now they have made their true love found, one of the few vocal sections in the piece. They will slowly intertwine and descend, turning as they do so. Brilliant timing there. When they land they are perfectly in hold to begin their lively quickstep section, which completes three full circuits of the rink and contains some very neat and fast step sequences. Look also for the lovely long flowing edges with plenty of rise, fall and sway.

"In a moment the tempo will slow down and our ice King and Queen will become just that little more intimate. There's a lovely side-by-side camel spin now, still under Earth gravity, with images of The Island in the background. At this point it has come into play in their lives. Into the secret garden they go, arm in arm, where we will see some fabulous intricate turns. A rose bush appears and he is seen to pluck one and offer it to her. The words 'War is Over' can be heard as she accepts the rose. Now they rise again, excellently timed to match the gravity change. They now perform some very intricate whorls around each other with a carefully timed landing to follow. She lands momentarily before he does, so she is leading at this point. We call this a reverse lead because normally it is the man that leads in ice dancing.

There are some great lifts in the next section and a spectacular throw axel, where she reaches a quite extraordinary height with the aid of lunar gravity. She will now perform no less than seven full rotations in the air, something that no skater could achieve on Earth, at least not until we have a rink with a reverse gravity unit. Next generation maybe.

Now the routine is almost over, as they enter the dawn of a new age. They reach out to the stars that now rise over them and open out with their arms outstretched. They kneel before a shaft of light, which is beamed out. Then they wait patiently for it to return. We wait. We listen. We watch, as our two committed lovers rise for the last time ready to watch over planet Earth as its guardians. It's almost over except for one last surprise, a particularly impressive illusion that sees the couple appearing to rise but not descend. They are actually descending slowly at the dark side of the rink, but they are carefully obscured by the graphics, such that it appears to all the world that they have become transformed into a constellation frozen in the heavens somewhere close to Aldebaran, the star after which a hamlet was named long ago in the early years of The Island and is now home to The Island's Opera House, which I know is full to capacity right now.

And that's it. The ice dance with a difference. Nothing has ever been seen like it, and probably won't for some time to come. We will now leave you with a trailer showing some of the features of this amazing Moonbase."

With the routine over Jobine and Joanie came down to embrace the royal couple, ready to return with them to their quarters where again a candlelit dinner was waiting along with a second bottle of Moonbase wine to try, this time a red.

"You read the words on that plaque that the engineers placed beside the door to The Electron-Beam Probe, didn't you?" Aub asked Katie.

"Yes," she replied.

"What did they say?"

"God save the King! God save the Queen! And may The Good Lord grant us all wisdom in newness of life."

CPSIA information can be obtained
at www.ICGtesting.com
Printed in the USA
LVHW031021090919
630399LV00002B/385/P